LAST KNOWN CONTACT

PHILLIPA NEFRI CLARK

Phillipa Nefri Clark
Mystery · Love · Suspense

LAST KNOWN CONTACT

AN IMPORTANT NOTE...

This book is set in Australia and written in Aussie/British English for an authentic experience.

Last Known Contact is a standalone title which is connected to the DS Liz Moorland series by the same author. There are cross-overs of some characters and they are set in the same "world".

Like to know more? Visit Phillipa's website where you can join her newsletter. www.phillipaclark.com.

ONE
WHERE IT ENDS

12 December

Ellie Connor burst out of dense bush onto a broad expanse of open ground. The gloom from the tail of the storm might protect her for a moment. That and the rain.

She skidded to a stop at the very edge of a cliff, catching a glimpse of wild waves a long way below. Doubled over, hands on her knees, she gulped salty air. Her legs shook from running but the adrenaline coursing through her had kept her moving. Adrenaline and self-preservation. She didn't want to die. Be killed by him. Most of her blonde hair had escaped its ponytail and she pulled a strand from her dry mouth.

So thirsty.

She reached for her backpack but there wasn't time. It wasn't safe to stop for so long. Below and to her right was the river mouth, just visible in the near-dark.

Safety.

"Oh, El-lie."

Her head shot up.

"I'm here to help you."

His voice drifted from the trees.

She ran along the side of the cliff, eyes searching for the way down.

A narrow track opened up. Not the one she remembered walking with Gabi last visit, but it would do. She had to put distance between them.

Underfoot the ground was mud and loose stones and Ellie's feet slipped from under her. She cried out as she landed on her elbows and behind.

Tears sprung into her eyes and she rolled against the cliff wall to catch her breath.

Out to sea, a helicopter sped past, its blinking lights mesmerizing Ellie. If only her phone wasn't smashed into a million pieces somewhere back in the bush, she would turn on its flashlight. Get their attention with her vague memory of Morse code.

But it passed by and the rain stopped. The wind dropped to almost nothing and the heavy smell of eucalypts and sea spray enveloped her.

Where was he?

Ellie pushed herself to her feet, wincing as she straightened. Blood trickled down her arms and she wiped it away, then cleaned her palms on her shorts. Her legs were filthy, and blood splattered. This time she was careful of her footing. One step at a time, a hand on the sheer rock face to her side.

At a sharp curve there was a shallow cave. Impossible to see how far back it went, or what might lurk within.

"Are you down there, Ellie?"

Ellie almost jumped into the cave entrance. His voice was closer. Surely, he would hear the hammering of her heart.

"You don't need to run anymore. I've come to help. I can get you to Gabi. You came to see her, didn't you?"

Don't you dare say my mother's name!

Ellie closed her eyes, arms wrapped around her body as

bile rose in her throat. She'd fallen into his well-planned trap. Alone, so far from any town. Nobody to turn to, no help.

She opened her eyes and started as a beam of light barely missed her feet.

"Getting a bit over the games, you know. All I ever wanted was to make you happy."

He was going to kill her, then find Gabi and do the same. Her fingers and toes were freezing even though the humidity was rising again after the storm.

"Oh, there's a blood trail. I'll bring you a bandage, Ellie."

Pebbles rolled down the path ahead of heavy footsteps. The flashlight waved from side to side.

"Ellie!" A different voice, echoing from the top of the cliff.

"I'm here. But he's close by!" Almost sobbing in relief, she stepped onto the path.

Her hunter caught her in his spotlight. "Gotcha, baby."

Ice clutched her stomach. Her feet wouldn't move. There was a gun pointed at her.

Again, from the top of the path, "Run! Ellie, run for your life!"

The flashlight turned onto her face. "I wouldn't do that, not if you ever want to see him alive again. Make a choice, Ellie."

I need to get to Gabi.

Ellie ducked out of the light and slid her way around the sharp corner.

A shot rang out.

TWO
HOMECOMING

5 December

IS JACK BANNERMAN DEAD?

The image beneath the newspaper headline was as familiar to Ellie as her own reflection. The same photo of her father was on her desk at Bannerman Wealth Group.

In the middle of Tullamarine Airport International Arrivals, she released the luggage-filled trolley to put her hands to her mouth.

"How are you coping, Ellie?" The reporter holding the newspaper shoved it closer to Ellie's face. "Do you have a comment?"

Dad?

"Is that why you cut short your trip to London?"

"What? No. I didn't." Ellie grabbed the paper. As she'd exited customs a moment ago all she had on her mind was a shower and a glass of Yarra Valley wine. Not...this.

Microphone in hand, another reporter pushed in front. There was a camera trained on Ellie. "Teresa Scarcella from *At Six Tonight*. Ellie, what are your thoughts at this difficult time?"

"No comment. Ellie, say nothing." A tall man in a sharp suit, with a buzz cut and muscles forced his way between the media and Ellie. "I've called for airport security so get out of our faces."

"Mr Dekeles, as head of security for Bannerman Wealth Group, what do you know—"

Paul Dekeles rammed the trolley forward with one hand and media scattered. His other arm went around Ellie's shoulders. The media formed a walking circle around them.

"Mr Dekeles! Please, a comment!"

"Can't print the comment I'd make," he muttered.

"Paul, is Dad…"

"We'll talk in the car but stop panicking."

Ellie blinked back tears as they passed through the airport's sliding glass doors to a warm Melbourne evening.

A limousine waited in the 'no standing' zone. The driver hurried to collect the trolley from Paul.

"Ellie! Just one more question!"

Paul stepped between the mob and Ellie and she threw herself into the back seat, pulling the door closed behind herself. The minute Paul moved, Teresa and her team were there, the camera hard up against the window.

The door on the other side opened. "Bloody vultures." Paul slid next to her and a moment later, they drew away from the curb.

Ellie scanned the newspaper. Words jumped out.

Where is Jack?

Iconic Melbourne entrepreneur feared murdered.

Yachting mishap.

Missing.

Did Dennis Connor kill him?

Lost at sea?

Worth billions.

Who will take his place as CEO?

"Don't believe the worst." Paul opened a bottle of water and held it out. "Sensationalism."

"But it says he's missing. When did he go missing? Why didn't anyone let me know?"

"You were already on the flight when we realised."

"Realised? How long?"

"Two days ago. Well, that's the last time he was seen."

"Seen where, Paul? Did *Sea Angel* sink?" Ellie sipped water, forcing down a bitter taste. Her hands shook when she replaced the lid.

"The yacht is fine. And he's simply disappeared into thin air. Or something."

"I'll call him." She turned her phone on.

"Pointless. We've all left messages."

"How could this happen?"

"No idea."

Ellie stared at him. "You're head of security."

"I'm not Jack's bloody keeper." Paul took the newspaper from Ellie and threw it onto the floor.

The traffic on the Tullamarine Freeway parted to give the limo room and Ellie checked her watch. Just after nine. Why hadn't Dennis called her yet? Would her own husband not be the one to break such terrible news?

"We're going to the house." Paul said.

"Does Meredith know what happened?"

"She doesn't know the time of day. Look, things will be upsetting. But its best this way."

"What on earth do you mean, Paul. Tell me what you know. Please?" Ellie exhaled heavily and leaned back against the leather seat as exhaustion gripped her.

"Not much to tell. Jack and Dennis planned to go sailing."

"And?"

"Jack didn't show."

"Then, where is he?"

Paul shrugged. "How was London?"

The limousine wound along streets in upmarket Canterbury, finally nosing through automatic gates between high stone walls.

Ellie climbed out and stretched to relieve the soreness in her legs from the long flight. Dennis' Alfa Romeo was parked near the four-car garage. She checked her phone for the tenth time but still no message from Dad. Nor from Dennis.

Paul led the way up half a dozen steps and through the open front door into a spacious foyer. "In the sitting room."

Off the main living area, the sitting room was dimly lit by a few lamps casting shadows onto cluttered, cheap knick-knacks lining the mantelpiece and sideboards.

Meredith Bannerman slumped on one of two leather sofas, a half empty glass of brandy dangling from her fingers. The ornaments were hers, which Ellie knew Jack couldn't stand. He liked things of quality. There were moments Ellie wasn't proud of when she'd wondered why Jack married Meredith, given his standards.

His back to the room, Dennis Connor stared out through the French doors. He didn't bother turning to acknowledge the arrival of his wife, although their eyes met in the glass reflection. Ellie crossed to Meredith and kissed her offered cheek. She wrinkled her nose at the stench of alcohol permeating from her stepmother's skin.

"Where's Dad?"

"About time you got here." Meredith sucked in more brandy.

Ellie addressed Dennis. "Where is he?"

"God knows." Dennis turned around. "Or not."

"Dennis, please—"

"Ignore Dennis. He's licking his wounds. From being interrogated." Meredith said.

"Who interrogated you? Why?"

Meredith began pouring another glass of brandy from a decanter on the side table, her hands shaky. "Nobody cares about the ones left behind."

"For goodness sake, would someone please tell me what happened?"

"Perhaps I can shed some light." Campbell Boyd, sixties, grey-haired, suited, stepped out of a dark corner.

Relief poured into Ellie and she threw her arms around her father's oldest friend. "What are you doing here?"

Dennis wandered to the sofa and took the decanter from Meredith before she spilled the contents. "Don't be stupid, Ellie."

Campbell frowned at Dennis.

"Come and sit. Clearly you don't know everything."

"I just got off a plane, Campbell. And it was a reporter who told me Dad is missing." Ellie sank onto the other sofa. "A reporter, Dennis. Not my husband."

"Not your husband." Meredith mimicked. "Oh, sweetie, such true words!"

I've come home to a mad house.

"Campbell?"

"The police are interested in Jack's disappearance. After they spoke to Dennis—"

"Why?"

"Effectively, he was Jack's last known contact."

"I wasn't the last to see him." Dennis collected a brandy balloon from a sideboard.

"Were you arrested?"

"Of course, he wasn't. One needs a backbone to commit murder." Meredith declared, as if it was something to aspire to.

"Murder?" Ellie barely heard her own voice.

Dennis grinned at Meredith. "As she drinks herself into oblivion once again."

"Well, at least I have the courage to carry out such a deed."

"The only courage you have comes from a bottle." Dennis sat next to Meredith. "Silly bitch." There was no malice in his words and they exchanged a look which Ellie didn't understand.

"Campbell—is Dad dead? Please tell me."

"Well, it was all a bit of a mess and-."

"For God's sake. I'll tell you what happened."

All eyes turned to Dennis.

"It was two days ago. Jack was stressed after the board meeting, so asked me to go sailing. Take a breather from important decisions at work. I was on time. He never showed up. I left a couple of voicemails and figured he got busy, so went sailing alone."

"Did you check the other boats?" Meredith said. "Perhaps he found a little sea nymph to shack up with?"

"Have another drink, Meredith." Ellie snapped.

Campbell cleared his throat. "When he came back to shore, Dennis tried Jack's phone again, and the house. Then called the office."

"He wasn't there. I swear to it, baby." Dennis stared at Ellie, his grey eyes cold behind small round glasses. "I swear it."

Ellie turned away. "Campbell, would you come with me to the police station? To wherever the investigation is based?"

"I'll take you." Paul spoke from the doorway.

"For God's sake." Dennis reached across Meredith for the decanter.

"Leave it until tomorrow. There's nothing to be done so late." Campbell picked up a briefcase. "I'll collect you in the morning."

"I'll get you home." Paul said. He came to Ellie, offering his hand. She glanced up at him, then to Dennis as he poured more brandy into Meredith's glass.

"Dennis?"

"I've moved out of the apartment." He didn't even look up.

Ignoring Paul's hand, Ellie pushed herself to her feet. "What the hell is wrong with you?"

Meredith directed a drunken smile at Ellie. How could she smile when her husband was missing? When nobody knew where he was?

"Getting ready for our inevitable divorce. It's what you wanted, isn't it?" Dennis held his glass up like a toast. "Welcome home, baby."

THREE
FALLOUT

5-6 December

Ellie wouldn't let Paul or the driver help with the luggage. Her apartment came with a twenty-four-hour concierge service and the young man on duty whisked her bags away.

"I should check the apartment with you."

"For what, Paul? If Dad happens to be there, I'll call." She'd had enough. The lack of answers, Dennis' announcement, Meredith's innuendo. Paul's protective fussing.

Inside her apartment, door locked, she leaned back against it and closed her eyes. The quiet and darkness drained some of the tension away, soothing raw emotions and calming the jumble of thoughts. Ellie slipped out of her shoes and sighed as the tiles cooled her feet.

When she opened her eyes, she frowned to see all the curtains were drawn, blocking out the stunning view to the Yarra River on one side, and all the way to Port Phillip Bay on another. She never closed them. Dennis must have, or…

"Dad?" It was a rasp, so dry was her throat. Nobody answered.

Ellie peered into the fridge. It was empty, apart from two unopened bottles of French champagne and half a bottle of white wine. The latter she took out. She didn't like champagne and never kept it here, so what had Dennis been doing? Four weeks away in London. Just one month and everything had changed.

Their king-sized bed was stripped bare. She sat on the end and poured wine into the glass she'd collected on the way. The door to the walk-in robe was open. Dennis hadn't quite moved out. There were some shoes, suits, and a bag tucked in the corner.

She grimaced at the stale taste of the wine. Probably the same bottle she'd opened the night before leaving for London. They'd argued. Disagreed was a better description, not the full-on fights from her childhood, with Dad and Gabi yelling at each other from across a room and doors slamming until she'd hide in the library, losing herself amongst the books her parents collected.

No, she and Dennis were always civil. She'd asked him one last time to consider marriage counselling. Try to find a comfortable middle ground, at least. He couldn't see why. To Dennis, keeping things to himself was second nature and sharing was something women did. "I'm not one of your girl-friends. That's what you all do, isn't it, complain to each other about your husbands?"

He'd obviously decided leaving a marriage was better than working on it. As bad as the wine was, Ellie finished the first glass and poured another. In the hallway between main and guest rooms she stopped to stare at photos on the wall. She lifted a hand and touched the smiling face of a handsome young man with long hair and a surfboard.

"Daddy's missing. How do I tell you, Michael?"

She opened the door to the guest room. This was as she'd left it, bed made up and fresh towels folded on the end, ready for guests.

Too tired to do more than strip off her clothes, Ellie climbed into bed. She hugged her body until sleep dragged her into a world of bad dreams.

———

"You don't look as though you slept at all, child."

Campbell and Ellie sat at one side of a table in an interview room in the police station. The room was cold, and she shivered. "I'm alright, I promise. I'll be better when we find Dad."

"I wanted to warn you last night...about the detective looking after this."

"Warn me?"

The door opened and they both looked up as an immaculately dressed man entered. He sat on the opposite side of the table, shook Campbell's hand, and only then made eye contact with Ellie.

She took in his three-day growth and collar-length black hair with dismay. Those dark, dark eyes of his were unreadable.

Ben Rossi.

Her hands slipped under the table to grip each other.

His lips tightened for an instant before he glanced at Campbell. "Thanks for coming in."

"Have you found him?" Ellie forced the words out.

"We have yet to establish this is a genuine missing person case."

She pushed her chair back. "Then we are wasting our time here."

Campbell placed his hand on her arm for a second. "Ellie, wait on. You wanted to speak to the police."

"But, this won't work..." She bit her lip. Dad was all that mattered. Ellie glared at Ben as she settled back in her seat.

He appeared unfazed by her reaction to seeing him. "When was your last contact with your father?"

"I am under suspicion? What are you doing to find him? All I know is from second-hand information and newspaper sensationalism."

Campbell leaned forward. "Detective Rossi, we've had no contact with Jack for three days. A man like him doesn't just disappear. He doesn't miss appointments and is never late. Never."

"No history of going off on his own? A short break with someone?"

"Someone who? His own wife doesn't know where he is. And Dad wasn't that kind of man."

"What kind?"

Not the kind you think. Not a man who doesn't care. Not a bad...father.

"Last time I saw Dad, we met at his house, in the library. I was leaving for London a few hours later and we had some last-minute papers to go over."

"You met at his house, rather than the office?"

"We both have desks in the library. Why did you question Dennis?"

"As the potential last known contact, your husband was able to provide useful information. Gave me a starting point. Your father's disappearance is unusual."

"We were meant to meet at eleven today. To talk about my London business trip."

"Meet where?"

"On the yacht."

Ben stood. "Here's my card. If you hear anything, think of anything, call." He held out a business card and their fingertips touched. Ellie almost dropped the card, but now Campbell was shaking his hand and without another glance, Ben left.

"Are you okay?" Campbell was on his feet. "I thought it was him. And you'd never speak that way to a stranger."

No. I wouldn't be like that with a stranger.

FOUR
SEA ANGEL

6 December

A few minutes before eleven, Ellie stepped onto *Sea Angel*, a sleek—if older—yacht. She glanced at her watch. He should be here, striding down the pier with his broad grin, or already on board with a limited-edition blue gin on ice. Just to take the edge off.

"Dad, are you here?"

She knew her breath was wasted, but still ran downstairs. It was the same as always. Water, beer, and wine in the fridge. A few frozen meals for emergencies. Beds in the two cabins made and clean towels in the tiny bathroom. Everything ready for a quick sail or overnight trip.

The yacht rocked gently beneath her feet as she made her way up, longing for the sun on her face. London in winter might be beautiful, but Melbourne summer was her favourite time of the year. Dad's as well. She sank onto one of the plump seats at the stern.

This place was private, quiet, yet only moments from the city. Tucked away at the bottom of a dead-end road, even the locals left the pier alone. Large signs warning against trespass probably helped, but Ellie couldn't remember this being anything other than a peaceful retreat.

Without Dad, what would she do? They'd been close forever and Gabi leaving so long ago brought them closer. If only he'd appear from below...her eyes turned to the steps and then she saw it.

Under the furthest seat was a pen. She got onto her knees and reached for it. Dad's pen, the one she'd had designed and made for him for his sixtieth birthday. It was always in his hand or pocket.

Footsteps approached and she panicked, slipping the pen into her handbag. If the media had found her, they mustn't see this. She grabbed her sunglasses and pushed them on.

"Mrs Connor." Ben Rossi stood, hands in pockets, on the pier. His black sunglasses masked his eyes.

Ellie's heart pounded and the words snapped out. "Why are you here?"

"Eleven o'clock at the yacht. I hoped Jack might appear."

There was a sympathy in his tone that cut through her anger and as tears prickled the back of her eyes, she was thankful for her sunglasses.

"Me too." She climbed onto the pier. "But he hasn't, so I'm going to do my best to find him."

"Keep a list of who you contact and the responses. It might help."

"So, you've decided he is missing."

"He's obviously missing. I'm investigating the possibility of foul play."

"Why would anyone hurt him?"

"Any suggestions?"

Not willing to talk to Ben, Ellie stalked away from the yacht, past a couple of other boats and across a dirt track to the carpark. At her car, she dug in her bag for keys.

"What if Dennis only gave you part of the story."

With a small jump, Ellie glanced around. She'd not heard him follow her and he stood staring back down the pier, arms crossed and legs apart.

"Dennis said he'd waited for Dad, who never showed. Instead of looking for him, he went sailing alone."

"But, did he?"

"I don't understand." Ellie joined Ben.

"Jack Bannerman doesn't miss appointments and is never late. Perhaps he was here at the arranged time. Perhaps they did sail out, a long way out."

"And?"

"Something happened. Jack fell overboard. Might have been helped over."

"Are you crazy?" Ellie dragged her sunglasses off. "Dennis and Dad are family. Dad isn't dead and Dennis is not a killer. How could you say such a thing?"

"Is there a reason Dennis would want Jack gone?"

"Gone? Or dead? Neither, for your information. I told you, they were family as well as business colleagues."

"And families are the most likely to kill their own."

"Oh, for god sake." She swung away.

"Is Dennis divorcing you?"

Ellie dropped her keys. Ben scooped them up, playing with them in one hand as he removed his sunglasses with the other. If it was compassion in his eyes, she didn't want it.

"My keys, please." She held out her hand.

"You deserve better."

"My keys, detective."

With a shrug, he dropped them into her palm.

FIVE
UPSTAIRS. DOWNSTAIRS

The sub-penthouse floor of Bannerman House offered expansive views across the city. The executive of BWG worked here in glass offices with a central reception hub. Jack had one end of the floor for his huge corner office and his Personal Assistant—Joni's work station.

Between the corner, along the windows, Dennis, as Chief Operations Officer, had the office beside Jack, then Campbell, Chief Finance Officer, was next. Their shared PA, Mark, used the reception area with two receptionists. At the other end of the floor, Ellie's office was smaller, quieter, and she liked it this way. She had no PA, having the reception team at her disposal, or any one of the sales and marketing staff housed on the floors below. Where everyone else had their name on their doors, Ellie's was a simple "Bannerman Foundation".

Any other time, this floor was abuzz with movement and chatter. Considered the heart of the company, this was where decisions were made and where the future was built.

Today the mood was anything but upbeat. At the long, curved reception desk, four staff, including Mark and Kay, answered phone call after phone call.

Jack's office was empty, the door closed. Joni sat at her desk with a lost expression. Dennis' office was also empty, briefcase on his desk along with a steaming coffee cup.

Only Campbell was there. His door closed, he spoke at length on the phone, then hung up and turned to a laptop. Beside it was a PC with two monitors.

Two files lay on the desk, one titled "Future" and the other "Foundation". He flicked through the former, intent on the contents, then tapped his laptop keyboard to complete an email. With a sigh, he hit send, his eyes straying back to the "Foundation" file. His shoulders tightened.

Several floors below was a much smaller room, its single window overlooking the next building. No Melbourne skyline here, just a workspace filled with monitors, filing cabinets, and a large desk.

"Glorified security guard." Behind the desk, Paul stared at a photo on the wall. Jack and Ellie at a black-tie event, with Paul standing behind.

"Time you realised that." Dennis walked in and dropped into a chair opposite Paul. "You're overpaid."

"Get out." Paul snarled.

"We need to chat, don't you think?"

"You don't want to do this."

"But I do. Actually, I want to fire you, but might have to wait a bit longer."

Blood rushed into Paul's face. "Such confidence from a murder suspect."

"I'm not going to be blamed for something I didn't do."

"Of course, you did it. Or made it happen." Paul swung his chair and stood. "I heard that conversation after the board meeting, and I'll prove you got Jack out of the way."

Dennis was on his feet in seconds, hands balled at his sides.

"You've lost your mind. Bit hard to prove something that didn't happen."

"You believe that, Dennis. Then you won't see it coming."

"Are you threatening me? Are you setting me up?"

Paul sniggered.

"You think this is funny? Jack's missing and until he returns, I'm going to be running things, so I'd be stepping carefully, baby. Very carefully."

A sharp tap on the door interrupted.

"Detective Rossi. Please come in, Dennis was just leaving." Paul stood and offered Ben his hand across the desk.

"Any news about Jack?" Dennis asked.

"Nothing about his whereabouts."

"Do you need to see me?"

"Just Mr Dekeles for now. I'll be in touch."

Dennis straightened his tie and turned on his heel.

"Take a seat, Detective."

"How's your relationship with Dennis Connor?" Ben sat and crossed an ankle over a knee. "How long have you known him?"

"Too long. He wants to fire me but doesn't have the power, so that should answer the first question. And he's been here for five years. Appeared one day and won't leave."

"Chief Operations Officer. Second in command?"

"He thinks so. Not sure what he does. I think Jack owed him a favour and when Ellie decided to take a year off to travel, he needed someone to fill her role. She came home and Dennis managed to keep the job and win the woman."

"And what does she do now?"

"Ellie runs the Bannerman Foundation. Looks after the causes. You know, big businesses today have their pet projects to help the less fortunate. She's good at it and it's as much her passion as a career."

"She didn't want her position back? Didn't want to be Jack's right hand again?"

Paul glanced at the photo again. "It wasn't that simple. Anyway, she has a big heart."

"You've been with Jack for a long time."

"My whole working life. He's a good man." Paul faced Ben again. "Look, I want to find him. I've spent hours driving to all the spots I've ever seen him at. Spoke to the barman at his favourite drinking hole. And some of the men he plays golf with. I'm working my way through a list of contacts but…"

"Go on."

"What if he's dead? I mean, how will Ellie cope?"

"Do you think Jack's dead?"

"How can it not be a possibility? Jack's wealthy beyond measure. He stands between certain people who want his money and power. Even at the board meeting, Dennis made it clear he's getting impatient."

"Enough to kill his father-in-law?" Ben said. "What exactly happened at the board meeting?"

"It was more after than during. The others were stuffing themselves with food while Jack, Dennis, and Campbell got into something at the far end of the boardroom table. I got a coffee for Jack, not that he noticed. He and Dennis were having words."

"As in?"

"Well, I remember Campbell saying he'd do the paperwork and he left. Then Dennis was on about Jack's decision affecting a lot of people, especially Dennis. Jack told him to shelve it and they'd speak privately on the yacht."

"Do you know what they were discussing?"

Paul shrugged. "I stay out of the business. Was only in there because I do a security update each meeting. But Dennis was agitated. This was three hours before Jack disappeared."

Ben glanced at the monitors lining one wall and Paul nodded. "Impressive, isn't it. The control room is downstairs, but I keep an eye on things."

"How long do you retain surveillance tapes?"

"Not tapes these days. But, a while."

"Can you get me any from the boardroom meeting?"

"Should be able to. I'll get someone onto it."

"Have you checked to see when Jack left that day?"

"I'm an idiot. Should have been the first thing. Sorry, Detective, I'll get you some footage."

Once Ben left, Paul swivelled his chair so he could stare at the photograph on the wall.

SIX
MESSAGE FROM THE MISSING

Ellie dragged herself into the elevator of her apartment building. Emptiness and exhaustion battled for her attention and her shoulders slumped beneath the weight. She'd been out by car, going to Dad's golf club, his Brighton box on the beach, a hotel he occasionally stayed at when he wanted some personal time. Nobody knew anything.

Then, she'd taken to the streets of Melbourne on foot, visiting every coffee shop, bookshop, and bar he liked. At one of the bookshops she'd seen a man at the back of the store in a designer suit with short cropped grey hair and her heart flipped, but then he turned. Not Dad. She'd hurried from the bookshop before she made a fool of herself by falling apart.

Now, as the elevator doors began to close, a man squeezed between them. Mid-twenties with curly blonde hair, he wore a singlet and track pants and carried a gym bag. She'd seen him once before, but there was also a familiarity about his face she couldn't place. Probably had seen him more than once and not paid attention.

"Thought I'd missed it." He grinned, positioning himself close to Ellie. Too close. "Need a shower something bad."

She agreed but put on the smile she used for strangers. Polite and remote.

"Hey, I know you."

Ellie looked at the ground. She wasn't up to questions about Dad.

"You live a few doors up from me."

"We're on the same floor." Ellie relaxed and offered a friendlier smile.

"You've noticed me."

Did you just flex your muscles?

"Guess you would. I work hard for this body."

Instead of laughing, she managed, "I'm married." At least for now.

"Good for you. I'm not into older women. But nice to know you've checked me out."

With a soft whoosh, the doors opened and gym man stepped out. Ellie counted to three then exited, hoping he'd kept walking. Older woman. Since when was thirty old? He unlocked a door to the left, grinning when she glanced at him.

Her corner apartment was the opposite direction and she let herself in, not sure whether to laugh or cry. Instead, she opened the only remaining alcohol—the French champagne and toasted herself.

To old women who are married but not married.

Shoes off, a mouthful of not-as-bad-as-she-expected bubbly warming her stomach, Ellie stood in the middle of the living room. If Dennis was gone, then this was all hers again. She'd owned the apartment for longer than she remembered and made the mistake of allowing him to add what he called 'improvements' with furnishings and art. Better than his preference of selling it and moving to the same suburb as her father, which Dennis considered a good idea.

The evening sky was red and gold and she longed to sit outside. How she loved Melbourne, the city she'd been born and raised in. From here she could see toward Dad's house.

The champagne was suddenly tasteless and she put the glass on the table beside the phone.

The answering machine blinked.

She'd go out and get dinner and a bottle of real wine and come back and sleep. Take a pill and block it all out just for one night.

Her hand hovered over play. It would be a telesales call.

She touched the button.

"Honey. It's Dad."

SEVEN
A CLUE

Ben almost bumped into a man rushing out of the elevator as he stepped in. They both apologised, then went their separate ways. The doors closed behind Ben, amplifying the stench of dried sweat he'd noticed coming off the other man. Normally people got sweaty after the gym, but the bag and clothes indicated he was on his way to one.

Ben stared at his reflection on the mirrored sides. Straightened his tie and combed his too-long hair with his fingers. Get it cut. Shave the stubble.

Why do you care what she thinks?

Ellie's floor. He turned right and headed to the corner apartment, where he tapped. "It's Ben."

"Not locked."

He raised his eyebrows and let himself in. The sliding doors to a long, wrap-around balcony were wide open and Ellie was outside, leaning against the rail.

Ben glanced around. Glass windows on both sides with incredible views. A gas fireplace set in the middle of a lowered living area. White kitchen with nothing on the benches. Not like the colourful mix of fruit bowls, herbs hanging to dry, and assorted bowls she used to keep there. And the minimal furnishings and rather odd pieces of artwork were new. New to him.

"This is all mine again, it appears." Ellie watched him from the sliding door. "If you know anyone who likes these sorts of furnishings, the whole lot will be going. Not my style."

Reading my mind?

"You should keep the door locked."

"The building is secure. Besides, I unlocked it when I buzzed you in." She stepped inside. "Who is going to harm me?"

"Not really the point."

She stopped near a sideboard. "Am I in danger?"

"I see no reason to believe you are a target, but don't let your guard down." His eyes roamed the apartment again. "Are you okay being alone?"

"Why?"

The question in her eyes was genuine. Behind the façade of coping with the chaos around her, and refusing to acknowledge their past, a tiny flicker of something ignited.

And disappeared. "Please don't patronise me, Detective Rossi."

"I'm not. You were concerned you might be in danger. Having someone else in the apartment might help you sleep better."

"Someone with a badge?"

Before Ben could digest her comment, let alone answer, she'd turned away. "I asked you here to listen to something. To a message."

Jack Bannerman's voice was the last thing he'd expected.

"Honey, it's Dad. Wish you weren't on a plane, and I'm sure there's all kind of talk now, but it'll make sense once you read the letter. I promise. It is in our secret spot so don't let Meredith know. Or…anyone. And I'm sorry to leave things like this." A long sigh. "I love you so much, honey. Be strong for me."

As the recording ended with a series of beeps, Ellie walked away. "Drink? Haven't got much else except expensive champagne Dennis decided to binge buy whilst I was in London."

"I need to hear it again. I missed the time of the call."

"Take the machine. Listen all you want but it won't change the facts." Ellie poured two glasses of champagne and carried them to Ben. The rims of her eyes were red.

"We don't know the facts, Ellie." Ben accepted a glass.

"He's sorry to leave like this. Wants me to be strong. What do you think he means? Ben, he was saying...goodbye."

"No. He was telling you there's a letter which explains something. Perhaps where he is."

"But why would he do that?"

Ben had no answers, so sipped the drink, watching Ellie's face. So expressive, the flash of hope followed by thoughtfulness, and then, a sudden understanding.

"I know what he meant. I need to go to the house."

"Jack's house? Why?"

"Dad and I have a few places we call ours. But only one, I think, where he could leave a letter. Are you coming with me?"

As if he'd refuse.

A solitary light was on in the library in Jack's house, the one over his desk. Thick carpet and timber walls created a sense of quiet and old-fashioned comfort. Several rows of floor-to-ceiling bookshelves filled one side of the space. Two desks faced each other, whilst in a corner, tub chairs circled a low coffee table near a bar.

Dennis sat behind Jack's desk, systematically going through each drawer. He'd already checked the safe which held its customary wad of cash, Jack's passport, and a small photo album. This he'd flicked through, passing over photos of

Ellie from birth to graduation, stopping on a casual one from their own wedding.

Ellie and Dennis were dancing. Near them, Jack and Meredith also danced but Jack's attention was on another woman. Gabi, her face animated as she waltzed with Campbell. Dennis had only met Ellie's mother once, at the wedding, then she was gone again to wherever it was she went.

Jack rarely mentioned her, but he kept a photo of her with Ellie on his desk at work. Despite him being the one to divorce Gabi. Perhaps he regretted it.

He closed the album and shoved it back under the passport, then locked the safe and straightened the painting in front of it.

There was nothing of interest in Jack's desk, so he turned to Ellie's. Behind some files in the bottom drawer was an old, black bottle of rum. Rum didn't interest him, but the lid of this bottle did. It was loose. Something else was inside, hidden behind the dark glass. His fingers were too big to reach what looked like tightly curled paper. He closed the drawer.

Bottle in one hand, he turned off the light. Fingers on the door knob, Meredith's raised voice, followed by Ellie's calmer one, stopped him. High heels approaching on the timber floorboards sent him scurrying to the furthest corner of the room, squeezing into a corner near a bookcase.

"Keep it short. I need my sleep."

The door opened.

"At barely eight?"

Ellie had a point.

"Anyway, what are you looking for? I'm not keeping Jack captive in here."

"Meredith, we won't be long, but for goodness sake, what does it matter? I'm getting something from my desk, not Dad's."

"Fine. Turn the lights off when you leave." The door closed with a loud click.

Just hurry up.

"So, why are we here?"

Dennis almost dropped the bottle. What the hell was the detective doing in Jack's library?

"When I was a child, Dad began hiding messages for me to find. Inside books usually, with a couple of clues to follow."

Unable to help himself, Dennis crept from his hiding spot and found a vantage point where he could watch Ellie between a gap in a row of books. She stood at her desk, the detective to one side.

"What was the purpose?"

"Probably to distract me when Gabi left. I was only little and suddenly had no mother. The messages ranged from envelopes with gift cards to handwritten notes telling me how...proud he was of me." Ellie shook her head. "Anyway, it evolved into our way of communicating to each other. Things we didn't want anyone else to know."

"Such as?"

"He lost a bundle on poker once. Didn't want Meredith to find out because she hates gambling but had to share. Oh, and I told him I was taking the year off via a note. I knew he'd be upset and it was easier for me to do it that way." She sat and opened the bottom drawer. "We use an empty rum bottle as the receptacle. Like pirate's treasure. Which should be here."

Which is in my hand.

And made it even more important he was the first one to read the note.

"But it isn't."

"You sure?"

"Perhaps he left it in his desk. But this is what he meant, I'm sure it is."

Dennis retreated to his dark corner.

More opening of drawers and then a sigh. "It doesn't make sense, Ben. It should be here."

"Who else knows about this? Dennis? Meredith?"

"Nobody. It was our thing and meant nothing. But the bottle is gone."

"Cleaner? Not that anyone should be in the desk drawers. Is there another hiding place?"

"I guess it might be in one of the books."

Dennis was as far in as he could get. If they came around the first row of bookcases he was stuffed. What excuse could he come up with?

Is this what you are looking for? Pina Colada, anyone? Oh, it doesn't have rum inside?

"Meredith wasn't happy about you coming in here. Shall we ask her a couple of questions?"

For the first time, Ben Rossi sounded like a sensible man.

"You'd better ask. I'll probably throttle her."

"Would prefer not to arrest you."

The long silence bothered Dennis. Bothered him a lot. He couldn't see what was going on and that detective had better not be flirting with his wife.

No more words, just footsteps going away and then the opening and closing of the door and the lights being extinguished as they left.

He forced himself to wait for five minutes, then squeezed out of the space. If Jack had hidden something in it, then got a message to Ellie to look for it…what would it be? Code for another safe, a password to something? Or a clue to what happened to him.

Meredith denied all knowledge. Why would anyone go in there, amongst dusty old books and desks belonging to the eighteenth century? Jack and Ellie kept their little secrets and she didn't care. She said all of this before telling them to leave and flouncing from the room.

Ben and Ellie's eyes met and they almost burst into laughter.

"Shall we go?"

"Why? This is Dad's house, not hers. I'd like to take a look around."

"For?"

Ellie led the way from the living room to the back of the house. "Maybe someone found the bottle and thought it was full." She flicked on a light and went inside. A billiards table took up one side, whilst a long bar ran along the other wall.

"This is a possible place." Ellie rummaged around behind the bar. "Not that Meredith can tell the difference between quality liquor and some cheap stuff she'd drink."

"You're not her biggest fan." Ben perched on a stool.

"I don't dislike her. After all, Dad loves her, I imagine." Ellie straightened with a frown. "Not here."

"But?"

"But? Oh, Meredith. She doesn't appreciate what she has. Or Dad."

"And she should be grateful? For the lifestyle and money being his wife brings?"

Ellie stared at Ben. "I didn't say that. And I'd like to go home now if that's okay."

The drive was silent until they reached the city.

"Drop me anywhere, Ben. No need to weave all the way in."

"Sure." Ben kept driving. "How long have Meredith and Jack been married?"

"Six years. I thought he'd never remarry so it was a surprise. But he seemed happy again."

"He was alone a long time."

"Gabi left when I was nine. So yes, a long time." Ellie gazed out of the window.

"Do you see her? Your mother?"

"Now and then. She still has her little cabin in Gippsland

but is off on adventures on her yacht most of the time. Sometimes she goes to spend a week near… well, Michael. But she hasn't been to Melbourne since…since my wedding."

"Which was how long ago?"

Ellie glanced at Ben as he drove through the evening traffic. "I married Dennis five years ago."

His jaw clenched for a second or two then he stopped at a red light and looked at Ellie. "We should talk."

She shook her head.

"Ellie—"

"This is close enough. Thanks for the lift." Ellie wrenched open the door and was out and into the night before he could respond.

EIGHT
WHAT WE HIDE

Dennis locked himself into the guest house where he'd made himself at home the day Jack disappeared.

Meredith had been hysterical when he'd explained Jack's no-show and begged him to stay. Much as he liked the idea of moving straight in with her, that wasn't his head talking. At least, not the decision-making one. The guest house was a compromise.

He left the bottle on the kitchen counter and searched for something to draw out the contents. In the bathroom cupboard was a pair of tweezers.

Was this really a message from Jack to Ellie? How many other secrets were hidden around the place? He was learning a whole lot about his wife tonight, including her interest in, or by, the detective.

The tightly wound paper was an envelope and addressed to Ellie in Jack's handwriting on Jack's personal stationery. It looked as though it had been crumpled into a ball and then straightened and rolled. Dennis flattened it out, then stalked away to find a drink. What made Ellie come looking tonight? Something must have made her believe whatever was in the bottle was important.

After a gulp of Jack's blue gin, Dennis slid a single sheet of paper from the envelope.

As he scanned the note, the glass dropped from his fingers, smashing into shards on the floor.

———

Instead of going to her apartment, Ellie let herself into Bannerman House. Dominating the corner of two of Melbourne's busiest streets, it was fully owned by Jack and the home of Bannerman Wealth Group, but also leased in part to several smaller companies to house their operations. BWG used the top five floors, plus four lower ones, and shared a number of common spaces.

The huge foyer was deserted. Even the security guards were absent from the long reception desk. As she waited for the elevator, Ellie gazed at the space around her. The first three floors were almost completely open and filled with foliage, comfortable seating areas, and two water features. Behind reception, a massive seascape reminded her of childhood summers spent on board one of the yachts.

With a soft 'ding' the elevator opened. Ellie tapped her key card on the reader and selected the sub-penthouse floor. In a moment she stepped out to a darkened reception area. She glanced to her office, neglected since her return.

My poor baby.

Almost six years ago, she returned from a long break overseas to find Dennis settled into her former job as Dad's right hand. Jack Bannerman didn't give people a second chance if they let him down, but agreed she could have a new role when she proposed a charity foundation. She'd lost count of how many people they'd helped so far.

Her destination wasn't her own office, but Dad's. Ellie paused at Joni's desk. Had anyone spoken to her about Dad?

Jack trusted his staff, few more than Joni, so perhaps there was something he'd shared with her.

Ellie let herself into his office, closing the door behind herself. His chair was pushed in, his desk tidy as always. She rested both hands on the back of the chair, imagining for one moment her father was seated there, busy writing a report or on a Skype call. Joni might hurry in with papers to sign, or bring yet another coffee.

She sighed and pulled the chair out. Remnants of his familiar after-shave lingered on the leather.

Dad, where on earth are you?

Ellie sucked in a long breath to the bottom of her lungs to calm her racing heart. She'd find him. She had to.

She opened the top drawer. The contents were neat, minimal, and required. He was not a man for clutter or hoarding. If something wasn't useful, it didn't stay. The only exception was a small collection of items of sentimental value.

The second drawer held two large envelopes, typical of the ones he sent and received all the time. She didn't open them. Campbell kept an eye on those sorts of thing so would know if anything unusual was going on.

She reached for the bottom drawer, interrupted by a sound outside the office. A door closing. Ellie watched for a moment, but seeing no movement through the glass, lost interest.

On the desk, Jack kept several photographs. His wedding to Meredith. Ellie and Michael as baby and child, five years apart. And one always at the front. For some reason it was face down, so Ellie picked it up. Her own face smiled back, along with her mother's. Gabrielle Bannerman, Gabi, as she insisted everyone call her, including her own children. Long gone from their lives, at least by distance.

Gabi's free spirit never accepted her serious husband's precise way of life, despite their great love. Ellie knew she'd tried, staying in a city and lifestyle almost choking her. But the arguments got worse and one day she left. Jack gifted her a yacht—*Wind Drifter*—and she travelled for years, turning her passion for sketching into an income, drifting from remote beach to distant island, only appearing for birthdays and the occasional surprise visit.

Jack always kept this photo here, despite complaints from Meredith. It was a rare moment when Gabi and Ellie were in the same place and sharing a secret which made them laugh. Ellie kissed her mother's image and replaced it in the position she knew it belonged.

A chill crept through Ellie and she glanced through the door again. There was nobody there, nothing but shadows. It must be a security guard around, probably checking the other end of the floor, but then, why not show himself?

She opened the door. "Hello? It's just Ellie."

With no response, she collected her bag from the desk, pushed the chair in, and locked the door behind herself. This whole thing was playing games with her mind.

Downstairs, there was still no sign of security, but a quick look at the monitor display behind the counter showed one of the guards heading into a bathroom, and another leaving a staff kitchen with a plate of food.

The streets were busy enough and Ellie walked home, needing the fresh air to clear her mind. At the corner of her street she was overcome by unease. A scan of the road showed nothing to make her believe she was being followed, not that she knew what to look for. Annoyed at her jumpiness, she stalked to her building.

———

A grey sedan drew away from the curb down the road from Ellie's apartment block. It slowed as it passed the entry, where the concierge was closing the door after Ellie.

NINE
DARK PLANS

7 December

"Where were you last night? I'd planned something special."
Meredith stood in the kitchen, hands on her hips which were
draped with an almost see-through slip over a bikini.

Dennis couldn't take his eyes off her. Makeup perfect, hair
dyed into the fashion of silver-before-your-time and curling
around her pretty face in soft waves, she was hot. Beneath
what passed for fabric, her body had curves he ached to press
himself against.

"Are you quite okay?" her voice softened with amusement.
"See something you like?"

"Coffee for a start." Dennis enjoyed the flash of annoyance
Meredith shot him. "We've got plenty of time, Merry, but need
to play it right."

"I don't see why. Jack is gone. And you're single now."

"Hardly. It takes more than moving half my belongings out
of an apartment to be single."

Meredith began making coffee, biting her bottom lip as she
turned away.

"Okay. Go on, say it." Dennis crossed his arms and leaned his hip against the counter.

"You know, Jack and I weren't exactly right for each other, but he was a smart man. He believed in going after what you want."

"Meaning?"

"Why should we wait? What does it matter if the world knows we want to be together?"

"For God's sake. Look, Jack only disappeared a few days ago so how is it going to look if suddenly we're an item? Paul Dekeles already blames me for it and Ellie is going to believe him unless we play things out carefully."

"Don't you…" Meredith sniffed, her shoulders drooping. "I thought you'd want to be with me."

He looked skyward for a moment, then sidled up to Meredith, reaching around her with his arms. "Forever, baby. Not just for a fling."

She relaxed and leaned back against him.

"Got to do this right. There are complications. Things to take care of. We can't afford to be in the firing line for any reason. I shouldn't be in the guest house even."

"Then move out. Find a hotel or something. But sooner or later they'll find his body, so you need to sever ties with your wife. Okay?"

What do you know?

Had Jack shared the contents of his note with Meredith? Surely not, or she'd be telling the police everything, if only to accelerate her claim on his estate. Unless it was pure coincidence and she'd paid someone to take care of her husband. His arms loosened.

"Dennis? You didn't answer."

"Right. Yeah, sure. Of course." He released her and picked up both coffee cups. "Wanna sit by the pool?"

"Sure." Meredith went ahead. As she sashayed in front of Dennis it was all he could do to walk in a straight line without spilling coffee. So sexy.

The pool reminded Dennis of an island lagoon. Rocks with a waterfall circulated the salt water. The floor was sand coloured and the water crystal clear. It was a pleasant place to unwind. A great place to host parties. Who to invite? The new-look board of directors he'd handpick?

"I swear, Dennis, you've got to get your hearing checked. May I please have my coffee?" Meredith held her hand out from the lounger she'd sunk onto.

"Miles away. Here." He perched sideways on the next lounger, feet on the ground so he could look at her. "I've got to go to work soon. Help the police. Stuff like that. And I need to speak to Ellie—"

"Why?"

Dennis reached for Meredith's hand. "She's going to have to do her job as Jack's daughter and the head of the Foundation. Whether she wants to or not, Bannerman Wealth Group needs to make a statement about Jack and I'm going to write it. She can tidy it up and get it out there."

"I guess."

"And this includes you. So, start thinking about being the distressed wife, the frightened woman whose husband just up and disappeared. Might need to get you in front of the media with tears and confusion. Can you do that, baby?"

Meredith crossed one long leg over another. "I'll find my mourning clothes."

"I wouldn't go that far. But dark sunglasses and some nice white handkerchiefs. I'll brief you beforehand."

Once she nodded, Dennis stretched out on the lounger, eyes on the pool. The splashing of the waterfall created small waves. Add a yacht and it could be a day on the sea. Soon.

"Didn't expect you to be here so early, Detective." Paul nodded as Ben lifted the coffee pot in the open plan police station. "Was going to leave this with the sergeant."

"What do you have for me?" Ben plonked a cup in front of Paul, then dropped into his seat on the opposite side of the desk.

Paul pushed a USB across to Ben. "Anything I could think of. The board meeting, particularly afterwards and you can quite clearly see how tense things were. Followed Jack's trail back to his office for a short bit, then off down the elevator. And him driving out."

Ben took the USB. "Thanks. I'll get this looked at. Was there anything odd you noticed?"

"Odd?" Paul sipped his coffee. "No. Well, maybe. Jack took an envelope from his office. Not the regular type that he drops off with his secretary, but a small white one. Like you'd post a letter in."

"And that's odd, how?"

"Jack's not exactly the letter writing sort. I mean, he dictates stuff and Joni does whatever she does to make it right. But she handles everything. Posting, or couriers or whatever. For him to carry an envelope out of the building was a bit strange."

"And he did so on the day he disappeared."

"He did."

"Anything else?"

"Not from the footage. And let me know if you need more. Or of anyone else's movements."

"Like?"

Paul shrugged. "Dunno. Just thinking aloud."

"Appreciate the assistance."

"Like to say I appreciated the coffee…" Paul stood with a grin. "Let me buy you a real one next time."

Ben grimaced at the eternal dig about police coffee, then

watched until Paul was out of sight. There were pieces to this puzzle not adding up.

Ellie stared at the ceiling of the spare bedroom for a long time, barely aware of the transition from night to light as her thoughts collided. Sleep had finally come long after midnight, but only for a while. She needed to make her own bed and move back into her own bedroom. New sheets. Flowers.

Everything was out of control, and Ellie hated it. Her work gave her purpose, a daily routine where she contributed and helped others. But that work had taken her away for a month and she'd returned to a world on its head.

Dad was missing and his wife didn't seem to care. How could Meredith be so cold about his disappearance? Perhaps it was a combination of brandy and worry that made the woman so nasty the other night. Today she'd go back and speak with her, one on one. Find out what the past few weeks were like and where she believed Jack might be.

And Dennis. Champagne in the fridge. Their bed stripped bare. Half his closest empty. Had she been away one time too many? Was there someone else?

Meredith...

Ellie flung the covers off, unsure if the sick feeling in her gut was hunger, or truth.

There was no food in the place, nothing she'd risk eating. She showered and dressed, plaiting her hair before it was dry and overdoing the makeup.

She glanced in the mirror on the way out, pausing long enough to brush a stray hair behind an ear. Worry lines creased around her eyes. At some point she needed to talk to Michael, about this. And tell him...what? Ellie closed the door on her dark thoughts.

The sight of gym man at the elevator was almost enough to

send her back inside. But the click of her door locking got his attention and he grinned. Ellie raised her chin and smiled politely as she approached.

"Nice morning. You're up early." He said.

Even from a few feet away his body odour invaded Ellie's senses. He was presumably on his way to a gym...or was he? Again, there was a sense of having met him somewhere away from here, or someone like him.

"Always. Are you heading down to the seventh floor?" She glanced at the bag he carried.

"Seventh? No. Should I be?"

"You look ready to work out."

He frowned as the elevator opened. "Yeah." He stepped inside.

Ellie followed, keeping as far away as she could in the small space.

"Sorry, just assumed you'd use the gym in the building."

He drew his bag closer to his body. "Right. Nah. I do other stuff. Like boxing. And I have a membership down the road from the last place I lived. Can't waste it."

The elevator stopped a couple of floors down and other people got in. Ellie flattened herself against the wall to make space, rather than move closer to gym man. Whatever his name was.

Her phone vibrated and she managed to slide it of her bag. A message from Paul. "I'm grabbing breakfast at Hidden if you'd like to catch up."

The doors opened. Out of the building, she crossed to the tram station in the centre of the road. Did Paul have anything new to add? Ellie needed a coffee.

TEN
HIDDEN MEANINGS

Hidden was an aptly named tiny café in a dark alley running off a narrow street. Word of mouth kept it busy from dawn to close and today was no different.

Ellie slipped between tables to reach Paul who was protecting two seats at a long bench facing a brick wall. He stood as she neared, dropping an unexpected kiss on her cheek.

"Here, grab your seat before someone steals it. Have you eaten?"

"Haven't had time to shop yet, but coffee will be fine thanks." Ellie tucked her feet under the table as Paul headed for the counter. She touched her cheek, brow furrowed.

Her stomach rumbled. She should have ordered some food. The café was buzzing with sound. Music, chatter, the background kitchen noises. It was pleasant. Comforting. She liked it here.

"Right. Won't be long." Paul settled next to her. "I am so sorry, Ellie."

"Why?"

"Leaving you alone since you got back to deal with everything. Not being there when you probably needed a friend."

"I'm fine, Paul. It isn't your job to worry about me."

"But I do. Jack would have…Jack wants me to."

Ellie's eyes searched his face. "Wants? Have you heard from Dad?"

He shook his head. "Sorry, bad choice of words. But he always did. Keep an eye on my girl. That's what he said more than once. So, I will."

"It really isn't necessary. But I do have questions."

A waiter interrupted with coffee. The steaming cup smelled divine and Ellie murmured her thanks before taking a cautious sip.

"Ask away."

"Okay. Since when did Dennis live at Dad's house?"

Paul sat back. "Have you asked him?"

"I haven't seen him since the night before last. When I got back from London."

"Why not?"

"Police station, then nearly a whole day searching everywhere for Dad," Ellie's voice broke a little. "Then I went to his house, to get something from my desk. But only Meredith was there and she was in a mood."

"What were you after?"

Was it her imagination, or was Paul closer, his eyes intense? "Just a…notebook I'd left there. Nothing important."

"Excuse me." The waiter returned with two plates. Paul motioned for one to be set before Ellie.

"Oh, I didn't—"

"I did. You need to eat."

Two perfectly poached eggs perched aloft a swirl of spinach, with a fan of sliced avocado to one side. Exactly what she'd have ordered for herself.

"Paul? Thank you. But how on earth did you order this?"

"It is your favourite, right?"

"It is."

"Then eat."

He was already devouring his waffles. Ellie stared at him for a moment, then picked up a fork, famished.

———

Food helped. She savoured every morsel, then finished the coffee with a sigh.

"Earth to Ellie."

"Sorry, Paul. That was delicious, thank you."

"Pleasure. I ordered more coffee while you were worshipping your breakfast."

Ellie laughed.

"Good. Better than looking so distraught all the time." Paul put his hand over one of Ellie's. "We're going to find Jack, okay?"

With a nod, Ellie withdrew her hand. "We were talking about Dennis."

"Oh. Him. He moved out of your apartment about three weeks ago. Into a hotel. Then the day Jack disappeared, Meredith had a melt-down and begged him to move into the guest house. Something about being afraid on her own."

"Rubbish. She has staff. And she could have asked you to provide security."

"She could have."

"What has she done to find Dad?"

"Stared at her reflection at the bottom of a glass a lot." Paul piled their plates on top of each other. "Sorry. That was insensitive. I don't know, Ellie."

"I'm going to visit her later. I'll ask her then."

"Good luck. What else are you doing today?"

"I need to meet with Campbell and Dennis and formulate a plan to manage things until Dad returns."

And see what they both really know.

She continued. "Once that's done, I want to sit down with

you and go over everything from that last day Dad was around." Ellie knew Paul would say what he thought. He mightn't get on with Dennis, but he was close to her father and along with Campbell could be relied on to tell her if something wasn't right.

ELEVEN
CAMPBELL'S CHOICES

Campbell Boyd had attended the same school as Jack. They moved in different circles, Campbell coming from a wealthy family who'd already lined him up for a future in finance and business management. While Jack excelled at football and cricket, Campbell retired hurt in the lower grades. He wanted to be athletic and be liked as Jack was. Perhaps he'd idolized him.

In their last year of high school, their paths crossed more, with Jack aiming for the same university as Campbell, his sights on a business degree. After a nasty incident when another student tried to bully Campbell into helping him cheat, Jack stepped in and from then, they were friends.

Jack's rise to wealth was meteoric and unexpected to everyone, except those who knew him personally. He was born fighting for what he wanted, the youngest of a large family living in poverty. A keen intellect and sense of justice drove him from a young age and he worked multiple jobs, giving some of his money to help his mum out after his dad went to prison yet again. Scholarships got him part of the way, and he did the rest.

What was not to admire and even love about Jack Bannerman? Campbell came out of university and straight into one of the big banks. Ten years later, Jack came calling. "I need someone I can trust, Cam. You've always been rock solid."

Bannerman Wealth Group was a fledgling company with five staff, housed in a rundown shop in West Melbourne. Against his better judgement, and the protests of his family, Campbell left a lucrative position and dived in. Thirty years later, he could look back without any professional regret.

He stared at the computer screen, pulled from his thoughts by a new email. It wasn't one he wanted to see. This was Jack's project, so without him, how was it to go ahead?

"Campbell? May I come in?"

"Ellie, my dear. Of course." He pushed himself onto his feet, grimacing at pain in his knees. Arms open, he met her on the other side of his desk.

"I don't want to interrupt if you're busy."

"Actually, I'm not. Please, let's sit." Campbell gestured for her to go first.

Ellie sank onto one of the two seat sofas and he took the other. She was pale and her eyes were ringed with redness. He poured water into two glasses from a jug on the coffee table.

"Are you sleeping at all?"

She took the glass with a smile. "Yes. Not enough. But everyone needs to stop worrying about me."

"Everyone?"

"Paul, for one. Have you heard anything yet?"

"You know I'd call you first if I do. And Paul has always had a soft spot for you. He'll watch your back." Campbell hoped that reassured her.

"If I tell you something, will you keep it confidential for now?" Ellie asked.

"You know I will."

Ellie put her glass down, untouched. "Dad left me a message. Well, two."

"What? When, Ellie?"

She glanced at the door then spoke in a quieter tone. "There was a voicemail on the home phone. I only found it last night."

Campbell's fingers drummed against his leg and he curled them into his palm. "Whatever did he say?"

"He was sorry I was on a plane. He said I'd understand once I read his letter."

"Letter?"

"Told me to look in our usual place—we've always had a secret way of communicating going back to my childhood."

He was holding his breath. Bit by bit, he let it out.

"The problem is, I've looked, and the letter isn't where it should be. Not even the...well the place we leave notes and stuff is missing." Ellie picked up her glass and drank.

"Jack told you he'd left a letter in your secret hiding place, but nothing was there? And he phoned while you were in transit. Then he must be alive!" At last some good news.

"You can't say anything. Ben is verifying the time of the phone call but without this letter, I'm no closer to finding out what happened. For all we know he might have hidden a letter to say he was going on a week's holiday to somewhere with no means of contact." Ellie's voice pitched higher as the words tumbled out. "He might waltz back here in a couple of days all suntanned and with presents from some island."

"You look like you're going to cry, Ellie. Please, have some more water."

"I'm not going to cry, but I want to find Dad." She leaned back and whispered. "I just need to find him."

"We will. The police will."

"Until there is some sort of evidence of foul play, or whatever you want to call it, they won't do anything. Not yet."

Jack's disappearance surely wasn't the result of him deciding to take a break on some deserted island. A lifetime knowing the man ruled this out. Besides, he'd have left instructions, delegated Dennis or Ellie to oversee things. And then there was the project.

"My dear child, I don't believe for a minute Jack would vanish to some island and somehow, we need to persuade the police to take it seriously. There's a large venture underway and his presence is quite critical."

Ellie sat bolt upright. "How critical? Campbell, who would benefit from his absence?"

TWELVE
CHANGE OF GUARD

The sub-penthouse floor was almost deserted. With the sudden decision to run an executive meeting downstairs, all staff had followed Joni to set things up. Only Mark stayed, finishing a paper Dennis wanted on Campbell's desk in a hurry. Nobody messed with what Mr Connor demanded, and by the time quiet descended, he'd completed the task.

He wandered into Campbell's office and around the desk. If he left this to one side of the keyboard, then Campbell would find it when he returned. His hand hovered over the keyboard as he surveyed the reception area. He was alone.

Mark tapped the keyboard and the screen woke up. An email was open. An interesting email.

The boardroom doors closed behind Joni. She'd offered to stay to takes notes after setting up a pot of coffee and selection of pastries, but Ellie wanted this meeting off the record.

She'd taken Dad's spot at the head of the table for no reason other than to best see the others' faces. Campbell was to her left, with Paul beside him.

On her right, Dennis tapped the table impatiently, his chair pushed back and one ankle crossed over a knee. At first, he'd refused to attend. It was a waste of his time. Ellie had shrugged and said fine, she'd meet with the other two. Yet, here he was.

"Thanks for attending on short notice. I know you are all worried about Dad and I'm hoping we can agree to work together to find him."

"Why is Dekeles here?" Dennis stared at Paul, who winked at him. Ellie ignored them both.

"The police aren't convinced Dad is more than off on some jaunt. There's no evidence he was kidnapped, or any one of a number of things. But we all know he would never just disappear like that!"

"Exactly, Ellie." Campbell said. "Even if he wanted a break, he'd have let us know."

"Which brings me to a question. Who would benefit from Dad disappearing?"

"Are you some sort of detective now?" Dennis checked his watch. "Get to the point."

How can you be so cold? Just like Meredith.

"Very well." Ellie said. "Campbell mentioned there is a major project underway, one Dad would need to be involved with. What is it?"

"It isn't for Dekeles to know so off you go, sunshine."

"Paul is a necessary part of our planning to find Dad. He's hardly going to run off and share company information."

"You sure about that, Ellie?"

"I can come back if you want." Paul pushed his chair back. "Jack is more important than whatever's going on with this...joker."

Dennis grinned. "That the best you can do?"

"Do either of you actually care about Dad?" Disappointed, Ellie shook her head.

With a sigh, Dennis uncrossed his legs and pulled his chair in. "Wind farm."

"Sorry?"

"We're working with a private developer for a wind farm. They needed investors and we've been finding them."

"Sounds straightforward. Would Dad even need to be involved?" A look passed between Dennis and Campbell. Something wasn't right. "So, what's the issue?"

Campbell cleared his throat. "Just the timing. The funding is in place, but the grid, where the farm will connect to send power to the provider, well, that's a problem. Our systems aren't set up for the volume of wind and solar farms, not in some regions, so it is either a case of get in early or look at a lot more cost by running your own storage as well."

"So, we're trying to get in first?"

Again, the look between the men

"Who will this affect?" Paul asked Campbell.

"Affect? Wind farms are a good thing."

"So, Jack is all for it?"

"What's your point, Dekeles?" Dennis leaned toward him. "Mister business expert."

"You didn't seem all that happy about it at the board meeting. Just saying."

"Dennis?"

"Ellie, I have no idea what he's on about. Jack signed off on it ages ago. It has nothing to do with him disappearing, and I thought that is what you wanted to talk about."

"It is. But if this deal put him at risk—"

"No risk, Ellie. Straightforward, as you suggested." Campbell interrupted. "Should we discuss the running of Bannerman Wealth Group while he is…wherever he is?"

———

"Something's not adding up, Paul."

Ellie and Paul were in the elevator, heading down to the foyer. Dennis was now the interim CEO, based on chain of command and long held instructions from Jack, in the event of death or disablement, which were verified by Campbell.

"You mean about the wind farm? Yeah. Those two know something they're not sharing and I'm surprised at Campbell but expect it from Connor...sorry."

"I wish you two would get along. Or act like adults at least. Sorry. Not sorry." Ellie was over it. Her voice was calm but she was one more problem away from screaming.

The doors whooshed open and Paul followed Ellie into the foyer. "Are you walking?"

"I'm going home to get my car then visit Meredith. And no, I don't need company."

"I'll pull my head in. About Dennis."

"Good. This is difficult enough." They stopped just inside the front doors. Ellie stared up at Paul. "Have you looked for footage from the day Dad disappeared? To see if anyone was with him?"

"He left alone. I looked."

"Oh."

"Yeah. Pity there's no cameras at that marina. Can't understand it actually."

"Only a handful of boats tie up there. Some of their owners are obsessively private."

"Still. Would have helped."

People hurried in and out of the building. Ellie looked past Paul to reception, to the painting of the yacht on the sea. How wonderful to simply take *Sea Angel* and go. Follow the trade winds, sea mist on her lips. Find Gabi, wherever she might be in the world right now and let her take some of the burden. She always knew the right words and besides, she should know about her ex-husband. Same as Michael needs to know.

"Ellie?"

No sea mists. Not until she found Dad.

"What if I bring dinner over later? We can compare notes and plan what comes next." Paul put his hand on her arm.

"Oh. Um, no, but thanks. I have no idea what I'm doing later."

"Well text if you change your mind. Or we could meet somewhere."

"We did for breakfast. And it was nice, thanks." Ellie extracted her arm with a small smile. "I have to get going."

She didn't walk home but grabbed a tram. Hanging onto a rail as it bumped and lurched across other tracks and around corners, Ellie drifted back to the earlier image of a blue-green sea and salty winds.

Find Dad.

Then she'd take a proper break. Run away with the yacht for a while. Sort out her future as a single woman.

In minutes she was home, stopping long enough to collect car keys.

The gates to Jack's house were open. Ellie nosed her car around the fountain in the middle of the driveway and parked facing back out. In her rear-view mirror, she saw the curtains move in the living room. By the time she reached the front door, Meredith had flung it open. Ellie steeled herself for the expected cold reception.

"I'm so glad you've come." Meredith threw her arms around Ellie. Unlike the last two visits, she didn't reek of alcohol and the embrace was heartfelt. "Please come in."

Ellie followed her, closing the door. "I'm sorry to drop by unannounced. Finding Dad is all I can think about and I wanted to see how you were holding up."

"Let's get coffee." Meredith headed for the kitchen. "How sweet of you. Shall we sit in the garden? I'll tell Brenda to bring us out a tray if you'd like to find a spot."

The sprawling grounds were a mixture of entertaining areas as well as leafy retreats. Ellie found a place in the shade near the pool, not on the lounges, but where old tree stumps were carved into seats. The guest house was only a few metres away.

"There you are!" Meredith dropped onto a seat and pulled sunglasses down from her head. Her skirt was short, revealing tanned, slender legs that she crossed. "Coffee won't be long."

"Thanks. I'd love to have a talk, Meredith."

"How was London?"

It felt like a year had passed since she'd boarded in Heathrow, not just a few days. Her notes were on the laptop, weeks of work turned into a brief she'd finished on the plane, ready to go over with Dad. Her chest tightened.

"It doesn't seem to matter anymore." Ellie stared at the pool. Two of the sun lounges were close together, coffee cups on either side. What else would go wrong?

"But it does, darling. Jack certainly thought it important enough to send you there for such a long visit, not that I really understand why."

"Setting up a new office takes time. I had meetings with a range of companies and individuals, people we might contract to handle the European side of the Foundation."

Brenda arrived with a tray, which she placed on another tree trunk covered with a glass top. Ellie thanked her, but Meredith barely looked up from her phone when it buzzed.

"The cakes are gluten free and vegan," she said. "And despite that, they are actually delicious. Help yourself."

"I will. Coffee smells good."

"The blend is from some green ethical rainforest something, ra, ra, ra. Better taste good as it costs the earth. Not that Jack cares, he is just as happy with instant." Meredith screwed up her nose at the idea.

"So…when did you last see Dad?"

Meredith picked up an exquisite cupcake. "The night before he disappeared."

"Not at breakfast that day?"

"Don't be silly. We never saw each other before lunchtime. You know what Jack's like. Early to bed, early to rise etcetera etcetera."

Yes. He works hard for what you enjoy.

"You're more of a night owl?" Ellie suggested.

"I do like a nice night out. We used to do those all the time." Meredith nibbled the edge of the cupcake. "Been quite a while though."

"So, how was he the night before he disappeared?"

"Actually, Ellie, this is going to sound like I contradict myself, but he was out late. We had dinner, then I had a friend to meet for a drink and he said he had work to do. You must try one of these."

Ellie took a cupcake, admiring an intricate pattern of minute iced flowers on top. If this was Brenda's work, she needed more recognition. "Did he work in the library?"

"Oh no. We left at the same time and he dropped me off at Crown Casino. He was going to go to the office to finish something with this windmill project thing."

"Wind farm?"

"Whatever."

"Was he back when you got home?"

Meredith removed her sunglasses. "Sweetie, I have no idea. I got in after one. And he sleeps in another room so how would I know if he even came back or stayed somewhere... else?"

Too much information.

Yet, it made sense if Dennis was in any way involved with Meredith other than being her step-son-law. Ellie bit into the cupcake rather than comment. It was light and fluffy and way too good for Meredith.

"What are you doing to find him? Is that detective of yours…on the case?"

Innuendo dripped from her lips and if Ellie wasn't enjoying the cupcake so much, she might have thrown it at her head.

"If you mean Detective Rossi, then you'd be best to speak with him. Dad isn't of great interest to them yet."

"Yet?"

"He hasn't been missing for long, plus he's an adult with full faculties, and there is no evidence of foul play."

"You're not doing a thing." Meredith pouted and sat back.

"He's your husband. What have you done to find him?" Ellie forced a smile. "Phoned? Texted? Hired a private detective?"

"Well, I'd ask Paul to look but he hates Dennis so it would be counter-productive. I've called. His phone is off, although I did leave a couple of messages."

"Why does it matter that Paul and Dennis can't get along? Dad is the one missing and they can work together if they have to."

"Right."

Ellie checked her watch. "Thanks for the coffee and these fabulous cupcakes. I'm going to pop into the library to collect some papers I need for the office."

"But it is so nice here in the sun."

"I'll find my way." On her feet, Ellie leant down to kiss Meredith's cheek. "You enjoy your cupcake."

While you still can.

When Dad got back, he'd be appalled by Meredith's lack of interest in finding him let alone the new living arrangements for Dennis. And Ellie would make sure he knew about it.

THIRTEEN
DAD'S DAYS

Ellie locked herself into the library. There were no papers to collect but Meredith wouldn't know the difference. Of all the shallow, selfish people she'd met, Dad's second wife was the worst. No apparent distress at her husband's disappearance, instead, she was content to eat cupcakes in the sun.

Before she could wind herself up any further, Ellie searched through the drawers in her desk again. The place that the rum bottle normally occupied was still empty.

Dad's desk was just as useless. He kept even less here than at the office, apart from a small pile of novels on the corner of the desk. She sat there, eyes roaming along the bookcases to the far wall. Clichéd as it might be, his safe was behind a painting.

She rarely opened this and hesitated before touching the artwork, a simple watercolour of a garden. Was it slightly angled? Meredith may have been in there, although Jack had told Ellie the main safe in the bedroom was the only one his wife cared about.

When Ellie pulled out the passport, she closed her eyes for a moment in relief. Logic told her some record would have come to light had he left Australia, but still, she'd wondered. If he was anywhere in this country, she'd find him.

From under the bundle of money he stashed in every safe, she pulled out the photo album and slid it into her handbag. If it meant enough to Dad to keep it in there, then she wanted to know why.

After locking the safe and straightening the painting, Ellie wandered around the bookshelves. She flicked through the books they'd used in the past for messages but no notes fluttered out, no folded pages provided a clue.

Her phone vibrated and she grabbed it from her bag, heart dropping when it was Paul's name, not Dad's. *Would you like a drink tonight to swap updates?* No, she wouldn't. She ignored it. What she did want was to open the library door and find Dad on the other side, but he wasn't there. Ellie found herself in the huge, country style kitchen. Two women, in the black dresses and white aprons Meredith insisted on, worked in silence at a long counter.

"I wanted to thank you for the coffee and such lovely cupcakes." Ellie smiled at the women as they looked up. "I have friends in restaurants who'd love to meet you...whoever made them?"

"Young Derry did, miss." Brenda nodded at the younger woman.

"Well, they were delicious. You both do a terrific job."

"Miss, is there any news...of Mister Jack?" Derry stepped forward.

"I wish there was. You don't remember the last time you saw him, do you?"

Derry nodded. "He had breakfast here in the kitchen."

"The day he disappeared?"

"Yes, miss. I made him coffee and scrambled eggs. He read the newspaper."

"How did he seem, Derry? Happy? Tired?"

Derry frowned. "Just…like normal. I hope he comes back soon."

So do I.

"Brenda? Were you here for breakfast?"

"I started late because I'd made him a late dinner. He told me to sleep in."

"What time? Dinner, I mean."

"Maybe around midnight. And, he was…"

Ellie tilted her head. "Please go on."

"At first, I thought he was sad. But when I took the meal to him, he was different. Smiling. And gave me a hug." Brenda blushed and glanced away.

"Where did he eat?"

"Oh. The library, miss. He ate in the library."

———

Ellie sat outside a café overlooking Brighton Beach, her coffee cold and a salad untouched. She'd missed lunch and only had the cupcake since breakfast, but even halfway through the afternoon, it was a mistake thinking she could eat.

A man jogged along the beach followed by a spaniel, who periodically rushed into the low waves and then sprinted to catch his owner, shaking water from its long ears.

She'd like to have a dog. Once she found Dad, she'd sell or rent her apartment and buy a townhouse. Or even a house. A garden and somewhere to play with a new, furry friend.

With a sigh, she pushed the coffee cup to one side. What had happened to Dad the night before he disappeared? Over and over, Ellie ran through the words from Brenda and Derry.

Dad had come home late from the office where he'd been working on the wind farm project, at least, according to Meredith. Between arriving, and Brenda bringing him dinner, he'd cheered up to the point of hugging her. Not a normal response with the staff.

What was his state of mind like recently? Paul mentioned tension in the boardroom. She needed to talk to Dennis. Except his mood earlier made her stomach turn. Two cups near the pool at Dad's house meant something. Something she wasn't ready to explore.

"Would you like a fresh cup?"

"Oh." Ellie started. The waiter began clearing her plate. "No. Actually, I'm leaving but thanks." She stood. "Sorry about the salad. I'm sure it was lovely."

Outside, a recycling bin overflowed with bottles. She took her phone out and dialled Dad's house, wandering to the edge of the sand as she waited.

"Bannerman Estate. How may I be of assistance?"

"Brenda, this is Ellie."

"Mrs Connor. Please hold and I'll put you—"

"No, I want to speak to you, not Meredith. If you have a moment?"

"Me? Oh, certainly." The other woman's voice was strained.

"I just wondered if you've come across any empty bottles. Actually, an old rum bottle."

"I don't understand?"

"Sorry. There's an old empty bottle my Dad and I used to keep in the library. It seems to have disappeared and I would love to find it. Sentimental reasons."

There was a long silence.

"I'm hoping you or one of the other staff might have come across it. Or could keep an eye out for it."

"Any empty bottles are disposed of in the recycling. Do you know when it went missing?"

"No. I'm sorry, I don't know. But it is short and very dark with a faded label. Would you look out for it and let me know if it appears?"

"I should ask Mrs Bannerman."

Screw Mrs Bannerman!

"Please, Brenda, let's keep this between us. The bottle belongs to me, and Dad. I think it might help me find him and you said you want that."

"I do, of course. Very well, I'll ask the others and phone you if we find it."

Ellie stared at the sea for a while after terminating the call. Brenda was scared of Meredith. Why was this so hard? Nobody knew anything. Or wanted to talk about Dad.

The sea air enticed Ellie and she longed to kick off her shoes and be like the spaniel running into the waves.

"Do you think we should be in here?" Joni glanced at Jack's desk then back at Ellie's face. "In case the police need to check anything?"

"Why would they do that? Come on, let's sit by the window." Ellie sank onto the sofa facing out over the city and patted the seat beside her. "I promise it is okay."

Joni perched on the edge of the seat, hands folded around each other. In the years Ellie had known Joni, she'd never seen the woman without a ready smile. But there were only drawn lines on her face, a weariness Ellie knew must be reflected on her own.

"You need to go home soon. Try to rest a bit."

"I'm fine, Ellie. Really, I should be here. In case…"

"When we find Dad, I'll let you know. And we will."

"It doesn't add up. Mr Bannerman doesn't ever go anywhere without appointments, a timetable, and regular contact with me. What could have happened?" She turned glistening eyes to Ellie.

"Can you remember anything about the day he disappeared? When he left, where he was going, what other appointments he had?"

"Of course. You know there was a board meeting that morning?"

Ellie nodded.

"After that, Mr Bannerman returned to his office for a few minutes. He left with his briefcase and a small envelope and dropped past my desk."

"To leave the envelope?"

"No, although I offered to post it. But he said it wasn't going in the mail."

Was it my note?

"He wished me happy birthday for next week."

"What?"

Joni pulled a tissue from a pocket. "He said there was something extra in my pay and to have a special night out on him." She dabbed her eyes. "But normally he'd say something on the day and always gave me flowers. He was so generous."

"Yet he wished you birthday greetings in advance? How odd."

"There you are." Dennis burst into the office. "I need you downstairs for this media thing."

Both women turned to look at him. His face was red and his tie loose. Ellie stood.

"Suggest you go via a bathroom so they don't think you've been drinking all afternoon. You haven't, have you?"

He didn't bother replying, just glared then stalked out.

"I do have to go. Sorry. Walk me to the lift?"

They stopped outside the office where Ellie gave Joni a hug. "At the moment, Dennis is in charge, so just treat him as if he's Dad." She closed the door behind them both. "You didn't say...do you know where Dad was going after he stopped at your desk?"

"He was going to meet Mr Connor at the *Sea Angel*, but not until later. I had him pencilled out for the afternoon before a dinner meeting."

"So, he left, what, a couple of hours before meeting Dennis? Where did he go?"

Joni shrugged as they covered the distance to the elevator. "He only said he was going to go home first to change."

But nobody saw him there. Or was someone lying?

"Last question. Who was the dinner meeting with?"

"Actually, I don't know." They were at the elevator and Joni tapped the button. "It was for eight pm at The Riverview, but he told me to arrange it for two, and under his name."

"How odd that nobody came forward to say they were meant to meet him." The doors opened and Ellie stepped in. "I have to go deal with this media storm. You've been great, Joni, but please, go home."

Ellie's heart went out to the other woman. She'd been Dad's PA for a decade and must feel lost. Dennis had better treat her properly. She stopped the elevator on a lower floor, not ready to be the face of the business to a mob who wanted answers until she checked her make-up and found her game-face.

FOURTEEN
MEDIA AND MORE

Game-face firmly on, makeup and hair perfect, Ellie strode into the foyer where a podium was set up. Dennis' insistence on making a formal press statement might get them off her back for a while, but as the media group turned, she somehow doubted it.

"There she is!"

Dennis met her and took her arm, as though escorting her out of concern. His hand squeezed her hard though and he whispered, "About damned time," through a smile.

Paul was there with a couple of his security guards and they made a path past the group. Dennis and Ellie reached the podium and turned their backs on the media.

"Teresa Scarcella is your target. Get her onside and she'll back off."

"And how do I do that?"

"I've written the statement, so you need only to look like you know what you're doing and read it. Meredith is here and might say some words, as will I. No going off-script."

Ellie scanned the paper he shoved into her hands, annoyed to see them shake. Get the job done, then have a drink. Quiet, alone. She drew in a long breath and nodded, then adjusted the microphone. Dennis withdrew to one side, where Meredith stood. Ellie refused to look at them.

"Good afternoon and thank you for taking time out of your busy day to come along."

What the hell rubbish had Dennis written?

"I'm going to make a statement, then there will be a short opportunity to ask questions."

"Ellie, do you think Jack is dead?" Someone called out.

"Of course not." She snapped.

"Stick to the script." Dennis hissed.

"We didn't have to let you in here." Ellie ignored Dennis and his script. "I'm happy to have a conversation, let you ask questions, but keep them respectful. This is my father we're discussing."

The chatter subsided and cameras moved closer.

"Thank you. Bannerman Wealth Group is eager to get any information about Jack's whereabouts, so hopefully we can work together. He was last seen leaving this building late morning on the fourth of December. He apparently drove himself back to his house. His next appointment was to go sailing on his yacht, and then have a dinner meeting."

"Who was he sailing with? Was it you, Dennis?" Another reporter pushed forward and his camera operator followed. "Where you the last person to see him? The last known contact?"

Dennis shook his head and kept his mouth closed.

"We are unsure of where Jack went between leaving the building and his expected rendezvous at the yacht. This is the time he disappeared, to the best of our knowledge."

"Ellie, Teresa Scarcella. What involvement is there from the police? Is Jack officially a missing person?"

"I can't speak for the police, Ms Scarcella. You'd need to approach them."

"When did you last speak with your father?" Teresa pressed on.

"Dad and I spoke before I boarded the plane in Heathrow. About two hours before."

"And no contact since? No message, or phone call?"

Oh, she's good.

"What we'd appreciate from you all is help asking the public for anything they might have seen. Jack Bannerman is a person of habit, of order. His disappearance is completely out of character." Ellie stepped away from the podium, closer to the crowd. "Look, I understand this is news to you. You're all doing your jobs. But this is my dad and I'd rather be spending time finding him, than constantly answering questions or going around you to get into my own apartment."

Teresa turned up one side of her mouth, but kept it shut.

"I'll tell you once I know what's happened. But please, please respect our privacy as a family and as Jack's beloved company. It would mean a great deal to me."

"Thank you, Ellie." Dennis was at the podium, Meredith at his side. "Mrs Bannerman would like to make a short statement. Are you still feeling okay to do this?" his voice softened as he looked at Meredith.

Dressed in a plain blue skirt and white blouse, with minimal jewellery and her hair in a tight bun, Meredith gave Dennis a small shake of her head, then touched her eyes with a handkerchief.

Oh, please.

"It has been a difficult few days for Mrs Bannerman, so please excuse her. Ellie, would you mind escorting Mrs Bannerman to a quiet room, and I'll open the floor to questions."

Ellie wanted nothing more than to tell Dennis to take Meredith himself and stop playing whatever game they were playing. Imagine what the press would do with that!

"Come on, Meredith." She guided her stepmother past the crowd, catching Paul's eye. He rolled his and Ellie almost giggled. Turning it into a cough, she headed toward the elevator, not particularly concerned whether Meredith kept up.

Once inside the elevator, she took out her phone. No messages.

"I think that went well, despite your little display of emotion. Might have helped if anything."

"Why didn't you speak?" Ellie shoved the phone in her bag and stared at Meredith. "Or was the whole thing of 'are you still feeling okay' pre planned with Dennis?"

"No need to get snippy, darling. We did discuss this, of course. Nothing like forward planning. I was worried I might get a bit too upset, which really wouldn't help, would it?"

"Maybe some genuine concern about your missing husband—"

"Oh, Ellie, I'd be very careful who you offend." Meredith smiled a forced, cold smile. "None of us know what the future holds. None of us know where your dear daddy is, so let's play happy families and make the most of this situation."

The doors opened and several people, sharing a conversation, entered. Ellie balled her hands into tight fists. Meredith dabbed her eyes again and one of the others in the lift nodded their sympathies.

When the group alighted, Meredith went to follow, but Ellie tapped her card against the reader again and pressed the sub-penthouse level.

"You are going to go and wait for Dennis in his office, Meredith." Ellie was pleased her voice stayed firm, unlike her churning stomach. "His PA will bring you something to drink if you need it."

"I'd rather we are friends, darling."

"I'm sure Dennis will be along soon."

Ellie checked her phone, filling in the seconds until the doors opened. They did with their soft whoosh and Ellie touched the 'hold' button. "Mark, would you escort Mrs

Bannerman into Mr Connor's office and see she's comfort-able?" she called to the main reception desk.

As Mark hurried over, Meredith stepped out with a hissed "Watch yourself, princess."

———

Exhausted, Ellie drove to her apartment without speaking to anyone, but she still had things to do. She made coffee and sat on the sofa, feet curled under herself. She needed to sleep so much it hurt.

Coffee finished, she dragged herself to the bathroom and showered for the second time today. Water streaming over her head drowned out the remnants of Meredith's nasty tone. They'd never been friends, but this open hostility was new and confronting. Dennis might be showing too much concern for Meredith's wellbeing, but he'd never touch her. His job meant too much to upset Jack. And he was married to his boss's daughter at least in name.

Half an hour later, hair in a ponytail and wearing a short white dress, Ellie strolled along the promenade at South Bank. On one side, the Yarra River reflected the first rays of sunset, while on the other, restaurants lined the street level of Crown Casino. She loved this part of Melbourne, where indoor and outdoor met and no matter what your age or lifestyle, there was something to enjoy.

She stopped to watch a group of children squeal and dance as narrow columns of water shot randomly from holes between patterned tiles. Fire burst through the top of pillars.

A helicopter rose from a helipad on the water, sightseers inside with cameras. They had a treat in store, seeing Melbourne at sunset from the air. Dad had taken special clients up in the past and it always enthralled them.

Back to the task at hand, Ellie turned away from the river and wandered along the restaurants. The Riverview was her target. She'd made a booking earlier, lucky to have a table available on such short notice. Elegant yet casual, it was an iconic Melbourne delight and one she and Dad often visited.

"Mrs Connor! How nice to see you again." Georgio, the maître de, ushered Ellie to an outside table. "I'll send water across immediately, but can I recommend a cocktail before ordering?"

"Thank you, but just sparkling water tonight."

"Indeed. I see your booking is for one?" he tilted his head.

"I'm starving, Georgio. You must have heard that Dad is missing and I've barely eaten since getting home. I needed to be here."

"And I shall look after you myself, my dear young lady. Your drink is coming." He hurried away.

With a sigh that came from deep down, she forced her shoulders to relax. This choice of restaurant wasn't random. Her eyes drifted around the diners. Couples and business people.

True to his word, Georgio reappeared shortly with a tall glass of sparkling water with lemon. "Do you wish to order, or people watch for a while?"

She smiled. "You know me too well. But I'll order, then people watch."

Ellie sipped her water after ordering. At last her insides began to settle, instead of flipping between nausea and a clutch of ice. She had to stop letting Meredith get to her. To find Dad, she'd need to see through whatever her game was.

From her vantage point, Ellie surveyed the people in the restaurant, including staff. Nothing was out of the ordinary, at least compared to what she was used to. Efficient and courteous service. She recognized a few people dining here and hoped they didn't see her. Tonight, she wasn't up to pleasantries. Except with Georgio.

"And, here is your starter." With a flourish, Georgio placed a plate of delicacies before Ellie.

"Beautiful. As ever."

It was delicious, and despite her lack of interest in food, this sparked her hunger. Every morsel sent her taste buds into joy and the perfect starter was gone before she knew it.

Should I talk with Ben?

Sure. He's absolutely the best person to turn to. Ellie swallowed the remains of the glass. As if watching her, the waiter reappeared. As he poured, Ellie spoke.

"You've seen me here with my Dad, haven't you?"

"I have. And I am sorry. I saw on the news he is missing."

"He had a booking here a few nights ago."

"Ah. I've just returned from a short holiday, so shall I ask Georgio?"

"No. No, I'll ask, but thank you."

She had to wait. Her main arrived with the same waiter and as she ate, Georgio was nowhere to be seen. The lovely meal reminded her of ones with Dad. They'd talk the whole time, laughing their way through the courses as they compared books they'd read, or conversations they'd heard.

"I miss you so much," she whispered, head down. Her heart ached. Was she the only one to want him back home? Joni was upset of course, and the house staff, but his wife and close colleagues acted as though his disappearance was nothing unusual.

"Dessert?" It was Georgio, and Ellie lifted her head.

"Georgio, did you see Dad here the other night?"

"Which day?"

"December four. He had a dinner reservation that evening for two."

"Let me check."

He darted away to his station near the door and flicked through the old-fashioned book he kept for reservations. Back and forth his finger went across the page, then he spoke to one of his waiting staff, glancing at Ellie. Both men went through the book again. When he walked back to her table, Georgio's face was puzzled.

"You are correct. Mr Bannerman's secretary made the reservation that morning. In fact, we only just managed to fit him in, but…"

"But?"

"Someone called during the day to cancel the booking."

"Someone? Joni, his PA?"

Georgio shook his head. "Apparently it was a man, and not Mr Bannerman."

FIFTEEN
THE PLOT TWISTS

"Good thing your carer had that last-minute date, huh?" Ben pushed a wheelchair along a softly lit path, away from a graceful old building through pretty gardens. "And I got here just in time, considering what she was going to feed you compared to what I will."

The man in the wheelchair grinned an awkward sideways grin, his eyes brimming with excitement.

Ben went off the path and carefully manoeuvred the chair across a perfect lawn, down a gentle slope to the shores of a large pond. At a bench, he parked the chair and locked the brake. "Care to join me for pizza, dude?"

He slid his arms under the man's armpits and helped him upright, then together they covered the small distance to the bench. "Gonna sit you here, Michael, okay?"

It took a moment to steady Michael so he was corralled between the back and arm of the bench. Ben made sure Michael's legs were comfortable. Then, he slid a pizza box from a basket beneath the wheelchair. "Ta da."

Michael made happy noises, no words, just the sounds Ben had grown to understand. "Mate, you don't know the best part." He slung a backpack off and flopped beside Michael. "Wanna see?"

From the backpack, Ben extracted a six-pack of beer. Michael's off-centre grin widened. "Yeah, knew it. These, my friend, are from the Barossa Valley in South Australia. There's a cool micro-brewery there and I picked a few up. Now, they're a mix of two each of their best, so let's start and you can tell me which you like best as we go."

As the light faded and sounds of night birds joined the soft sploshing of water against the banks, the men ate and drank. Once pizza was in his hands, Michael could manage it with a bit of help.

"I reckon your motor skills are better than last time. No more missing your mouth like I do when I've had too many drinks."

Michael's laugh brought a smile to Ben's face and he opened fresh beers, their second each. He wiped Michael's hands clean with a moist towelette, then wrapped his fingers around the middle of one bottle. "Got it? Cool. This is a pale ale. These guys make everything in a building barely bigger than a shed. You'd love it."

Ben's phone vibrated with a message, and his lips tightened as he read it to himself.

Any chance we can meet tonight for an update?

Ellie. He tapped a response.

After nine. Tell me where.

Did she have news, or was she after intel?

Michael nudged him, curious, and Ben held up the phone so he could read the message.

"She wants to meet up for a drink. Do you think I should go?"

"Y...es."

"But I'm having drinks with you and there's still another one each left."

"G...o."

"Hang on, new message alert. She says to meet her near the helipad by the river. Hope she's not planning a night flight."

Michael snorted.

"Guess I'd better meet her. What if she decided to steal a helicopter?"

"Arr…arr…st."

"Did you say arrest her?"

Eyes glinting with mischief, Michael nodded.

"Now, that would be misusing my powers as a police detective." Ben picked up the empty pizza box. "However, if it stopped a potential theft of an expensive item…" he winked. "I won't tell her you suggested it."

An hour later, Ben found Ellie on a footbridge, staring into the dark river below as though contemplating life. What did she see in the slow-moving water? Lost dreams and forgotten hopes? An answer to where her father was? Or memories of the once strong and vibrant brother he'd recently wheeled back into his exclusive, expensive, residential care facility?

Ben stopped, hands clenched. Michael didn't deserve what had happened to him.

But nor did Ellie.

She appeared so fragile. Her body was too thin. She wasn't eating properly, surely, and how could she, being so worried about damned Jack Bannerman? Probably not sleeping either.

Ellie gazed up, straight to his eyes as though feeling his on her across the distance. Her face was tense but suddenly, she relaxed and offered a small smile. And that was all it took for his anger to drain away, replaced by a long-buried yearning to protect her at all costs.

By the time he reached the bridge, she'd walked to its end to meet him. Her white dress followed every movement and long, golden tendrils of hair had escaped a ponytail. Up close, those gorgeous eyes gave away a mountain of pain and he wanted to brush the hairs back and hold onto her.

"Bit late for a stroll?" he managed.

"I'm sorry. I should have left things until morning."

"Didn't mean that. And I'm hardly an early to bed kind of guy."

A spark of something—amusement or an old memory—replaced the haunting pain in her face and Ben caught his breath. Nothing would ever be over between them.

He nodded at the empty helipad. "Left without us?"

Ellie laughed. A real, straight-from-the-heart laugh.

"You can laugh. But now we'll miss the best cityscape view the world has to offer."

"You don't like flying." She reminded him.

"True. Do you want a drink?"

"Yes. I've kept a clear head all day so yes, I'd love one."

"Okay to walk a bit?"

"Unless the helicopter returns, I think we'll need to."

In silence, they crossed the footbridge and wandered for a while before settling on an outside table of an upmarket bar. Conversation and music spilled out from the packed area inside as Ellie sat.

"What would you like? Are you hungry?"

"Just a glass of wine thanks."

Ben wove through the customers and ordered a bottle of wine and a cheese platter. He waited for the wine, leaning against the counter and watching Ellie. She sat motionless, shoulders slumped. Did she know something new, something distressing, or was she utterly exhausted?

Two glasses and bottle in hand, he returned to their table. Her eyes widened a little at the sight of a whole bottle.

"And there's some food coming."

"Damnit, Ben. This isn't a date."

He opened the wine and poured. "No. It's a meeting to discuss Jack, at your request. But we're not at the station, or at your office. Are we?" He took his time putting the bottle to one side and picking up one glass, which he held out to her.

Ellie bit her bottom lip. Ben knew that look. She was churning inside, battling to control the need to walk away.

Stay this time, Ellie. Stay.

"I'm tired of people thinking they need to feed me." Her voice was low with a touch of bitterness. Then she accepted the glass with a soft, "Thank you."

Picking up his own glass, he tilted it toward her. "To resolution."

She nodded and sipped.

"Who else is feeding you?"

"Paul. Paul Dekeles. We had a coffee and he ordered breakfast when I said not to. Which I probably needed, but it was beside the point."

Unease settled in Ben's gut.

"Why were you meeting him?"

"To catch up from the previous night. He said Dad always wanted him to keep an eye on me. For safety."

"He dropped off some footage from the building. The day Jack vanished." Ben said.

"And?" Ellie leaned forward, eyes huge. Hopeful.

"Still working on it. I need more."

"More?"

"Ideally, footage from the house."

Ellie sat back and drew in a long breath. She drank half her glass quickly, then put it on the table. "There's a heap of cameras there. I thought about this earlier. Dad left the office to go home and change. Now, I haven't asked everyone, but I get the feeling nobody at the house saw him. Whether the staff were out or he just slipped in…I don't know."

"You think something is off." Ben finally lifted his own glass.

A waiter appeared and placed a platter on the table. Cheese, fruit, crackers, and quince paste. Ben glanced at Ellie.

"I ate at The Riverview. But..." she reached out and delicately took a tiny piece of cheese. "Sorry. For snapping earlier."

"If my opinion is still worth anything, it is for you to cut yourself some slack." Ben refilled her glass. "What have you found out since the other night?"

The wine slowly disappeared and little was left of the cheese platter by the time Ellie filled Ben in. Much he dismissed. And some was noteworthy, but probably of no consequence.

"Tell me again about Joni." Ben created a mini stack from the last of the brie, an olive, and a cracker.

Ellie leaned on an elbow, more relaxed now but still with a haunted expression. "She told me Dad was fine before the meeting. When he came back, he got his briefcase and an envelope then stopped at her desk to wish her happy birthday."

"But her birthday wasn't that day?"

"No. And he said there was something extra in her pay, so he'd already arranged that with payroll."

"Is that what he's done in the past?"

"Normally he sends flowers, perhaps a small gift. But it was ahead of time and it makes me wonder..." she played with the stem of her empty wine glass.

"What? That he knew he wouldn't be there for her birthday?" Ben split the remains of the bottle between their glasses. "Is it possible he had a business trip planned?"

"She'd know. Dennis would know. And he wouldn't have left that message for me and hidden a letter."

"Do you believe the envelope Joni saw was that letter?"

"Yes. Perhaps. Dad would have left it in the bottle when he arrived home to get ready to sail. And between that time, and last night, it disappeared. Tell me, Ben, isn't that the least bit suspicious?"

On more than one level.

"Are you going to take his disappearance seriously?" The sudden panic in Ellie's voice pitched it higher and she paled.

Without thinking, Ben covered one of her hands with his. It was cold. "I do, Ellie. I've taken it seriously from the time Paul Dekeles reported him missing. And regardless of whether it becomes a full investigation or not, I'm going to help you find him."

She shook her head but didn't pull her hand away. "I'm so worried, Ben. I know you don't like Dad but he's never acted this way."

"My feelings are irrelevant. My suggestion is that you go home and sleep. In the morning, come into the station. I'd like you to look at the footage Dekeles gave me. Okay?"

Why would Jack leave a note for Ellie, phone her to tell her to look for it, and simply vanish? His earlier speculation that Dennis had something to do with the disappearance was probably wrong. This felt like a plan from Jack which had gone pear-shaped.

Somebody knew something and he was making it his business to find out who.

SIXTEEN
LIES AND OTHER STORIES

8 December

Sea Angel moved under the weight of a man stepping aboard, her old boards creaking. The sun was an hour away from rising, but the air was already humid and warm. Only two other yachts were tied up and nobody was aboard them.

Gloves on his hands and by the narrow beam of a small flashlight, the man searched the seating area, moving the cushions. He crouched to look beneath the benches, pulling out life-jackets and shaking them. Then, he sank back on his heels, turning the flashlight in his fingers, a grim smile on his face.

Back on his feet, he took the steps leading below deck. In one of the cabins, he extracted a handgun from a pocket. He glanced around, then pushed the gun between the base and mattress of the bed.

He shoved the gloves into his pocket and climbed back to the deck, turning off the flashlight as he stepped onto the pier. He surveyed the horizon of Port Phillip Bay. A faint lightness in the sky heralded dawn.

It was going to be a perfect day. And everything was going

perfectly as planned. Better than planned thanks to an unexpected turns of events.

Earlier, he'd arrived to plant the gun, cutting through the deserted carpark after leaving his car a block away.

The crunch of gravel from the other side of the road had stopped him in his tracks. He'd pressed himself against the bushes, heart thudding as he formulated an explanation for being there.

"Someone there? You okay, mate?" Fishing rod in one hand and bucket in the other, an older man had peered through the dim light.

Yeah. I'm okay. More than okay thanks to you.

He'd stepped away from the bushes to show his face.

The fisherman had smiled. "Oh, it's you."

Now, he reached his car, which he'd had to bring closer. Only so much a man could carry, particularly out here where he might be seen.

Ellie sat in a small waiting area in the police station, early for her arranged meeting with Ben. She'd slept for several unbroken hours, waking in a calmer state of mind than she'd had in days. Talking to Ben, unburdening herself in a way, took some of the pressure off.

An elderly woman shuffled in and lowered herself onto the next seat. The woman had tears in her eyes.

Ellie offered a small smile. "Are you okay?"

"It doesn't get any easier."

"I don't understand."

The woman fumbled inside her handbag, finally drawing out a handful of cards the size of a bookmark. She handed one to Ellie.

On one side was the image of a boy, a teenager. Tousled brown hair and hazel eyes above a cheeky grin. Underneath were the words *Have you seen Adam?*

Ellie turned the card over. Adam Blackwell. His age, height, last known sighting, contact details.

"I'm so sorry." Ellie held it out.

"Please keep it. In case. My grandson, you know. Disappeared seven months and three days ago and it is almost his birthday." A tear ran down the woman's cheek. "Had an argument with his granddad and took off. We raised him and we just want him...home." Her voice trailed away.

Dad missing was bad enough but how to bear not knowing where a teen was? She glanced at his age again. Not even sixteen.

"Oh, Detective Rossi!" Adam's grandmother pushed herself upright and hurried to Ben, who was halfway down the hallway. They spoke for a few moments and the woman hugged Ben, who shot Ellie a faint grin over her head.

When the woman shuffled past Ellie to leave, she smiled, the tears gone and something like hope in her eyes.

"How do I help?" Ellie showed the card to Ben. "He's a baby, all alone somewhere."

"Don't you have enough to worry about? Come on, let's go this way."

She caught up with him. "Do you think he's staying with friends? Or is he really lost? He's so young."

"If you mean Adam, then I can't comment. But he isn't forgotten about, okay?"

His firm tone irked Ellie, but now they were winding through an open plan space filled with police officers so she didn't reply. She had an idea of something she could do to help find Adam.

Ben opened a door and gestured for Ellie to go ahead. This room reminded her of Paul's office with its wall to wall monitors. There were a couple of desks, two whiteboards, and a young, intense woman with red plaits working at speed on a laptop. She glanced up as they entered.

"Ellie, meet Meg. Meg, Ellie."

They said hello at the same time.

"Take a seat. Meg is a forensic analyst. Nobody puts data together better."

"I'm not giving you the formula, no matter how nice you are."

"Meg has a special coffee blend that only she knows. Thinks any compliment is an underhand way to steal it."

"Can't be too careful. Mrs Connor, I've examined the footage provided by your head of security."

"Ellie, please. May I see it?"

Ben nodded at the largest monitor. "We'll run through them in the order Paul Dekeles provided, then have a closer look at each area if you're okay with it?"

"Of course." Ellie turned her eyes to the screen and the boardroom footage began. Her heart jumped and she curled her hands into fists on her lap.

Dad was in his usual spot at the long table, with Campbell and Dennis on either side. Paul placed a cup next to Dad, who barely noticed. There was a conversation between the three other men and Paul retreated to near the window. Dennis leaned forward, talking, then abruptly stood, and left.

The camera changed to Dennis leaving the boardroom, already on the phone.

And then to Dad in his office.

What about the rest of the boardroom footage?

He packed his laptop into his briefcase, tidied his desk, and then picked up an envelope. Ellie leaned forward, frowning. The envelope was small, and she recognized it as one of his personal ones.

Dad stopped at Joni's desk for a moment before going to the lift, the envelope still in his hand.

Inside the lift, he pressed the basement button then stared at the doors the whole way down. When they opened, it was at the basement where his car was parked. He got out. The screen went blank.

"You alright?" Ben asked.

"There's so much missing. Why isn't there footage after Dennis left the boardroom? I mean, Dad had a coffee sitting there, Campbell and he were talking, and Paul was hanging around. So, what happened?"

There was no reply, so Ellie turned to Ben. His expression unsettled her. She saw the detective in him, the need to find out what she knew or thought. But there was more. A sadness. Ellie wanted to cry out, "Don't pity me! Help me find him!" but her manners and self-control kicked in and she gulped down the responding emotions.

Meg took her hands off her keyboard. "What we're seeing is edited. Not by us. I would like to get hold of an hour either side of each clip. And the quality is surprisingly bad. Quite old style."

"Then we'll get it for you. Or do you want to come to Bannerman House? I'll arrange full access."

Ben and Meg exchanged a glance.

"What?"

"Your husband has already said we need a warrant to get more." Ben shrugged.

"He what? That's insane. He wants this resolved as much as I do."

"Isn't he CEO now?"

"Acting CEO." Something bothered her. "Can you replay the part where Dad is in the lift going down to the carpark?"

Meg tapped a few keys and the footage resumed.

"This isn't right. There must be more." Ellie stood and went to the screen. "It isn't there."

"What isn't?"

Ellie turned to Ben. "The envelope, detective. Where is the envelope he took into the lift?"

"Where the hell's Dekeles? Campbell, do you know?" Dennis stormed into Campbell's office, tie to one side, and a shirt button undone.

"No. Are you alright?"

"Don't worry about me. I need to speak to the idiot." He dropped his briefcase onto a seat and straightened his tie, frowning as he found the button. "Slept in and then traffic was a killer this morning."

Campbell reached for the intercom. "Coffee?"

"No, I—okay, actually yes."

"Joni, would you arrange coffee for Mr Connor and me please?" Campbell nodded through the glass window as she rose. "Grab a seat, Dennis. Why are you after Paul?"

Dennis dropped onto the chair opposite Campbell, still fiddling with his tie. "Giving confidential footage to the police without approval. He handed a selection—meaning he selected what he wanted—to that Rossi guy."

"But isn't it to help work out Jack's movements before he disappeared?"

"By picking the bits he thinks make me look guilty."

Campbell stared at Dennis. "But you're not guilty of anything, Dennis, so there's no chance of you being implicated from anything caught on our cameras."

"Well I've fixed it. Told Rossi he needs to go through legal channels if he wants anything else."

"Is it necessary? Surely, they'll see us as putting up roadblocks to finding Jack." He leaned forward. "If it helps the police identify anything of value to their investigation, then why would you stop them?"

The reddening of Dennis skin, from his neck upwards, accompanied a cold anger in his eyes. "I'm CEO now and will do what I believe is best for the company. For that matter, what investigation? One cop who is spending more time with my wife than following up the few leads we have."

"I doubt he is spending much time with her."

"What do you know about him?"

Joni tapped on the door and came in with two cups of coffee. Campbell didn't answer until she'd left again, closing the door behind.

"I've met him less times than you have." Campbell sipped his coffee. He wasn't about to share his speculation about Ben Rossi and what he once might have meant to Ellie.

"On another matter, have you heard anything from the... the other party?" Dennis reached for his coffee. "The timing couldn't be worse."

"Actually, there is an email here, which I've sent across to you. They want a meeting."

"I'll look at it soon."

"When will you tell Ellie what is going on, Dennis?"

"That was Jack's job. So, until he returns, it's pointless. There's no value in making any of this public and causing more harm than has already been done. I expect you to keep quiet."

For now, Dennis. For now.

Dennis' phone beeped a message. "Dekeles just drove in, so I'm going to go find him."

"Jack trusts him. Paul's worked for him almost as long as I have, so take some friendly advice and put your dislike aside, for the sake of appearances, if nothing else."

On his feet, Dennis swallowed the last of his coffee. "I don't trust him. I do like you, though, so let's keep it that way and you not offer me anything more than the work you're paid for."

Campbell gripped his cup until Dennis left and was out of sight. Wherever Jack was, he needed to come back.

"There's something terribly wrong. We need more footage."
Ellie rubbed her eyes, strained from watching the recordings
for what felt like hours. "I'm not imagining it, am I?"

Meg shook her head. "My opinion is the elevator is taken
from another day. There doesn't appear to have been time for
Mr Bannerman to put the envelope out of sight between stepping in, and pushing the button. Not unless he stood there for
a while and the segment was clipped a bit too quickly."

"Didn't Paul put this together late at night? He must have
made an error somewhere." Ellie looked at Ben. "I'll speak to
Dennis and arrange access."

"And if he refuses?"

"He can't. And why would he?"

"Why indeed?"

Ellie bit her bottom lip. Dennis had nothing to do with this.
Whatever else he was up to, it wasn't about getting rid of Dad.
She knew Ben was staring at her, waiting for a response, but he
wasn't getting one.

"Ben? Sorry to interrupt." Another detective peered in.
"Got a missing fisherman."

"Off a boat?" Ben stood.

"Nope. A pier. Think you'll want to take a look."

"Be right there, Andy. Meg, would you see Ellie out."

"Sure."

"Let me know how things go with Dennis. If he doesn't
agree, we're not yet in a position to seek a warrant."

Ellie jumped to her feet. "Why not? We've acknowledged
the envelope is missing…not just from those clips. It has to
mean something."

"This department is over-stretched. I'd need more to go on
for a warrant. And if I had one, it'll be to look at more than
monitors."

Why will nobody help?

Ben's expression was of pity.

"I'll see myself out. Let you get on with more important business. Thanks for helping, Meg."

"Ellie—"

Ben's voice followed her as she left the room and stalked through the open plan station.

SEVENTEEN
LATE AND MISSING

"His wife is beside herself. Frank Barlow keeps to a routine. At the end of the pier before dawn, home by eight am. Stops to buy the paper on the way back, along with croissants for their breakfast."

"That's pretty specific." Ben surveyed the car park. Why was he here again?

Detective Andy Montebello grinned. "Wrote it down. They have an arrangement. He fishes for dinner three days a week and buys them both breakfasts. She cooks him his favourite meals. Been this way for six years, ever since they moved to a town house up the road."

"No previous history of deviating from this? Catching up with a friend? No arguments?"

"Not according to Mrs Barlow. Been married forty-two years, retired when they moved here. He was a teacher, she worked in retail. No children. Committed couple from the sound of it, and she is distraught."

"Do the usual. See if the local unit can help with a couple of uniforms to door knock. You backtrack based on Mrs Barlow's statement of where he left from, went to, and anything possible in between."

Andy nodded and wandered away, tapping on his phone.

Ben ran a hand through his hair. First Jack, now Frank. Was someone targeting this pier? From here, broken glass around the light pole reflected the sun. He turned to call after Andy.

"We're going to need some forensic help. Would you handle it?"

"Sure thing. Shall I tape the area off?"

"Not yet." Ben chuckled as he left the carpark. Andy would love to turn the place into a crime scene.

He squatted near the broken glass. A half brick lay not far away. Maybe bored kids.

Or a serial killer.

Not time to consider this yet.

Just because two men were missing, last seen—or expected to be seen—around this pier, meant nothing. Coincidence. Except, Ben didn't believe in coincidences.

It was hot today. Hot and sticky and no chance of a storm until tomorrow, according to the latest weather report. Careful to avoid any glass, he continued to the pier. Two small yachts bobbed on one side with no obvious sign of anyone on board. He'd send Andy down to check. There private property and no fishing signs but no fencing, gates, or cameras. And Frank Barlow fished here three times a week, so did he have permission?

Who owned the pier, anyway? It wasn't attached to a house, or on a private beach, just tucked away in this little indentation in Port Phillip Bay. He gazed back the way he'd come, scanning the neighbouring streets. One apartment building had floors high enough to see the pier. Otherwise, the short road finished at the carpark and that was densely treed. Enough to hide someone who was up to no good.

Sea Angel was moored at the furthest end. With no light from the broken globe, it would have been dark along here a few hours ago. Was Frank Barlow connected to Jack? Ben made a few notes on his phone to remind himself to check later.

The yacht creaked as the tide moved it. What secrets did she hold? There was more to Jack's disappearance than him taking off without a word, Ben knew it in his gut. And he needed to have a look around here, go below and see for himself there was no evidence of some terrible act.

Ellie is the best way to do that.

But she'd virtually stormed out of the precinct less than an hour ago. Had she gone to work, perhaps to confront Dennis? Ben sighed and dialled her number.

———

Paul locked himself in his office. He wanted to punch the wall. No, he wanted to punch Dennis Connor.

"Arrogant shithead."

He caught sight of Dennis on a monitor and put his fist up at it. If it wasn't that he needed to be here, he'd have knocked him down ten minutes ago and walked out. Dennis was just waiting for the opportunity to fire him and he wasn't about to let it happen.

His hands were clenched so tightly they hurt. He stretched them out and looked at his knuckles, then the palms. Fighting hands. A past well forgotten, yet still of value sometimes. It was how he'd met Jack and how he'd stayed with him when others would see him gone.

Paul sank into his chair. Dennis could yell at him as much as he wanted. With the key from a thin chain he took from around his neck, Paul unlocked the bottom drawer of the desk. Inside was a metal box, and he used a different key to open this. The tension drained away as he lifted the lid and he smiled. Worth every bad moment.

He reached both hands into the box, fingers extended.

There was a tap on the door.

He withdrew his hands, ready to tell whoever it was to clear off. Except it was Ellie.

"Give me a minute."

Paul closed the lid and returned the box to the drawer.

He checked his tie was straight and jacket in place before opening the door. Ellie stared up at him with those big eyes of hers and his stomach turned. She was upset.

"What's wrong?"

"May I come in?" she did anyway, dropping onto a seat, then swinging it to look at the monitors.

"Don't tell me you've had a run-in with Dennis as well?" he wandered back to his own chair.

"I thought you agreed not to—"

"Listen, Ellie, I have the greatest respect for you and I did say I wouldn't get into it with Dennis, but he just ripped my head off. Cut me some slack, please?"

She swung back. "What for?"

"Providing the video footage to Ben Rossi without his express permission."

"Oh, that."

"You knew?"

"I know he's gone primal and wants to make everyone jump through hoops, but Dennis is just trying to protect Bannerman Wealth Group. He's never been in this position."

Bloody shouldn't be.

"Fine. He's learning. But he does know better than to yell at senior staff, I think."

"Did he really?" again, Ellie's eyes were drawn to the screens. "What changed, Paul? What happened when I went to London?"

This was the last question he'd expected. "I'm happy to talk to you about what I've observed."

She gazed at him, her expression unsure.

"Not here though. And it will take more time than over a coffee."

"But you'll tell me what you know?"

He nodded.

"Dinner? Tonight okay?" she went back to watching the screens, to Dennis, talking to Joni at her desk. She didn't look happy.

"Yeah...yes that'll work. Want me to find somewhere?"

"Thanks. Text me the details."

Her phone rang. She ignored it.

"Answer it, Ellie. I'm just doing paperwork."

"Sorry."

She answered without checking the caller and Paul could swear her shoulders slumped.

"I have nothing to say to you right now."

Interesting.

"You're where?" She glanced at him as she listened for a moment. "Do you think it will help? I mean, really help?"

Paul shuffled some papers as if he wasn't interested in who was on the other end of the phone. He thought the caller was male from a snippet of voice he'd heard.

"Alright. I'll head straight over." She hung up and stood in one fluid motion.

Paul pulled his eyes away from that red-hot body and to her eyes.

"Want a lift?"

"No, I'm fine thanks. I do want to talk about the video footage though, so can we do that over dinner as well?"

"Sure." He got up and reached the door first, opening it. "I'll message you in a bit."

With a nod, she was gone, and he locked the door again. What was wrong with the footage? Had she seen it?

He sank on his chair. What had he missed?

———

By the time Ellie pulled into the carpark near the pier, she'd worked herself into a state of mild panic. Ben wanted to look around *Sea Angel* but hadn't said why. Only something about an incident in the area overnight. Had someone vandalized the yacht? Or was there some new evidence?

Half of the carpark was fenced off with police tape, and a patrol unit was across the road, stopping cars driving any further than the entry. Heart in her mouth, she parked and climbed out, looking for Ben.

"Mrs Connor?"

A young, well-dressed man approached. The detective from the station this morning.

"I'm Detective Andy Montebello. Detective Rossi asked me to escort you down."

"What's happened? Have you found…"

Was Dad here? Or his…body?

Tears sprung into her eyes and she grabbed sunglasses and forced them on. The detective didn't seem to have noticed and led her out of the carpark toward the pier. Ben's car was parked to one side, along with another car marked 'Crime Scene Services'.

At the base of some bushes, one officer took photographs of the ground and branches. What the hell was happening?

Ben stood partway along the pier, speaking to a man she recognized as the owner of one of the small yachts. His eyes met hers as Andy stopped to wave her past, and he shook the hand of the other man.

Somehow, she managed to control herself until he reached her and was hopefully out of earshot from anyone else. She hated to be upset, to risk losing control, and took what was meant to be a calming breath but felt like sea water.

"Ben…is it…" her voice was raspy and she wanted to kick herself. Stop being pathetic.

"Hey, no." On the other hand, his tone was soft, concerned.

"I'm sorry if you misunderstood, but we haven't had anything new about Jack."

Relief and disappointment mingled to form a knot in her chest. She managed a nod back at the carpark. "Then, what?"

"Let's go to *Sea Angel*." He waited until she stepped forward, then walked at her side. "Remember the missing fisherman Andy mentioned this morning?"

"Yes. He wasn't here, was he?"

"According to his wife, he fished here a few mornings each week. Has for years. And this morning he left home but hasn't arrived back. Not yet, anyway."

"I saw broken glass back there."

"From the light globe. Looks like half a brick took it out."

"Did the fisherman drive here? Is that why your people are in the bushes?"

They reached the yacht and Ellie slipped her shoes off. Ben did the same, placing them on the pier. "There were a few snapped branches and before you imagine the worst, it might be from anything. A car backing into them, for example."

"If this fisherman only went missing a few hours ago, why the big presence? Is it because of the location?" Ellie took her sunglasses off, wanting to see Ben's eyes clearly. He wouldn't lie to her, but he might filter information. His expression didn't change when he nodded.

"Unusual for two people to go missing in a matter of days and the only thing in common being one secluded pier."

"Unless something is going on! Who is the fisherman? Did he know Dad?" Ellie put her hands on her hips, chin up. "Nobody is meant to be on here anyway." She seen plenty of people ignore the signs.

"We're trying to establish why he was here or supposed to be here. Do I have your permission to board *Sea Angel*?"

"As long as you tell me why." Ellie stepped aboard.

"Gut feeling, Ellie. Something's not sitting right about Jack's disappearance, nor the fisherman's. This pier has no security, no cameras or way of knowing who comes and goes. Yet, these boats are valuable and could be stolen or tampered with."

Ben sounded puzzled, and Ellie agreed. She'd never understood why Dad left the yacht here instead of at the Yacht Club. But there'd never been an incident before, and the area was low crime and peaceful.

She stepped back. "Please, come aboard."

The boat rocked a little as Ben joined her on deck. He looked at home, his legs planted a little wider than normal, but his body steady.

"What do you need to see? You won't upend the beds and throw the cutlery onto the floor?"

"This isn't television, and I don't have a warrant."

"So, if you had a warrant, you'd wreck the place?"

He grinned broadly and warmth flooded through her.

Oh, for goodness sake, Ellie!

"Do you want me to wait up here?"

"No, I'd prefer you to see everything I do. If there's something I need to take a closer look at, you need to know why."

She went down the steps, all too aware of how close he was behind her.

"There are two cabins. When I was there the other day, I checked every room and they were perfect. Beds are always made with fresh linen, towels ready, water and beer and so on in the fridge. Dad has someone who cleans and makes sure she's always ready if he wants to take her out."

"I'll look in each of those first. Would you stay in the doorway to observe please?" Ben entered the left cabin. This was the one Ellie normally used if she was onboard overnight. Not very often these days. The room appeared normal, the way it was the other day. Ben took a few moments to carefully open drawers and cupboards, look under pillows, and slide his hands beneath the mattress.

"You forgot to check behind the curtains."

"Good point." Ben pulled the porthole curtain aside. "Nice view."

"The other cabin is exactly the same, except there's probably Meredith's stuff in the drawers. She tends to have clothes all over the place." Ellie let Ben squeeze past, their bodies almost touching. His familiar scent hit her senses and she bit her bottom lip.

"So, Meredith sails?" Ben repeated the search pattern. "Often?"

"Rarely. Only when Dad insists. She wants a bigger yacht, thinks *Sea Angel* is ancient and not worthy of Dad's status."

Ben stopped near the bed, his eyes on Ellie. "What do you think?"

Ellie ran a loving hand over the timber door frame. "*Sea Angel* is a beautiful old lady who can outsail anything modern."

"You love her."

"Yes. And with good reason."

"What reason?"

With a frown, Ellie stared at the bed. "Someone's touched the bed. It wasn't tucked like that."

"Here?" Ben took his phone out and snapped some photos. "The corner isn't a regulation Navy fold, is it?"

"Nope, and Dad insists on them."

"I'm going to lift the mattress up a bit." Ben dropped onto his knees and slowly raised the side of the mattress.

Ellie looked over his shoulder, leaning down to see…

"Oh my God, no."

EIGHTEEN
EVIDENCE

"Ellie, can you reach my phone?" Ben didn't move. "I need two things. One, some photos, and then for you to call Andy for me."

She moved closer to him, until her breath was on his face and her hand was on his chest. "Where?"

"Um, top shirt pocket."

In a moment she had the phone and was at his level, on her own knees. The heat left his chest the second her hand did, but her hip pressed against his.

"It is password protected. Shall I use my phone?"

"No." Damnit. "Twenty-five ten."

She tapped it in, then shot him a look. "You are kidding, right?"

"Old habits, sweetheart."

The word came out before he could stop it, but she ignored him, taking a series of photos of the gun nestled between the mattress and bed base. He needed to change his password from her birthday.

"Okay, there's a heap there that look okay. So, do I just look up Andy? Oh, found him. What shall I say?"

"Nothing. Hold it against my ear."

"You don't want much."

At least she was handling this.

The phone rang a couple of times and Andy answered. "Boss?"

"Come to *Sea Angel* and bring forensics. Right now, please." He glanced at Ellie. "Hang up?"

She slid the phone back into his pocket, her eyes intense. "We don't carry guns on the boat, by the way."

So, you keep them elsewhere?

"Are you okay having others onboard? Officially, we can now, but I want you to be okay with it."

She sat on the floor with a thud. All the bravado drained away. "I'm not okay with any of this, Ben. I don't know what to think."

He adjusted himself to touch her shoulder with his. "Hey, look at me. I'm going to work this all out and we will find Jack. Once Andy arrives, you go back to the pier and I won't be too long. Okay?"

Her eyes were wide and there was a trace of panic but she nodded.

"The next steps will be upsetting, so I'm telling you to prepare you. Crime Scene Services will take over from me and the yacht will be searched. *Sea Angel* may be locked down for a while and you can't touch anything on your way out. Once the gun is processed, I'll need to speak to you officially."

"I'm a suspect?"

"No, Ellie. This is a process. But you'll do a statement about this. And depending upon the forensic results and anything else found onboard, other people may be interviewed. You have to trust me."

"I don't have a choice, do I?" she pushed herself onto her feet as hurried footsteps approached. "I need to find Dad and you are the only one with any sort of means to help me."

"You have a security team, aren't they working on it?"

"I don't know anymore. Dennis is stopping Paul from

doing his job and doesn't talk to me unless he wants something."

"Boss? You down there?"

"Cabin on the right, Andy."

What was Connor up to? Bannerman Wealth Group had money and the freedom to look in ways Ben didn't. If your father-in-law and CEO was missing, why wouldn't you use every resource at your disposal?

By the time Ben briefed Andy and relinquished control of the mattress, Ellie was gone.

It might be any normal day of a Melbourne summer. A bit too humid for comfort, the sky a brilliant blue and not a cloud in view. The low tide lapped against the pylons beneath the pier, whilst seagulls cawed as they hovered on the slightest of breezes.

Under Ellie's bare feet, the timber boards burned, so she slipped her shoes on. She didn't want to leave *Sea Angel*, now bustling with police, but her heart raced so fast she had to walk away. Off the pier, past a remaining uniformed officer, to her car. There, she sank into her seat and closed the door.

Her hands shook as she tried to insert the key to the ignition and she gave up after two attempts. Ben wanted her here. But she couldn't bear this. She pulled out her phone and dialled Gabi. The call went straight to message bank, same as every other one since she'd returned from London.

The phone rang the moment she put it down and she grabbed it, answering without checking the caller. "Gabi?"

"As if. No, this is your dear step-mamma."

Ellie rolled her eyes. "What do you want?"

"No need to be snappy, dear. I want to discuss some boundaries."

Ben emerged from the path between the bushes, glancing

around then seeing her in the car. As he approached, Ellie swung the door open. "Meredith, this isn't a good time."

"You answered the phone."

"I thought you were someone else."

"Charming. Anyway, I'm not happy with you speaking to my staff without me being present. Don't do it."

"*Your* staff?"

Ben slowed as he noticed the phone in her hand, but she managed a grin and mouthed 'Meredith'. He rolled his eyes as she had, and a giggle started somewhere deep inside. Ellie clapped her hand over her mouth to stop it coming out as Meredith went off the deep end.

"What are you insinuating? I'm really tired of you playing Daddy's little girl. Jack is my husband and that makes the staff mine. The house mine. The business mine. Do you hear me?"

Ellie was holding the phone a little away from her ear so Ben could listen in. His expression turned serious, as she imagined hers had.

"Bannerman Wealth Group is not yours, Meredith. It will never be yours because you signed a pre-nuptial agreement and I'm pretty certain that includes anything suspicious happening to Dad. Isn't that true?"

The silence on the other end dragged on, then the phone call disconnected. Ellie threw her phone into her handbag. "Perhaps she forgot about such a small detail."

"Pre-nuptial. What else don't I know?" Ben squatted beside the car to use its shadow.

"No idea. Did you find anything else? Hand grenades? Assault rifles?"

"Not sure if you are teasing me or having a go, but no. The team will do their stuff and I'm going to meet with my boss to decide what happens next. When would you like to make a statement?"

Ellie glanced at her hands. They weren't shaking, so she put the key in the ignition and turned on the air con. "I'm going to go see Dennis. I get the feeling you'll want to look around the office at some point, so maybe I can help him see the wisdom of doing it voluntarily."

"Do me a favour and don't say why. No mention of the gun yet. I'd prefer to be there."

"He's still my husband, although I kind of expected Meredith to add him to her list of things she owns. I won't mention the gun, okay. But I have to talk to him."

Ben stood and stretched. "Call me if there's an issue. Or if he agrees to let us drop by for a look and see. Or just call me."

As he walked away, Ellie closed the door and started the motor. She waited at the carpark entrance for the police officer to move a car they'd put across. Ellie glanced toward the pier. Ben stood halfway to the pier, watching her drive out. It was time she went to see Michael. More than time.

Dennis stared out of his office window at the street far below. All those people hurrying from place to place, jay-walking as they tapped on their phones. Plans and dreams. Most of them had no idea. Sheep, following the rest, with an annual holiday in Bali and an oversized mortgage in the suburbs. They might get a promotion every few years, believe they are something special. Buy a new car.

Losers.

They should look up and see what they'll never have. CEO of a Melbourne icon. Control of a multi-billion-dollar business that wasn't even at its peak. But now, with him at the helm, there were new opportunities. New markets and a direction Jack would never consider. And a project to cancel.

Long live the frigging king, and don't come back.

The intercom beeped and he dropped onto his chair and hit the button. "Yes?"

"Mrs Bannerman on line one, sir."

"Joni...why are you still coming in to work, and where is Mark? Didn't we arrange some leave for you?"

"It was offered, Mr Connor, but everyone is still fielding calls so if it is all the same, I'll work the rest of the week. Mark is on a break."

"Sure. Whatever." He disconnected and picked up the phone. "What's up, Merry?"

"That bitch of a wife of yours—"

"Settle down. Have a sip of something and tell me what happened."

This should be good.

Dennis pushed the chair back and rested an ankle on one knee.

"I found out she's been interrogating the staff here. Asking questions about when Jack came home and when he left and if anyone found some stupid bottle."

He leaned forward. "Bottle?"

"Oh, some old rum bottle. Meant something to her and Jack."

"And?"

Exasperation filled Meredith's voice. "Why are you worried about a stupid bottle, Dennis?"

He wasn't. He knew where it was. But why was Ellie pushing the point with it?

"Anyway, I phoned her to ask nicely if she'd please run things past me before speaking to the staff. But she just threw it all back in my face."

The elevator opened and Ellie stepped out, her eyes going straight to Dennis.

"As if I have no rights at all over the house, or the staff, or the business, just because..."

"Because?"

Ellie walked directly to his office, bypassing the reception desk.

"I'm going to have to go, Merry."

"Fine. But I want to go out somewhere nice tonight. Can't stand all the doom and gloom."

"Sure. I'll arrange something." Dennis hung up as Ellie came into the office. "Most people knock."

"Most people who are married don't leave their spouse without explanation, move into their father-in-law's house while he is missing, and refuse to have a civil discussion with said spouse. Do they?"

She had a point.

"Sit down. I need to talk to you anyway."

"Has your stepmother-in-law been complaining about me?" Ellie pulled out a chair across the desk and relaxed into it as though she was here for a pleasant visit. She crossed her legs and smoothed her skirt to almost cover her knees. Despite today's heat, her hair and makeup were flawless and she might have spent the morning in front of a cooler. But that was Ellie, always looking great no matter what life threw at her. Even the other night—straight off the plane and with the news about Jack—she was amazing in jeans and T-shirt. Pity things weren't different.

"Tell me what happened in London." He said.

"London? You're worried about that?"

"I'm CEO. Need to worry about everything."

There was an uncharacteristic flash of anger in Ellie's eyes as she leaned forward. "Acting, Dennis. Acting CEO. Once Dad returns there'll be a whole lot of changes."

"Meaning?"

"Why haven't we hired a private agency to find him? Or given Paul resources to head one up?"

Dennis laughed shortly. "He's not even qualified to watch monitors. And there is a police force looking for Jack, so why would we get in their way?"

"If you were missing, Dad would do everything possible to find you."

"With your support?"

"Of course."

"Even now?" He didn't really want her to answer. "Anyway, what changes?"

"Dennis, even now I would be distraught if you simply disappeared with no trace. Aren't you the least bit concerned about Dad? I understand you were meant to meet him that day and some people are speculating about whether you did."

"I didn't." he snapped. "Which people?"

"You know, the best way to show the police and everyone else there's nothing to hide, nothing any of us know about Dad's disappearance, is to give the police what they want without them resorting to warrants."

And there it is. What does she think she knows?

"Dekeles had no right to give them anything without permission. Are you protecting him?"

He watched Ellie closely but her expression was genuinely confused. "I just want Dad home. Or to know he's okay. I have no reason to protect anyone or hide anything, and nor does Bannerman Wealth Group. Wouldn't it be logical to make it easier for the police to help find Dad and get him home?"

"Not if he doesn't want to be found." Crap, he hadn't meant to say that. He opened his laptop.

Ellie stood. "What do you know? Have you heard from him, or did he say something before he disappeared? Is that why you were arguing in the boardroom?"

"We were not arguing. Sit down and stop the drama. I just think you're expecting him to magically reappear. If his disappearance is out of character, then you need to consider other options, baby."

"Like what? If he was kidnapped, we'd have been given demands, and if he'd had an accident—"

"Or maybe he was depressed, Ellie. It happens."

Campbell hurried in. "I'm so sorry to interrupt…oh, is everything okay?"

"Campbell, was Dad depressed?"

Dennis pushed his chair back and got to his feet. "What's the problem, Campbell?"

"Apparently there are police onboard *Sea Angel*."

"They can't be there!"

"Actually, they can. I gave them permission and before you start, you know damned well I have the right to do so." Ellie grabbed her handbag and swung away.

Dennis reached her at the door, bypassing Campbell. He put a hand on her arm and lowered his voice. "Whatever you're up to, I'll find out. And about London? Forget about any briefing because the way things are going, there'll be no need to set up an office there. If there is no Foundation, there's no need for London."

Her eyes widened. She recoiled, shrugged his hand away and rushed out. He'd said too much today but it wasn't his fault. No, it was all on Jack's shoulders, wherever he was.

NINETEEN
UNRAVELLING THREADS

It took every bit of self-control for Ellie not to run from the building in tears. She didn't even know if it was anger, or fear of losing the Foundation churning inside. Ten minutes of fast walking later, she understood. Dennis was quite mad if he believed Dad capable of taking his own life.

Panic and fury fought for top billing as her brain went over and over Dennis' words. He doesn't want to be found...he was depressed...no Foundation.

Breathe, Ellie. Sit and breathe.

There was nowhere to sit along the busy street, so she took a few steps into a narrow alley, relieved it was empty. She leaned against a wall, forcing herself to calm down, aware her blouse was soaked with perspiration.

Why would Dennis threaten to close such an important and successful part of Bannerman? It made no sense, not commercially. If out of spite it made even less sense.

Meredith and Dennis both wanted her out of their way and she could no longer pretend they weren't together, or heading that way.

Did Dad know? "Oh, God."

If he knew, would it be enough to make him...no. Jack

Bannerman was one of the strongest people she knew and he loved life. He'd fought for everything he had and there was no way he'd simply hand it over. But something was terribly wrong at work, and it was time to take a step back and look at everything with less emotion.

She had to go back to the office. Find out what Dennis meant about the Foundation and involve the other board members in a discussion about getting some heavy hitting assistance finding Dad. Ellie glanced around to get her bearings. This little alley wasn't familiar, but it looked as though it would lead to Collins Street. From there, a tram would get her home to fresh clothes.

The alley was wide enough for a single car and ran between two tall buildings. She hurried along the brick road, her footsteps the only sound. Halfway to the corner, something made her stop and glance back. Out in the bright sunlight, cars crawled along, and pedestrians rushed. Nothing out of the ordinary. Yet a shiver went up her spine. As she continued to the corner, her phone rang.

"Hi, are you alright?" Ben asked.

"Have you found anything more?"

"Straight to the point. But no. Are you able to come in to do that statement?"

"Now? Um, I'm going home to change and... Is later okay?"

The strongest sensation of alarm filled Ellie and she looked behind. There *was* someone there, so close to the wall they almost blended into it. And coming her way.

"Ellie?"

"I think I'm being followed." Her voice was a whisper as she rounded the corner. Collins Street was in the distance and she picked up her pace.

"Where are you? Ellie, share your location please."

She tapped her map app and sent it him.

"Are you alone?" There was tension in his voice.

"Apart from the man behind me."

Ben cursed. "I'm sending someone now. Can you see people ahead of you? Is the street busy?"

"Yes. But it is miles."

"No, sweetheart, it is only two hundred metres. I can see now. Keep walking, stay in the middle of the laneway, and make it clear you are on the phone to police. Say something, loudly."

"Thank you, officer! Yes, I do love the dog squad and am so pleased they are around the corner today!"

"Ellie. Something realistic."

She giggled. Some poor person was walking in the same direction and she was turning it into some scene from a horror movie. He'd probably be tasered for taking a short cut.

His footsteps were fast.

Louder.

Closer.

Her heart lurched when another figure stepped out of shadows ahead.

"There's someone else. Ben, there's two of them." She almost tripped as the feeling drained from her legs. Her fingers slid into her handbag, searching, but if there were two men working together, what would she do? "I'm scared."

"Listen to me. They are most likely just taking a shortcut, just like you are. But get as close to Collins Street as you can and if you feel threatened, I want you to scream help as loudly as you can. Okay?"

Ellie doubted she could get even a whisper out.

The man in ahead moved directly in front of her, planting his feet with one hand up like a stop sign.

She veered to the other side of the alley, blinking to clear sudden tears.

"Ellie, hey, wait up, it's me."

"Paul?"

"Don't be afraid, I'm here."

"There's someone following me."

Paul looked past her. "Stay put." He charged toward the man behind her, who turned and ran back the way he'd come.

"Ellie! God sake, answer me." Ben shouted through the phone. Ellie had lowered her hand with the phone to her side.

"Sorry. I'm okay. The man in front of me was Paul. Paul Dekeles. He's chasing the other man though."

"Get to the road and be visible."

"Paul said to stay—"

"I'm saying get to people. Move now. Are you moving?"

"Yes. Paul's gone back in the direction I came from."

Ben spoke to someone on his end, then was back. "There's uniformed officers not far from you. We're on our way but stay with them once they arrive. Okay?"

"Okay. I'm not far now. Why would anyone follow me...I don't get it?"

"Are you still wearing the grey skirt and white blouse? The uniforms will be looking for you."

"Yes. And I'm at the street." Ellie paused to let people pass. "There's an outdoor café. I can stand near it. Lots of people."

"Good thinking. I can see where you are on the map. Don't hang up, I'm going to send your location to them."

She found a spot close to the edge of the pavement, but hard up against one barrier of the café. Her eyes darted around, every man on the footpath a threat. She hated this.

"I'm less than five minutes away. Are the uniforms there yet?"

"No. But I'm safe. I don't know where Paul is."

"We'll find him. Stay on the line, I'm talking on the other phone but will be back."

She had no intention of moving. Her hands were clammy, and she rubbed one, then the other on her skirt to stop the phone slipping from them.

Two uniformed police sprinted through the crowd and she went toward them.

"Ellie Connor?" the male officer puffed, while the female officer got on her radio.

"Thanks, yes. But my friend is chasing whoever followed me."

"A unit is on its way to the other end of the alley."

Paul appeared at the entrance, head turning side to side until he saw her. He raced her way and both officers stepped in front of Ellie, hands on their holsters.

"He's my friend."

"Ellie, I said to stay where you were. I thought you'd been grabbed." He skirted around the officers and threw his arms around her.

She wiggled out. "Paul, I'm fine and was on the phone to the police the whole time."

"You should have done what I said."

"No. She did what I asked. Which was to get out of a potentially dangerous position." Ben, with Andy on his heels, emerged from the café side. He glanced at Ellie, then back to Paul, who opened his mouth, then shut it again.

People stared as they went past. Someone in the café had their phone out, videoing from what Ellie could tell. Great, back to being on the news again. She caught Ben's eye.

"Before Teresa Scarcella and her crew arrive, can we go? I'm ready to do the statement."

"Andy, would you take Ellie to the car? I'll finish up here and be a moment."

Ellie followed Andy to the other side of the café, where Ben's car was double parked. She glanced back. Ben and Paul were in conversation, their body language puzzling. Almost as though they were enemies.

"Who was following Ellie?" Ben turned back to Paul.

"That's what I just tried to find out. Little shit got a head start."

"Description."

"Dunno. Youngish guy. Darkish hair, maybe."

"Very helpful."

"Listen here, Rossi, I tried to catch him. He was almost at the first corner when I found Ellie, so don't start—"

"Start what? You were closest to him. You are a security specialist. I think you can do better than a general description." His voice was calm, business-like.

"I want to be sure she's okay."

"She's okay. Height? Weight estimate? Clothes?"

"Happy to do a statement. Why don't I come with you now?"

"Why don't you and Constable Tan here find a quiet spot and she'll ask some questions. I'll call you if I need a statement. Which way did he turn from the alley?"

Paul stared past Ben toward the car. "Right."

"How did you know where Ellie was?"

"I followed her."

"Explain."

"Nothing sinister, Detective." The eyes now back on Ben's face were hard. "She had a fight with her idiot husband and ran out of the building so I followed to make sure she was alright. But she suddenly disappeared behind a building and I happened to know the alley came out here. Closer to where I was."

"You happened to know."

"My city. Just as well I did. Don't you agree?"

There was a challenge in Paul's voice, in his stance. He was built like a fighter and wouldn't be a good person to run into on a dark night.

Or in a dark alley.

"Ellie was relieved to see you. She was frightened." Ben said.

"I should come with you."

"Thanks, but Constable Tan is waiting for you. We'll talk again."

Ben walked into the café and bought bottled water. Before climbing into the car, he made sure Paul had done as he asked. Paul glared at Ben over the officer's head.

Andy was in the driver's seat, so Ben sat beside Ellie in the back, handing her the bottle of water.

"Did you still want to go home first?"

"No. No, I'd rather talk while it's fresh. Thanks." She opened the bottle and gulped several mouthfuls.

Ben reached over her for her seatbelt, careful not to touch her as he clicked it into place.

"Andy, station please. And why are you driving my car?"

"Double parking is illegal."

"Don't get a scratch on it."

Ellie drank some more, then tried to replace the cap. Her hands shook so much that Ben took it from her and twisted it back on.

"Adrenaline. Happens to us all."

She nodded, then turned a little so she was facing more to the window. A barrier between them. Again.

TWENTY
REVELATIONS

Andy drove into an underground carpark. Ben was out of the car the moment it parked, and Andy opened Ellie's door. The shaking was gone from her hands and the water helped push down an unwelcome wave of nausea. This was one shock too many and she longed to curl in a ball and sob.

The elevator doors opened, and they all got in, Ben and Andy in muted conversation. She needed to pull herself together. She caught a glimpse of herself in the mirrored walls. Her skin was white. Worry lines creased her forehead and her eyes were like a startled rabbit.

"You are the strongest woman I know." Ben spoke so softly she thought she'd imagined it. But he was only inches away, between her and Andy, who was now on the phone. "This will all pass."

She closed her eyes and inhaled to fill her lungs before letting the panic out with a long breath. The nausea lessened. Ellie opened her eyes as the elevator halted. Ben still watched her, his expression unreadable.

"Who wants coffee?" Andy cheerfully offered as he led the way out.

Ellie followed with Ben at her side. Her awareness of him

was through the roof. How could he still see her as strong, after what happened to Michael, to them? Why would he even care after everything? Yet, he did, at least enough to help her through her fears. If only things had been different.

But they're not. I wish I wasn't here.

Andy went in one direction and Ben opened the door to the interview room. She dropped her handbag on the table and swung around as he closed the door.

"I'm not strong, Ben. And nothing will pass until we find Dad. I appreciate you trying to make me feel better, but this can't happen."

"What can't happen?"

"This… whatever it is."

He perched on the edge of the table. "Let's get something straight. I didn't want Jack's case dropped on me anymore than you want me involved, but it is what it is. We both want to find Jack, so we're on the same side, Ellie."

"For now."

"I always have been." He pulled out a chair and sat, gesturing for her to do the same. "How are you feeling?"

Ellie sat, arms crossed. She shouldn't have made things personal. "I had a scare, that's all. I'm fine now."

"Can you run through the events of the last hour or so? From the time you left your building."

Why does it matter when I left. How do you know I wasn't shopping?

"I was walking and lost my bearings. The heat was getting to me as well, so I stopped just inside the alley for a breather. Once I worked out where I was, I figured I could cut through to get a tram home."

"When did you suspect there was someone following you?"

A shiver ran down Ellie's spine and she squirmed in her seat. "I got a feeling. I know it sounds silly, but it was like I was being watched. I turned around, but there was nobody there."

"Go on."

"I got to the corner and that same creepy feeling made me look again. This time I saw someone behind me. He was close to the wall but apart from that... My reaction was ridiculous because the city is full of people and lots of us take shortcuts..."

"But?"

"This whole thing with Dad is wearing me down, to be honest. Jumping at shadows. Except, he was following me, wasn't he? And then he ran."

Ben leaned back in his seat with a shrug. "Which may be nothing more than taking fright at Paul challenging him. He's a powerful looking man and if he scared the other man...who knows? Did you get a proper look at him?"

Ellie shook her head. He'd been too far away and the alley had little natural light. "An impression of someone lean, tall. Definitely male. Sorry."

"Paul might have more information. There's cameras in the area which Andy is getting onto."

"Speaking of Andy," Two coffees in hand, Andy nudged the door open. "A little bird told me you have yours black. So that's what it is." He put a cup down in front of each of them. "Just to interrupt for one sec, early enquiries report no one running out of the alley. But I have someone checking up on cameras in the area." He pulled the door closed as he left.

"There was someone there, Ben. Paul saw him as well."

"I know there was. Paul tailed you from your building."

"He did what!"

Eyebrows raised, Ben picked up his cup and took a sip.

"Why would he follow me?"

"What were you and Dennis arguing about?"

Hand half-way to her cup, Ellie froze. "How do you even know we were. And it is not your business."

"I'm not going to use it against you. Let me decide if it has anything to do with Jack, or for that matter, whoever was in the alley today."

"If you must know, I told him he needed to give police full access to the footage and anything else you need. I asked why Bannerman isn't doing its own investigation into Dad's disappearance. God knows we have the resources."

"He didn't agree?"

"Of course not. So, you'll need to get a warrant because I'm only a board member. I can let you into my office and that is all."

"I'll take you up on that."

"Oh." Ellie picked up her coffee and sipped, expecting the worst. Rich flavours surprised her. "This isn't bad."

"Thank Andy. He worked as a barista through university. What else?"

"He suggested Dad might have been…well, depressed."

Ben laughed. "He doesn't know Jack as well as he thinks."

Lightness filled the dark hole in Ellie's heart for a moment. She'd known it couldn't be true, but to hear Ben—of all people—confirm it, gave her a sudden hope.

She smiled. "No. No, he doesn't know Dad at all."

They finished their coffee in silence, but the tension had left the room. After this, Ellie would go home and shower, wash away the fears and go visit Michael.

"Where are things with *Sea Angel?* Are your people still onboard?"

"Yes, and probably for the rest of the day. They are checking everything, from fingerprints to trace. And in advance, I can only apologise for the mess they'll leave."

"Trace? Do you mean blood? Do you think that gun…" she put her hand over her mouth as her mind raced back to Ben's scenario of Dennis shooting Dad.

"Hey, Ellie calm down. Yes, blood is one thing, along with

all manner of other substances. A gun under a mattress is a highly unusual find. Did you recognize it?"

"No. I'm not one for guns but Dad has a couple. Registered. He keeps them in safes along with cash. Sounds a bit underbelly." She leaned her arms on the table. "You don't think some mafia or something is involved?" The look Ben gave her almost made her laugh. "Okay, just clutching at straws. Because why would there be a gun under a mattress on a yacht?"

Ben's phone vibrated. "Sorry." He read a message before glancing back. "Is there any chance Dennis will change his mind about giving us access to Jack's office? And the footage?"

Ellie shook her head. "Doubt it. But something he said just came back to me. He said there's no point letting you have access if Dad doesn't want to be found. What on earth does that mean?"

After sliding his phone into a pocket, Ben copied Ellie's crossed-arms-on-the-table, leaning toward her a little. "People go missing for a lot of reasons. The overwhelming majority are quickly located, even if they don't want to contact their families, they at least advise police they are safe."

"And the ones you don't find?"

"Missing adults of sound mind and means—like Jack—are often just wanting time out. Things might be rough at home, or a bad investment scared them. They go without telling anyone because they are under so much pressure. Or from shame. Jack reached out to you with his phone call, and the so-far unlocated note. It fits the profile of someone wanting a break, but not disappearing without a trace." He shifted his position, linking his fingers together. "Perhaps he is taking a few days for himself and the message didn't get through."

"He had a lot on his plate. But Campbell has been watching for any transactions and there are none, not on Dad's business cards or personal. Campbell takes care of everything for Dad."

"And his phone appears inactive since shortly after leaving

the building the day he disappeared. Which brings me to some other reasons people vanish."

Ben's expression darkened. He looked away, down at his hands, then back into her eyes.

"Not going to lie, Ellie. Some people take their lives and are never found. Or are murdered and hidden. It happens, you know it does. And while I don't believe Jack would be depressed, he did have things he wasn't proud of."

"I'm not here to discuss his childhood, or his relationship with Michael." Ellie sat upright.

"Not asking you to. Look, I need to consider everything because that's what I do. Don't get shitty with me because I ask questions or paint scenarios. None of this is personal."

And that's what hurt most. It used to be personal. Once, Ellie would have been on the other side of the table, in Ben's arms, sobbing her heart out if need be, but not anymore. Now, his familiar face was both friend and enemy and the resurgence of old feelings was unacceptable.

But real.

She pushed herself onto her feet. "Unless you need me, I'd like to go home."

He stared up at her. Was it disappointment lurking behind those eyes? Couldn't be, not if this wasn't personal.

"I'll ask someone to give you a lift."

"I'll grab a tram, thanks. And I'll stay out of alleys."

He grinned as she pushed the door open.

Andy was on the other side, about to knock. "Heading off. Need a lift?"

"Nope. But thank you."

A few feet away, her phone beeped a message and she stopped to read it. Behind her, Andy's voice carried as he spoke to Ben.

"I have issues with this Paul Dekeles fellow."

She took a discreet step back, lips open.

"Me too."

"You don't just follow someone to see if they are okay. What about a text, or phone call?"

"Something doesn't sit right."

About to go back to ask what that something was, Ellie heard the door click closed. She dropped the phone back into her handbag, message unread, and found her way out.

She'd known Paul for years. He'd worked for Dad for as long as she could recall, starting off in some position away from the business, but eventually becoming head of security. He did everything to look after the building and Dad.

"I'm not Jack's bloody keeper."

The words shot through her mind from the night he'd picked her up at the airport. He was Dad's keeper, at least as far as security, so why or how had he lost sight of the man who paid his wages?

Ellie shook her head as she exited the police station. She headed for the closest tram stop. Paul was loyal to Dad. She would never believe otherwise. Police could think what they wanted but he wasn't the issue. It was more likely Dennis knew something from his hostile and odd behaviour.

At the tram stop, Ellie remembered the message. It was from Paul. *8pm. At Cameron's.*

Dinner at such an upmarket restaurant was the last thing she wanted now. But she had to go. This was a chance to work out exactly what she was up against. What was going on behind the scenes during her absence. Nothing more or less.

TWENTY-ONE
DINNER

Paul took his time getting ready for the date with Ellie. He'd left work early, which was deserved after saving her in the alley from God-knows-what. A long shower and shave, fresh clothes, and a pre-dinner shot of vodka over ice all put him in the mood for fine dining and company. Such a pity Ellie was under pressure, but he'd prepared a range of subjects to talk about, and would ensure she'd enjoy the evening.

When she'd accepted his invitation, he'd known immediately where to take her. Cameron's was intimate, expensive, and perfect for couples. He'd already spoken to the maître de and arranged a discreet table outside overlooking the river. Ideal for watching the colours of the sunset change above the Yarra River. Then perhaps she'd enjoy a walk alongside the water.

He'd not offered to collect her. This was a ten-minute walk from her apartment, or a two-minute tram ride. Tonight, she'd be here with an open heart. He knew it.

Go slowly.

They'd known each other for ever. And there were many things in common, but others so different it would be a delight to discover them. He smiled at his reflection in the hallway mirror and ran a hand through his short hair.

On the street, he grabbed a tram. His apartment in Footscray was far enough out to escape the worst of the city, but close enough to easily commute. Not that this was long term. His plans went way beyond a small apartment in the suburbs. With few expenses, he'd saved most of his income for years and was almost ready to enjoy the fruits of his labour. Almost.

He arrived early, but rather than go in, wandered up the street and answered a few messages, keeping an eye out for Ellie. Like Jack, she was always on time. And there she was, at one minute to eight. She stood outside and gazed around so he waved to get her attention, running across the road.

After her scare today, he knew better than to give her a welcome kiss. Let her fears subside and then see where the evening took them.

"Sorry! Almost ran late." He slowed as he approached. "Last minute issues at work. You look lovely." She did. Hair loose around her shoulders, some sort of pretty short dress, showing off her legs. "Ready for dinner?"

A few minutes later, seated in the table he'd requested, they read their menus. "Shall we have an entrée? I believe the shared antipasto is excellent."

She closed her menu and put it aside. "I'm happy with just a main, but please get something for yourself. I'm not super hungry."

"Nah, happy with a main. Maybe we'll have dessert if you want it later?" he signalled for the waiter and they ordered.

"Are you sure you don't want wine? Or a cocktail?" Paul asked for the second time, surprised she only asked for sparkling water tonight.

"Bit of a headache from the heat today."

"We can move inside to the air-con."

"Oh, no, I like it here and this is nice, sitting here and

watching the river." She smiled and leaned back in her chair as their drinks arrived.

Paul lifted his beer. "To summer evenings with good company."

"Cheers." Ellie responded by tapping her glass against his. "I really appreciate us having a chance to talk away from the office."

Oh, that.

Well, he had agreed to fill her in on the last month's events. "Agree. Things are pretty tense there at times. Have been for a while." Yep, time to tell tales.

"How so?" Now, she sat forward, one hand on her glass, playing with the condensation on the outside. She had pretty hands. Long fingers. Her nails were short, but perfect.

"Paul?"

"Miles away." He took another sip of beer. "About a week after you went to London, Jack and Dennis got into it. After hours, nobody else on the floor. I was about to go home and saw a lot of arm waving on a monitor, so shot upstairs."

"What happened?"

"They were yelling at each other and didn't even hear the elevator because I got right to Jack's door before they saw me." He paused for effect. Ellie was hanging on his words. "I couldn't make sense of most of it, but heard a few things. Meredith's name. Retirement and succession. The Foundation."

"What? In what context?"

"I did hear Jack say…or yell, that he had no intention of handing his company to Dennis or of retiring."

"No. He won't retire for years yet. But Dennis would be the logical next CEO."

"Apparently not in Jack's opinion. Dennis said something about getting rid of the Foundation because it costs too much to run."

"Oh. He made a comment today about it."

I know he did.

"You mentioned Meredith?"

"Right." Paul dropped his head. "I don't want you upset."

"Paul? I'm pretty sure I know what's going on."

When he looked up, her face expected the worst. She deserved better than Connor and perhaps with a bit more of a nudge, she'd turn her back on him completely. "Dennis said one way or another he is having the business, and that includes going via the boss's wife."

Ellie put one hand over her mouth, eyes glistening.

"Damn, I'm sorry. I shouldn't have said anything." He put a hand over her spare one and squeezed. "If it is any consolation, Jack laughed at him. I figured he must be confident she wasn't interested in Dennis."

"Um, I need a tissue." Ellie used both hands to look in her bag and dabbed her eyes. "Sorry, just a silly reaction. What did Dennis do then?"

"Walked out, forced his way past me and slammed the door to the stairs. Must have needed to take them to cool off." Paul grinned. This bit was fun.

"And Dad?"

"I might refrain from quoting the words he used. But he was riled up. Actually, it was more than that, he seemed concerned about Connor's threats of taking the business, more so than the wife. We had a few talks away from the office. Coffees, late-night dinners when he couldn't bear going back to the house."

The waiter brought a basket of bread and refilled their water. Paul waited until he was out of earshot. "Jack looked after me when I younger, so I was happy to be there if he wanted to talk."

"And these talks. Tell me more." Ellie took a slice of bread. Good, she needed to eat.

"Not much to tell, Ellie. He vented a bit, mostly about Connor being a pain in the butt. Said he should never have hired him but didn't know how to change things. Wished he'd kept your job open for you."

Halfway through buttering her bread, Ellie stopped, looking at him in shock.

Found the key!

Paul made himself busy with his own bread. "And I know you don't want me bagging Connor, but I never understood why Jack hired him. Oh, I'm sure he's good at his job, but," he smiled at Ellie, "he isn't you, and a lot of business left with him in the role."

"That's nice of you to say, Paul. But I love the Foundation and all the people we've helped since I started it. And Dennis is wrong about it costing so much because it brings in a lot of business through my networking. He only has to ask Campbell if he wants figures."

"I hate to ask this, I really do, because I think Jack will come home from wherever he is at the moment," Paul put down his bread and leaned toward Ellie, lowering his voice. "but what if he doesn't? Where will it leave you, and Bannerman Wealth Group? Theoretically speaking."

"I might have a glass of wine." Ellie nodded at a passing waiter, who took her order. "Sorry, I'm ready for one now. There's not a lot I can say, Paul. I'm bound by some confidentiality clauses but you be assured your position is safe."

"Not worried about that right now. Worried about you."

"Don't. Dad always plans ahead and when the time comes for him to retire, I'll be offered certain options. Dennis is backing the wrong horse, to be crude, if he wants permanent control of the group." As though she was at peace with it all, Ellie bit into the bread.

Paul followed suit, not tasting his piece as the implications sunk in. Dennis Connor was about to lose a whole lot of happiness. A whole lot.

Ellie didn't have a headache and had delayed drinking to keep a clear head. But now, she sipped the cold white wine with appreciation. Across the table, Paul munched on bread. He'd gone quiet since she'd mentioned Dennis being on the wrong track. Was it too much information?

Or, just enough.

Whether Paul misunderstood Dad, or was lying, she had no idea. He was hiding something and probably exaggerating other things and it annoyed the hell out of her. She'd play his game for a while and if it led to a dead end, so be it.

"I never thanked you for today."

Paul frowned as though puzzled.

"In the alley."

"Oh. My pleasure. Wish I'd have caught the little shit though."

"So do I. Would love to ask him what he was doing."

"Probably some pick-pocket or mugger looking for easy prey."

"Thanks." She rolled her eyes.

"You know what I mean. You were alone in a secluded place with no weapon. He'd have grabbed your bag and taken off before you knew it."

She tilted her head. "How do you know I don't carry a weapon?"

His burst of laughter turned several heads. The waiter must have recognized her expression before she controlled it, as he hurried over to top up her glass. Once Paul calmed himself, still grinning, she offered a toast.

"To strong men coming to the rescue." She held her glass up and after a moment, he tapped his beer against it, his face more sober.

"Come on, Ellie. I wasn't having a go."

She smiled and sipped.

Their meals arrived, and the table was silent as they ate. Unlike last night with Ben, when the sight of food he'd ordered made her hungry, she barely tasted what was probably a delicious meal.

"This is lovely, thank you."

"You deserve a nice night out. Too many bad things going on. Like the alley."

"Speaking of which, Paul, how on earth did you find me there?" she picked up the fork and played with a piece of carrot, trying not to be too obvious watching him.

His expression changed. Was that anger that flashed across his face? Then it was gone again. Maybe she was wrong.

"Believe it or not, I was shopping. Or was going shopping. For new...shoes. Saw you on the street and was about to wave when you disappeared into the alley. I had to go the other way which was past the other end of it. Happened to glance in and saw you. And him."

Come on, Paul.

"I'm lucky you needed new shoes. Did you end up finding some?" She gave up on dinner and picked up the wine glass. Not much left. Time to go home and open a bottle for herself.

He shook his head, cleaning up the last of his meal with a piece of bread. "Spent too long with the constable. Would have been easier to come with you to do a statement as I ended up somewhere anyhow doing one." Paul put the bread in his mouth and continued. "No thanks to the detective."

Enough of poor manners and complaints about Ben and outright lies. She might not know where Dad was. Whether Paul was just bad at his job, or no longer cared, he'd let Dad disappear. Then said he wasn't his keeper. Tears welled up and she rapidly blinked them away, finishing her wine to hide the sudden rush of emotion.

"Another?" Paul offered as he dropped his knife and fork on opposite sides of the plate. "Happy to order dessert."

"I'm so sorry, my appetite is non-existent. I am so worried about Dad."

"How do I fix this?"

"Paul, where do you think he is?"

"I wish I knew, El. I want to believe he is taking personal time and some message got lost. But the way Dennis and Meredith are...I mean, he's now in the job he and Jack argued about, and as for her? Meredith is positively celebrating. Makes it bloody difficult to look past them."

Beneath the table, Ellie's hands clutched together. She would never believe Dad was gone. Never.

TWENTY-TWO
DINNER FOR TWO. ANOTHER COUPLE

In the heart of Lygon Street, a restaurant was known among locals as the place to go if one wanted a discreet dinner. Behind a plain brick exterior lived a true Italian heart, a dark and tiny space with a dozen tables only far enough apart for the waiters to navigate with plates of extraordinary food. People booked weeks ahead.

Most people.

Dennis and Meredith shared a table in the quietest corner. Lit by a candle, their chairs were close, their hands closer. There was an unspoken rule of privacy here.

Some poor patron had their reservation cancelled the moment Dennis called. He had a certain pull in some areas, and this was one of his favourites. Meredith was hardly the first person he'd brought here but he hoped she'd be the one to return with for future anniversaries and celebrations.

He watched her across the little table, longing to taste those lips. Real or not. She'd wasted enough time on Jack Bannerman, but it was worth it. Or would be.

They shared a dessert and sweet dessert wines after a bottle of Italian red. He'd never seen Meredith laugh so much, her eyes free of the misery he'd always considered part of who she was. No, her marriage made her sad. He would spend the rest of his life making her happy.

"When, Dennis?" she whispered with a giggle.

"When what?"

"You know."

He scooped some tiramisu onto a spoon and slipped it into her mouth, smothering a groan as her tongue drew it past her lips.

I do know.

"Not yet, my darling. We have to be sure."

Her hand found his leg and crept upward. He met it with his own and a curve of his lips. She enticed him in ways he'd never experienced, but there was work to do first. No more being with the wrong person to help him achieve his dreams.

"Mr Connor, apologies for the interruption," the maître de leaned down to Dennis' level, his voice low. "There is a growing group of paparazzi outside. We asked them to disperse, but they say they will wait for you."

"What! How do they know we're here?"

"Not from us, sir. Perhaps you were seen arriving."

"Does it matter, Dennis?" Meredith asked, her hands back on the table.

"It does."

"When you wish to leave, I will escort you out the back way. Nobody is out there." The man weaved away.

"Shit." Dennis scanned the room. "Someone here must have recognized us and called the media. No frigging privacy."

A few moments later, Dennis opened the door of a taxi for Meredith in a deserted laneway behind the restaurant. No more dinners out for now, not until his position was made permanent. A quick divorce and remarriage and everything he wanted would come true.

TWENTY-THREE
BREWING STORMS

9 December

Ben saw the sun rise from the end of the pier. *Sea Angel* tossed around in a higher than usual swell from a hot wind streaking across the bay. The temperature was already high, uncomfortable, and predictions of a thunderstorm tonight were backed up by heavy humidity.

The yacht was done with and Ben felt sorry for whoever had the task of cleaning it. Fingerprint residue covered hundreds of surfaces. Despite his request to search with minimum disruption, someone went over the top in the galley and emptied every drawer and cupboard.

All for little result. No blood, no unusual items or suspicious trace. One gun, hidden under a mattress. His hopes of quick identification of an owner turned to a forced patience with the discovery of deliberate damage to the serial number. Meg insisted if it was registered, she'd find it, but needed longer than normal.

He sighed and turned his back on the bay. All of this bothered him on an unusual level. He didn't care that Jack

Bannerman had disappeared, not personally, but he did care about the impact on Ellie. Her life might appear privileged and perfect from the outside, but he knew better. Many kids grew up without their mother around, but it was what happened to Michael which tore a hole in her heart.

And tore us apart

She'd made up for every loss in her life by working harder and making herself indispensable to Jack as if he was the one person she could count on. And if he was dead?

Then there was her marriage. If there'd ever been love there, Ben didn't see it. Not from Ellie.

Ben left the pier to stare up at the top floors of the apartment block overlooking the carpark. It was a street or two back, towering over closer low-rise apartments and houses. Andy had sent officers doorknocking but the residents knew nothing of the missing fisherman, or the missing businessman. No strange noises, or unfamiliar activity. One apartment was empty, for sale, and a couple of others weren't home, so he'd follow those up himself later.

Andy's ringtone jangled and he dragged his phone from a pocket. "Morning."

"Have you seen the paper yet?"

"Which one and why?"

"I'll send the link. Couple of interesting pictures."

"You're not at work, are you?"

"Nope, just browsing over coffee."

The phone dinged with the message and Ben clicked the link. The front page of the paper had the same picture of Jack from the other day, with a headline.

Whilst Jack's away, his family play.

Beneath were two images. The first was dark, in an intimate restaurant. Meredith sat close to Dennis as he fed her.

Then, another restaurant scene. Ellie and Paul. He was laughing, but her expression was disdainful.

What are you doing, Ellie?

"Interesting is right." Ben said.

"She's not into him."

"If you mean Ellie, I agree. So, what was she doing there?"

"Maybe she's doing her own investigation." Andy said.

Ben raised his eyes to the sky. "Far out, she'd better not be."

"Got the impression she doesn't think we're working fast enough. And she strikes me as a determined and capable person with considerable resources at her disposal."

"Tick, tick, and tick. I have to speak with her about the state of the yacht, so will have a chat about the photo. The other one interests me more. Are those two celebrating something? Neither look upset to be missing their husband and father-in-law."

"Poor form. See you in the station?"

"Yeah. And thanks for the heads-up."

Time to get the whiteboard out. Too many loose threads.

At his car, Ben looked back at the pier, to *Sea Angel* and past her to the sea. Somewhere out there were some answers. If not about Dennis, then perhaps about Frank Barlow. How to find them was his problem.

Dennis burst into Meredith's bedroom without knocking. The curtains were drawn and she was buried beneath the covers. He sat on the edge of the bed and flicked a lamp on.

"Wake up, we have a problem."

"Huh?" with a groan, Meredith turned over and peeked out. "Oh, hello. Change your mind?"

"I said we have a problem, Merry, so stop thinking about the bedroom all the time."

She emerged from the covers, sitting up and letting them drop, exposing a see-through negligee. "But we're in the bedroom, sweetie. And you woke me. Not the other way around. What problem?"

"Our private dinner last night made the headlines." Dennis held out a copy of the paper. "Someone in the restaurant took a happy snap."

Meredith snatched it. "When Jack's away, the family plays." Her eyes followed the page and widened. "Not my best side. And what's this? Your little wifey is off playing her own games."

"I doubt it. If she was going to get with Dekeles she'd have done so years ago. No, these two are plotting something. Probably to overthrow me."

"Are you a king, now? Overthrow is dramatic, sweetie." Meredith leaned against him. "He can't do anything to hurt you, and why would daddy's little girl care? She is too busy looking for Daddy."

"Maybe. But you and I do have a problem. This will turn the spotlight onto us about Jack, so we need to get our stories straight. I'll arrange coffee and meet you by the pool."

"It is early. I don't do early."

"You do now." Dennis kissed her lips but moved away as her arms came up to hold him. "In ten minutes, max, because I have to go to work soon."

"Fine." She flopped back onto the pillow. "Last chance?"

From the door he blew her a kiss, then closed it behind him.

Campbell arrived on the executive floor first. Only Jack ever got here before him, or sometimes Ellie. He turned on the coffee machine in the small kitchen before unlocking the door to his office.

It was already unlocked.

He checked the calendar, but the cleaners were due tonight. They only came twice a week so it wasn't a case of them leaving a door open. If they had, there'd be words said because he kept too much sensitive material here to risk anyone snooping around.

The drawers on his desk were locked, and nothing appeared out of place, so Campbell turned on the monitors and plugged in the laptop. He adjusted the blinds to reduce the early morning glare, stepping on something on his way back to the desk. A pen.

"How odd." He picked up the now-broken pen. Not his.

Who's been in here?

A prickling sensation ran across his skull. Something was wrong. Campbell locked his door from the other side, rattling it to be certain. As he waited at the elevator, he glanced around. Most of the lights were still off and much of the space was shadowed.

"Is anyone here?"

Of course, he was alone, and why would anyone with bad intentions reply? The elevator dinged and he jumped, then laughed shortly as he stepped in.

Several floors down, he exited, heading to Paul's office. This floor was not open plan, but had hallways and offices, and was also in semi darkness. Paul's office door was closed and the lights off.

The control room was always manned. He headed there next, tapping on the thick door then holding his lanyard up to the camera.

"Mr Boyd? Do you need one of us?"

"Actually, I'd like to come in, Glen."

Glen stepped aside, pulling the door closed and locking it behind Campbell. The wall of monitors always impressed Campbell. Ellie was walking through reception.

"Sir?" Glen waited, and the other guard, whose name escaped him, looked up.

"Oh. I'd like to view some pictures taken during the night please. Of my office."

"Do you have a time in mind? Would you start a search,

Will?" Glen spoke to the other man, who began tapping on a keyboard.

"After nine and before half an hour ago."

"Quite a long time. Are we looking for anything in particular?"

"I feel someone was in there."

"We did a check around midnight. All locked up."

Thank goodness I'm not imaging it.

The security guards both watched the monitor as the time stamp raced. The monitor went black.

Glen fiddled with the cord behind it and it came back on, then off again. "Not again. Direct the footage to another screen, please."

"Why is that happening?" Campbell asked.

"Dodgy screens. We've had a few do that lately."

"Isn't it unusual? They aren't very old."

"Old enough. Makes our job harder. Sir, rather than wasting your time, why don't we check those hours and let you know if we find anything."

Back in the elevator, Campbell received a message from Dennis with a link to the paper. He groaned as he scrolled the headlines, then shoved the phone in a pocket. His wanted to look at recent security purchases. Paul might need to speak to whoever he ordered from if they were breaking down so soon.

The lights were all on when he exited the elevator, and Ellie stood near Jack's office, staring in. Campbell's heart went out to her.

"I keep expecting him to be there, child." He joined her, putting an arm around her shoulders. She leaned her head against him.

"Today, Campbell. I want to find him today."

"I would like that very much. Keep believing." Campbell removed his arm and reached for his phone. "Have you seen the paper yet?"

"No. But I've had a dozen missed calls from Teresa Scarcella wanting a comment. She's probably upset she didn't get the scoop herself." Ellie followed Campbell to his office, which he carefully unlocked. "Don't know why she's bothering with me though. From the sound of it, scandal is Dennis and Meredith's new middle names."

"I have the link if you wish to see."

"Not really. Anyway, I'm going to visit Michael this morning. Meant to yesterday but…"

"Oh, I didn't even ask how you are feeling today. What a horrible scare you had in the alley." He gestured for her to sit and once she did, lowered himself into his chair, grimacing as pain shot into his knees.

"Probably an overreaction because who would follow me and why? I'm not going to stress about it, that's what Ben is paid to do."

"Ben?"

"Well, the police." Ellie looked at her hands.

"I'm pleased you're visiting Michael. I imagine it has been quite a while?"

"Much too long." At last she turned her gaze onto him. "I need to ask something, but if you aren't allowed to tell, I understand."

No. Please don't ask me about it.

"Yesterday, someone told me something which has me a bit confused. It doesn't add up."

How did you find out?

"And it makes me wonder if this someone is lying to me about a whole lot of things. I can't stand liars."

Campbell's palms were sweaty and he struggled to maintain eye contact. She knew. And she was warning him not to lie any more.

"Ellie, there's certain things I shouldn't discuss."

"Like how many people know about the pre-nuptial?"

"What?"

"The one Meredith signed before marrying Dad. Who

knows about it?"

His stomach unknotted.

"Ah. Not many. Unless one of them has disclosed this information, it is only the legal team who drew it up, the—ahem—happy couple, you, and me. And your mother, of course."

"Why does Gabi know?"

Campbell shrugged. "Jack wanted her to know. Gabi asked for nothing from her marriage, not a cent. It was Jack's choice to gift her the boat and some money all those years ago." He leaned forward. "I may be speaking out of turn, but I think Jack wanted her to know this second marriage was different. Not so much about the heart."

Ellie bit her top lip with an expression he knew so well when she was thinking.

"Who on earth raised the pre-nup with you?"

"Can't say yet. So, Dennis doesn't know?" Ellie stood.

"Not to my knowledge."

"I'd better head off. At this time of day the traffic will be a nightmare. Don't get up, I've interrupted your morning peace enough." She smiled and with a wave, was gone.

With a heavy exhale of relief, Campbell sank back in his chair. He'd been certain she'd found out about Jack's project. Well, Jack needed to get back before she did uncover his plans because Campbell had no intention of being the person to tell her.

TWENTY-FOUR
A SISTER'S LOVE

All the way to Ambling Fields, the home of her brother, Ellie worked on what to say. How to tell Michael their father was missing. Vanished with no trace and no suspicious circumstances. And in words he'd understand, without hitting him too hard. She'd not mentioned Dad in years and his reaction the last time she had discouraged her from repeating it. But he had the right to know.

Once off the freeway, she followed a narrow road through increasingly secluded countryside with low hills and glimpses of the sea. Was Michael ever taken to the beach? A pang of sadness hit hard. Once an accomplished surfer, his damaged brain would never again allow his body to control a wave. He barely spoke, only fragments of words. His ability to understand changed by the hour.

A high wall went on for minutes before Ellie stopped at the closed, iron gates. The place was like a fortress in some respects, as much to protect the residents from unwanted intrusion as to prevent them leaving without proper supervision. Every resident was from a background which kept them of interest to the media. Former sports stars, past music greats, a handful of the elite wealthy. What brought each here differed, except they were all people with life-changing, debilitating conditions. Almost all brain damaged from accidents, disease, or addictions.

"Name, relationship, password." A speaker prompted, and when Ellie responded, the gates swung open.

She drove almost a kilometre through vast gardens before parking in the allocated bay for Michael's visitors. Or visitor. Ellie was nearly positive she was the only person who came here, except when Gabi made her once or twice a year visits. She'd stay for a week nearby, spending her time with Michael for hours a day, then disappear back to her solitary life in her secluded cabin or on her yacht.

The main building was once the gracious home of a family of great wealth. The property was put into a trust when the owners died, many years after their own child was brain damaged. They wanted somewhere safe and protected to offer the rare chance of healing, or more often, a dignified and comfortable way to continue.

Michael wanted for nothing. Twenty-four-hour care, the best medical and psychological treatment, access to cutting edge technology. And all for a million dollars a year.

Money was no object when it came to Michael. Jack even wrote it into his will how his son would benefit and nobody had a hope of contesting it. Whether Jack had stepped foot here since Michael arrived, she had no idea, but suspected not. She shook her head to dispel the thoughts.

A text message directed her to Michael's location so she diverted and found him in the water garden. Part pool, part huge glasshouse, the beyond-luxury area provided warm, safe swimming for those who could, or assisted water activities for those less able. To one side were a few comfortable deck chairs amongst an abundance of greenery, and here Ellie found Michael. She stopped to watch him. Stretched out as though lazing around a pool, he might be any mid-thirties man with wealth. Great haircut, open shirt and board shorts, and designer sunglasses.

But she knew better. Her strong, funny, and talented brother was a shadow of the person she grew up with. Instead of the banter between them, the competitive nature of their relationship, the respect and love for each other, there was only awkward silence with occasional connections. Michael still knew her, but so many pieces of the puzzle that made him unique were gone.

After taking a deep breath, Ellie made her way to Michael and sat next to him.

"Now, before you say anything, would you like to see what I brought you?"

The expression on his face warmed her heart. From a bland daze at the roof, his smile lit the room. He grabbed at the sunglasses but couldn't quite manage them, so she reached over and slid them off.

"Hey, there you are!"

Those brown eyes of his danced with delight and Ellie's heart was full. She reached into her handbag and slid out a block of chocolate. This she dangled in front him.

"This is just for you!"

His mouth opened and he tried to push himself upright. In an instant, an assistant was there, guiding Michael to sit up and adjusting the deck chair to support him. Just as fast, he was metres away again.

Worth every cent Dad pays.

Ellie opened the chocolate and broke a few pieces off. She grinned as Michael forced his palm out and then she closed his fingers around the strip. "Go for it."

The effort of simply putting chocolate into his mouth cut holes in Ellie. But she smiled and nodded as he managed at last and grunted in pleasure. This was their special treat. No doubt he had chocolate and every other good thing he desired here, but their bond over basic caramel filled chocolate was worth more than anything.

As he munched his way through the block, Ellie entertained him with snippets of her London trip, keeping the conversation light. Every specialist reported Michael had limited understanding of anything outside his routine. He might recognize faces and feel a connection, but many words lost their meaning and his memory was poor. But there were times he would emerge, like when he saw the chocolate.

"I have two important things to tell you."

Michael was busy licking melted chocolate from a finger.

"The first is about Dennis. Do you remember him? My husband?"

It would be surprising, as Dennis only met Michael a couple of times and then found reasons not to visit anymore. But Michael nodded.

"Well, he and I have decided not to be married now. He has moved out so I'm a single sister again."

Single sister used to be Michael's way of introducing her to his male friends. "Here is the lovely Ellie, my single sister."

He grinned.

Ellie grinned in return, a little stunned he remembered.

His mouth opened, not for more chocolate, but one of his rare attempts to speak. "Ba."

"Ba? Bad news?"

Michael's face contorted in effort. "Beh. Nnn. Be…n."

With a small gasp, Ellie sat back. Ben? "Did you say, Ben?"

You think I'm with him again after everything he did to you?

The grin was back and Michael bit into the last of the chocolate. He looked pleased with himself.

"Right. Okay, but no. Ben Rossi is not the reason my marriage is over."

He might be the reason her marriage lacked the intense love she'd dreamed of. Some things only happen once in a lifetime.

Some loves.

"Michael, sweetheart, there is something else I need to talk about and this is pretty serious. Are you still listening?"

He finished his mouthful and his eyes found her.

"I don't want this to worry you but it is important you hear it from me in case anyone mentions it and you don't know what's happened. When I got home a few days ago, Dad had disappeared. He's missing at the moment."

He recoiled, almost overbalancing. The assistant was at his side to help him.

"I'm sorry I upset you." She reached for one of Michael's hands, but he pulled away. "I'll find him."

Michael's head tossed from side to side and guttural sounds poured out. The man grabbed Michael's wheelchair and helped him into it. "Ms Connor, I'll take him inside now."

On her feet, Ellie tried again to take Michael's hand, but his face screwed up and he pulled his arms against his body.

"I love you, big brother." Tears flooded her eyes as the man wheeled Michael back to the main house. "I'm so sorry."

She gulped the pain down and when he was out of sight, rushed to her car. A bitter taste rose in her mouth and she leaned against the bonnet for a few minutes until the nausea subsided. This wasn't fair. Michael made mistakes, everyone makes mistakes, but his left him broken.

I'll find you Dad and you will come and see him.

As she slid behind the wheel, her phone rang, the caller ID belonging to Ambling Fields.

"Ms Connor, this is Kerry, I'm Michael's case officer."

Ignition on, the Bluetooth picked up the call and Ellie left the carpark.

"Is he okay? I didn't mean to distress him."

"He will be. I'd meant to call you anyway. The other day he saw news coverage of your father's disappearance."

"Oh, damnit."

"We can't filter everything, unfortunately. He reacted then

as he has now. I should have warned you he'd be easily upset. My apologies."

"I just wanted to reassure him I am going to find Dad. Once I do, we'll both visit."

"Well, I wouldn't recommend doing so. Of course, please do find him, but it is better he stays away from here."

Ellie pulled the car to the side of the driveway. "Sorry. Did I understand you correctly? Not bring Dad to see him?"

"This may be difficult for you to hear, Ms Connor. Mr Bannerman's disappearance is not what set Michael off. It was seeing his face. We've worked with your brother for a long time and there is always the same response when your father's name is mentioned, or his picture appears."

"*Dad* is the problem?"

"Yes. It may be best if the two never meet again if Michael is to live the best life he can. I must go now."

The bitter taste rose again, and Ellie only barely managed to open the car door in time.

TWENTY-FIVE
TWISTS

Dennis had the limousine collect him after a much later start than planned. There was a ton of work he'd let slide, thanks to Jack and his poor decisions. He was hardly perfect, though. Instead of telling Meredith no to dinner, he'd assumed nobody would find them together. By the volume of phone calls this morning, and media camped outside the gates, too many people were interested to expect any sort of privacy.

Traffic was heavy and Dennis opened his briefcase. At last he was in the position he'd coveted since joining Bannerman Wealth Group, and regardless of the reason, or the opposition, he intended to keep it. The top file in the briefcase kept him busy for most of the trip, reviewing and approving several new accounts.

As they entered Domain Tunnel, he put the file away. Beneath it was the sealed yellow envelope marked 'Private'. It was Jack's baby, not his, but now there were big decisions to make. He could follow Jack's wishes and respond to the piling up emails from Jack's contact with a firm date. The fallout was the unknown factor. Loss of jobs. Risk to his own status. Or, he could exit the negotiations and lead the group into a different future.

What were you thinking, Jack?

His hand strayed to an inner pocket of the case. Zipped inside was the letter he'd found in the bottle. There was no need to open it as he'd memorized every word, but he unfolded and read it again. This wasn't the Jack Bannerman he knew. Thought he knew. With everything running the way Jack wanted, why pick this moment? And without offering a word about what came next.

My darling Ellie,

No matter what anyone tells you, remember I love you. You are brave and strong, loving and beautiful.

Dennis shook his head. The bond between Ellie and Jack was a pain in the butt. More than five years ago she'd returned from her unsanctioned time away, hopeful of resuming her position as Jack's right hand. For a week, Dennis watched with growing confidence as Jack's resolve hardened. Once bitten, never again. Let Jack down and expect things to change. Ellie's abandonment of her job and her life at Bannerman had left her father perplexed and then angry. The anger had cooled, and Jack's solution was for his daughter to create the Bannerman Foundation. Dennis stayed in the role everyone expected Ellie to return to.

What nobody foresaw was the rapid success of the Foundation, bringing help to thousands and new clients to the group. It took little time for Jack to re-establish the relationship with his daughter and when speculation began about Jack moving her back to her former position, Dennis acted.

He married the boss's daughter.

One way or another, he wanted Jack's job and was prepared to wait. Surely Jack would retire soon, but his sixtieth came and went with no sign of a change. Day after day, he'd get out that gold pen Ellie had commissioned for his birthday, sign the contracts Dennis wanted to sign, and reinforce the likelihood he'd never leave. Damn him and his pen. He glanced back at the letter.

Not everything is as it seems. Gabi once told me happiness lies in our hearts if we look hard enough. I've searched, Ellie. I truly have, but all I see are shadows closing in.

"Sir? Shall I go into the carpark as there are media out the front again?"

The driver spoke through the intercom and Dennis' head shot up. The entry to the building was invisible behind cameras and reporters. All thanks to his bad judgement. And Ellie's.

"Thanks."

Dennis folded the letter and zipped the pocket. He was no closer to a decision on how to use Jack's note to his benefit. Not yet.

———

It annoyed Ellie to see media outside her apartment building. She nosed her car into the underground carpark and phoned Teresa Scarcella as she waited for the elevator.

"Ms Connor, I'm happy to hear from you."

"I'd like to make a deal."

"Love deals. Go ahead."

"I'll give you an interview."

"And?"

"Two things. Clear your lot from in front of my apartment because you are impacting the daily lives of people who are not involved."

"Okay. I can't speak for other channels though. And what else?"

"I'd like your help."

There was a long silence. The doors opened and Ellie let some people out, then got in. "Teresa?"

"Help, how?"

"With Dad missing, I've been exposed to another missing

person story which is every bit as important. I want some coverage."

"Of someone else's story?"

"Take it or leave it."

"Take it. Shall we schedule for this afternoon?"

"I'll text you." Ellie disconnected the call as the doors closed. If the media hadn't moved by the time she got to her apartment, there'd be no interview.

The doors opened on the ground floor and gym man got in.

"Are those reporters all here for you?" He asked.

"Sorry. They should be headed off soon."

"I saw the paper."

Ellie rolled her eyes and he laughed.

"You had a big day, being chased down an alley and all. Need a security guard?"

The hairs on the back of her arms stood up. "How do you know about it?"

"Huh? Video taken from a phone somewhere online, I think."

Yes, someone was videoing her with the police and Paul, or at least it had looked like it. Were they close enough to overhear though?

"Apparently some copper was asking around the area about a dude running from the alley. Kind of made sense."

The doors opened and Ellie hurried out.

"So, do you need a security guard?" Gym man called after her.

"No thanks."

"Can't be too careful."

Was that a warning? Ellie glanced back but he'd already reached his door and wasn't looking her way. She got into her apartment and locked herself in.

Floors below, the media mob dispersed. As one lot left, the others followed. At least Teresa kept her side of the first part of the agreement. Ellie sent her a quick thank you text, and asked for details of time and place for the interview.

The balcony was too warm for comfort, with a hot wind rattling the chimes. Ellie closed the sliding door behind herself and took her shoes off. The quiet of the apartment settled around her and she sighed deeply, releasing the tension of the past hour. Her stomach had stopped churning but her thoughts collided. She filled a glass with water and perched on the end of the sofa.

Michael's reaction broke her heart. Kerry's recommendation Dad never see his son again was a shock. But had Dad ever visited Michael? Not to Ellie's knowledge. He'd always refused to go with her, and changed the subject of Michael so often that now she wondered if he'd truly turned his back on his son. How would Michael understand his once-beloved father's absence from his life?

She remembered the photo album she'd taken from the safe at Dad's house and found it in the handbag she'd had that night. Back in the living room, she curled her feet under her on the sofa and opened the album.

Her own eyes stared back. Serious, possibly cross by the body language of her seven-year-old self. Ellie laughed. She didn't remember this being taken, but it was on *Wind Drifter,* the yacht Gabi eventually took. Michael was in the background with their mother, playing a board game of some sort. The photo was faded and the clothes dated it.

Ellie turned page after page. All the photographs were of her family. Memories Dad kept of his children growing up, including one of Michael surfing and another from the set of the TV show he starred in for two years. Dad's disappointment when Michael chose a path away from Bannerman gradually turned to pride as his fame and fan base increased. This was the last photo of Michael in the album.

The rest featured Ellie—first day at Bannerman, her wedding, at a fundraiser for the Foundation. Even one she'd sent from Africa during her year away. She'd thought he'd disposed of it, but here it was. And at the back, one of Gabi. Bare footed on a beach, wrapped in a sarong, she was young and so pretty. Over one shoulder she'd slung a bag, and in her hand she carried a small book. Ellie knew it straight away. She'd always called it 'Mum's happiness book' and quoted phrases for any occasion as a child. After Gabi left, Ellie would retreat to the library and sit on the floor reading it when she missed her mother or argued with her father.

What an interesting find. She'd return it to the safe tomorrow so Dad didn't find out she'd taken a look at his private memories. And maybe she'd see where the happiness book was and borrow it for a while. God knows she could use some right now.

"Finally spoke to the remaining resident in that apartment block." Andy helped himself to coffee and poured one for Ben, who leaned against the counter in the police station kitchen.

"And?"

"Nothing. Shift workers with no recall of the dates we need, nor any suspicious going ons in the carpark or marina. Had hoped we'd get something."

"What about the one for sale? Thanks." Ben took a coffee.

"Agent is arranging a time to go in for a look. Owners are overseas."

"And no joy with the alley?"

Andy shook his head. "Sorry. Nothing out of the ordinary. Couple of cameras over the road but nobody running from the direction of the alley. Traffic may have hindered seeing anyone."

The men walked through the open plan squad room to their desks opposite each other.

"Did you speak to Ellie about the yacht and things?"

"Actually, no." Ben reached for the phone. "Thanks for the reminder." He dialled, sipping his coffee. It went to her message bank. "It's Ben. Need to update you on the yacht if you'd call me back. Thanks."

"Maybe she's scrubbing fingerprint powder off and cursing you."

"Crap. Hope not."

Andy put his elbows on the desk. "What is it with you both? Don't give me that look, I don't need a detective's badge to see something going on there."

"We've met before."

"Met?"

"Long time ago. Before she was married. End of story." Ben put the phone down and pushed his coffee cup away.

"Some things don't end. Just saying."

"Ben, do you have a minute?" Meg stuck her head out of her office.

"Perfect timing."

"But I have so many more questions." Andy teased as Ben stood.

"Put all that investigative energy into finding out who owns or controls the pier. And if there is any relationship between Frank and Jack." Not about to give Andy any more time for questions, Ben strode to meet Meg.

"You called?"

Fingers flying over a keyboard, she didn't look up. "I did. Two secs."

The footage from Paul was on a monitor, paused on Jack in the elevator. His hand reached to press a floor button, but the image was fuzzy.

"Are they all like this?"

"Some are fine. Like this," Meg jumped to Jack speaking to

Joni. "Perfectly clear as though a photograph. Not like these." She moved through a series of stills, mostly from the elevator and hallways. "There's a difference in the quality of the equipment."

Ben perched on the edge of Meg's desk. "Is it a matter of some being older than others?"

"I'd need to look at them onsite, but probably, as well as lack of regular maintenance."

"Must be tight with the budget at the Bannerman building." Ben's phone rang. "Anything else?"

"Nope. Still running a search on the gun."

He nodded, answering the call as he left the room. "Ben Rossi."

"It's me. What's wrong with the yacht?"

"Nothing that some cleaning won't fix. Crime Scene Services are done with it."

"Is there anything new about the gun? Or…anything." Ellie's voice was strained.

"I just left Meg, who is still running a search on the gun. If anyone can find information, she's the one. Andy spoke to the rest of the residents in the tall apartment block near the pier, but nobody had any information. Which isn't necessarily a bad thing."

"I guess. So, if Dad didn't make it to the yacht, who really did see him last?"

Good question.

Ben dropped onto his seat. "I'm going to go over my notes from the interview with Dennis, but he said something about Jack's driver ferrying Meredith somewhere that day so he'd expected to see the Lexus in the carpark."

"Except, it is in the garage at the house. Dad drove it home —we saw the footage of him leaving the Bannerman carpark. Can't you get some warrant to make Meredith let you look at the cameras at the house? Actually, I just remembered our security room monitors it. Which means Dennis won't let you look. But I can."

"I'd rather you don't, Ellie."

She didn't answer immediately, but he heard her sigh. "Then what am I to do? There's no reason for me to not check whatever footage I want. I feel powerless."

"You're not powerless. I'll need your help soon, but until I gather more information, there's little to be done. Are you at work?"

"No. Home. There's a storm coming in a few hours. Perhaps I should go and clean *Sea Angel* before it hits."

"*You'll* clean her?"

Ellie laughed, long enough to send a flicker of a smile to Ben's lips.

"Of course, I will. Or did you expect Meredith to put on rubber gloves and carry a bucket?"

Ben covered the mouthpiece and spoke to Andy. "Were there people around the pier earlier?"

"Yeah. Another yacht arrived, and someone else was working on theirs."

"I can hear you both. I'm perfectly fine to spend an hour on my...on *Sea Angel*. So, if there's nothing else?"

"There's nothing else. But keep an eye on the weather, okay?"

"You're worse than Dad. Sure, I'll take an umbrella." Ellie hung up.

"Andy, can you find out who owns *Sea Angel*?"

"Jack Bannerman."

"Are you certain?"

Andy scribbled a note. "Is this before or after the thousand other jobs you gave me?"

TWENTY-SIX

STORM WARNING

The fingerprint residue had to wait. Ellie spent the first hour picking up cutlery, the contents of the pantry, bottled water, and the linen. The latter went into a large bag for washing. After being on the floor and handled by who knew how many people, she wasn't about to refold it.

She opened one bottle of water and gulped it as sweat trickled down her back. The wind carried the welcome scent of approaching rain and the peculiar motion of the boat reminded her the storm was closing. Ellie didn't care if she stayed on board until it passed. *Sea Angel* had weathered a lifetime of inclement weather, mostly out on the open sea, so a Melbourne storm wasn't about to cause her any grief.

This done, she evaluated the work ahead. Fingerprint residue covered just about every surface. On the way below she'd seen the dust on deck, but that could wait. Hopefully, the rain would help a bit and if she remembered in time, she'd spray the railings and wheel with ammonia before the storm hit and let the rain help out.

For another hour or more, Ellie methodically worked her way through the yacht until it smelt as much of ammonia as the sea. Her half-interest in staying onboard disappeared as the first patter of rain began. She'd need to keep the hatch closed and would be ill from the fumes.

She requested an Uber pick up. After a final check, Ellie closed the yacht up and made sure *Sea Angel* was secure. Over Port Phillip Bay, black, heavy clouds scuttled to land. The wind was erratic, agitating the water close to the pier. All the yachts tossed around and sea spray splashed across the timber boards. Hair whipping around her face, Ellie put her head down and hurried to the carpark.

Out here was no real shelter, so she pushed her way into the bushes as much out of the wind as possible. Lightning streaked across the sky and she counted until the boom of thunder followed. The light rain intensified. She should have brought an umbrella, or at least a jacket, but here she was, about to be drenched wearing only shorts and T-shirt. Her phone showed the Uber driver as still minutes away. She backed a bit more into the foliage, careful to avoid sharp branches.

Ellie peered through the rain for a bus shelter, or even an open carport where she might wait. The residences along the street had high walls and she couldn't see to the next road whether the apartment building's entry was covered. She glanced up at highest floor. Someone stood on a balcony. She brushed rain from her eyes and looked again. A man—she thought. He stared in her direction. Was he watching her, or the storm? But even as lightning brightened the sky around her, he remained still, his face in her direction.

A car turned off the road and Ellie emerged from the bushes to wave. Thank goodness the driver found her. But Ubers weren't generally large sedans and as the window wound down, she saw Ben.

"There's an Uber coming."

"Hop in, Ellie."

"But I—"

"Get in out of the rain."

She glanced up at the balcony as she opened the door. The man was gone. The window wound up as she threw herself in and shut the door behind herself.

"I'm so sorry to soak your car, I'm drenched."

"Where's your own car?"

"At home. Why are you here?" She pushed wet hair from her eyes.

"Cancel the Uber. I'll take you home."

"They'll be here in a minute."

"Please. There's some news."

A cold, sinking feeling hit her. With shaking fingers she cancelled the booking. "What...what news, Ben? Dad?"

His expression gave nothing away. "There's been a report of a body in the sea."

The pit of Ellie's stomach dropped.

"No idea who it is, so don't think the worst."

"Where? Can we go there now?"

He shook his head and drove out of the carpark, windscreen wipers barely coping with the deluge. "Nothing to do until the storm passes. The...um, body is in a tricky spot among rocks across the bay. Stuck just under the surface."

Ellie stared ahead without seeing. This wasn't happening. Dad wasn't dead, he was coming home soon from wherever he'd gone. Not lost to the sea. Jack Bannerman was a survivor. He'd survived his childhood.

Her hands gripped each other as Ben weaved through traffic without another word until he pulled up outside her building.

"Ellie, look at me." His voice was calm, insistent, so she did. "Go into the foyer. I'll park and meet you in a minute, okay?"

"You don't need to."

"Yes, I do. There's a bit to tell you, and at least you can change out of the wet clothes. I won't be long."

She nodded and pushed the door open, climbing out into a

flood from the sky. The concierge started toward her with a huge umbrella but she was at the entrance too quickly. "Thanks, please let Detective Rossi in when he gets back in a moment."

Arms wrapped around herself, she retreated to one side of the foyer. The stairwell door opened but it was gym man coming up from the carpark level. He looked her up and down with a smirk.

"Share a lift?" he pressed the hold button.

There was no way she was getting into the elevator with him, not now, not ever. Something about the glint in his eyes sent shivers down her spine.

"Come on. You can drip on the floor as easily in the lift."

Her head shook.

"I don't smell bad, do I?"

If only you knew.

"I'm here, Ellie."

Ben was at her side and gym man closed the doors.

"Something I said?" Ben asked, shaking rain from his hair.

"He's…strange."

They waited for the next elevator.

"Crossed paths with him last time I was here. Strange, how?"

The door opened and Ellie led the way in. "He runs around with a gym bag but doesn't use the one here. I thought he was chatting me up one time then he told me he isn't into older women."

"A charmer. Do you know his name?"

"Gym man. No, I don't and you are not to start suspecting my neighbours of anything."

Ellie was shivering as her hair dripped down her shoulders. Her clothes clung to her and she avoided looking in the mirror in the elevator. Even her handbag was wet, dark patches seeping into the fabric.

The doors opened and Ellie glanced in the direction of gym man's apartment. No movement up the hallway.

"Is that where he lives?"

"Yes." Ellie headed for her own door and unlocked it. "Forget him. Tell me about this...body in the sea." She dropped her handbag onto the kitchen counter to remind her to empty and dry it.

Ben closed the door. "Dry off first. You're shivering, I can see it from here. Or have a shower and I'll make coffee. Okay?"

He was already in the kitchen, so she kicked off wet sandals and went to her bedroom. After a quick shower, she'd make Ben tell her everything. It wasn't Dad, she knew it in her heart.

TWENTY-SEVEN
DISCOVERIES

Ben had no idea how Ellie survived in this apartment with next to no food in the fridge, freezer, or cupboards. She loved cooking and used to keep the freshest of produce on hand for the intimate dinner parties she hosted weekly for her close friends.

Used to.

Where were those friends now when she needed them? Probably driven away by Dennis Connor, a man who struck him as being more than a bit of a narcissist. When he'd been here a few days ago, Ellie made some comment about Dennis binge-buying French champagne during her time in London. Had the man really left his wife with so little to come home to?

Beside Ellie's handbag on the counter was a small photo album. As the coffee machine heated, Ben flicked through the pages, stopping on the one of Michael surfing. Their shared passion of chasing the waves around the world once made the inseparable and introduced Ben to Ellie.

She'd captured Ben's heart over late night tequilas with stories from her volunteer work in remote villages across the globe. At the time she was studying a double degree in culinary management and cooking and worked part time for Jack.

Once a year, she'd steal a couple of weeks to help change lives. Until Michael's life changed forever.

"That belongs to Dad."

He'd not heard the shower turn off. Ellie didn't look upset, it was a statement as she dried her hair with a towel.

"Some good memories in there." Ben closed the album and went back to the coffee machine.

"It was in his safe in the library, which was kind of a weird place to put photos. I'll take it back tomorrow for when he gets..."

The sudden distress in her eyes cut into Ben. He turned his back, finishing the coffee. By the time he carried two cups out, she was on the sofa, legs under herself. Her hair was still damp, softening into the waves she'd always hated and he'd always found cute. She stared out of the windows at the storm.

"Here, this will warm your hands."

She took the coffee without a word, sat back, and gazed at him. Waiting.

"Let's talk about this." Ben sat on the sofa, but far enough away to give her space. "Late this afternoon a report came in about something floating on the surface at the base of the cliff at Black Rock. Initially, it looked like clothes, but a boat coming in from the storm said body. They weren't in a position to get closer. Lots of underwater rocks there and as the tide came in, the body didn't move."

"Are they sure it's a person?"

"Pretty sure. Some uniformed officers got there in time to have a look but the way down to those rocks is treacherous. Seemed to be wearing dark pants and light top."

"We don't even know what Dad was wearing. Ben, we need to go to the house and speak to Meredith, and to the staff. Someone must know!"

"And we will, Ellie. Not until this storm passes though."

As if to reinforce Ben's words, a clap of thunder rattled the rain streaked windows. Although it was early evening, the sky was dark. The last weather prediction he'd looked at warned of a long and damaging storm front.

"How would a body get there?"

"I'm not a tidal expert, but someone who is will work out possible source locations, particularly once we have a time of..."

"Death, Ben? I'm a big girl. Don't feel you need to avoid using the words you need to use." She sipped coffee, eyes never leaving his face.

"Sorry. It feels odd to be having this conversation."

"Because it is me, or because it might be about Dad?"

Both, actually.

"Anyway, speculation is a bit pointless, but one possibility is the person fell. Or fell elsewhere and was carried by an undertow. Or drowned somewhere in the bay and the tide moved them. Until recovery and inspection, we can't consider much more as we don't know how the person died."

"I'd really like a drink." Ellie slid her feet onto the floor and stood. "Want one?"

"Yes. But you have nothing in the kitchen."

"Bother. I keep meaning to shop, but you know what? There's a supermarket on the bottom floor of the building next door and this building has an access door to it so I won't even get wet."

"I'll go." Ben's phone rang. "After I get this."

"Be right back." Ellie grabbed her purse and phone from the wet handbag and was out of the door before Ben got to his feet. But she was gone and the phone kept ringing.

"Yes!"

"Detective Rossi?"

"Sorry, speaking."

"It's Paul Dekeles here. Is this a bad time?"

Ben stared around Ellie's apartment. "No, go ahead. How can I help?"

"We're short staffed so I've spent some time in the control

room. When it was quiet, I was reviewing some footage from the other day and found something a bit interesting."

"Which day?"

"When the fisherman went missing. Ellie was with me when you called to get her down to the pier. Anyway, something about that morning stuck in my mind so I had a look."

"And?"

"Dennis Connor fronted up late. I mean, late late. Got out of his car with his sleeves rolled up and no jacket. Tie all to one side, hair a mess."

"I'm not sure where you're going with this."

"He is normally early to the office and immaculate. Never a hair out of place. But if you don't want the footage, that's fine."

"I didn't say that. At this point though, we don't have permission to look at it."

"So...I might just keep a copy in a safe place. And when you do have permission, I'll be here."

The connection was terminated. Dennis wasn't fully on his radar. If this body was Jack, things would change. But Paul interested him. The man was a bit too protective of Ellie and Ben was fairly sure she wasn't encouraging a relationship.

What are you up to, Ellie? Is he part of your own private investigation?

On the way back from the bathroom, a short hallway displayed several framed photographs. The one near the bedroom door was from Ellie's wedding, a formal image including Jack and Gabi. Two others were scenery from Ellie's travels, and then one of her with Michael on the set of his TV show. Ben remembered the day because he'd taken the photo and somewhere, he had a copy. "Damnit, Mikey."

There was a tap on the front door. "I hope you're in there!" Ellie called.

He swung the door open and took a box of shopping from her arms.

"Left my key card and had to get the concierge to let me back through downstairs." She went to the kitchen. "Just put it there, thanks. Thought I'd get food at the same time. Can you find glasses and open the wine?"

As Ellie unpacked, Ben collected glasses from a cupboard where he'd spotted them earlier. The wine was a dry white, ice cold, and he suddenly wanted nothing more than to share it with Ellie. Sit in the semi dark watching the storm. Talk about anything. Or nothing.

Except he was here as a detective. Not her... whatever he once was.

"I might need to go."

"Now?" Ellie straightened from the fridge. "But...okay. I guess you have work to do." Her hands gripped each other and Ben frowned. She was scared. Unsure.

He opened the wine. "Finished work, so if you really want to share a glass, I will."

The relief on her face shocked Ben. This was all so much harder on Ellie than she gave away. So brave and so good at making everyone else feel good.

"Yeah. Okay, it will give you time to tell me more about what's happening. With stuff."

Two wines poured, shopping packed away, they moved back to the sofa.

The wine was smooth and oh-so-drinkable and Ellie swallowed half a glass before speaking again. Ben's presence brought a strange comfort. Not because it was Ben, of course, almost any company would help stop the crazy thoughts from spinning out of control.

Except Meredith, or Dennis. Or Paul. Or gym man. Not their company.

She almost giggled as she mentally crossed off at least three people she'd previously enjoyed spending time with. Maybe not Meredith so much. Definitely not gym man, whatever his real name was. It was a stretch to come up with anyone. Campbell? Some of the staff? Where were all the friends she'd had?

"Ellie?"

"Hm? Sorry. I haven't cooked a meal in ages. More than a month." There was no reason for him to know that, but the words tumbled out. "And I miss it. I miss making the apartment beautiful and inviting my friends over. I miss cooking all afternoon and selecting nice wine and creating cocktails. Laughing out on the balcony in summer and sitting around the fireplace in winter. I do."

"And croquembouche?" Ben grinned.

"I do not miss croquembouche at all! You remembered that?" Ellie shook her head. "The perfect dessert they said. It will be easy, they said. Except they lied and it collapsed in a heap and the profiteroles ended up on the floor."

"Not all of them. We managed to save some and they were yummy with ice cream."

We. You and Michael.

As Ellie had stood by the table with her hands in the air, Michael and Ben had scrambled to catch the little balls of deliciousness before they hit the ground. And when Ellie was ready to cry at the waste of time, effort, and food, those two found three bowls, scooped ice cream into each, and split the saved profiteroles three ways.

A sudden pounding in her chest brought Ellie back to now. Ben watched her, his expression closed. If he wanted to talk about Michael, then he needed to raise the subject. But he'd better not want to.

"May I have some more wine please, seeing as you have the bottle on your side of the coffee table." Ellie finished the rest of her glass as he reached for it. He topped up hers, but not his. He was going to leave soon.

"You want to talk about the case."

"I looked in Dad's safe at work earlier. Before anyone else arrived. Well, Campbell was there, but downstairs for something. Dad's gun was there. And don't look at me with such disapproval, Detective. He owns three handguns, and each is registered and properly maintained. He retrains annually and has never had to use one."

"Then why?" Ben leaned back. "He has a security team. Cameras everywhere and Paul Dekeles on call. Tell me why he needs three handguns?"

"Because he does. For goodness sake, Ben, you know his history."

"His father?"

Ellie nodded. "Dad grew up in fear. Not for himself, but his mother, his siblings. It is why he took martial arts lessons and learned to box. One doesn't live with a drug trafficking parent and not know how to protect themselves."

"Jack's father is long dead."

"But would it ever really end? He's never told me much but I've done my research and can only imagine what his life as a child was like. Strangers arriving at any hour of the night. Evicted from one house after another. Never in a school for more than a few months. And the violence."

She put the wine glass on the table.

Lightning struck somewhere close and she jumped. A long roll of thunder shook the building. The room was almost dark but when she looked at Ben, her heartbeat steadied.

"Jack spent his life proving he wasn't like his father, Ellie. His hard work and dedication gave you—gave you and Michael—everything he lacked growing up. But he is still the sum of his past. And it shows sometimes."

She bristled, crossing her legs away from Ben. "I don't need a trip to the past."

"There are things you don't know about."

Stop.

She closed her eyes. Not now. Not ever. Ellie knew more than enough. But the phone call with Kerry played over in her mind.

Dad is the problem.

Ellie opened her eyes and swung back to Ben. "No. First we need to find Dad, okay? I'm not ready to talk about him, or Michael, or…or us. Not until Dad is safe."

She reached for her wine and sipped, watching Ben over the rim. His eyes were so dark, impossible to read. And he sat so still, so able to hide his emotions. It never used to be like this.

He put his glass beside the wine bottle. "I saw the photograph I took. Of you and Michael. Has Jack ever been to visit him?"

It was all she could do to not scream. "Did I not explain myself? Get…out."

He didn't move.

Ellie found herself on her feet. She didn't know what to do, where to go, so focused on her handbag, still on the counter where she'd left it.

"Ellie—"

"Please go."

She was all too aware of Ben standing, then striding to the front door. She up-ended the bag to empty it. The door opened as she ran a hand over the contents. Something was wrong here. Among her makeup and receipts and keys was something she'd completely forgotten she had. The door began to close.

"Ben! Ben, wait."

His face appeared around the door, cautious.

"Oh my God. I've made a terrible mistake."

Ben shut the door and crossed the distance. "What's wrong?"

She looked up, tears streaming down her face. "How did I forget? Its Dad's pen."

TWENTY-EIGHT
HOUSE OF CARDS

He had his answer. Ellie wouldn't accept what was going on with Jack and Michael, or what had gone on. There were so many details she'd never heard and as much as she loved her father, Ellie deserved the truth, not some fragile belief.

She was angry. Upset. And tonight, with Jack potentially being the body in the bay, Ben should have left things alone. Door almost closed, he could have kicked himself.

"Ben! Ben, wait."

The panic in her voice wasn't about him leaving. He peered around the door. She was still at the counter, handbag on the floor and its contents spilled everywhere.

"Oh my God. I've made a terrible mistake." Ellie stared at the middle of the pile.

He was at her side in a second. "What's wrong?"

When she looked up at him, tears falling, he barely made out her words. "How did I forget? Its Dad's pen."

"His pen?"

Among lipstick and receipts, business cards, and keys, was a gold pen.

"Can you explain the significance? Why are you crying?"

"Because I found…under the seat…that morning."

"Hey, Ellie, deep breath. Here, have a sip of wine." Ben refilled both glasses and handed one to her. "Sip. You're not making sense so take a moment."

She managed a small mouthful, blinking away the tears and visibly forcing herself to calm. He could count on one hand the times he'd seen her cry. Ellie was not a crier. Was this simply a reaction to finding something of Jack's?

"I should have told you at the time but I thought you were the media and I'm so tired of being followed and hounded by them."

"Told me what?"

"When I was on *Sea Angel* the day after I got home, do you remember talking to me?"

"Of course. You hoped Jack would appear for your arranged meeting." Where was this going?

She put the glass down and wiped her eyes with both hands. "Damnit. I hate being so emotional. Just before you arrived, I noticed something glinting under one of the seats. Dad's pen. This." Ellie reached for it.

"Leave it there. Tell me exactly what happened. Even the smallest detail."

"Okay. I sat at the stern thinking how much I wished Dad would come up the steps. The sun glinted off the pen and I crawled under the seat to get it. It was near the steps and at the back."

This might change everything.

"I heard footsteps and threw it in my bag thinking it was Teresa Scarcella again. But it was you."

"But you didn't show me."

"No. No, you were the last person I expected to see on the pier. Or at the police station. Or ever again."

Tears reformed in Ellie's eyes and she swung away.

Ben pulled an evidence bag from a pocket and eased the pen inside. He left it on the counter, picking up Ellie's glass and following her to the corner of the living room where she stared out at the storm. For a moment they stood in silence, then she accepted the glass with a small 'thanks'.

The rain was less intense now, more a steady tap on the windows. Thunder still rolled long and low but the lightning had moved on except for the odd flash here and there. Something made Ben cross to the sliding door and pull it open. The smell of the storm flooded in. The balcony was covered and only wet from the earlier sideways rain, so he stepped out, breathing deeply.

Below, the streets were filled with traffic but few pedestrians. He glanced at his watch, surprised it was barely past closing time for most businesses.

"So much humidity."

He hadn't noticed Ellie follow him out.

"Storms all night, if you believe the weather reports."

"I believe my senses. Plenty of experience out on the sea with nothing more than instinct and intuition."

"Which for the most part, you have volumes of."

She looked away.

"Ellie, tell me about this pen. Why is it important?" Ben turned his back on the city to focus on Ellie's face.

"I had it made for Dad for his sixtieth birthday. For years he'd lost every pen he ever had and he used to say it didn't matter as they weren't made of gold. So, I found a craftsman who created this from gold plating with a band of titanium and nickel—which formed a memory metal of sorts. It was a private joke."

"He couldn't lose it because it would remember where he was?"

"Yeah. Figuratively. He loved it."

"Incredibly thoughtful gift. Who thinks of something with so many layers of meaning? No wonder he kept you close, despite…"

Damn. Leave things be.

"Say it." Resignation filled her voice. "Nothing else will upset me tonight."

"When did Jack have the pen last? I recall the footage of him signing papers at the board meeting." Ben wandered inside, across to the counter.

Ellie left the door open as she trailed him.

"The thing is, Ben, he always had it with him. At work it was either in a pocket or his hand. At home he'd leave it on his desk or in his briefcase." Her voice rose a little. "He would have signed papers at the boardroom, gone home with it, and then what? I would think leave it at home as he was going sailing!"

Ben took her wine glass and set it down. At the risk of her telling him to leave again, he reached for one of her hands. So cold, yet the evening was warm. "So much isn't adding up. I agree, why take a pen sailing, unless he expected to have documents to sign or some other use?"

Ellie shook her head.

"I'm going to run the pen to the station. Get it checked for fingerprints. But I'll be back soon, okay? As long as you want me here."

Her fingers curled around his, gripping as though afraid to let go. "Maybe I should come with you?"

"Or, you could stay here, close the sliding door and warm up. You don't need another soaking."

"I...okay. If you need to do other things," she released his hand and wandered into the kitchen. "I'm fine. Really."

Sure, you are.

"I'll call when I'm leaving. See if you want some company." He picked up the bagged pen and slipped it into a top pocket. "You okay?"

"Be careful out there. In the storm."

Ben was more worried about Ellie being alone, not because of the storm, but how distressed she must be not knowing whether the body in the bay belonged to Jack. And now this new clue threw everything into doubt.

"You're certain?" Paul stood in Jack's office, all the lights off, talking on his phone. The storm had played havoc with the power in the building and workers were happy to leave in droves. He'd spent the last hour resetting cameras, fixing the automatic carpark gate, and keeping people off the lifts.

The rest of the security team had things under control again and Paul came up here to check the doors were locked after Campbell's complaint this morning. There'd been no footage of his office thanks to another failure.

Time for an upgrade.

"Yeah, I'm still here. You've done well today. We'll grab a coffee tomorrow."

He disconnected the call. Jack's desk always fascinated him. So tidy with its perfectly placed family portraits. Paul picked up the photo of Ellie and Gabi. Two pretty women. Both free spirits but the difference was Ellie understood responsibility. She'd never leave her kids behind when things got tough. He liked Gabi because she did what was right for herself, but at the same time, despised her for abandoning Ellie.

How courageous was Miss Ellie Bannerman? She faced every challenge with grace and determination. Look at how well she'd taken the collapse of her so-called marriage. Paul grinned as he replaced the photo frame. Their future held so much happiness and such wealth. They'd travel, have homes in Switzerland and Hawaii. Always wanted to visit Honolulu and have a go at surfing.

Paul took the stairs to the carpark two at a time. The automatic gate rolled effortlessly out of his car's way and he eased onto what was still a busy road. His first stop was a Thai takeaway he'd phoned earlier. He managed to pick up dinner without getting drenched.

A few moments later, he buzzed Ellie from downstairs.

"Hello?" Why was her voice so cautious?

"Ellie, its Paul."

"Oh."

Oh?

"I bought dinner for us. Thai. Thought it would save you cooking or going out on such a bad night."

"That's sweet, Paul. Um...I am right in the middle of cooking though. And, you've heard about the...um, body in the water?"

"What? Buzz me in, El."

"Someone spotted a body over at the base of the cliff in Black Rock. The police can't get to it until the storm passes. Probably in the morning."

"Okay. Buzz me in and you can tell me the details." The rain was heavier, coming in sideways and Paul was getting wet. The concierge watched him from the reception desk inside but wasn't making a move to let him in.

"I'm not good company right now. But thanks for thinking of me. Goodnight."

"Ellie—"

Finger raised to press her number again, Paul changed his mind. For Ellie to say no, she had to be feeling upset. Probably thinking it was Jack's body and who wouldn't be worried? He'd have taken care of her, kept her from being sad. But, he'd respect her wishes and keep an eye on her instead. Make sure she was safe.

His car wasn't far down the road, and he left the wipers on as he unpacked dinner. Later, he'd make some phone calls and transfer some funds, so she'd have a guardian angel for a few hours yet. Paul turned on the radio and listened to the news about what they were now calling the 'body in the bay' mystery. The reporter speculated whether this was Jack, or

Frank Barlow? And was there a connection between the two missing men?

The storm strengthened again. The traffic all but disappeared and no pedestrians ventured along the pavement, apart from one man who hurried from a car further down the road and ran up the steps of Ellie's apartment building. Must be a resident.

But the man stopped at the intercom. Paul increased the speed of the wipers. The front door opened as lightning lit the sky and Paul almost dropped his takeaway container. Bloody Ben Rossi. What the hell was he doing here? Was it about the body?

Paul gripped the steering wheel. Of course not. Ellie said she was cooking dinner. She said she wasn't good company tonight.

"You mean, you're expecting company tonight, you little liar."

TWENTY-NINE
WHAT GETS US THROUGH

Somehow, she had to gain control of her emotions. Crying in front of Ben, telling him to get out when a calm response would have been just as effective, all of this was born from the stress since arriving back in Australia. But she hated it. Dad wasn't being found any faster if his daughter melted down.

Once she'd come to that conclusion, Ellie began to cook.

From the back of a cupboard she dug out her pasta maker. A mound of flour on the counter, eggs, knead. Through the machine until she had a pleasing row of linguine hanging over a makeshift rail of chopsticks between two tall jars. She washed a bunch of sage and put half a block of butter aside. Might as well make a decent sauce.

The intercom interrupted her process and once she finished talking to Paul, she returned to the kitchen frowning. Paul was pushing boundaries. Breakfast when she didn't ask for it, dinner at an expensive restaurant instead of a casual meal to talk about Dad, and now turning up uninvited with takeaway. He was either over-compensating for Dad's disappearance, or making a move on the boss's daughter.

Her glass was empty, so she refilled it. There was a decent bottle of red on the dining table, where she'd placed it with two fresh glasses and setting for two. If Ben wanted to eat with her. He'd called before Paul fronted up, and said he had something to discuss if she was up to it.

Ellie stared at the table. Had she made it too pretty? Too much like a…date? She ran over and took away the candle and wine. Then the glasses. No, this wasn't a date. In a moment she'd cleared the table and was swallowing a mouthful of wine with half an eye on the weather. The storm was back, or a new one here. Either way, the wind had increased, and she'd closed and locked the door to the balcony. Lightning flashed and she jumped as the intercom buzzed.

"Kind of wet out here."

"I'll find a towel. Come up."

The concierge would send him up in the elevator. The security in this building was more than she needed, but proved its value on nights like this.

About to unlock her front door, she hesitated. The building was safe.

What if gym man came calling?

She ran to get a towel from the main bathroom and waited near the front door.

The elevator dinged.

"It's me."

"What's the password?"

"Profiteroles."

With a smile from somewhere, she opened the door to Ben and looked him up and down.

"You are barely damp."

"Thanks for getting a towel."

She handed it to him and closed the door. "Good luck getting any drier."

Ben made an exaggerated attempt to dry his hair and she laughed.

"Good to hear that laugh. Are you cooking?"

Ellie returned to the kitchen. "The pasta maker was feeling

unloved in the back of a cupboard. Look at all the linguine it made to say thanks for using me again."

"Very nice of it. Are you eating it all by yourself?" Ben leaned on the counter, eyes on the pot of water ready to heat.

"I am hungry."

"Oh."

"Well, I guess there's enough for two if you—"

"Yep. I think I should stick around a bit and make sure there are no…um, leaks. From the storm."

"Leaks. Right." She turned the stove on and settled the pot over the heat. "Once the water boils, dinner will be ten minutes or so."

"Jack's pen has been dusted and is staying in the evidence room for now. I'll get it back to you as soon as possible."

"How long until you hear anything?"

"Fingerprints? Tomorrow, next day. Depends on who touched it and if they have the fingerprints on file anywhere. I know you do so we can exclude yours. Jack does."

"And Paul would, being security."

"Why would Paul handle Jack's pen?"

She reached for a heavy based pan with a shake of her head. Why would anyone, other than Dad?

"Ellie, there's something else."

"Go ahead." She tossed the butter and sage into the pan and adjusted the heat. "I can listen and cook."

"*Sea Angel.* You've never mentioned who owns her."

This was the last thing she'd expected Ben to say. As the butter gradually melted, she poked at it with a spatula. Why did it matter?

"You've always referred to her as Jack's. He and Meredith go sailing on her. She's tied up at a pier Jack pays a lot of money to use."

"When I turned eighteen, Dad gifted *Sea Angel* to me. But there were some conditions."

"Such as?"

"Nothing important."

Ellie bit her bottom lip as she added the sage to the butter. The water in the pot was almost boiling but she wasn't ready to add the pasta. Not until Ben stopped with the questions.

He noticed the bottle of red and opened it. Ellie snuck a glance as he poured two glasses. Tendrils of his slightly damp hair curled around his neck.

"Shall I set the table?" He didn't wait for an answer, coming into the kitchen and helping himself to cutlery, salt, and pepper. "I'm not trying to scare you, but as the owner of *Sea Angel*, if the gun is identified as having any illegal associations, then you'll be under the scrutiny of other police departments."

Her mouth dried out. In her haste to get a glass of water, she knocked the spatula and it landed on the floor with a clatter, bits of sage and butter in a trail behind it.

Ben tore paper towel from a roll and went to clean up, but Ellie took it from him without a word. She had none. This nightmare had no ending. Squatting, she dabbed at the small mess, barely able to see as yet another round of tears flooded her eyes. Her fingers wouldn't hold the paper towel and with a thump, she sat on the tiles.

"Ellie, it will be okay, I promise." Ben was kneeling at her side. "Last thing I wanted to do was make you feel worse but you need honesty, and I don't think you've been getting it lately."

"Why…are you…kneeling here?" Nothing made sense anymore. Dad was gone. There was a gun on her yacht. A body in the water which might be Dad. Her husband was involved with her stepmother. Ben was back.

Ben offered a handkerchief. "I thought you were making your world-famous burnt butter linguine."

She wiped the tears away and blew her nose as discreetly as possible.

He leaned closer without touching her. "I said the other

day you are the strongest woman I know. But it doesn't mean you can't cry or grieve. Being able to feel and know how you feel is a mature response."

"Don't feel mature right now. More like I want to throw a tantrum and beat the ground with my fists."

Ben stood and offered his hand. "Perfectly good bottle of wine up here which won't drink itself."

Ben finished setting the table to give Ellie a chance to compose herself. She'd disappeared into the bathroom for a few minutes before returning to the kitchen. He'd switched everything off the minute she hit the floor, gutted at her reaction.

Think before speaking, Rossi.

But if he didn't prepare her, who would? The confirmation from Andy that Ellie owned *Sea Angel* was not entirely unexpected. It was so well kept and loved. Much as Jack Bannerman appreciated order, he had none of the light touches making the yacht so welcoming. So why the secrecy and what made Ellie hesitate when she answered? For that matter, why did the whole Bannerman family—excluding Michael—have to be so complicated?

"Almost ready."

"Any candles?" Ben joked.

"This isn't a date."

The lights went out. Not only in the apartment, but the buildings around them. Further away the lights were on and a few generators must have started as shops below lit up again.

"No generators in the building?"

Ellie carried two bowls to the table. "I imagine so, but if they are anything like the ones at work, don't count on a quick solution." She nodded to the sideboard as she returned to the kitchen. "Candles in there."

It might not be a date, but dinner by candlelight was

happening anyway. Ben lit the candles he found, collected a basket of bread from the counter, and waited for Ellie. She glanced outside as she set down a salad. "How strange to look out on darkness."

They ate in silence for a few minutes, surrounded by lightning and torrential rain. Perfect pasta in a buttery sweet sauce, soft bread, and rocket in balsamic—memories of past meals with Ellie poured into Ben. Picnics and breakfasts, late night snacks by the sea and romantic dinners for two. He put down his fork and picked up his glass.

"To Chef Ellie." He touched the glass to hers when she rose it.

"Haven't heard that name in a long time." She sipped. "I have to cook more often."

"You should. And being a chef is still possible, you know."

"Maybe one day I'll own a restaurant. Run it with people who fall through the cracks and create a safe place for the displaced."

Always there for the underdog. Ellie's heart knew no boundaries.

Except when it comes to me.

Ben forced away a sudden heaviness in his chest. She'd made her decision years ago and it was fate that brought them here tonight, not love nor a hope to start over. By candlelight, her eyes softened as she spoke more about the restaurant of her dreams. If only they'd met another time. If only Michael hadn't been his best friend. He nodded at her words although he heard none of them. She stopped speaking and drank some more wine, then turned intense eyes to him.

"I want to tell you about *Sea Angel*."

This he heard.

"I'm listening."

"Dad transferred the papers to me on my eighteenth birthday but I had to sign an agreement. Because I was so young, he would pay all the costs around *Sea Angel* until I was earning enough to take them over. Yachts are expensive creatures. In return, I'd give him use of her when mutually convenient."

"Seems fair."

"But. And it was a big but." Ellie played with the stem of her wine glass, her eyes on her fingers. "For the arrangement to continue, I had to work for Dad."

"Do you mean in order for him to pay the costs, you had to be employed by Bannerman Wealth Group?"

She nodded.

"And what about when you were in a position to take over?"

"Kind of fell to pieces when I left for a year. Although I still own *Sea Angel* on paper, in Dad's eyes I broke the agreement. We've been at a polite impasse for years." She emptied her glass, then scooped up the last of her pasta.

A slight shaking of the hand with the fork belied her calmness. Ben refilled her glass, then his, giving her time to continue. Her meal finished, Ellie pushed the bowl aside and held the wine glass between her fingers.

"I won't sign the papers back, and he won't take his stuff off the yacht. There's no animosity, but we're not getting anywhere."

"The yacht belongs to you, Ellie. Why haven't you returned all of his belongings to his house, and moved *Sea Angel* to where you want to moor her?"

"When I left for a year without leave or notice, it damaged our relationship and it took ages to rebuild. If you hadn't noticed, Jack Bannerman isn't a man you defy."

"I know this." Ben folded his arms on the table. "But that is his problem, not yours. And before you defend him, I know Jack loves you, Ellie. There's a difference between love and ownership. And he is controlling you. Why do you still let him use you? The way he uses everyone."

Her eyes narrowed and she bit her bottom lip. In a moment

she'd tell him to leave again and this time it would be permanent.

"I'm his daughter. He needs me." Her voice was so quiet he barely heard her. "I'm all he has now."

"No, sweetheart. He has Meredith, or did. And he has…"

"Michael?" her chin went up. "Yes. Until he was arrested."

Surely, she could hear the pounding of his heart? He dropped his hands beneath the table and let them clench so hard it hurt.

The silence dragged on between them while outside, thunder shook the building. The chimes were out of control, jangling heavily in the wind. Ellie closed her eyes as if shutting him out. Everything out.

"Tonight isn't the time to speak of this, Ellie and I am so sorry I let the conversation go this way. You've done a beautiful job with dinner and I'm going to make us coffee, okay?"

She pushed herself to her feet.

"Coffee would be good. I might sit on the sofa and watch the storm."

As the coffee machine warmed up, Ben cleared the table and packed the dishwasher. If Jack was the body, then Ellie's life was about to change. But if the man was alive somewhere, Ben intended to find him and have a long overdue conversation.

With the coffees, Ben joined Ellie at the sofa. She was asleep, her head nestled in her arms and her body curled up. He sat on the end, drinking his coffee and watching her sleep.

THIRTY
WHOSE BODY?

10 December

Ellie woke when the front door clicked shut, sitting upright with wide eyes. A blanket covered her and she was still dressed.

Early morning light streamed through the windows. The storms were gone, leaving clear skies through the gaps between buildings. A lamp was on, so the power was back. She dropped her feet onto the floor, waiting for a headache, or worse, from so much wine last night. But none came, and her mind was clear. In fact, this was the first time she'd woken without battling exhaustion.

When Ellie opened the front door the hallway was empty. Why had he left without waking her? She cast her mind back. They'd not argued, but emotions had run high. Cooking for Ben, sharing a table with him, touched a part of her heart she'd long buried. The stirring of memories was not what she needed now, if ever.

Propped against the coffee machine was a note.

Call when you are ready and I'll have you picked up.

Retrieval underway.

Ben.

PS. Chef Ellie deserves happiness.

Much as she wanted to throw clothes on and get to wherever this retrieval was, she needed a shower. And to prepare herself.

Under a steady stream of hot water, she practiced a meditation technique to protect herself from what was ahead. Until the body was identified, there was doubt, and staying calm and logical was better than what she wanted to do—fall apart. By the time she dressed, her mind no longer chased thoughts into circles.

She sent a text to Ben as she made coffee. *Ready for pick up.* Once she'd poured coffee into a reusable coffee cup, she'd wait downstairs.

Ben's note caught her eye. Chef Ellie was what he and Michael called her back in the days of university, dinner parties and big barbeques on the beach.

Not knowing what to expect today, Ellie threw a packet of tissues into her handbag and sunglasses, then peeked out of the door. Running into gym man would be too much. She pulled her door shut and sprinted to the elevator, willing it to be quick. Her phoned beeped as she stepped in. *Andy is downstairs.* Ellie tapped the ground floor button.

"Hey, hold the lift!"

Gym man's face appeared for a second before the doors completely closed. Exhaling in relief, Ellie watched the floor lights as the lift descended.

A police car was outside. Not like Ben's plain one, but the lights and sirens type. A prickle of dread traced up her spine, so she raised her chin and pushed the door open before the concierge got to it.

Andy was coming up the steps and smiled. "Hey, Ellie. All set?"

"I guess. Where's your car?"

Andy opened the back door. "Ben commandeered it. Some issue with his. This is Constable King."

They exchanged pleasantries as Andy climbed into the front passenger seat, then Constable King pulled away from the curb. Ben's car was parked further down the road, with both street-side tyres flat.

"How?"

"All four are slashed. Someone took a dislike to the car. Or Ben."

"Where are we going, Andy?"

He turned as far as he could to speak to her. "Black Rock. About half an hour away, depending on traffic. Our crew was there at first light, setting up what they could. The tide is going out but the storm made a mess of the area."

"Is…um, is it still there?"

"The body? It is. By the time we arrive, they may have retrieved it and you won't be going near it unless we need help with identification. Ben wanted you there so you're kept in the loop. Nothing worse than being alone and thinking the worst."

The police car wound through the early morning traffic, through the Burnley tunnel and cutting through suburbs to emerge on the road not far from where Dad had his beach box. The sky was the clearest blue and the sea reflected it. Calm and endless. Nothing like yesterday.

Ellie went through the messages on her phone, anything to distract her thoughts. One from Campbell expressing his concern for her after the news broke. She replied, telling him she was on her way there now. One from Teresa updating their interview time after cancelling yesterday. Then another, expressing her hope this wasn't Jack. Why was she trying to be nice? Finally, a message from Dennis.

We need to talk.

What on earth was there to discuss? His relationship with

Meredith? Failure to be a husband? Or was it about Dad? Did Dennis know something?

Ellie put the phone away. Dad's pen didn't get onto *Sea Angel* by itself. Either Dad was on the yacht and dropped it, or someone took it from him and lost it there. Dennis went sailing without Dad. So, he said.

Ben once painted a different picture. Two men out in the bay, a long way out. An argument, or even an accident where Dad fell overboard and Dennis kept the secret. If there'd been a struggle, the pen might have slipped out and rolled under the seats. Ellie's chest tightened. And the gun. Was it used to…to shoot Dad?

"Almost there. At the end of this road there's a carpark." Andy's voice cut into her spiralling thoughts and she glanced up with a start.

The sea was a long way down from the road. They turned into a carpark dotted with emergency services vehicles. A couple of uniformed police were in attendance and they waved Constable King through. Andy was on the phone as they climbed out.

"Yeah, just got out of the car." He hung up. "This way."

Ellie rubbed her arms as she followed Andy. A narrow track led to a clearing where equipment and emergency services people created a sense of urgency.

"Wait here for a moment."

Andy vanished down a side path. Ellie stayed put for ten seconds then took off after him. Underfoot was slippery, with muddy patches and loose stones. Voices called to each other ahead but the words weren't clear. Ellie's heartbeat pounded in her ears. Was it Dad?

Around a bend the ground evened out. On a stretcher on the ground, covered almost completely with a sheet, a bloated body lay. Ben squatted beside the grotesque form while Andy was back on his phone.

With a gasp, Ellie stopped dead, hand over her mouth. Ice

poured through her veins as Ben straightened. His eyes met hers.

Daddy.

"Ellie."

She shook her head and took a step back. Ben strode toward her, hands outstretched. He was about to tell her this was Dad. A small cry began low in her throat and then he was there. His warm hands cupped her face.

"No. It isn't Jack."

Her legs buckled but Ben's arms whipped around her waist and pulled her in against his chest. "Did you hear me, Ellie? This isn't Jack's body."

Campbell put down his phone and wiped his forehead with a handkerchief. News at last and so much better than expected. Not for the poor man who had drowned but thank God it wasn't Jack.

He pushed himself to his feet. At his doorway, he gazed around the floor. Joni sat at her desk, officially on leave but seeming unable to stay away. Dennis tapped on his computer in the next office. For some reason, Paul was at the reception desk speaking to Mark. Perhaps he had more information about the unlocked door?

"Everyone." He cleared his throat. "May I have your attention for a moment please?"

One by one, heads turned to him. Dennis glanced up, still typing.

"I've heard from Ellie."

Dennis stopped typing.

"About the unfortunate person found in the bay."

"Get to the point, Campbell." Dennis stood, hands on his desk.

"Well, the news is good, at least for us. It wasn't Jack."

"Oh!" Joni burst into tears.

Dennis closed his laptop and went to Joni, patting her on the shoulder. Mark hurried across with a box of tissues, pulling a handful out for her. "It is good news, love. I'll make you some tea."

Paul stepped forward. "Who is it, then, if not Jack?"

"Not formerly identified, but appears to be the missing fisherman. Poor soul." What Campbell didn't share was that Frank Barlow had a gunshot wound to his chest. Ellie whispered it to him, then asked him to keep it quiet for now. And he'd do anything for Ellie.

"Right, well now we know Jack's alive, everyone back to work." Dennis glared at Paul on his way back to his office. "I mean everyone."

Campbell followed him. "It may be pointing out the obvious, but we don't know if Jack is alive."

"You know what I mean." Dennis returned to his seat and opened his laptop. "Wish he'd hurry up and get found. All this speculation is damaging our chances of finalizing Jack's project. Although, it might be better to back out and go a different direction, don't you agree?"

"That's not what Jack wants."

"How do we know?" he nodded at reception. "Jack might have had enough of this. Too many bad decisions and difficult memories. For all we know he might be off with a mistress, or at the bottom of the ocean."

"Or kidnapped. Or lost somewhere."

Dennis threw his head back, laughing so loudly everyone turned.

"Campbell, he isn't wandering around some forest, eating berries. The police ruled out kidnapping as we've had no demands. If someone was going to be kidnapped, Ellie is the logical one."

"I beg your pardon?" What manner of man said such a thing about his own wife?

"Look, all I meant was Jack—who controls a fortune— would be free to negotiate and pay whatever ransom was demanded. If Jack was kidnapped, there's no quick way to access funds. Pretty pointless in my books."

Well, haven't you got it all worked out?

"Tell me, Dennis. What do you believe happened after Jack left here that day? Where did he go?"

Hands back on the keyboard, Dennis shrugged. "I know what everyone else knows. He was going home to change to meet me at the yacht."

Dismissed, Campbell checked on Joni, then stopped at the reception desk where Paul still stood. "Did you need me for something, Paul?"

"Oh. No, Mark is helping me check all the monitors, so waiting for him to get Joni's tea. That's all. Good news about Jack, though."

"It is. Very good. I'm sure Ellie was beginning to despair."

"Where is she?"

"Out at Black Rock. No doubt with Detective Rossi."

Paul's face darkened and his body tensed. Did he not get on with the detective?

"She was taken out there in case identification was required. I imagine she'll come to work soon."

"Right. I'll keep working on the monitors and we'll make sure everything is up to scratch for when Jack gets back."

"Thank you, Paul. I feel much happier knowing you are looking into this yourself."

Back in his office, Campbell watched Paul speak to Mark after the other man set a cup of tea in front of Joni. They glanced his way and he nodded.

THIRTY-ONE
A SHOT TO REGRET

By the time Ellie left Black Rock, this time in the front seat of the patrol car with Constable King driving, the media had arrived. They were kept back as Frank Barlow's body was loaded into the waiting coroner's vehicle, their questions relentless as it drove away.

Ben had protected Ellie, shielding her from the mob as he escorted her to the police car. Once she was inside, he squatted beside her.

"Okay now?"

"Thank you. I'm so sorry for Frank's wife. What terrible news for her."

"It was going to be bad whoever it was."

"But murder? Oh, Ben. Who would do this?"

"Homicide will be doing their job to find out. And I will escalate the search for Jack. Are you going home?"

"I'm doing an interview with Teresa Scarcella. It might get her off my back for a while and besides, she owes me a favour I intend to call in."

"She owes you?" Ben raised his eyebrows.

"Let's say we have an arrangement."

"You continue to surprise me, Ellie Bannerman."

"Connor. For now. Ben, thanks."

"Thanks?"

"Yeah. For stuff." She smiled and he couldn't help responding in kind.

As the patrol car nosed along the track, he saw her watching him in the side mirror. Her eyes still had a haunted expression but now at least she had hope again.

"Boss?"

"Stop calling me that."

Andy grinned. "Got a call. Homicide are keen to have a chat."

"With us, or just you?"

"Funny. Both. Meg wants to see you."

Ben and Andy followed the path all the way to the base of the cliff. With a lower tide, some of the rocks were exposed. Meg—pants rolled above her knees—stood ankle deep in water, taking photographs of the rocks. A uniformed officer kept an eye on her from the safety of a tiny pebbled beach.

The men stopped short of the water's edge. "You need me?" Ben raised his voice over the waves.

Meg glanced up. "Yeah. Can you come here?"

Sure. Love ruining a perfectly good suit.

As Andy laughed, Ben threw off shoes and socks, then rolled his pants up as high as possible. One tentative step at a time, he waded to Meg, somehow managing to keep his clothes dry. The water was warm and the rocks not sharp.

"What's up?"

"This is where the body was caught. See that crevice there…no, look a bit to the left and below the surface. Two rocks almost meet."

Swirling water confused Ben's eyesight but when the sea drew back a little, he saw it. A handkerchief sized piece of fabric. "What on earth?"

"Exactly. And that's the spot the body was trapped, yet

different from his clothing. The tide will be low enough soon to extract it, but in case it disappears I've taken a million images."

"No. Can't risk it. Give me two minutes and yell if it moves."

Back on the beach, he stripped to his boxer shorts, handing his clothes, wallet and holster to Andy with a warning look not to comment.

He did. "Hope the media don't come down here."

Ben ignored Andy, returning to Meg with the same thought. The field day they'd have with him in next to nothing, doing what he was about to do. Meg's eyes widened but she kept her opinions to herself.

"Still there? Good. There's no way of getting any DNA or trace off it now?"

Meg shook her head.

"I'll try to get it, but if I drown, please tell Andy to keep my clothes. Smarten himself up a bit."

With that, Ben walked into the deeper water near the crevice, stopping every couple of feet to rebalance. Here, water churned around his waist as waves met from different angles. He watched their pattern and waited until there was a regular gap of ten seconds or so, then sank beneath the surface.

Saltwater stung his eyes and the roar of the ocean filled his ears. The undertow tugged at his body. Bubbles rose around him as he let air escape through his nostrils.

The fabric waved at him, further away than he'd judged. He forced his body to drop and propelled himself forward to reach for the cloth. Caught on a jagged edge, its corner was badly frayed and ready to come free and float with the currents.

No, you don't.

Enclosing it in one hand, Ben worked it free with the other, desperate to do no further damage. His lungs burned but now he had it. With a push upwards, he found the top of the water and broke through, gasping.

"Dude, I was about to arrange for coast guard to fish you out." Meg took a photo of Ben.

"Oi. Delete that thanks." Ben was all too aware of his soaking wet underwear and hair dripping all over his face. He shook his head to clear it away as he waded back to Meg, gripping the fabric.

"It doesn't matter about my photos." She gestured up the cliff. "We've been watched for some time and I'll bet you'll make the evening news."

Ben swore. "Instead of taking photos of me, how about phoning Andy and getting some control lines in place?"

"Oh, I did. He said he had his hands full with your designer suit, your gun, and your expensive sunglasses."

He opened his mouth to say what he thought of Andy, but Meg grinned and held out a towel. "There you go. I'll take my evidence and you cover…yours." She looked him up and down.

Meg took the fabric by one corner and worked her way back to the beach. Ben dried his face first, then followed. There was the glint from partway down the cliff. He groaned inwardly at the idea of what their footage might look like.

On the beach, Meg took an evidence bag from the kit she carried everywhere. Ben dried himself, grimacing as he redressed his still-damp body.

"They've been told to clear off twice, but have the same rights as anyone, unfortunately." Andy nodded upwards. "Trying to get them out of your way so you're not held up. Homicide are up there and waiting. So, they've let me know."

"Well, you'd be happy chatting to them." Shoes back on, Ben had another go at his hair and gave up, raking it back with his fingers. "Any news?"

"About a transfer? Not yet." Andy's dream job was Homicide and he'd applied as soon as qualified.

Homicide Detectives Liz Moorland and Pete McNamara were in conversation with the last of the emergency service people as Ben, Andy, and Meg reached the carpark, somehow avoiding a small contingent of media huddled around a camera.

"Checking you out, sunshine." Meg dug Ben in the ribs before packing her kit into her car.

Ben ignored her and waited with Andy near the detectives. "Were you able to arrange for my car to be picked up?"

"Yeah. Sent it to your mate who does tyres. Said he'd have it dropped back to the station this arvo. And I've asked uniforms to check around, see if anyone saw what happened."

"What happened is someone doesn't like me. This was no random act of stupidity, Andy, and if we find the perpetrator—"

"Ah, decided to join us? Enjoy the swim?" Pete McNamara extended a hand to Ben. A bit older than Ben, Pete was shorter and muscular with wavy bleached-blond hair touching his shoulders.

"Funny. But Meg has something interesting so let's hope it was worth it."

As Pete and Andy shook hands, Liz Moorland grinned at Ben. "Long time. When are you going to head our way?"

"Not on my radar, Liz. Good to see you."

Liz was built like a runner, which she was in her spare time. Lean but with power that occasionally shocked adversaries, her smile was disarming and genuine. She and Ben went through academy together.

The four met Meg at her car, parked beside Andy's.

"A preliminary look at this tells me it was probably ripped from a shirt. Expensive. But I'll tell you for sure once I have it back at work." Meg pulled the bag out of her kit and passed it around. "Much as it is soaking wet, my guess is this is off some high-end business shirt. Tailored."

"What was Frank Barlow wearing?" Liz returned the bag to Meg.

How would he ever forget? The body on the stretcher barely resembled a man with its bloated features. An almost bald head matched the photo of Frank his wife provided and a wallet in his pants included his driver's license. No doubt it was Frank. Once was Frank.

Worst part of the job.

"Black short sleeve polo top. White knee-length shorts. Sandals, one missing. Black belt. His wife mentioned a light-weight waterproof jacket but it wasn't on him." He could still smell the effects of decay and sea water inside the body. Ben drew fresh air through his nostrils.

"So, no fancy business shirt." Pete leaned against Andy's car, watching Meg pack her stuff into her boot. "How does a piece of shirt get stuck beneath a body in the ocean?"

"Be interesting to see if anything is under his fingernails. If his attacker wore the shirt, and he ripped it trying to escape…" Andy's phone rang, and he walked away to answer it.

"Until the coroner examines the body there's little point speculating. I'm more interested in the bullet." Pete said.

"You should be interested in both." Meg closed the boot and faced him. "And the tides. That will show you where he entered the water."

"There's always a place in Homicide for you."

Meg rolled her eyes. "No thanks. Not with you hotshots. I'll stick with my team."

Ben covered a grin. "Anything else, detectives?"

"We'll take it from here."

"Actually, Pete, we need to collaborate on this one." Liz said. "I reckon Frank's death is linked to Jack Bannerman's disappearance somehow. Don't you, Ben?"

"Gut tells me so but no link yet."

"Got your link!" Andy sprinted back, eyes brimming with

excitement. "Whilst you were busy photographing our model here, Meg, an ID came back on the gun from the yacht."

"And?"

Don't let it implicate Ellie.

Ben's shoulders tensed.

"And…we are going to go chat to its owner. One Dennis Connor."

THIRTY-TWO
AS THE WORLD FALLS DOWN

"Is there anything you'd like me to ask?" Teresa Scarcella made notes on an iPad as a make-up artist brushed powder over her neck.

Ellie gazed around the studio, digging her fingernails into her palms as memories of visiting Michael on television show sets turned her stomach. Once, his life was split between in front of a camera and a surfboard and how he'd loved his world.

"Ellie?"

"Sorry. No, if you're sticking to what we've run through, then nothing."

Teresa waved the woman behind her away. "This will be live, so relax and let me do the work. All you have to worry about is answering as sincerely as you can. There will be one break of three minutes, then three questions and one minute for you to say whatever you want. As long as it isn't about my appearance haha."

With a nod, Ellie shifted in her seat. The glare of floodlights was annoying but this wouldn't take long. If it helped find Dad, it was worth it. And Teresa already had provided the media contact she'd promised. Someone to speak to next.

The interview touched on Bannerman Wealth Group's history, on Jack's meteoritic rise to fortune, on his raising his children virtually alone. Teresa kept the questions to the point, without side-tracking to Michael's fall from grace and the following tragedy. Not that Ellie would have answered such questions.

"When Jack left Bannerman House to meet Dennis at the yacht, did he leave alone?"

"He did."

"And did he go straight to the pier?"

"No. He headed for his house first to change, but nobody saw him there."

"Isn't that strange?"

"The house is large and his wife was out at the time."

"So, you believe he changed into sailing gear and went to *Sea Angel* to meet your husband." Before Ellie could reply, Teresa continued. "Dennis claims to have gone sailing alone because Jack neither arrived, nor picked up his phone. So, do you believe your husband?"

This was off script. "There is no reason or evidence to believe otherwise. Dennis and Jack got on very well and worked together with the same passion for the company."

"Tell me about your long visit to London. You arrived home after your father vanished. What was the purpose of so much time away? Was it to do with your failing marriage?"

"Completely unfair question, Teresa. I regularly travel for my role as head of the Bannerman Foundation. We are investigating the logistics of opening an office in England and this was the sole purpose of my trip."

Take that, reporter.

Without blinking or referring to her notes, Teresa leaned forward a little. "Speaking of time away, you left your father's company for a whole year. How did it affect your relationship?"

Cold clutched Ellie's chest. She wanted to leave. Walk out

but in front of a million viewers what would that say? She had to present Bannerman Wealth Group in a favourable light.

"I didn't get a chance to have a gap year, or backpack around Europe. So, I took some time to work with disadvantaged communities in Africa, and in Australia. And when I returned, those experiences helped me set up the Bannerman Foundation."

"And then you married the man who took your position at Jack's right hand within a few months of returning."

What was Teresa driving at? She didn't seem bothered that Ellie didn't answer, turning to smile at the camera.

"After this short break, please join me as I speak with Ellie Connor, daughter of missing gazillionaire Jack Bannerman."

The moment the red camera light dimmed, Ellie was on her feet.

"Sit down, dear."

"This isn't what we agreed. My personal life has nothing to do with Dad disappearing!"

"Are you sure?"

"Of course, I am."

"Have some water. Sit down and this will finish before you know it. No more off script questions."

An assistant hurried to Teresa's side and she turned her chair away from Ellie. How could anything from Ellie's life impact on Dad to the point of him vanishing? Obviously, the media had nothing better to do than reach for answers. Ellie sat, wiping the palms of her hands on her pants. A make-up artist dabbed powder on her forehead and freshened her lipstick.

"Ready?"

Ellie forced the frown away and made her face neutral as the camera light turned to red.

"Thank you for joining us again. I'm with Ellie Connor, talking about the shocking disappearance of her father, Jack. I imagine this is a very distressing time?"

"Yes. Not knowing where Dad is, what might have happened to him, feels unreal."

"But at least you've had good…friends around to support you. Like Paul Dekeles, head of security for Jack. Taking you to a nice restaurant, such a good man. Although, where was he when Jack disappeared?"

"We met to discuss a plan of action to find Dad."

"But he was there when you were stalked in a dark, frightening laneway."

"None of this is relevant to finding Dad." And none of these questions had been provided for Ellie to see before they started.

"Well then, what is relevant? The fact that your estranged husband was photographed feeding dessert to your stepmother. Is it relevant that Dennis has said he wants to be CEO?"

Ellie pushed her seat back.

"And Ellie, is it relevant that your husband—Dennis Connor—is about to be arrested in connection with the alleged murder of a missing fisherman?"

As Ellie gasped, Teresa stared at her through cold eyes. "Care to comment?"

In the middle of an early lunch at his desk, eyes on the monitors for entertainment, Paul frowned as Ben Rossi and his offsider came through the front doors and to reception. They flashed their badges and a moment later one of the receptionists led them to an elevator and tapped the reader with a card.

He was on his feet in a second, grabbing his jacket as he rushed to the stairs. Three floors up, he burst through the fire door just as the elevator opened. Everyone on the floor turned to look at him as he gasped for air.

As soon as the police stepped out, all eyes moved to them.

Dennis came out of his office to meet them, offering his hand to Ben Rossi. They spoke for a moment, Dennis recoiling, just out of Paul's earshot. He followed them as they went into Dennis' office.

"What's going on? You can't just front up here with no notice." Paul stopped inside the doorway.

"Get out, Dekeles. And shut the door." Dennis gestured for Ben and Andy to take seats on his sofa.

"Dennis, I think you need me here. As a witness." No way was he missing out on this. "Campbell's out and the others aren't senior enough." He shut himself in with them, standing against the door.

Despite another glare, Dennis didn't argue. He sat opposite the other men. "Okay, you have my full attention. Have you found Jack?"

Ben Rossi shook his head. "No. Do you own any weapons, Dennis?"

"What?"

"Rifles. Handguns?"

"Yes. I have a revolver, why?"

"Where is that firearm now?"

"In a safe."

Paul recognized the twitch above his left eye. He'd seen it before when Dennis was agitated.

"We need the exact location." Ben's voice gave away irritation at the responses.

"Why. Tell my why first."

Andy took over. "Mr Connor, if you'd prefer, we can discuss this at the station."

"Look, I don't know what's going on, but alright. My gun is secure in a safe in the guest house."

"Gentlemen, it is quite legal to own a licensed handgun. Dennis does regular practice with his, as does Jack. It is part of knowing how to protect yourself in a city where crime runs rampant." Paul said.

"This isn't underbelly, Paul." Ben didn't even look at him, his eyes on Dennis. How rude.

"He's right though." Dennis waved his hands around. "I'm up to date with all the requirements. I don't like guns but Jack wanted me to have one. He likes all of his executives to have one."

"All of them?" Ben asked.

Dennis shrugged.

"When was the last time you saw the weapon?" Andy stood.

"Huh? Probably when I moved into the guest house. So, it was the night after Jack vanished."

Ben got to his feet. "We'd like to see it."

"What on earth?" Dennis remained seated. "Why? And I want an answer or I'm not moving."

"Very well. You may recall we searched the yacht *Sea Angel*?"

"Which you had no right to do."

"We had permission from her owner."

"Jack owns the yacht. So, you do know where he is?" Paul couldn't help himself.

"Jack doesn't own the damned thing." Dennis glanced at Paul. "Ellie does."

Paul felt his mouth drop open. Since when did she own *Sea Angel*? This wasn't possible.

"Mr Connor, when Ben was given permission to search, he discovered a gun hidden below deck. That gun has been identified as yours."

Dennis leaned back in his seat. "But…how?"

"Look, that's impossible." Paul stepped forward. "It is either Dennis' gun or not. If he says his is locked in a safe, then he should know. You've made a mistake."

Ben and Andy exchanged a glance. One Paul couldn't read.

"Dennis, we're going to open the safe but it will be easier if you help us." Ben moved toward the door and Paul stepped aside. "Are you coming?"

With something like a moan, Dennis pushed himself upright, collected his phone and wallet from his desk, and shuffled after Ben.

"I'll come with you." Paul addressed Dennis as he neared.

"No, you stay and fill in Campbell. And Ellie. And I have no idea why you're backing me."

"Jack trusts you. That simple."

The fear in Dennis' eyes was something Paul had never seen. He waited until the elevator doors closed on the three men, then went looking for Joni. "Might pay to put the solicitor on notice. Just in case."

THIRTY-THREE
NOT WHAT YOU THINK

Ellie ran out of the studios, trying to dial Dennis as she dodged around cars in the sprawling carpark. She stopped long enough to do it properly, then sprinted for her car as the phone rang.

"You've reached Dennis Connor, CEO of Bannerman Wealth Group. Leave a message or call my secretary."

Far out, who includes their acting title on a voicemail? Ellie didn't bother to leave a message. At her car she dug around in her handbag for keys.

"Ellie! Wait, we'd like to ask some questions."

Not far behind, a reporter with a camera crew was hurrying her way.

She fumbled, dropping the keys. No way was she talking to any more media. Ellie snatched the keys off from the ground, lips tight to hold back a scream at how Teresa Scarcella tricked her. She slid into the driver's seat and had the motor started before they reached her. The cameraperson stopped in front of her and she nosed the car forward until they stepped aside. Freed up, Ellie accelerated.

Before turning onto the main road, she pulled over and

dialled the office, putting the phone onto Bluetooth. It rang for what seemed like ages before Mark picked up.

"Mark, it is Ellie. I just heard something about Dennis and can't reach his phone."

"He had a visit from some police officers and they've all gone somewhere."

"Somewhere? Where?"

"I'll transfer you to Paul, as he was in with them during a short conversation."

The phone went to the ridiculous music Dad insisted on having. Ellie took the turn-off to the office. Which police? And why? Nothing made sense.

"Ellie? Where are you?"

"On my way. What happened?"

"Ben Rossi and his mate fronted up with no notice and insisted Dennis accompany them."

"To the police station?"

"No. They want to see his handgun."

"Why?"

"Apparently they found a gun on...*your* yacht."

Why did that sound like an accusation?

"And?"

"And it belongs to Dennis."

Ellie's foot touched the brake and she saw a car swerve behind her. She flicked the indicator and nosed into a side street.

"Dennis? Where did they go?"

"To the guest house. He said he has it locked up in the safe there."

"This isn't happening, Paul. Dennis wouldn't harm anyone."

"I told Ben Rossi that Dennis does the right thing with his firearm. He didn't care."

"Since when are you looking out for Dennis?" Ellie did a U-turn.

"Not nice, Ellie. He might annoy me but he is still your husband and acting CEO. As I told him, Jack trusts him and I don't really care about anything else."

"Sorry. You both always seem to be at each other's throats. Thank you. I'll head there now."

"Jack's house?"

"Yes. This is going too far."

"But should you? I mean, Ellie, this is a police investigation so maybe leave them to do their job? We could use you here right now because this unsettled everyone."

"I will, I'll be there soon, but there's things going on you don't know about."

The pause on the other end of the phone dragged out as Ellie turned onto the freeway. Her mind already was at the house. Meredith would be upset. The staff concerned. Dennis. Who knew? And Ben needed clear access to determine what was fact or fiction.

"Paul, I saw the poor man who was in the water."

"The fisherman?"

"I didn't see much but it hurt to know his wife will never see him again. And for what? Who would shoot a man on his way to fish for dinner?"

"Shoot?"

Oh, crap.

"I wasn't meant to say that. Can you keep that to yourself for now? Please?"

"You can trust me."

"Thanks. You're such a good friend. I'll phone soon, okay?"

"Always here for you."

The connection ended and Ellie frowned. Had she said the wrong thing by calling him her friend? It didn't matter though because somehow her husband was in deep trouble.

"Where is your warrant?" Meredith was in the middle of the pathway between the house and guest house, arms crossed. She wore a bikini and high heeled sandals, dark sunglasses pushed back on her head. "You can't simply appear and demand to search my home."

"Dennis Connor is your guest?" Ben asked. Dennis was right behind him, next to Andy.

"You know he is."

"He has given us permission to search the safe in the guest house, so please step aside."

"But it isn't his house! Dennis, why would you do such a thing and not even let me know?"

"I'm proving my innocence, Meredith, so please do as they ask."

With an exaggerated sigh, she turned and walked ahead. "Innocence for what?" she asked over her shoulder.

"Merry, they claim—"

"That's enough, thanks." Andy put his hand on Dennis' arm. "Mrs Bannerman will be apprised of the details in due course."

At the door to the guest house, Meredith swung around. "So, you waltz onto my property and won't even say why? Fine. Knock yourselves out."

Ben was close to the end of his patience with the lot of them. Paul for putting up ridiculous barriers, Dennis for digging his heels in until almost forced to assist, and Meredith, who wasn't going to be as easy to keep out of the way as he wanted. As Dennis unlocked the front door, Ben leaned down and spoke quietly to her.

"We appreciate your cooperation, Mrs Bannerman, and I personally guarantee to bring you up to speed as soon as possible. This isn't a full search, so be assured there will be no disruption of anything. We'll be on our way soon."

She stared at him, eyebrows raised, then suddenly swayed

toward him, her hand resting on his chest. "I'll await your…
personal update then."

If he didn't need to keep her from putting up roadblocks later,
he would have told her to remove her hand and step back.
Instead, he nodded and politely moved away to follow Dennis
and Andy, who'd already gone into the guest house. As he closed
the door, he avoided looking at her, but could feel her eyes on him.

"You can just tell her you have to do this. No need to play
nice with her." Dennis almost snarled.

"Where is the safe?"

They stood in an open plan living area, separated by a
counter from the kitchen. Windows across the front looked
toward a pool. The main house was behind trees and shrubs.

"Bedroom." Dennis didn't move.

"Let's go." Andy gestured for Dennis to lead the way and
after a moment, he grunted and stormed through an open
door.

Beyond this was a short hallway leading to the main
bedroom. Dennis went straight to a hanging mirror and lifted
it down. The small safe in the wall had a combination lock. "I
suppose you want me to unlock it?"

Ben moved to Dennis' side. "First, what do you expect to
see in there?"

"Everything? The gun of course, in its case. Bullets in a
separate box. Personal papers."

"Such as?"

"Personal. Letters I've kept. A couple of achievements from
school. That kind of thing."

"Anything else?"

"Two watches. My wedding ring and don't give me that
look. I might not consider myself married now but the ring is
worth a lot."

"Open it, Connor."

Dennis tapped away and the door swung partly open.

"Step back. But keep your eyes on the inside so we are all in agreement about the contents. Andy, can you take photos?"

Phone camera ready, Dennis in the right position, Ben put gloves on. He opened the door to its full width. "Gun case is here. Andy please."

Andy took a series of photos and then one by one, Ben removed the items, placing them on the end of the bed.

"It has to be there." Dennis muttered.

"Large yellow envelope with what feels like documents inside." Ben would look later. "Rolex watch. Seiko watch. Jewellery box with..." he opened it, "gold wedding ring with diamonds. Or at least, that is my impression."

"They are. Open the gun case."

Ben glanced at Dennis at the urgency in his voice. Sweat poured down his face, even the bald part of his head glistened.

"Box." Ben looked inside. "Bullets. Full complement."

From the corner of his eye he saw Dennis's body relax. Did he really believe it was in there?

"And keys with a key card. Looks like the one Ellie uses at her apartment. Duplicate?" Now he faced Dennis, holding the card up. "You're not going to use this, are you?"

"I have every right. Half my gear is there and I'd never go there unless Ellie knew first. Don't want to arrive and her think we're together again."

"How thoughtful. Where's your gun, Dennis?"

"In there! Exactly where I put it when I moved in. Here, let me see." He pushed past Ben, who stopped him with a hand on the shoulder. "Let go. I want to see."

"Then use your eyes. But you're not touching the safe right now."

Dennis' eyes flickered around the safe as Ben took out the gun case.

"It's light."

It was a hard cover in the shape of a handgun. Before he

opened it, Ben knew it was empty. He let Dennis look as he unclipped it.

Dennis paled from his skull down. "But...I...it was there."

Andy reached for handcuffs but Ben shook his head. "Dennis, we're going to go to the station with you. At this point it is for a formal interview."

"What? I haven't done anything wrong. And my gun was there. I swear it was. Someone's done this to me. Set me up. Paul Dekeles most likely."

"And we will discuss a number of possibilities during the interview. Andy, would you gather the contents of the safe to bring please?"

"Do I have to come with you? I've told the truth." Dennis' legs buckled and he sank onto the bed. "Jack's my boss. My father-in-law. I'd never hurt him."

Ben gave him a minute to gather himself, helping Andy slip the items into evidence bags. Good thing Andy acted as though he was already in Homicide and carried an endless supply of the things. He left the safe open.

"Time to go. Please accompany Andy while I have a word with Mrs Bannerman."

"Why? Are you telling her I killed Jack? Because I didn't. Man, I didn't even see him after the board meeting." His voice rose.

"Yet your gun was found on the yacht where you arranged to meet him. I'll be along shortly."

Ben stalked out, not wanting to hear another whining word from the man. He followed a path which skirted the pool. A large covered area led to the part of the house he'd been in with Ellie in the games room. Where was Meredith?

"You will not say a word to them, do you understand?"

Ah, she was in the kitchen. Ben followed her raised voice, pausing out of sight as she continued to bark commands at some unfortunate person.

"They want to take this house from me. Do you know what

that means? Huh? Do you? It means you'll be out of jobs and out of a nice place to live. So, you say nothing, not to them or Princess Ellie."

There was a subdued 'yes, ma'am' in response.

Princess Ellie. The wicked stepmother is showing her true colours.

"Furthermore, as soon as these people leave, I want Mr Bannerman's suite thoroughly cleaned. And I mean thoroughly."

"Why?" Ben stepped into view and Meredith jumped. Two women in black dresses and white aprons stood one side of a table facing her. They kept their eyes down.

"Detective Rossi." Meredith's change of tone from cold anger to a welcoming purr was remarkable. Still in the bikini, she'd added a wrap which still left little to the imagination. "You two may go. Take a ten-minute break."

As the other women scurried for a door at the side of the kitchen, Meredith leaned her hip against the table. "Care for a drink?"

"Why do you want Jack's room cleaned?"

"What a silly question. Surely he'll be home soon and nothing is as welcoming as fresh linen and his favourite flowers."

"I've come to let you know Dennis is coming to the station for a formal interview. Please don't enter the guest house or allow your staff to do so until we advise otherwise."

"Dennis? But he likes Jack. Surely you don't think he's responsible for my husband being missing?"

"I'm going to need to speak with you also."

Meredith smiled, but her eyes hardened and Ben pitied her staff.

"Anytime. Over a cocktail?"

"Which is a conflict of interest."

"Doesn't stop you spending time with Jack's daughter."

Meredith straightened, and ran her fingers through her hair, turning to emphasize her figure as she did. "Nobody will confirm it, but I have a theory. About you."

"I'm going now. But I'll be back to speak with you, and your staff. Telling them not to cooperate is morally and legally wrong, Mrs Bannerman." Ben wanted to be out of this house. He knew the way to the front door.

Meredith followed, her heels tapping on the timber floor. "So, I think you are the police person who broke her heart. And her Daddy's. If I'm right, you arrested his only son. Poor Michael."

Ben stopped, hands clenching as he forced down the anger. Would nobody ever understand?

"I am right." She continued, catching up. "I must say little Miss Ellie has quite extraordinary taste in men. Dennis is fabulous but you, darling, you are spectacular." Her hand reached out as though to touch him again.

If he wasn't so angry, he might have laughed. "What is his favourite?"

Confused, Meredith dropped her hand. "Favourite what?"

"Flower. Jack's favourite flower, to welcome him home."

"For God sake. Fine. Lilies."

Andy tooted the car horn. "Back soon." Ben promised, then opened the front door and shut it behind himself with slightly more force than required.

THIRTY-FOUR
TRUTH OR LIES?

Ellie didn't make it to the house. Dennis returned her call from the police car as she exited Burnley Tunnel.

"I didn't hurt Jack. You need to know that."

"Dennis, I have no idea what to think. I saw the gun on *Sea Angel*. If you didn't put it there, who did? Who else had access to it?"

"Thing is, I changed the combination on the safe when I moved in. So, unless someone was looking over my shoulder, I have no answer." His voice was strained.

"Do you need a lawyer?"

"Dunno. Do I, Ben? Ben shrugged so let's hold off for now."

"Okay."

"Can we keep this quiet?"

As she took an exit to turn her car around for the second time, Ellie couldn't restrain a short, cynical laugh. "Not a chance. I was doing a live interview with Teresa Scarcella and she told me—on air—that you were about to be arrested. How the hell did she know?"

"God. Why were you doing that?"

"Why were you and Meredith out on a romantic date? Why

did you move out without a word? And why didn't you try to find Dad? Dennis, why didn't you?"

Back on the freeway toward the city, Ellie gripped the steering wheel, every muscle tense. The silence dragged. He'd messed up from the moment Dad vanished and if he really didn't have a hand in it, Dennis had still failed to do his job.

"It doesn't matter now. I have to go."

"Wait, what doesn't matter?"

He'd gone. At least Ben had him and if there was anything to be discovered, he'd do it. What Ellie needed to do was put together this jigsaw puzzle and find all its missing pieces.

———

From here, the view was every bit as good as he'd been told. On a perfect day like this, the horizon barely blurred where sea and sky met. The land around Port Phillip Bay expanded out, curving around the vast waterway until it disappeared from the reach of the human eye. Mornington Peninsula on the far side, and to Port Lonsdale should he follow the coastline to his right.

He dared not go onto the balcony and be discovered. The apartment was for sale and there was a degree of risk in being here. Made the adrenaline run faster through his veins.

Heightens the experience.

And the experience was what he wanted now. No more dead-end job serving others. Soon he'd have it all. The future stretched ahead the way the ocean did from his vantage point.

Below, the carpark near the pier hid little from this vantage point. As surrounded as it was with heavy bushes and trees, his view was unencumbered. Amongst the four cars there was a police unit. Forensics. He'd seen it drive in and watched with interest as three officers went over the area where Frank ran into him the other day.

Fortuitous. A good word and accurate description of the

moment Frank recognized him. Pity for the old guy, but exactly what was needed at the time.

The police moved along the pier, checking the boards and sides. Only one yacht was tied up today. *Sea Angel.* The owners of the others must have got tired of being questioned. Would these police find anything else? He'd left nothing. Nothing he didn't intend for them to find.

His phone rang and he turned from the windows. "Yes."

"She's arrived."

"Thanks. There'll be a bonus for you." He disconnected. Yeah, a bonus bullet. Nobody was getting between him and his dreams. Nobody.

"Mark? Where is everyone?" Ellie stopped at reception on the executive floor. He was the only person in sight, even Joni wasn't around. All the offices were empty.

"Lunchtime." Mark looked up from his keyboard. "Did you need a hand with something?"

"No, but thanks. Just getting some things from my office then going to the boardroom. It is free, isn't it?"

Mark tapped on his screen. "Hm...yes. No meeting scheduled there until five today."

"Oh? What meeting?"

"Mr Boyd and Mr Connor are meeting with Mr Van Doran, and Ms Langford."

"And they are from where?"

He shook his head. "I only booked the room on Mr Connor's instructions. And have a note here for it to be a private meeting."

Private about what?

"Dennis may not be back though."

"Oh dear. Was he arrested? Is he being blamed for Mr Bannerman's disappearance?" Mark jumped to his feet.

"No, so calm down. He is simply helping the police with a line of enquiry. Why don't you get yourself a coffee or something and I'll hang around here."

"Are you certain? I'd love to run downstairs and get a juice."

"Go. I'm only going into my office."

Once Mark was in the elevator, Ellie tapped on his keyboard, but he'd locked his computer. She'd have to ask Campbell about the meeting.

She'd barely stepped foot in her office since coming back from London. A pile of folders filled her in-tray. Ellie stood at the window as the quiet of the room calmed her jangled nerves. Her phone kept beeping as messages came through and she switched it off.

The reception phone rang and she picked it up on her desk. "Bannerman Wealth Group, how may I help?" She perched on the edge of the desk.

"Stop the sale from happening." The voice was male. And muffled.

"Who is this? What sale?"

"That's for you to find out. Your daddy was keeping secrets from you."

"Okay, tell me who this is or I'll hang up."

The man laughed. "I know where to find you. And your brother. Stop the sale."

"Wait—" Ellie dropped the phone and covered her mouth to prevent a cry from forming.

The elevator dinged. "I'm back, Mrs Connor." Mark called.

All the feeling left Ellie's legs. She couldn't move or speak. The dial tone taunted her from the phone on the floor. Stop the sale. Stop the sale.

"Are you alright?"

Ellie jumped. Mark was at the doorway.

"Oh my, you look as though you've seen the metaphorical

ghost!" He saw the phone and scooped it up. "Whatever is wrong? Are you feeling unwell?"

Unwell? There wasn't a word for how she felt. But the circulation returned to her limbs and she managed to drop her hands and shake her head.

"Shall I make coffee? Or a glass of water?"

"Water, yes water please." Ellie sank onto her chair as Mark ran out. She found paper and pen and wrote everything she remembered. His words, hers. His strange voice, his laugh. The time of the call. Was nothing going to stop this madness?

"There you go." Mark placed a glass in front of Ellie. "Do you want me to call someone?"

"Thanks. But no, I'm fine. Just some news I wasn't expecting."

Mark gave her an odd look. As though he didn't believe her.

Stop jumping at shadows.

"When Campbell gets back, please let him know I need to see him." She stood. "I'll be in the boardroom."

The phone rang and Ellie stepped back. "I'll let you get back to your station."

He nodded and disappeared but still Ellie felt uneasy. She sipped on the water. It tasted bitter. She tipped the remains into a potted plant in the corner. After gathering a notepad, she locked the door of the office.

The minute she was in the boardroom she dialled Ambling Fields. As she waited to speak to Kerry, Ellie tossed her notepad onto the end of the long table. From behind Joni's extra desk, she dragged out a wheeled whiteboard.

"Mrs Connor, how may I help?"

"Hi, Kerry. How is Michael?"

"I was just with him, actually. He is in good health."

"But?"

"Still withdrawn. Past experience tells me it might be a day or two until he settles down."

"Please let me know if there's anything you need. Anything."

"Was that all?"

"No. I need to ask about security. I understand some patients have private security available and wondered if our father made such facilities part of Michael's package?"

"Exactly why are you asking?"

"Um…I guess with all the media attention on Dad's disappearance, there might be some attempt to bring up Michael's history—"

"I saw your interview with that woman."

"And that is what made me think about security. They have no scruples and will do anything for a story."

"My advice is to avoid speaking with them, instead of putting yourself into such a risky position which might very well impact on your brother." Kerry's tone was judgmental and abrupt. "No, Jack Bannerman did not make provision for additional personal security. We do have secure premises, as you well know."

When this was all over, Ellie intended to make some changes. Michael needed a new assessment to see if there was any chance he could come away from residential care. At least some of the time. She'd asked in the past but the answer was always no. His level of need was too great to be managed at home.

"I will speak to our head of security and arrange for him to call you, if that is suitable?" Somehow, Ellie kept her voice pleasant. "His name is Paul Dekeles and he will discuss your process to provide Michael with private security. Until we find Dad."

"Very well. I hope you do find him because he has much to explain." Kerry disconnected the call.

Ellie stared at the phone in her hand, mouth open. No filters there. She dialled Paul's number, which went to voice mail.

"Paul, I'd like to speak about some security issues if you can call back. Or in the next couple of hours I'm in the board-room so can meet you there instead."

She'd probably end up with Campbell and Paul at the same time. Ellie left her phone on the table and turned the white-board to get better light. On its shelf were coloured markers, an eraser, magnetic pins, and a long ruler. Everything for a board meeting. Or a giant mind map. She picked up a marker.

THIRTY-FIVE
FOUNDATIONS CAN FALL

Through the partly open doors, Campbell watched Ellie for a moment or two. Marker in one hand and ruler in the other, she added lines and words to some kind of diagram. He knew her well enough to imagine she was putting everything she knew about Jack's disappearance into some form of order. Not that there was any reason to believe she would solve what might be unsolvable.

His chest was heavy with the news he carried. It was time she knew the truth and it would hurt her so much. Jack's decision was meant for Jack to explain. Not those he'd left behind, wherever it was he'd gone.

Campbell tapped one door as he pushed it open. "May I join you?"

Ellie spun around, eyes wide. "Oh. Sorry, yes." Her mouth softened into a smile. "I was miles away."

As he drew closer, he read some of the words on the whiteboard.

'Dad' at the very top. Then his name, hers, Dennis, Meredith, Paul, Michael. Why Michael's? This was at the very bottom, along with notes too small for his eyes. In the centre of the board, in red, the words 'Last known contact'. Apart from

Michael and Ellie's names, the others had arrows pointing to the phrase.

"Don't take any of it literally, Campbell. I'm sorting, that's all. You should've seen how much I've already erased, you know this is simply my way of putting this into a kind of perspective."

"I thought as much. You've always loved puzzles and mysteries, but when it comes to your own father, it must be incredibly difficult."

She nodded. "Would you join me at the table for a few minutes? I'd like to talk if you have time?" She sat at one side of the table and he chose the opposite side.

"Campbell, today has been awful." She crossed her arms on the table, leaning on them. "I saw the body of poor Frank Barlow. He wasn't Dad, and for that I am so grateful, but he was someone's husband. And Dennis is being interviewed about a missing gun. And a man phoned and threatened me. And Michael."

"They did what? Who would do this?"

"I answered the reception line. There was a man on the other end who wouldn't tell me who he was. He said I needed to stop the sale. That he knows where I live, and where Michael is." Her eyes glistened although her voice was strong and steady. "And I know something is being kept from me, and I need you to tell me what it is."

The heaviness moved to his stomach like a stone and he closed his eyes. Who else even knew about Jack's arrangement, let alone wanted it stopped? With a deep breath, he opened his eyes and held out a hand.

"Child, I am so sorry someone threatened you. And you are correct. There is a secret."

Sudden panic flashed across Ellie's face and she gulped, as though holding her emotions in with a steel vice. She took Campbell's hand.

"I've known you for all of your life. Even while you were at university, I still saw you those couple of days a week you worked here. I never met Detective Rossi, but I knew a bit about him. He was such a friend to your brother." Campbell said.

"This isn't about Ben."

"Yes and no. When you left for a year, Jack was shattered. He was already in a bad place after...after Michael's —accident."

"It wasn't an accident."

Ellie's hold on Campbell's hand was tight, almost painful as her long nails dug into his skin. She wasn't aware, her eyes intent on his face.

"Regardless, in Jack's eyes he'd lost you both. Dennis came along and they hit it off. The skill set was right but you know all of that. You returned, created the amazing Foundation, and for the first time in years I saw Jack happy again. Like when he first married Gabi. The business grew and he even remarried."

"Why the history lesson?"

"To give you some context. Your father came from nothing to build a fortune. Then effectively lost his son and he thought his daughter. His wife had long gone. With you back, it was as though he finally found some peace. Someone he loved actually came back to him. But, Meredith wasn't making life easy. She wanted more. More of his time, of her friends, of the things she thought he owed her."

"And the pre-nup meant she would never leave him. Are you saying he left her?" Ellie released his hand and leaned forward. "Is this about where he is now?"

"No, no, I would have told you if I knew." He sighed. "This is about the company. He lost heart. When you went to London, he found out Dennis was seeing Meredith and it kind of broke him. It wasn't just about his feelings anymore. He wouldn't confront your husband or fire him. Dennis has a solid contract."

224 PHILLIPA NEFRI CLARK

Ellie's lips parted but she said nothing. She clasped her hands together on the table and waited for him to continue.

"Against my advice, Jack decided to sell."

"Sell? The house?"

"No, Ellie. The business. He has a buyer for the group."

"He…but he wouldn't. This means everything to him, and the Foundation. Oh, God, what about the Foundation?"

"That was the draw card for the buyer. The shining jewel in an already beautiful crown. I am so sorry, Ellie, but Jack was only waiting for you to come home before signing the papers."

THIRTY-SIX
TELLING THE TRUTH

"I've told you everything I know." Dennis glared at Ben across the table in the interrogation room. "You have no answers, I have no answers. Someone is obviously setting me up."

Ben stood and stretched. He'd sat for too long going around in circles with this man. "But why? What would motivate someone to go to such trouble? To steal your gun—and somehow know where it was to steal—then plant it on the yacht you were supposed to meet Jack on the day he vanished. How is that proving you killed Jack?"

"Exactly! There's no evidence I have anything to do with Jack going wherever he went. And now you've admitted it, I'd like to leave."

"Soon." Ben turned his chair around and straddled it. "You see, there's still a few things I need to know. Are you having an affair with Meredith Bannerman?"

"Hey. You can't ask that."

"Just did. How long has it been going on? Does Jack know?"

"I bloody hope not. I mean, there's nothing to know. We've not done a thing."

"Photos of you sliding a spoonful of dessert into her

smiling mouth say otherwise. She's got a lot going for her. Attractive. Funny. Good fashion sense. Young."

I meant one of those. Wait. None of those.

"Too young for Jack. Okay, I like her a lot. But we've not... not yet."

"Because you are both married?"

"Get real, detective. But the writing is on the wall, isn't it? Jack was an absent husband, the way Ellie was an absent wife. She's allowed to move on."

"Meredith? Or Ellie?"

Dennis glared at him.

"And there's the small bonus of anything she might bring from her marriage."

"None of it matters. Whether she is loaded or poor, Meredith means the world to me. She is all class."

Trying for the insanity plea?

"So, you don't care if she gets nothing from a divorce, or Jack's death?" Ben asked.

"We're a long way from worrying about it. Assuming Jack is alive and well, there is still a year to wait before divorce and that's if it doesn't get messy."

"If he's dead?"

"Then I don't know. Presumably, Michael is looked after for life, Ellie gets a slice of the business, and Meredith gets the rest. I already said I don't care."

A tap on the door and Andy poked his head in. "Borrow you for a min, boss?"

"Sure." Ben stood. "Would you like a coffee, or water, Dennis?"

"How much longer will I be here? I have a meeting at five."

"Try to get you out in plenty of time."

"Coffee. Black with two sugars. Can I make a phone call?" Dennis reached for his phone.

"A quick one."

Door closed, Ben and Andy walked to the coffee station.

"Getting anywhere?"

"He has motive but if he did anything to Jack, it'll be for nothing."

Ben poured two coffees.

"Frank Barlow's autopsy is underway. A bullet was removed from his heart and is the same calibre as Dennis' gun. Forensic testing will take a little while."

"Crap." Ben stirred sugar into one cup. "I'd love to keep him here."

"Not much of a flight risk and if you arrest him, he'll be on bail in minutes."

Coffees in hand, they headed back to the interrogation room.

"I might drop some information on him and see what emerges. Anything else?"

"You had a call from Ambling Fields, from a Kerry."

"Is Michael okay?"

"Yeah, she said something about Ellie asking for extra security for him and wanted to know if you had suggested it."

"No. I'll call Ellie later and ask why. Mind getting the door?"

Andy grinned, opened the door with a flourish, and closed it behind Ben.

Dennis was on his phone. "I have to go. Just confirm they'll be there and make sure the room has a decent selection of consumables." He hung up. "Thanks for the coffee."

"Sure." Ben leaned on the edge of the table. "That was about the meeting you mentioned?"

"Uh huh."

"With?"

"Need to know. Company business."

"Is Ellie attending?"

"Just Campbell and the other party. Nothing to do with her at this stage."

There was a smugness about Dennis that irked Ben. Something was going on behind the scenes.

"Enjoying your job? Acting CEO, isn't it?"

"I would if Jack wasn't hanging over my head. Everyone wants him found and until he is, it's a bit hard to move forward."

"But you are. Moving forward? Meetings you don't want to talk about. Secret dinners with his wife. Misplacing a firearm."

With a scowl, Dennis leaned forward. "Already told you that was stolen. Unless you can prove otherwise, I'd like to leave now."

"Go ahead."

Dennis pushed his chair back.

"Curious about one thing though." Ben took a long sip of coffee. "You say you don't care about what Meredith brings from her marriage to Jack."

"And?"

"Even if it is nothing?"

"What are you driving at, Rossi?" Dennis was in Ben's face, his own flushed in anger. "You think you know so much? You think you know my wife?"

Without moving from his perch on the desk, Ben raised an eyebrow. "This isn't about Ellie. No, this is about Meredith and the pre-nuptial contract she signed before marrying Jack. You might want to ask her about it."

Whatever colour was in his face drained to white, and Dennis stumbled back a step. "You're wrong."

Ben shrugged. "Anything is possible."

For a moment, Dennis glared at him and Ben maintained steady eye contact, willing the other man to do or say something stupid. But he turned and flung the door open and stalked out.

Paul tapped on the conference room door and strode in. Empty. From the look of the place, Ellie must have stepped out for a moment.

On the end of the table were markers, a ruler, and eraser, and the whiteboard was covered with diagrams. Not diagrams. He stepped closer, scanning what reminded him of a mind map.

Most of it made sense of sorts. It was Ellie's handwriting and her attempt at playing amateur sleuth was admirable, if misguided. She was missing a whole lot of details for a start. Nothing about Dennis and his plans for the company, so she must be in the dark.

His own name featured, linked by lines to security footage. Why was she worrying about it?

Leave it to the professionals.

Despite her recent poor judgement with the detective, Ellie's heart was generous. Not making Meredith look bad, although she could. And the comments about Michael?

Paul squatted to read. "Is Michael safe where he is or is it time to bring him home? Speak to Paul about security and a specialist doctor about options."

Was that why she'd called for him to come here? He straightened and glanced again at the items on the table. Lids were off some of the markers so he replaced them and laid them in a neat row. Two chairs were pulled out—opposite each other at the end. Did Ellie meet with someone else?

He sent her a text. *In boardroom. Where are you?*

As he waited, Paul checked the cameras. Three in total, all working as expected. But it was time for upgrades. He'd almost completed his purchase order and only needed one of the executives to sign off on it. Jack normally did it. He wasn't about to waste his time with Dennis so Campbell would have to do.

The doors opened and Mark wheeled a trolley in, covered in a white tablecloth and filled with cloches. He nodded to

Paul and parked it by the narrow table near the door. Paul wandered down as Mark transferred cloches to the table.

"What's all this?"

"Meeting in half an hour. Joni went home so I'm the bunny in charge of this now."

"You're doing alright." Paul's mouth watered as he looked under one then another of the domed lids. Pastries, cheeses, perfect little sandwiches. He'd missed lunch. Would anyone notice if he took some?

"Don't even think about it. I'm under strict instructions and have no desire to draw the wrong kind of attention to myself."

"Who is at this meeting, then?"

"Campbell, Mr Van Doran, Ms Langford, and Dennis, as long as he's back by then."

"I gather Ellie doesn't know?"

"Not from me, she doesn't. I have to go find the key to the bar."

With no response from his text to Ellie, there was little point hanging around. Paul followed Mark as far as the elevator then they went to different floors.

Back in his office, Paul picked up the purchase order. It was for a complete refit of cameras, monitors, and alarms, to allow for a software upgrade for the building and Jack's house. His eyes flicked over the words and the numbers, down to the one at the bottom. All six figures of it.

THIRTY-SEVEN
ONLY SOME THINGS MATTER

Sea Angel strained against her ropes, longing to be free. From her position slumped on the deck, Ellie lifted her head from folded arms for long enough to make sure the yacht was still tied up, then dropped it again. The sounds of the sea swooshed through the timber boards she lay upon.

The late afternoon sun was kinder today than the recent stifling heat, and between the warmth and the movement of the boat, she could almost have dozed. Perhaps she had, for the tears were gone and the thumping of her heart no longer resonated in her ears. Her stomach was an empty pit and her body might have been run over by a truck, so much it ached from the tension in her muscles.

How she'd got here from the boardroom was hazy. There were flashes if she thought hard enough.

"That was the draw card for the buyer. The shining jewel in an already beautiful crown. I am so sorry, Ellie, but Jack was only waiting for you to come home before signing the papers."

"I'm okay, Campbell."

I'll never be okay again.

"My dear, I'm so sorry to drop this on you." He'd retreated into the haze.

She'd made it to her car, she knew that much because the keys were secure in her hand. But the drive here? Lost somewhere.

Why, Dad?

He'd spent his life building his empire from nothing. Less than nothing if you knew his history, and Ellie only knew what he'd told her and what she'd found in old records. With every step he took, it was one more away from his childhood and from the father who cared for his drugs, not his family. The chaos of juggling school, protecting his mother and siblings, and earning enough to feed them until he'd broken free. As *Sea Angel* wanted to now.

Ellie pushed herself upright, wiped her face, and leaned back against a seat. Instead of going below and curling onto a bed, she'd collapsed here when her shaking legs refused to carry her another step. All she had with her were the car keys, so her handbag must be in the car. Hopefully locked.

"Ellie?"

She hadn't heard Ben approach. He looked so worried, there on the pier with his sunglasses off and jacket under his arm.

"Hi."

"May I board?" he took off his shoes.

"I'm not good company."

He stepped onto the deck. "I've phoned and left messages. I called your office and was told you'd left some time ago. What happened?"

She shook her head, not knowing how to start or where.

"Shall I get some water for you?" He didn't wait for an answer, heading below and returning in a moment with two bottles. He handed one to her and tossed his jacket onto the seat before joining her on the deck. Ellie opened her bottle and gulped down half without stopping.

"I have a bit to tell you. Would you like to go first though?" he asked.

"No. What's happened?"

"I've interviewed Dennis at length. And although he has motives, and there is now some evidence, my gut still says he isn't responsible for Jack disappearing. Not directly."

"And what does that mean?" Ellie stretched her legs and turned to see Ben better. "Not directly?"

"He's up to something. A secret he's keeping from you."

"More than just about Meredith?" She put the bottle down. "I know what the secret is. Campbell told me today."

"That's why you're here?"

"One reason." She didn't know how her words would come out. If she could even say them. "Give me a minute, Ben. Tell me the rest."

"Okay. He admits to having a relationship with Meredith although he claims it is platonic for now. But he had no idea about the pre-nuptial agreement."

The corners of Ellie's mouth lifted. "You told him?"

"Might have mentioned it. He'd just finished explaining how he didn't care if she was loaded or poor."

"God, he's such a liar."

"He was pretty desperate to leave for a meeting at Bannerman House."

Was it happening now? It must be at least five o'clock and as Acting CEO, he might believe he could sign on Jack's behalf. Did she have a job to go to tomorrow?

"Ben, that meeting is about selling the business." The words rushed out. "Dad decided to sell Bannerman Wealth Group and was waiting for me to come back to tell me first. But now Dennis and Campbell are meeting with the buyers, or I think they are."

Ben swore beneath his breath.

"Yes. And all this time they've told me Dad was worrying about a wind farm project but it was this."

"But the Foundation?"

Lips pressed together, Ellie nodded. She reached her hand out and Ben took it, curling warm fingers around hers.

Seagulls hovered overhead and a breeze picked up, *Sea Angel* rocked a bit more, still wanting freedom.

I should set her free and go with her.

"It isn't right, Ellie. Or fair."

"We were making a difference. It isn't fair for the thousands of people who still need a hand."

"Wouldn't the buyers keep going though?"

"Maybe I should apply for a job. From the sound of it I won't have one for long." Ellie sighed, squeezed Ben's fingers, and retrieved her hand. "There's something else and I was waiting for you to finish with Dennis before bothering you."

Ben nodded as he swallowed some water.

"When I got to my office today, only Mark—you know, Dennis' PA—was on the floor. Nobody else. Anyway, he was desperate for a juice or something so I sent him off and played receptionist. A man phoned."

"Who?"

"Impossible to tell because his voice was muffled. As though something was over the receiver. He told me to stop the sale."

"Sorry?"

"This was before I knew about it. I wrote it all down, what he said. But at the end, he said he knows where I live and where…where Michael is."

"That's why she called."

"What?"

"Kerry Gibbons left a message asking about increased security for Michael. Now it makes sense because I assume you rang her?"

"Why did she call you? I can take care of things. I've got to keep him safe." Ellie's heart was pounding again and she quickly sipped some water. "I'll speak to Paul about hiring someone to go out there for a while. And I was thinking, well hoping, if his specialist will allow it, maybe he can come out of the facility."

Ben's face was unreadable.

"Sorry. You don't need to know about this stuff."

"I do. After this is all over, we need to talk. Really talk. But, Ellie," his voice softened. "I wish you'd phoned me as soon as it happened. Never mind what else I'm doing."

A sense of calm replaced all the hurt and fear and confusion. In this moment she trusted Ben again. Amongst all the chaos, he was a beacon of safety. She exhaled, long and slow.

"I might go and see if the meeting is underway. Gatecrash it." She used the seat to push herself to her feet, stiff from being on the deck so long. "Thanks for looking for me."

He stood, grabbing his jacket as Ellie headed for the pier. "Maybe keep your phone a bit closer. Don't want to be searching for two Bannermans."

In the carpark, Ellie gazed up at the apartment building up the road.

"What's up there?" Ben rattled in his pockets for keys. His car had four new tyres and someone had washed it.

"In the downpour yesterday, I saw someone up on the balcony."

Ben turned to look. "Probably wondering what anyone was doing out in the middle of a storm. Which balcony?"

"The end one." She pointed. "He just stared at me. It was a bit...creepy."

"Are you certain it was that one?"

"Very certain. Why?"

"No reason."

"Ben!"

"Doubt if it means anything, but that apartment is empty. However, before you add this to the inevitable list of clues I suspect you keep somewhere, it was most likely either the agent or the owner doing a check."

Ellie grinned. "List of clues? Me?"

"Yes. Now, are you okay to get to this meeting, and not begin a war?"

"As if. I'm going. Will you tell me what you find out?" Ellie unlocked her car, relieved to see her handbag on the passenger seat. "I'll keep my phone closer."

"Good. And I will." He pulled his phone out.

As she drove out of the carpark, he was talking on the phone, his eyes up on the balcony.

THIRTY-EIGHT
WATCHERS

Ben's stomach churned. He sat on the top step leading into the apartment block near the pier, waiting for Andy and the real estate agent.

When Ellie didn't answer her phone earlier, and he couldn't find her at work or home, his mind had gone into overdrive. Then, he remembered he still had the link to her location on the map app and breathed a sigh of pure relief when it showed him she was at the carpark.

Jack was lucky he wasn't here right now. It was time the man stopped running Ellie's life, even though she still couldn't see it. Sell the damned business but do it with her full knowledge. He must be scared of her response, to not tell her until the last minute.

Andy's car drew up out the front, followed by a second car. Probably another dead end but unless she was mistaken about the balcony, Ellie might have seen someone who could help them. He pushed aside his other concerns about her and stood.

The other driver approached Ben with an extended hand. "Norm Piper. My company handles this building."

"Detective Ben Rossi. Appreciate you meeting us on short notice."

Andy joined them, talking on his phone. Did he ever not have it in his hand? Ben gestured for Norm to lead them into the building. Inside there was no reception desk or even much of a foyer. The single elevator took its time coming down.

"What exactly do you expect to find in the apartment, if I may ask?" Norm tapped on the elevator button for the third time. "The owners have asked why the building has been visited by police so often recently."

"There was a report of someone standing on the balcony."

"Today?"

"Yesterday."

The doors opened. It was even slower going up.

"Well that is simply impossible, Detective Rossi! As you saw, one must have a key card to enter, or use the intercom to request entry. And the same for each apartment."

"How can you be certain someone hasn't called another resident and been let in, then broken into this one?" Andy had hung up his call when they stepped into the elevator and now slid it into a pocket.

Norm sniffed. "We are particular about our residents. I'm quite sure nobody would do the wrong thing."

With a loud ding, the doors opened on the top floor. At the far end of a narrow and dim hallway, Norm slid a key card into the door and pushed it open.

"Thanks, we'll take it from here." Andy let Ben in first, closing the door on Norm's look of outrage.

"How to make friends..." Ben grinned. "Get that phone out please and take some happy snaps. Everything you can find."

The apartment consisted of a kitchen, dining room, and living room rolled into one space, two bedrooms, and one bathroom. Nothing special considering the position of the place. There were some furnishings. Three stools under the kitchen counter. Refrigerator. A bed with a bare mattress. A small table out on the balcony, and inside the sliding door to it, a fourth stool.

"Odd place to leave a stool." Ben sat on it. He had a perfect view of the pier and *Sea Angel*. The churning increased in his gut. "Andy, there's fingerprints on the glass."

"Good. Gives us a reason to get Homicide up here."

"Really."

Ben found gloves in his pocket and slid one on to open the sliding door. Out here, there was no barrier to viewing the carpark near the pier. On the floor was a cigarette butt. "Refilled your supply of evidence bags?"

"Why? Oh, man." Andy took photos, then collected the butt. "Dirty habit. Might be time for someone to give them up."

"I agree we need some help here, so let's leave everything else as we found it." Ben closed them back inside. "What's that sound? Who leaves a refrigerator on?"

"Hope there's beer in there." Andy waited with his phone as Ben swung the door open. A dozen unopened bottles of water lined the top shelf. "Branded. Now I like this person because they want us to catch them."

"Clean Living Gym." Ben read the label. "That's in North Melbourne."

"So, not only do we have fingerprints, but this. And the butt. Does this guy want to be arrested?" Andy rolled his eyes.

"Might just be a trespasser, who smokes and goes to a gym —at least that one?"

"You ponder the mystery and I'll call it in."

"No, hang on." Ben returned to the sliding door. "If someone was onboard *Sea Angel* right now, I'd be able to see them. And with binoculars, I'd be able to identify them and read their lips. Might be worth seeing if the reverse is true. Fancy a stakeout?"

240 PHILLIPA NEFRI CLARK

"This is all your fault, you doddering old fool!" Dennis bellowed the words from one end of the boardroom table to the other, where Campbell sat. "Now she knows, she'll interfere."

"Stop shouting. Ellie had to know at some point." Campbell had a plate of goodies from the table Mark prepared and was holding a pastry like it was glass.

"But why today? Why cancel our meeting?"

"Delayed, Dennis. And if you want to point fingers, go look in a mirror." He bit into the morsel with a sigh of pleasure.

Dennis glared at Campbell, then loosened his tie. Sweat poured down his face and his chest was tight. He wasn't having a heart attack, but between Rossi and Campbell it was a wonder he hadn't keeled over yet.

He stalked to the selection of spirits and red wine and poured a whiskey. Then he poured a second glass and carried both to where Campbell sat, dropping one in front of him.

"Thank you. This is a particularly decent selection so perhaps your Mark could be utilized a bit more in this regard."

"Why?" Dennis pulled a chair out and sat. "You believe Jack won't return so Joni is redundant?"

"Not at all. Joni is highly skilled in areas she is under-utilized in. Would be a win-win for everyone. Cheers."

Not ready to calm down yet, Dennis pushed his glass around the table between his hands. "Why, Campbell? What good did it do upsetting Ellie?"

"She knew something was being kept from her. Wind farms? Come on, Dennis, since when would Jack care enough to finance such a thing?"

He had a point. Dennis picked up his glass and swallowed the contents. He reached across and took a slice of cheese. "Sorry. Didn't mean to yell."

"Been a bad day."

"Bloody police who think they know me."

"At least they know enough to believe you haven't had anything to do with Jack disappearing." Campbell finished his whiskey.

"Things are getting out of control."

"What things, Dennis?" Ellie stood just inside the door. She looked exhausted, ready to collapse, but the fire he'd seen before was in her eyes. He got to his feet.

"Join us? Come on, I'll get you a drink."

He poured a glass of red wine, threw some cheese and crackers on a plate, and hoped she'd listen, rather than berate him. She'd sat beside Campbell, her skin pinker than usual.

"Have you been in the sun today?" Campbell asked.

"Kind of. What happened at the meeting?"

Dennis set the plate and glass in front of her, then refilled his own glass. "Didn't happen. With everything going on today, Campbell thought it best to delay things."

"But you have the right to sign those papers, Dennis. Why wouldn't you?" Ellie's eyes bored into his. "Sell, make a huge profit for stakeholders. Or even take on the role for them with a pay rise?"

He shook his head. "It isn't my call. Come on, Ellie, do you think I like Jack's decision?"

"I don't understand."

Campbell picked up another pastry. "Neither of us supported the sale. Jack was frustrated with us but he had the right to sell without anyone's approval."

"And he was going ahead."

"Yes. He wanted you home to go through a final checklist about the Foundation." Dennis collected the whiskey bottle and splashed more into his and Campbell's glasses. "He had set his mind on making this happen and needed your help."

"Mine? What, packing his office up." Ellie took a mouthful of wine, her expression serious.

"No. Helping train someone to take over from you. There were no jobs offered to existing personnel, not me, Campbell, or even you, Ellie. The potential new owners have their own people and your role was just about handing over." Dennis said.

"I don't believe you."

"Of course not. But Jack isn't here to tell you himself. Either you believe or not, it is the truth."

"Campbell?" Ellie looked unsure.

"It is the truth. And while I'm happy to retire now, nobody else will be. Anyway, I must get going so I'll ask Mark to come down and clean up." He pushed what was left of his plate of goodies between Dennis and Ellie. "Might as well enjoy before everything changes."

Dennis finished his whiskey as Campbell left, closing the doors in his wake.

"So, you and Campbell were the only ones who knew about this?"

"As far as I'm aware. Why?" He couldn't read her expression. The uncertainty was gone, replaced by something like disappointment. Or even anger? Either way, Jack deserved every bit of her wrath. She didn't answer though, just finished her glass. Still reeling from Ben's lies—or where they?—about a pre-nuptial contract, he made a decision.

"Ellie?" It took effort, but he forced a caring smile. "Hey… this has got to be a shock. I'm sorry I didn't tell you earlier—even when you were in London."

"Why didn't you?"

"Jack made me promise. Both of us. And the lawyer brokering it is bound by confidentiality. The buyers insisted on this."

What are you thinking? And why aren't you yelling at me?

"I've made some mistakes lately. Moving out of the apartment without giving us a proper chance."

Ellie pushed her seat back and stood. "Oh, please. If anything, Dennis, you did me a favour, because now I see things lot more clearly."

He nodded. "I understand. I've hurt you and I'm sorry for that."

Without another word she grabbed her handbag and stalked out, startling Mark who was on the other side of the door, hand outstretched to open it. He glanced at Dennis but said nothing. Just as well.

THIRTY-NINE

WHEN TRUST IS GONE

Ellie took the stairs down to Paul's office, needing the physical activity and time to settle her thoughts. Dennis was an idiot if he believed she couldn't see what he was doing. All of a sudden, he was regretting losing his marriage, conveniently on the day he discovered the woman he really wanted wasn't worth the millions he expected.

What bothered Ellie most was the revelation that only Dennis, Campbell, and Dad knew about the sale. Unless someone from the legal firm, or the buyers had shared the information, then who did? Who had phoned her to stop the sale and why on earth would they? Who was going to lose out by Bannerman Wealth Group changing hands?

Partway between floors, Ellie stopped and leaned against the cool, concrete wall. She'd known Campbell all her life. Dad relied on him and called him his closest friend. To think he might betray the firm, or have some ulterior motive was ridiculous. She cast the idea away.

Dennis? What good would it do him to tell a third party about this? He said he didn't want the sale to go ahead, that his own job was at risk, so was he behind the earlier phone call? He knew how protective Ellie was of her brother, and he wasn't above upsetting things to get what he wanted.

But he was in an interrogation room with Ben when the call came.

She sighed and continued down the stairs. To keep mulling this over would turn her into a paranoid woman afraid of her own shadow. And there were plenty of shadows on Paul's floor. The overhead lights were off. She checked the time. After six. The office doors along the hallway were all closed.

Paul's office was ablaze with light and the door open. She tapped and he looked up from his phone with a startled expression which changed to one of welcome.

"I'm sorry to surprise you."

"Ellie, come in. I didn't hear you." He tossed his phone into a drawer. "Sit, please. Want a drink?"

"Thanks but no. Just a quick visit to ask something." She took the chair opposite him, eyes drawn to the monitors. One was flickering on and off. "I had to…run out, before."

"I gathered after I stuck my head into the boardroom and no Ellie." Paul raised his arms behind his head, linking his fingers.

"Yeah, sorry. Anyway, it is about Michael."

"Is he okay?"

"Fine, thanks for asking. I was thinking about all the publicity Dad's disappearance is getting and how Michael might be affected. You know…old fans, or media trying to see him again like they used to."

"Ambling Fields is well protected. Plenty of high-tech stuff and their own security team."

"I know. But I'm worried. Do you know anyone I could hire until Dad gets back? Someone able to do personal security up there?"

"Sure. Couple of guys come to mind so would you like me to see who is free?" Paul dropped his arms and leaned them on the desk. "No point you being stressed about Michael. Who'd ever harm him?"

"Thanks." Paul's response set her mind at ease.

"Is Dennis back? Any updates?"

"It surprised me you stood by him when the police arrived."

Paul shrugged. "Didn't seem right, them fronting up without warning and marching him off. You mentioned the fisherman...Barlow? That he was shot."

"I shouldn't have said anything. And it is all I know...apart from how awful I feel for him and his wife. Who would do such a thing?"

"Probably in the wrong place at the wrong time."

"But at the pier?"

"Shouldn't have been there. Plenty of no trespassing and no fishing signs."

"He may have had permission, Paul. Dad might have known him."

"But Jack's not here to ask."

The monitor which had been flickering suddenly turned to black.

"What is going on with the screens, Paul? There's been a few playing up."

Paul got up and played with the back of the monitor, which came back on. "Long story, El. Basically, when I wanted to upgrade a while back, Jack was reluctant to spend money on it. In the end he did, but not as much as I needed. You know, we've had new tenants who wanted more and I could only make the money stretch so far."

"But Dad is big on security."

"He said he had pressure from other parts of the business. Increased staffing costs for the executives, for one. And some deal which fell through. He lost some money on it."

None of this made sense. Probably Dad didn't realise how

old the equipment was getting. This was something she could look into.

"Dinner?" Instead of returning to his seat, Paul perched on the corner of the desk near Ellie. "There's a new little spot at Brighton. You'll like it."

She smiled. "Sounds lovely but I have a ton of work to do upstairs. I was there earlier and unless I take care of at least one tray of files tonight, I won't catch up."

"I can order in. Help you."

"And again, sounds lovely but no. I'll work through and eat once I'm home. Finally did some shopping." She stood, finding herself closer to him than she expected.

His arms shot around her shoulders, pulling Ellie against him in a hug. She froze. He squeezed her close, as though unaware of her stiff body.

"Paul, let go please." Her voice was muffled against his jacket and her arms were pinned at her sides so she couldn't push herself away. "Paul."

This time he released her. "Oh, sorry, didn't mean to stop you breathing." He laughed.

He actually laughed.

Ellie stepped away. "You can't do that."

Paul looked confused. "We're friends. Wanted to make you feel cared about."

"But this is a workplace, so I'd appreciate you keeping it professional."

"Sure. Of course, I hadn't meant to cross the boundaries. Not here."

"Paul. Not anywhere. You can't just grab me like that."

He walked around his desk to his seat, dropping into it with a thud.

"Will you let me know once you've spoken to the security people you mentioned?" Ellie wanted to go. This wasn't a comfortable place and the way he now stared at her made her stomach knot. Her clothes smelt of cigarette smoke.

"Sure."

"Paul, I—"

"You made your point. I said I'd find out."

With a nod, Ellie left the office. She was sure if she glanced back, he'd be watching her. He was lucky she'd known him long enough to believe his motives but would mention to human resources it was time to send out a reminder to all staff about the standard of behaviour Dad demanded. Dad, and the law.

FORTY

WHAT LOVE IS WORTH

He still couldn't believe the gun wasn't there. Dennis had the safe open and its contents on the bed. At least, what Ben let him bring back. Bullets and the gun case remained at the police station, but after a cursory glance, the yellow envelope was returned, as well as the watches, his wedding ring, and keys.

"Make sure you tell Ellie you have this." Ben had handed the key card back. "Or I will."

Who did Ben Rossi think he was? Access to the apartment was his as long as he kept this.

Dennis tossed everything into the safe and locked it.

Before he'd left the office, he'd called Meredith and arranged to have dinner by the pool tonight. Brenda was cooking something special and then all the staff would leave for a night off. Time to sort a few things out.

Back in the kitchen, he plugged his phone in to charge and poured a whiskey. This went with him to the bathroom, where he stripped and shaved. A long, hot shower washed away the stench of the interrogation room and accusations.

Dressed in a white linen shirt and chinos, Dennis knew he looked good. He finished the last dribble of whiskey and decided against another when he checked the time. No being late for this date.

He arrived poolside a minute early. A table and two chairs were set near the waterfall end, which was lit from below. Very pretty. Dusk approached. He lit the candle in the centre of the table.

"Is this all for me?"

Dennis looked up. Meredith swayed toward him in a body-hugging red dress and heels. Her hair was sleekly pulled back, which accentuated her eyes. Damn, she'd better have some answers. He held out a hand and she put hers in his palm.

"You," he kissed one cheek, "look incredible," he kissed the other, "and smell like…"

"Like?"

"Something edible." Now he kissed her lips, just a touch. "Do you care to join me for dinner?"

"If you insist…although I'm happy to jump straight to dessert, if you get my meaning."

Brenda appeared with a tray. She placed a plate of bruschetta beside the candle, and two champagne glasses near an ice bucket.

"Thanks, Brenda, I'll open that." Dennis led Meredith to her chair, which he pulled out for her. Brenda hurried away. Probably thought he was a murderer.

The champagne opened with a pop, spilling a little onto the ground. Meredith giggled. "Oops. Whatever are we celebrating, darling? Your release from custody for the second time?"

"Funny. Not." He poured two glasses, handed one to Meredith, and raised his. "To discovering what love is worth."

Their glasses clinked. "What love is worth?"

"We'll get to that later. For now, enjoy the bubbles." Dennis sipped his. "You know, I never thought I was a champagne man until you came along. Ellie hates the stuff."

"Ellie might have fabulous taste in men, but that's as far as it goes."

Men? Who else?

It wasn't important. He offered Meredith bruschetta and took some for himself. He'd missed lunch thanks to the police and only had a nibble at the food on offer in the boardroom earlier.

The waterfall splashed in the background and evening birdsong filled the air. Native birds loved the gardens here. He'd watched them over breakfast a few times, darting from branch to branch with their colourful wings. Lorikeets. Although it was magpies talking now.

"Dennis? You are miles away."

"Been a long, painful day, Merry."

"What did come of it all? That annoying detective phoned to say he wants to interview the staff tomorrow. Does he have the right?"

"Probably. I might put my lawyer on standby. Make sure they have a team at the ready should any of this escalate."

Meredith's jaw dropped open. "How?"

With a shrug, Dennis refilled their glasses. "How is my gun missing? I changed the combination and it was locked inside the safe. I keep saying I'm being set up but nobody listens. It's as though someone has a hidden camera." He shoved the champagne bottle back into the ice, shards spilling out. "Maybe someone does."

"Hold on, are you saying there are cameras in the house… like in the bedrooms?"

The return of Brenda, with a trolley, interrupted. She wasted no time setting down luscious plates of spaghetti marinara and a side salad. "Sir, ma'am? There are two desserts beneath the cloches. And a selection of white and red wines. Will that be all tonight?"

"In a hurry?" Meredith gazed away, bored.

Dennis ignored Meredith and smiled. "Thank you, Brenda. Please have a nice night out and enjoy the small bonus in the envelopes I left for you all. You've more than earned it lately."

Once Brenda was out of sight, Dennis took Meredith's hand. "You need to be more gracious. These people adore Jack and will do anything for you because he'd want them to."

"Yes. Okay, sorry. I just feel sometimes like they watch my every move and judge me."

"And you are worth watching." He squeezed her hand and released it. "I love seafood. Now, red or white wine?"

There was no point going home to change out of the clothes smelling of cigarettes, then coming back to work in the office, particularly alone on a dark floor. Ellie didn't want to be in the building anymore tonight.

I'm tired. Done.

Campbell was at his desk, head buried in paperwork. Or rather, in his computer. He looked up long enough to smile through the glass walls as she hurried past. On her way back, box of files in her arms, she stopped at his door.

"What can't wait?" she grinned.

"Hm? Oh, I am so far behind. With Jack gone...more work."

"I'm sorry. Can't someone help you?"

"I've palmed a lot off to the team downstairs but some things need my approval."

"Question." Ellie shifted the box to be more comfortable. "Do you approve all the purchase orders?"

"Mostly. Why?"

"Paul mentioned he has to replace a lot of the equipment because Dad didn't want to spend money last year."

"Jack looks after security. He's always insisted on it."

"Well, someone will have to until we find him. Go home soon?"

He might have nodded yes, but Ellie imagined Campbell would be there for hours. Everyone was at capacity, except

Dennis, who barely made an appearance. She pushed the thought away as she drove to her apartment.

As she waited to turn into the underground carpark, gym man wandered out of the building, stopping to answer a phone call. His gym bag was over a shoulder and he wore shorts and top, as if going to work out. Like usual.

The traffic cleared and Ellie nosed the car over the pavement. Gym man turned, their eyes meeting through the window. No smile or acknowledgement from him, only a stare until her car went underground. She parked, annoyed to see a tremor in her hands. Something about the man was unsettling.

Ellie collected the box and her handbag and locked the car. The carpark was well lit, but shadows were inevitable and concrete pillars were thick enough to conceal a person. She glanced over her shoulder more than once as she hurried to the lift.

Dinner was done, the plates piled up on the trolley. The champagne bottle was empty and Dennis poured the last dregs of the red wine into Meredith's glass. She watched him through half-closed eyes, relaxed in a way she'd never been with Jack, or any other of the men she'd been involved with. Dennis was hardly a traditionally attractive man with his balding head, plain face and glasses—no, it was the way he carried himself, his confidence which melted her. And had since they'd met. She understood why he'd married Ellie, but what a waste.

"Why do you think Jack vanished without so much as a see-you-later." she asked.

"Do you really believe he did? Vanish?"

"I don't see his body washing up on the rocks like that trespasser's did." She swirled the wine around in the glass. "I have a theory."

Dennis raised both eyebrows and she giggled. Soon, she'd get him to take her back to the guest house for a nightcap. And more.

"My theory is that Jack is playing a game with us."

"What kind of game?"

"You said earlier you think someone is watching you. Your gun was stolen but nobody broke in. What if Jack set this whole thing up to see what we'd do?"

Oh, she loved her ideas. Jack must be having a fit somewhere about now if he was keeping an eye on her.

"Interesting theory. But why?"

"I wonder where all the cameras are?" Meredith turned her head to gaze around the garden. "Probably just part of his usual control freak thing."

"Did he control you?" Dennis leaned forward. "Has he ever hurt you?"

"Oh, sweetie, not at all in the way you're thinking. But he believes he owns his daughter, and she doesn't do herself any favours by doing whatever he asks."

"Nice of you to care."

"I don't. Not much anyway. So, where is he hiding? And why."

Dennis averted his eyes and leaned back in his chair.

Oh, you know more than you're telling me, Dennis. I'll play along. For now.

"Shall we open the white? Kind of back to front." He reached for the bottle.

"Sure. I'm not precious."

For a few moments he fussed with fresh glasses and pouring, then pushed her glass across. "Another toast?"

Meredith raised her glass, waiting.

"To honesty."

"Okay." She clinked her glass against his. "Want to elaborate?"

"You know I have a thing for you?"

Meredith lost interest in the wine. Dennis was about to ruin everything. It didn't stop her swallowing a large mouthful of the stuff.

He pushed his chair back and crossed an ankle over his knee, playing with the stem of his glass.

"I heard a rumour about you. About you and Jack."

"A rumour?"

"Is there anything you want to tell me, Merry? About any arrangements with Jack?"

Tears welled in Meredith's eyes before she could stop them. "You mean the stupid pre-nuptial agreement he forced me to sign? Is this what it is about? Wine and dine me and make me feel like a princess only to tell me you don't want me anymore." She stood, unsteady from too much alcohol.

Dennis didn't move. "I do want you. But I want you *and* whatever Jack owes you for wasting all these years with him. Sit. Please."

With a sniff, Meredith dropped back on her chair. Dennis offered her a handkerchief and topped up her glass.

"You should have told me. Regardless, we'll get someone to look at it."

"He says it is to protect me as well as him. And his kids."

"Do you remember the details? Is there a suicide clause?"

Meredith's mouth dropped open.

"Got to cover all possibilities, Merry."

The candle was almost burned down, the last of its light reflected in Dennis' behind his glasses. Meredith couldn't see past the flickering to his eyes. An unpleasant shiver ran up her spine.

FORTY-ONE
ONE DOWN

Campbell took a break to eat a microwaved meal and check the news on his laptop. So much speculation, particularly about Dennis now word was out about his trip to the station. Some tried to connect Jack's disappearance to the dreadful death of poor Frank Barlow.

He scrolled down the stories, stopping, mouth open, at an article titled 'What Jack Bannerman wants to forget.'

A photograph of Michael from his TV show was under the headline. Unable to stop reading, Campbell scanned the article.

Jack Bannerman may be missing, but his son is the one who really lost out at life. Michael Bannerman was the golden boy everyone expected to be at his father's side. Preferring to surf and act, this rich boy took everything to the extreme, including his use of illicit drugs.

Campbell shook his head. There were a series of images of Michael, a childhood photograph, on a surfboard, in a tuxedo at an awards night, and then one in handcuffs.

Michael was undoubtedly the spoilt brat of a rich man. His arrest by his so-called best friend, then-Constable Ben Rossi, made headlines at the time. Money must talk, with the soft sentence Michael received. Things were looking up for him. But the golden boy went straight back to his old habits, this time with an almost-lethal overdose. Thank goodness for Daddy's money or the now-brain injured Michael would be locked up in some asylum. Perhaps Jack disappeared due to shame.

"Bastards. Never get anything right."

He pushed his empty tray aside and peered into the darkness around his office. Jack was not environmentally friendly but loved telling the world the building switched to reduced power and lighting at night. Made for a good story for him and saved thousands a year. Jack loved to save money almost as much as he loved making it.

Which made Ellie's earlier comments even more curious. Jack was frugal, but not stupid. He'd never refuse to pay for the necessities. He treated every one of his staff as an asset and kept an open-door policy. Paul's contention that Jack wouldn't spend money on security was ridiculous. He had to have misunderstood.

He'd had a call from downstairs earlier, about his unlocked door. They'd found no footage of anything unusual, but admitted they'd had some issues with the cameras. So what was going on?

His hand hovered above the phone. It was too late to get Paul now, but he could at least leave a voicemail.

"Paul, once you get this, please arrange a time for a chat. We need to discuss the last equipment upgrade. Goodnight."

For the next hour, he went back through the best part of fifteen years of records, years of regular upgrades and improvements as the business grew. The more he checked, the more he knew there'd been a mistake between acquisitions and accounts. It wasn't the first time there'd been anomalies, but never around Paul's department.

Yet another thing to fix.

As he shut down his laptop, a faint 'click' from the reception area took his attention. The laptop went into his briefcase and he reached for the lamp to turn it off. Again, a sound but louder.

"Anyone here? Security?"

Briefcase in hand, Campbell locked his office door and dropped some work onto the reception desk.

The door to the stairs was slightly ajar. There was a stapler acting as a door jam. He pushed the door open and peered over the rail.

"Who's playing games? Show yourself!"

A shard of fear lodged in his heart. Weakness swept into his legs and he scolded himself.

Someone dropped the stapler. Nobody is here.

He returned to the hub and let the door close behind. Time to go home and have a drink.

At the elevator, he reached for the button.

Pain shot through his head.

FORTY-TWO
WHO WATCHES THE WATCHER?

11 December

Sea Angel rocked about with the incoming high tide, her sides dipping on the swell. Ben stretched his legs out, enjoying the sensation. For a western suburbs' boy, he did like being on the water. Not that his income was ever likely to result in him buying a boat unless it was a dinghy. For the past few hours he'd imagined owning such a beauty as this one.

But she belonged to Ellie, and Ellie came from a whole different demographic. As humble as she was about her family's wealth, it was still a fact. And the mega rich didn't play well with the average man.

His phone vibrated and he shook his head to clear the thoughts.

"Anything, Andy?" He'd left Andy in the car at the top of the road past the apartment block.

"I'm hungry. Aren't you?"

"Don't you have an endless supply of those bars you call food?"

"Clearly not endless."

Ben glanced at his watch. "Alright. You head home and I'll stay for a bit longer."

"Wait up. Taxi just stopped."

All evening people had come and gone from the building, but still the empty apartment remained in darkness.

"And?"

"One eighty centimetres give or take. Caucasian male, blondish hair. Short top, shorts, bag over his shoulder. Looks chilled."

"Don't say chilled in your report."

Andy laughed. "Looks calm. Better?"

"Slightly."

"He has a key. Inside now. Taxi is gone."

"See you in the morning, Andy."

"It is morning. Two in the morning."

For another half hour Ben fought a heavy tiredness. He drifted off for a few moments, jumping as a night bird flew past. The air had cooled, and he took a final swig from his water bottle. He trained binoculars on the dark apartment again.

The sliding door was open.

A car approached, and Ben turned the binoculars to the carpark as a black Alfa Romeo weaved into it, coming to an abrupt stop in the middle.

Dennis Connor. What the hell?

Ben stood, planting his feet wide to steady himself and looked up at the apartment. Someone was up there on the balcony, staring in the direction of the carpark. A man in dark clothing from head to foot. He couldn't see his face and then, the man was gone.

After stepping onto the pier, Ben texted Andy. *Need you back here.* Ahead, a car door slammed. Hand on his holster, Ben worked his way to the bushes, then skirted the carpark until he had better visibility.

Dennis was at the bonnet of his car, swaying on his feet. He took his phone out and promptly dropped it. With a loud curse, he leaned down to retrieve it and lost balance, dropping onto his knees. Comical if he hadn't just driven the streets of Melbourne in that condition.

Somehow upright again, Dennis lurched in the direction of a council rubbish bin. He leaned against it as he checked something on his phone, then reached inside.

Ben videoed on his phone as Dennis extracted a paper bag. Drugs? Money? He almost held his breath as Dennis opened it and peered in. His expression was one of pure confusion. He turned the bag upside down and white material fell out. A shirt.

Dennis stared at it on the ground. Ben lowered the phone, mind racing. The material he'd retrieved from the rocks where Fred Barlow was caught. It was shirt material. Quality. Dennis reached for it and Ben propelled himself into the carpark.

"Leave it, Dennis!"

"Whaa?"

"I'm identifying myself as Detective Ben Rossi. Do you understand me?"

With a frown, Dennis leaned forward for the material.

"I said to leave it. Stand up straight and put your hands behind your head!" Ben bellowed the command as he ran.

Dennis staggered back a step or two and lifted one hand. Behind him, Andy's car pulled up across the entry to the carpark and he jumped out.

"Someone's in that apartment, Andy. Get up there but be careful."

Andy was back in the car in seconds, turning it in a tight circle before flooring it up the road.

Ben reached Dennis. He wrinkled his nose at the reek of alcohol emanating from the man. "Dennis, do you understand who I am?"

"Ben Rossi. Mr Policeman who likes my wife." Dennis smirked. "Watcha doing here?"

"More to the point, what are you doing here? Answer carefully, no more of your smart mouth."

Camera out again, Ben took shots of the shirt, crumbled on the ground.

"My shirt."

"Are you identifying this as belonging to you, Dennis?"

"Huh? Sure."

"Car keys." Ben held his hand out.

After checking every pocket, Dennis pointed at the car. "Might go home now." He took a few steps and slowly sank onto the ground.

Ben strode to the car and took the keys from the ignition. His own car was parked two blocks away, complete with his breathalyser.

"How much have you had to drink?" he squatted beside Dennis, examining his eyes.

"A glass of champagne with my lady."

"With Meredith Bannerman?"

"Maybe. Why are you staring at me?"

"Working out if you need an ambulance, Dennis. Bit more than one glass."

"And we had some red wine. And some white. And then, a whiskey or two."

"Why did you think it was a good idea to drive?"

Dennis frowned and reached for an inside pocket.

"Stop. Keep both hands where I can see them." Ben checked Dennis' pockets. Phone, wallet, a set of keys. "What's on the phone?"

"Had a call. Was in bed but thought it might be Jack. Miss him, you know."

Sure you do.

"Wasn't Jack."

"Who called?"

"Said he was a friend. Said I had to find a bag in the bin

here and it would lead to Jack." Dennis lay on his side. "Go away."

Ben's phone vibrated. "Where are you?"

"On my way back." Andy sounded puffed. "Apartment was wide open but empty. Just missed him, sorry."

"I'll call it in. Bring your breathalyser. And the biggest evidence bag you have."

FORTY-THREE
UNREST AND DISTRESS

Ellie's phone rang out just as she heard it. She wrapped her wet hair in a towel and reached it as it rang again. Ben's number. With multiple missed calls and messages.

"You found Dad?"

"Ellie, thank goodness. No, not yet."

She took the phone to the bedroom. "I was in the shower. What's wrong?"

"I wanted to come over to talk face to face but…something's happened."

"Ben!"

"There's been an accident at the office. Campbell appears to have fallen down some steps—"

"Oh my God." She sank onto the end of the bed. "Is he okay?"

"He's in intensive care, Ellie. Broken arm. Lots of bruising, and a head injury."

Mouth suddenly dry, Ellie stared through the window. The sky was deep blue with barely a cloud. The city was waking up.

"Ellie?"

"I'm here. Which hospital?"

"Royal Melbourne. I'd come and get you, but I have my hands full."

"I have to get dressed." Ellie got up again.

"Don't go yet. You need to know something before the damned media or someone tells you."

What else?

She grabbed a dress from a hanger.

"Dennis is in custody. I arrested him early this morning."

The dress slipped straight through her fingers onto the floor as she stopped dead in the middle of the room. "You did what?"

"Details later. At the moment it is only for driving under the influence. He's sleeping it off. Once you've been to the hospital, I need to talk to you. Okay?"

"You can't come to the hospital?"

"I would if I could. Call me once you get there and if I'm finished, I'll meet you."

She scooped the dress up and straightened. "No. No, you keep looking for Dad, if that's what you are doing."

"Ellie."

"You are still looking. Aren't you?" she hung up and tossed the phone on the bed. It was only when she glanced in the mirror, she realized tears streamed down her cheeks.

An hour later, Ellie climbed into a taxi to leave the hospital. Even Campbell's family weren't allowed to see him yet and they didn't want her there.

"He should never have been at work so late." His wife dabbed her eyes. "There are laws about forcing people to spend so much time at their job."

It wasn't worth arguing, nor the time to. For as long as Ellie could remember, Campbell had worked the same long hours as Dad. He ran his office the way he wanted, and nobody could make him go home before he was ready. Not even Ellie last night.

She didn't call Ben on the short trip to the office although she had a million questions. Dennis always drank a lot, but she'd never seen him drive after more than one glass. How was she supposed to spin this one to the press, let alone the staff? She ran through scenario after scenario until noticing the taxi was stationary, the driver waiting. How long had they been outside Bannerman House?

Take me home. Or to Sea Angel. Take me away from this.

Instead, Ellie climbed out. Thank goodness there was no media presence. Just the normal foot traffic along this busy street. She stood on the edge of the pavement, gazing around. Everyone was going about their usual business and living their lives. But hers was on hold.

"Ellie?" Paul called from near the doors. Mark and a couple of others from the finance team were to one side, smoking.

She pulled herself together and walked toward him, shoulders back.

"You've seen Campbell?" he asked as she went past. He caught up inside. "How is he?"

"I haven't. Nobody is allowed in because he is terribly injured. What I need to do is speak with everyone on the executive floor, as well as the head of the teams Campbell supervises."

At the lift, she jabbed the button.

"I want you there as well, Paul. There's other news and as a company, it is important we discuss things internally before anyone else is involved."

"Anyone else, who?"

The doors opened and Paul gestured for Ellie to go ahead of him. Someone called for the lift to hold but he hit the close doors button.

"Did you just smoke?"

"Sorry, haven't had a chance to freshen up. Saw you as I was coming back in."

"It'll kill you eventually."

"If someone doesn't get me first."

Ellie glanced at him. He was straightening his tie in the mirrored side of the lift and met her eyes with a questioning look.

"Who would hurt you, Paul?"

"Nah. I'm talking from habit." He smiled. "Wasn't always such a model of society."

"Dad trusts you."

"Yeah. Yeah, he does."

The doors opened on the executive floor. Joni was at reception.

"Would you ask all of this floor, and Campbell's team, to come to my office in thirty minutes. And once you've got some support again, may I get a strong coffee?"

Joni nodded and began making calls.

Ellie turned to Paul. "Who found Campbell?"

"Will. He's in the control room."

"Please ask him to come and see me."

"Sure."

"I'll talk to you soon." Ellie didn't wait for a response and headed to her office. It was unlocked. Last night she'd locked it before speaking to Campbell. She made a mental note to talk to the cleaners. First Campbell's office, then hers.

For a moment, the room was hers. A reprieve for the madness surrounding her. Once Dad was back, a few people would come under his scrutiny. Dennis and Meredith sprang to mind. Either way, she'd help him sort through it all and then maybe, in a few months, take a step back. Train someone to take over the Foundation.

That's if the Foundation exists in the future!

"Mrs Connor? I made you a coffee and found a muffin. In

case you've not eaten yet." Mark put the cup and plate on the edge of her desk. "Is there anything else you need?"

"Thanks, no. This will help."

"May I say how shocked I am to hear about Mr Boyd."

"Thanks. Me too."

Mark left, closing the door behind himself. Ellie took the coffee to the window and sipped, letting the caffeine do its work. She needed to know why Dennis was really arrested. Her mind wandered over the possibilities, until a tap on the door alerted her.

"Come in." Ellie put the now-empty coffee cup on the desk as the staff trailed in. With so many people in here, there weren't enough seats, but she encouraged them to find a spot and perched on the edge of her desk.

"Thanks for being here. As you may be aware, there are a couple of items we need to discuss. The first is about Campbell Boyd."

"Is he going to be okay?" Will stood to one side with his hands clenched.

"Will. I'm so glad you found him and would like to talk to you after this please. I've come from the hospital. Mr Boyd is in intensive care. He has a head injury which has put him into a state of unconsciousness, plus a broken arm, and bad bruising."

"He'll recover though?" Paul asked from the back of the office.

"From the limited information I have, it is too soon to know the outcome, but he is in excellent hands."

Paul and Mark shared a look. Ellie tilted her head to one side. But the look was gone as soon as it began.

"Our thoughts are with him and his family, and of course, all costs will be taken care of. If you wish to send your best wishes and so on, I'm sure they will be appreciated. Team leaders, please let your people know and if anyone is struggling, take today off. This applies to everyone."

A murmur ran through the small group. Ellie's phone buzzed. Message from Ben. She turned the phone face down.

"There is another matter and this one is equally serious, although completely different. I have few details, but in the early hours of this morning, Mr Connor was arrested."

The earlier murmur became loud whispers. Ellie raised her hand. "Please. It appears to have been for an offence unrelated to my father's disappearance, but I expect the media will jump on this with delight. I'm reminding you all, us all, to keep what we discuss confidential. Once I have further details, I'll tell you. Okay?"

Joni raised her hand. "Mr Bannerman is gone. Mr Connor under arrest. Who is going to run the business?"

Who indeed? "I think we should wait until we have further information. All of you are amazing and important to us, so please, continue to do what you do best, and when the time comes, the remaining board members will work together to keep everything going."

Most of the staff nodded to each other. Will stared at his hands.

"Thanks for coming up here so quickly. Your ongoing support means more than I can express. Will, would you please stay?"

When everyone else was gone. Ellie moved to a pair of chairs near the window. "Come and sit with me."

The moment Will sat, the rims of his eyes reddened.

"I'm so sorry. Would you talk me through it?" she kept her voice soft and encouraging, she hoped.

"Doing normal rounds about three am. Was up here at ten, and Campbell was working. Left him in peace. Anyway, on my next run his office door was still wide open. Seemed odd and he'd already raised concerns about his office being left unlocked by the cleaners. Mind you, they say not."

"So how did you find him?"

Will frowned. "I always take the stairs down." He drew in

a long breath. "Couldn't believe what I saw. He was at the bottom of the steps, and you know there's about fifteen of them on each level. Thought he was dead, Mrs Connor. Not a movement and he was bent out of shape. Briefcase had gone ahead of him and mustn't have been closed because his laptop was smashed further down. Called Glen, and he got an ambulance."

"Do you know if anyone has looked at footage?"

"No idea. Paul came in and he told me to go home once Mr Boyd was taken."

"You did really well. Is there anything else that struck you as odd?" Ellie asked.

"Really weird but when I checked his chest for a heartbeat, a stapler fell out of his pocket."

"Stapler?"

"Yeah, like the ones all the PA's have on their desks."

FORTY-FOUR
NOT ALONE

Ellie closed the door behind Will and locked herself in. At the window, she rested her forehead against the glass, willing the cold to spread through a body overheated by worry. One, then another, her palms reached for the clear barrier. All she wanted was to curl into a ball and cry until nothing was left.

Campbell was like a second father. Always there if she needed advice or a shoulder. Dad's best friend. She should have worked in her office as planned. They would have shared a meal, talked through some issues, and probably left at the same time. But why had he taken the stairs?

Her phone buzzed again, and Ellie walked away from the window, and answered without checking the caller.

"I'm sorry. I can talk now."

There was only silence. Ellie sat behind her desk.

"Ben?"

"No. Paul."

"Oh."

"Why doesn't he investigate Campbell's accident?"

"Because it was an accident." Ellie said.

"Was it?"

A chill swept through Ellie and she bit her lip.

Paul continued. "Why would he take the stairs when the lift was working fine?"

"I wish I knew. Have you had time to look at the footage? See if something was wrong?"

"Doing it now, Ellie. But where was Dennis last night?"

Really? You hate him so much?

"Let me know when you've checked the footage. Surely that will show you who, if anyone, was on the floor with Campbell apart from me much earlier. Is there anything else you need?"

Another long silence and Ellie rolled her eyes. Why so many dramas?

"Will you step in as CEO?"

"I'll do whatever the board needs, but in the interim, all the department heads are capable of managing their teams. As you continue to do."

"Was beginning to wonder if you'd lost confidence in me, El."

"Is there any reason I would?" Another call beeped.

"No."

"Then stop worrying about it and let me know once you have some footage to view. Please. I have another call, so talk later."

This time she checked. Ben.

"Hi." She said.

"Are you okay?"

"Just spoke to the staff who work with Campbell. Sorry, I couldn't interrupt to answer before."

"Any update on him?"

Ellie turned her chair to stare out over the city. "No. His wife is angry with me and the doctors won't let anyone in yet. I'm so scared for him."

"He's in good hands."

"I know. Ben, everyone is at me about Dennis."

"Shall I come to you?"

"I'd really like you to look at Dad's office, and where Campbell was found. Can you do that?"

"What am I looking for?"

"That's just it. I don't know, but I'm the closest thing to being in charge and you don't need a warrant if I invite you. Do you?"

"Then I'll bring Meg as well. See you soon." He terminated the call.

Ellie buzzed Mark. "Would you arrange for the whiteboard from downstairs to come to my office? And the markers and stuff."

No more leaving her ideas out in the open. Ellie had work to do.

"Is there a way to tell if Campbell simply lost his footing?" Ben had waited until the elevator doors closed before asking Meg.

"Let me see first. Probably ruined by staff and paramedics."

"With Dennis out of the way, at least we get a shot at Jack's office without a warrant."

"My bet is he's gone on a road trip."

"One with no footprint, Meg. No use of credit cards. No accessing his emails or any social media. Not a sign of him despite circulating his details across the state."

"Maybe a sea trip then."

The doors opened on the executive floor. Joni came to greet them.

"Mrs Connor asked me to take you to where Mr Boyd was found."

"Thanks, Joni. Where is Ellie?"

"I'm here." Ellie peered through the doorway of her office. "Can I show you something, Ben?"

Meg nodded to Ben and followed Joni to the fire door.

Ellie closed her door once Ben was in the office. There was a whiteboard on wheels pushed against a wall. A smile passed his lips. She was doing exactly what he had.

"Don't laugh at it."

"Far from it. Very impressed, actually. Is it helping?" He stood in front of the writing and Ellie joined him, picking up a marker.

"I hope you can help fill some gaps. Dennis?"

"You might need another whiteboard."

By the time he'd told Ellie about the events of the small hours of the morning, she'd added more words.

Under 'Dennis' was 'who was he meeting?', 'how did his shirt get in the bin/who put it there?' and 'why is he being set up?'.

"He isn't a killer, Ben. An idiot, but no killer."

"And my gut says the same, but the shirt adds a level of evidence we hadn't had before. It is enough to ask for a warrant to search the guest house, and…" he frowned, cross about what had to be done.

"And? The apartment? No need, I'll give you permission."

She understood. Out of everyone, Ellie was the only person who genuinely wanted to find Jack Bannerman. The rest all paid it lip service, even—Ben suspected—Campbell. Despite a lifelong friendship, the man had hardly gone out of his way to find Jack.

"Why is this in your office? You told me it belongs in the boardroom." He gestured at the whiteboard.

"I'd rather keep it from prying eyes. For example, I've added Mark now, because he seems to be involved with Paul on some level. Yet their respective roles require almost no contact. And in here, I can lock the door when I leave." She wandered to the window. "If it stays locked of course."

"Explain."

"I found it unlocked this morning but am certain I locked it last night. Campbell also has mentioned this. The cleaners weren't even on the floor so who is doing it?"

"Security?"

Ellie turned around, her slender body silhouetted against the city skyline. Exhaustion and worry lined her face and Ben longed to smooth them away. Ellie didn't deserve this. She tilted her head, the barest smile of query touching her mouth and there it was. The fire in his veins as if never gone.

"Ben?"

"I'm going to find your father. I promise you." How he'd crossed the room he couldn't remember, but he was near enough to see some of the tension drain away. "I think he's alive. There's nothing pointing to anything else."

"But...Frank Barlow? And Campbell?" her voice trembled.

He reached out a hand and she came to him, leaned against his body until all he could do was inhale her warm scent and feel her relax as his arms wrapped around her waist. The years apart meant nothing, not to his heart and body.

"We can't." she whispered into his chest.

She turned in his arms and he dropped them, letting her step away. Her colour was heightened, and she avoided his eyes.

Say what you want. You feel it too.

"We don't know why Jack vanished so finding his last known contact is my top priority."

"Isn't it Dennis?" Ellie dug around in her handbag, eventually finding a tissue, and drying her eyes.

"Probably not. If he did see Jack last, I don't believe it was at the pier. I've arranged with Meredith to speak to Jack's staff at the house, see if any of them can add to the little we know about that day."

"Do you want me there?"

"Nope. Let's keep you out of this for the moment. Shall we go to Jack's office?"

Ellie nodded and led the way. Ben noticed Mark watching

her as she passed the reception hub. Once inside Jack's office, he glanced back. Mark was on the phone, eyes still on Ellie. Then he glanced at Ben, and Mark hung up. Something to add to his own whiteboard at the station.

"Nobody has been permitted in here since Dad left. Not the cleaners, or the staff, except for Joni, Dennis, and Paul."

"Paul?"

"To check the safe with me and Dennis, and make sure the cameras were working. Some of the previous night's footage had dropped out."

Ben went to the door and closed it. "Ellie, what's going on with the surveillance? That's not the first time I've heard about issues, and a lot of the footage Paul provided was low quality."

"He told me Dad rejected much of the last upgrades. But Dad is pedantic about security, whether here or at the house. Even my apartment building—it had to be one with top quality security systems and then he had it checked out before I bought it."

Yet you think he doesn't control you.

"How do you feel about Meg taking a look at the system? Discreetly."

"As long as Paul doesn't know. Anyway, would you do your thing and see if I've missed something here?"

"My thing?" Ben grinned. "Am I a mentalist now?"

"Funny."

"Holmes?"

"Not even close."

At least she was smiling again.

Perched on the arm of a sofa, Ellie watched Ben open drawers, books, and papers. He wore gloves and replaced everything he touched. His eyes were focused on his job and barely a word had passed between them since he began.

This gave her time to put jumbled emotions back into their box. He'd caught her at a weak moment, worried about Campbell and doubting everyone's motives. His arms gave her much-needed strength, but that was all it could ever be. She played with her wedding ring. Time for it to go. As soon as Ben and his team had searched her apartment, she'd pack the remainder of Dennis' things and send them to him.

How long does a divorce take?

"Ellie?"

She glanced up. Ben held a photograph from Dad's desk.

"Why does Jack keep a photo of his first wife on his desk?"

"I'm in it too." Ellie joined Ben and took it from him. She loved the way Gabi smiled in this photo. "There's only a few pictures of us together since I grew up."

"Most men don't keep their ex-wives images in front of them."

"Dad isn't most men. And besides, you know it wasn't a lack of love which led to their divorce. Gabi needs freedom, and Dad needs security. Different personalities." Ellie kissed her mother's image and replaced the photo on the desk.

"You're a mix of them both."

"Stop it." Ellie went back to the sofa. "Stop detecting me."

"Not a word."

"Is now."

"Where is Gabi?" Ben stared at Ellie.

"If you think she's run away with Dad, forget it. Her life is on the sea and at her little cabin and she's made it clear more than once she'll never return to this world. And he will never leave it. Besides, I have tried to contact her every day I've been back, but she isn't at her cabin and isn't answering her phone. But I have the number of her closest neighbour who lives further up the river."

"So, call them?"

Ellie rolled her eyes. "Did that days ago. *Wind Drifter* hasn't been there for a few weeks, and last they heard, Gabi was heading off to work on illustrations of some rare bird around King Island. Or somewhere."

"You might have told me this earlier."

"I didn't think it mattered. If there was a hint Gabi and Dad were together don't you think I'd be hunting her down?" Try as she might, Ellie couldn't keep impatience from her voice. "I wish that was where he is, Ben. For a lot of reasons."

"Boss, a minute?" Meg was at the door, her face blank.

Ellie jumped up. "Come in."

Ben nodded and Meg closed the door behind herself.

"That warrant? I think you should ask for it."

Ellie's hands clenched.

"I can't be certain without more time and equipment, but I'm betting Mr Boyd didn't fall. Not without some help. I think he was attacked somewhere else and dragged to the steps."

FORTY-FIVE
PERFECT PLANS

Everything was coming together perfectly.

Soon, very soon, he'd collect his final payment and do his own disappearing act.

One more deposit.

It was risky. Between Ben Rossi and the homicide squad, there was a whole lot of sniffing around going on. And Ellie thought she was some sort of amateur sleuth with her whiteboard and clever musings. But take care. Remember what happened to the old man who couldn't leave things alone. He might have unfortunately survived the fall but talking wasn't going to be an option for some time.

Losing the top apartment overlooking the pier was disappointing. More for the thrill of it all than anything. After all, there was nothing more to do there, unless to steal the yacht and add yet another element to the mystery. Then again, boats weren't his thing.

He packed the last of his clothes. Travel light. Leave behind what you don't need. Time to move on from the city he'd called home for a bit too long. There was no million-dollar view from this place, but a million dollars in a very secret account was about to make up for it.

Bags packed, he wandered around the apartment. Not worth leaving any pointers about what he'd done or where he was going. What a shock it would be when they worked out he'd been right there in plain view all this time, always in the background.

His phone beeped and he read the message. *Cops think Boyd was pushed. And they're going to her apartment.*

Time to go. This was happening a little too fast, but patience was his friend and he'd live out of his car if he had to. He'd be long gone from Melbourne before anyone worked out what happened.

After fixing some loose ends.

He opened the top of his other bag. A rifle, handgun, bullets. He zipped it and slung it over his shoulder.

"You have no right to be here harassing me, and even less right to arrest an innocent man!" Meredith screeched at Ben.

He'd need to wear ear plugs if this kept up. He set the warrant on the coffee table in the living room where she'd taken him. "This gives us the right. You can let me do my job or spend some time in the back of the car and then the station."

Her mouth opened. And closed. Tears filled her eyes and he wanted to tell her to pull her head in. She was a big part of the problem and this behaviour only made things worse.

"I'm sorry you are upset, Mrs Bannerman, but I've explained why and now I need access to the guest house. Afterwards, I will speak to your staff as already arranged, so please ask them to be available. Okay?"

Meredith lifted her chin and crossed to the tray with brandy. "I am not okay with it, but you've made your position clear." She poured a glass of brandy and swung back. "I want to know why you arrested Dennis."

"As I've told you, he drove his car while well over any limit in the world. Surprisingly, he made it to his destination without killing anyone. Do you know why he was there?"

After swigging back a mouthful, she shook her head. "Dennis is his own man. What he chooses to do is up to him. But when I saw him last, he was going to send some emails and then sleep."

"What time was this?"

She shrugged. "Late. Midnight or later. We'd drunk a bit and I went to bed."

"Any staff around to confirm a time?"

"Dennis and I had a romantic dinner by the pool. Once it was served, they all left for the night. Only two of them live here anyway, and Dennis arranged for them to go to a movie in the city and stay somewhere nice. I didn't even know he'd gone out."

"Have them available for a chat. I won't be long."

Ben strode through the house and past the pool. There was a table there with two chairs. One of the staff stopped clearing it as he went past. The lifestyle of Jack and Meredith sickened Ben. Too much money, alcohol, and in Michael's case, drugs. Yet the minute he got himself into trouble, his father turned his back on him. Damned hypocrite.

As he closed in on the guest house, he forced his anger down. He had to be clear minded and controlled. And he couldn't do this alone. Two uniformed officers waited at the door.

———

"He's not lying about being watched." Ben directed a flashlight onto a curtain rod as one of the officers took photos. "Looks as dodgy as all hell, not at all professional, but this is in the right spot to let someone see his code for the safe."

They'd found the tiny camera hidden amongst the curtain

folds in the bedroom. Not a brilliant disguise but one that was missed by a casual search of the room.

Ben took the phone from the officer and messaged the photos to Meg. Someone wanted Dennis to be a fall guy.

The rest of the guest house offered nothing. It was as clean as a place could be. Apart from the one camera.

"Where does it lead?" one of the officers asked.

"Good question and one I hope Meg can answer. I think those cameras are app based, so presumably whoever put it there has access. Might be watching us right now." He gave the camera the finger and the officer laughed.

Dennis Connor was guilty of drink driving. Probably of a whole lot of stupid decisions, not the least being his appalling treatment of his wife, none of which would result in further charges. He had a decent lawyer and might walk away from jail time, despite the high alcohol reading.

Andy's ringtone interrupted.

"Did you see the pics I sent Meg?" Ben asked.

"Dude, told you not to do that."

"Ha ha. Why are you calling?"

"Got some results forensics results. How did the search go?"

"Found a camera trained on the safe. He's been set up."

"His lawyer is here and says the same."

"I'd like to keep him for a bit longer. See what else we can get from him."

"Then, you might be interested in where the bullet came from. The one that killed Frank Barlow."

Ben knew. His gut knew, and it rarely lied.

"Dennis' gun."

Andy sounded way too happy. "Got it in one."

"Then charge him. We'll sort it out but for now, let's keep him close."

After leaving the uniforms to prevent Meredith storming into the guest house, Ben met with Brenda, outside by the pool at his request. Until the whole property was searched, he wanted no risk of being overheard.

They sat on either side of the now-empty table. Brenda gripped her hands together, eyes down, lips in a straight line. Nerves, or guilt?

"Please relax, Brenda. I'm Ben, and all I want is to help find Mr Bannerman. Do you mind if I ask a few questions about the last time you saw him?"

"Mrs Bannerman says I must."

"You're not in any trouble and you are not obliged to answer any questions."

She glanced up, eyes uncertain.

"It would help though."

There was the slightest nod and Brenda softened her mouth.

"Thank you. I understand you've worked for Mr Bannerman for a long time?"

"Since before he remarried. He is a good man. Works hard."

"Do you remember the day he disappeared? The last time you saw him?"

She glanced away with a small shake of her head.

"You don't remember, or you don't want to tell me?" Ben kept his voice friendly.

"I...I shouldn't say."

"It will help if you do."

Brenda looked Ben in the eye.

"The last time was as he left for his taxi."

Taxi?

"Do you recall the time?"

"Exactly midday."

"That is exact."

"His driver was away with Mrs Bannerman's commitments

so he phoned a taxi and wanted to be sure he'd be at the pier in time."

"To meet Mr Connor?"

Brenda frowned. "Yes. Him."

"Do you know which taxi company?"

"No. He insisted he'd call and then told me he'd wait outside the gate. I closed the front door behind him."

"Why haven't you come forward?" Ben kept his voice neutral.

Brenda glanced over her shoulder.

"Mrs Bannerman is in the house. Are you afraid of her?"

Those hands were tight together again.

"One more question. Do you remember what Mr Bannerman was wearing and carrying?"

"Oh, yes. He wore his favourite sailing shirt and shorts. I remember because he had his gold pen in the top pocket. Because of the papers he had to sign. And he had his briefcase and the bag he takes sailing. I think he usually packs spare clothes in case of bad weather, extra shoes, and…"

"And?"

She suddenly leaned forward and whispered. "I think he took the last bottle of his special gin."

"What makes it special?"

Brenda shrugged. "His son gave him a case of it before… well, you know. It was the only one left, which he kept on his desk in the library. It isn't there now."

FORTY-SIX
SAVING HIMSELF

Ellie sat in Jack's place, alone at the boardroom table. The remaining board members had agreed, even encouraged her to take the role of CEO. One more down and the board would not be able to make decisions. Was this part of someone's plan? Disable the executive and go in for the kill?

But who would make such elaborate plans? There was no family left on the board, not until Dad came back. If Dennis was convicted of drink driving, he'd lose his position. There were rules set in stone about standards.

Did the potential buyer have some insider working with them to bring the price down? Someone Ellie knew and worked with? Her stomach turned at the idea.

I don't want this.

She never had. Ellie's calling was food. Not high business or dealing with a world crashing around her shoulders, but the thrill and controlled chaos of a restaurant. Ben was right. She *would* pursue it again. A tiny light ahead, the rediscovery of a long-lost dream.

Just find Dad. Then everything would be okay again.

Ben called.

"Are you finished with Meredith?" She asked.

"Almost lost my hearing, she yelled at me so much, but yes."

On her feet, Ellie pushed the chair in. "Anything worth telling me?"

He hesitated.

"Ben?"

"There is, but I can't say at this point. Nothing leading to Jack."

"I'm acting CEO." Ellie headed for the boardroom doors. "So, no warrants required, just do what you need here."

"Do I congratulate you?"

She almost snorted. "Get real. I'm done with this mess, but someone must keep things running. When will Dennis be released? I need to talk to him."

"I'm heading into an interview with him right now. And his lawyer."

Ellie stopped in the hallway. "Why?"

"The bullet that killed Frank Barlow came from his gun."

Ellie slumped against the wall. "No."

"I'm sorry, Ellie. And it doesn't mean he knows a thing about it, so keep this to yourself. He's going to maintain the gun was stolen and perhaps it was."

"Am I married to a killer, Ben? What if he did kill Dad?" Her voice rose.

"Then he'll tell me. But my gut says otherwise."

A couple of staff approached, talking to each other. Ellie straightened and nodded to them. She was sick to the stomach of keeping up appearances.

"Sweetheart?"

"Why do you still call me that?" She forced her feet forward, toward the elevator.

"Old habits. Should I stop?"

"Probably."

"Are you telling me to?"

She stepped into the elevator and tapped Paul's floor. "I'll think about it."

"Hang in there. Where are you now?"

"Going to check on the staff. I'll probably send them home."

"Are you going home?"

"I'm the new CEO, remember? No rest for me."

"Uh huh. I've got to go."

She slid her phone into her handbag as the doors opened. The chatter of staff and tapping of computers filled the air. The doors along the walkway were all open. She spotted Joni at a desk among the team that worked directly with Campbell.

Paul's office door was closed. She tapped, and when no response came, peered through the glass door. He wasn't in there. One row of monitors was blacked out, and she frowned. How bad was the surveillance situation? The second row was on, one monitor trained on the carpark. Two men talked in a dark corner. Their arms were raised, body language angry. Ellie opened the door and went in.

She picked up Paul's land line phone to call the monitor room just as the men went separate ways. One stalked off in the direction of the street. She was sure it was Mark from his lean and tall build. The other man stormed to the elevator; anger etched in the face she knew so well. It was Paul.

———

"You found that call I got on my phone?" Dennis tapped on the table in the interview room. "I can go?"

Ben settled into the chair opposite, while Andy preferred to stand near the door, arms crossed. No matter how many times he told his partner there was no 'good cop, bad cop', Andy still approached every interrogation the same way.

"You can't go."

"Detective, my client is entitled to apply for bail immediately. We're talking about a simple DUI." Lawyer Brian Landing sat beside Dennis.

"Actually, we are talking about murder, intent to cause bodily harm, illegal use of a firearm, and enquiries relating to the disappearance of Jack Bannerman."

Dennis swung to his lawyer. "What the hell?"

"Indeed. Please explain yourself, Detective Rossi."

"Homicide will be along shortly, and they will have a lot more to say than I do about the death of Frank Barlow. The bullet that killed him has been identified as originating from the gun I found on *Sea Angel* during a legal search. A gun licenced to you."

"But...I—"

"You don't need to respond, Dennis."

"It will help him if he does, Mr Landing. My interest is around Jack. Evidence points toward your client for the unlawful death of an innocent fisherman, so the next step is determining any connection between this, and Jack's disappearance." Ben turned his attention back to Dennis. "You are the person he was meeting that day, on the same pier where Frank was killed."

The colour drained from Dennis face and his mouth opened and closed.

"You can do as Mr Landing says or help me to help you."

"I'll talk to you."

"Dennis—"

"No, I said I'll talk to him, Brian."

The lawyer grunted and began taking notes on a writing pad.

"Dennis, what do you know about Jack's disappearance?"

"I don't know where his body is."

Ben drew in a breath. "So, are you admitting to killing Jack Bannerman?"

Dennis burst into laughter.

Are you quite insane?

Even Brian Landing moved his chair further from Dennis.

Serious again, Dennis leaned forward. "You've got it so wrong, Rossi. I had nothing to do with Jack's disappearance and I can prove it. Jack killed himself."

"And you know this—how?" Andy spoke when Ben remained silent.

"He left a note. And I know where it is."

FORTY-SEVEN
SMALL GOOD THINGS

Ellie waited for Paul outside his office, not wanting to start their conversation off by defending being inside it.

You're the damned CEO. Say what you need to!

But no, it was best to give him the benefit of the doubt. If there was a problem with Mark, let him feel he could talk to her.

"Mrs Connor?" Joni ran down the hallway. "You need to see this!"

"What's wrong?"

Joni turned and took off in the opposite direction and Ellie followed at a sprint. She caught up in the lunchroom, where a group of people sat around a television.

"They're about to show the lady you helped." Joni beamed.

Confused, Ellie stared at the screen as an advertisement ended. A local current affairs show flicked on and there sat Mrs Blackwell. As she was interviewed about her missing grandson, the same image Ellie had seen of Adam was shown, and a banner along the bottom advised the numbers to ring with any information on his whereabouts. As Mrs Blackwell pleaded for her grandson to get in touch, a warm glow tiptoed into Ellie's heart.

As one, the staff turned and clapped at Ellie. She grinned. "Wow, after all the crap with Teresa Scarcella, I didn't believe this other show would help out. But look at it!"

"We don't watch Ms Scarcella, do we?" Joni put her hands on her hips and there was another round of applause.

Ellie blinked back a tear or two. This support, this moment, reminded her why she loved her job. The feeling was the same as every time she ran an event or sent a huge donation to one of the charities the Bannerman Foundation cared for.

On the way back to Paul's office, she tried to hold onto the feeling. If Adam Blackwell saw his grandmother on television, surely, he'd at least let someone know he was fine? If he's fine. So young and at the beginning of his life.

Paul was in his office, door open, arms crossed as he glared at the monitors.

"What's wrong with them?" Ellie stood in the doorway. "May I come in?"

"Sure. Take a seat." He dropped into his chair on the opposite side. "They are effed up, that's what's wrong. I've been downstairs in the control room trying to see what the hell happened to Campbell, but after you left last night, the cameras went down again."

"There's nothing?"

"Not a thing."

"This can't continue."

"Well, don't blame me. I've asked for an upgrade and Jack wouldn't do it."

"Talk me through that. Why wouldn't he?"

Paul ran a hand over his chin. "No time even for a shave. I'm not having a go at your father, Ellie, promise. He had a lot of other stuff going on. For one, he said the cost of caring for Michael went up suddenly and he had to dip into business funds out of the blue."

The funds for Michael don't come from the business!

"Anything else he had going on?" Ellie was impressed with the calmness in her voice.

"Yeah. Meredith. She gambled a ton of money away and left him with some shady characters to deal with. He cleaned out his cash reserves and then some."

"I had no idea she gambled!"

Paul nodded. "She learnt her lesson because he threatened to divorce her if she ever did it again."

"Wow. You never really know someone, do you?"

Oblivious to her sarcasm, he pointed at the top row of monitors. "The issue is more than this, El. I had the head technician from the place I order from come in and he had concerns even last year about the failing equipment."

"How much will it cost to do what needs doing?"

"Doesn't matter. Campbell was going to sign off on it but now…who knows what will happen. I'll fix it up as best I can. As usual."

"As of an hour ago, I'm acting CEO. Campbell may take a long time to heal. I have no idea where Dad is. And Dennis is unlikely to return to his position."

Paul's eyes shot to Ellie's. "Dennis is out?"

She shrugged. "Not my call, but a conviction for drink driving would put him in a poor light, don't you agree?"

He glanced at his watch. "Too early for a congratulatory drink for your new position?"

"A little. And I'm not sure how I feel about this. CEO has never been my goal and certainly not under these circumstances."

"You'll change this company for the better."

"Except, the minute Dad returns, he gets it back."

"But you can make decisions. You can approve the purchase order for the new security system."

"I can. Send it to me and I'll go through it."

"Even better, let me take you to dinner and we can talk it

through then. Kill two birds with one stone, so to speak." Paul stared at Ellie.

Are you hiding something?

"Happy to have a drink. As long as it is early and local."

"Sure. Anywhere in particular?" he asked.

"The wine bar down from my apartment."

"Seven?"

"Six. I have so much to do. And please, send the purchase order to me first to look at." Ellie got to her feet. At the door, she turned. "I meant to ask if you've seen Mark lately."

"Mark? Isn't he with Joni in finance?"

"No. Maybe he left for the day."

"Why do you need him?" Paul came around the desk.

"I'm trying to update all the executive staff on the changes. See you tonight, Paul."

Before he got any closer, she hurried away, heart thumping. A text message buzzed and once in the elevator, she read it.

Ellie, can you meet me at Jack's house? Ben.

Now? She replied.

As soon as you can.

With a sigh, she tapped the down button on the lift.

FORTY-EIGHT
THE WEIGHT OF HAPPINESS

Ellie stepped out of the taxi she'd grabbed rather than drive with so much on her mind. Ben's car was parked in the driveway along with a Crime Scene Services vehicle.

The front door was open. "Hello? It's Ellie."

Nobody replied.

She went inside. Meredith was asleep on the sofa in the living room, snoring. An almost empty brandy decanter was on the side table. If Paul had told her Meredith drank her way into debt, she might have believed him.

Brenda stood in the kitchen, staring out of the window. She jumped when Ellie spoke.

"Brenda?"

"Oh! Um, I think the detective is in the library, Mrs Connor."

The hallway felt long and her legs wanted to turn and ran away. Ellie had worked herself up on the way over, expecting Ben to be here breaking the news of something bad happening to Dad. Or arresting Meredith.

This house once rang with laughter. And sometimes loud words. But mostly the happiness of a small family. Dad, Gabi, and Michael. And Ellie, always wanting to be the centre of attention. Except Michael took the role with his career. And then his notoriety.

At the library door, she hesitated. This room was a sanctuary for Dad. And for Ellie. Their escape from the outside world when things got tough.

The door opened. Ben held out a hand and she took it, biting her bottom lips as tears threatened.

"I'm sorry to message you. I couldn't call."

"You found Dad?" she whispered.

"No. But Dennis told me some things and I need you to help me figure it out."

"What things."

He led her to Dad's desk. "I need to tell you what he said first."

As she sank onto the chair, he squatted at her side, still holding her hand. "This is going to be upsetting. But we don't know if anything he said is true. And even if he thinks it is, there's no proof."

"Ben, tell me!"

"Dennis denies harming Jack. But he did steal something."

Ellie wrinkled her brow. "Stole? From Dad?"

"And from you. The night you and I looked for the rum bottle, Dennis was in here."

Her mouth dropped.

"Apparently he hid in the corner when he heard us approaching. I believe him because he repeated some things we said."

Ellie's mind raced back. There'd been a moment. Something about Ben not wanting to arrest her. She'd understood what he meant. Not two people from one family. He couldn't lose another person who he cared about.

"Oh."

"Yes. Not that he's bright enough to understand."

She almost smiled.

His hand tightened. "He had been going through the drawers of both desks and he found something."

"The rum bottle? Oh, Ben."

"And he removed a note from it."

"What did it say?" she whispered.

"He said he put it back. In here."

Ellie freed her hand and reached for the bottom drawer. Behind the files, there it was. The old rum bottle. She picked it up. "Did Dennis say what is in the note?"

Ben straightened, then perched on the corner of the desk, his eyes intense. "He did. But I don't know if he is lying."

Then it must be bad. Ellie removed the lid and turned the bottle upside down. The corner of an envelope emerged, and she carefully slid it out. "This is the one he carried from his office. The one on the surveillance footage."

"Or one like it."

She tried twice to remove the note, her hands shaking so much Ben took over. He opened the one page and held it out. Lines ran through it, criss-crossed as if screwed into a ball and then flattened. But then came the words.

My darling Ellie,

No matter what anyone says, remember I love you. You are brave and strong, loving and beautiful.

Not everything is as it seems. Gabi once told me happiness lies in our hearts if we look hard enough. I've searched, Ellie. I truly have, but all I see are shadows closing in.

I've stuffed things up. I agreed to sell the business and now I can't get out of it. Your Foundation will go as well as my life's work. It seemed the right time. You see, I have some tumour growing in my brain and there's nothing to be done about it. And I'm not good at illness. Just look how I've treated your brother all these years.

With me gone, there's a chance of getting out of the agreement. I'm leaving everything to you, so do with it what you want. Just make sure Michael knows I never stopped loving him.

Sorry you had to find me this way.

Dad.

Ellie had no words. Somewhere deep inside, a heaviness dragged her down. It was over. He'd gone away to die and left behind a mess for someone else to fix. Not any someone. No, he'd chosen the one person he relied on the most. The person he kept on a tight leash. The child he knew would do his bidding because she always had.

He couldn't just wait until she was home and work through everything with her and the board. Even to the grave, he wanted to control her. The heaviness turned into a fire, burning its way from her stomach to her lungs. He loved Michael. But never told him.

My job to tell him? You self-centred, narcissist.

He'd stuffed up alright. Not a word of warning he wanted to sell, or more important than that, about his illness. Did Gabi know? Of course not, it was something little Ellie would handle. After all, she had nothing better to do now he'd guilted her out of being a chef, given her job to a man who might be a killer, and torn her away from her one true love.

"Ellie, please. Take a sip."

Ben's face was near hers and she jumped, spilling water over them both.

"Sorry…" When had he got water?

He handed her a glass. "Drink." From a pocket he pulled a handkerchief and dabbed it on the wet spots on her legs, then dried himself.

She took a sip, then gulped through dry lips. Her eyes returned to the note, which Ben must have taken from her and put on the desk.

"I think I'm done looking for him. And running his business. Whatever game he's playing, I'm not buying anymore."

"This reads like a suicide note." Ben finally read it, his eyes flicking to Ellie's as he reached the end. "But this bit… Sorry you had to find me this way?"

"In the phone message he left after he disappeared he said to look for the note. If he put the note here, presumably he meant to...end things here. So, either he did, and someone removed his body with no trace, or—"

"Or he changed his mind. But maybe just about the where." Ben interrupted.

"Do you think the note looks like someone scrunched it up? Even threw it away? What if he changed his mind and wrote another note but this one ended up in here?" Ellie said. "Dad is alive somewhere."

"Have you considered a career as an investigator?" Ben smiled. "Are you okay, though?"

Was she? All the earlier sensations were gone, leaving only a kind of numbness. She longed to see Michael.

"I'm okay. What now?" she stood, brushing a few remaining drops of water from her dress. "Do we tell Meredith?"

"No, we let her sleep. Much quieter that way."

"You didn't hear her snoring."

"Still quieter than her screeching. There is something else. I spoke to Brenda earlier and she had a bit more about the day Jack disappeared." Ben gestured to the desk. "She remembers he carried the bag he usually takes sailing. Change of clothes etcetera. But she is also convinced he took a bottle of gin with him."

Ellie looked at the desk. "How did I miss this? Michael gave him six bottles which were custom made for Dad. When Michael went to prison, Dad threw just about everything out which reminded him of his only son." She heard bitterness flood her tone. "I saved what I could, and years later, gave Dad the one bottle of gin I'd rescued. It was always here, unopened."

"Any idea why he'd take it?"

Nothing makes sense anymore. Nothing.

"I have to go, unless you need me for anything else?"

Something in Ben's eyes told her he had more to say, but he shook his head. "Where are you going? I'll give you a lift."

"Home. I'd like to go home."

FORTY-NINE
DECEPTIONS AND LIES

As Ben navigated through peak hour traffic, Ellie read the documentation attached to Paul's purchase order on her phone.

"Do you know anyone in security I could run this quote past?" she asked, not looking up as she scrolled to the top again.

"Show Meg. But I know it can run into thousands."

"How about close to two hundred thousand?"

Ben whistled.

"Mind you, it replaces lots of monitors and cameras plus updates whatever system we have. I know nothing about this sort of thing."

"How long since the last upgrade?"

"Paul told me he requested one a year ago but Dad didn't have the money. All kind of weird reasons, none of them true. Such as Meredith having a gambling debt he had to pay."

"Jack's the gambler."

"I know. And he has wasted a lot of money with poker, but always keeps cash to cover himself. His play money."

"So why does Paul believe that stuff?"

Ellie put the phone away. "I've known him for years. He

worked for Dad before joining Bannerman Wealth Group, when Dad had another business on the side." She took off her sunglasses as the car nosed into the Domain tunnel. "He's always been there—by Dad's side or doing what was needed but I never really knew him. I thought I did."

"What changed your mind?" Ben braked and swore under his breath as a truck slid into the lane in front of him.

"He keeps lying about little things. Like Meredith gambling, and Michael's costs skyrocketing, and not seeing Mark when I'd just watched them through a camera, arguing in the carpark."

Ben didn't say anything, but his knuckles whitened on the steering wheel.

"Perhaps he's always been a liar. Look how he kept insisting Dennis was behind Dad's disappearance."

"Is it a case of him believing Dennis is guilty, or is he taking advantage of the situation. Why don't I run a background search on Paul."

They emerged from the tunnel into late afternoon sun, Ellie making a big deal of looking for her sunglasses to avoid responding. She was the best person to find out what Paul was up to.

———

"I know you have your hands full, but I have a question." Ben looked over Meg's shoulder as she searched on one of her computers using a code which was gibberish to him.

"Leave a note."

"What would it cost to upgrade the security systems in a large building."

"Ben."

"Say at Bannerman House."

"Are you donating so next time the CEO goes missing we

get decent footage?" She still didn't look up as her fingers flew over the keyboard.

"Ellie is CEO now and she'd better not go anywhere."

"Heaps, dude. Lots of megabucks."

"Two hundred thousand?"

She shrugged. "Depends on the quality. Who is the company they're dealing with?"

Good question. Ben sent Ellie a message to ask.

"What are you doing, Meg?"

"Answering questions when I said to leave a note. Aha!" She grabbed a mouse and clicked, and the screen filled with data. "I'm finding out where that camera was directing its signal."

"From the guest house?" Ben pulled up a chair and slid beside her.

"Shh."

Ellie replied to his message. Rather than annoy Meg, he did an internet search. A landing page with a contact form appeared. No phone number or much else. He forwarded the information to Andy to check.

"Right. Well that was fun." Meg pushed her seat back and looked at Ben. "This sweet little thing gave up the number of the phone it was relaying to."

"Impressive. Is there a name attached to this number?"

"There will be. What's the name of the security company?"

Ben showed Meg what he'd found and she raised both eyebrows. "Crap website. Probably a shell. Get Andy to take a look."

"Already doing so."

"Then go away and let me do my job."

"Call me." Ben stood. "And if you're going be here half the night, order some food."

"Leave your credit card and I will. Actually," she grinned, "I'll find your card details so toddle along. I promise to keep the spend to a minimum."

Andy met him at the door. "Got something from the gym. Clean Living Gym."

"The water bottles?" Ben headed for their desks with Andy spinning around to follow him.

"They had a theft a week or so back. Gym bags, cash, and water bottles. A few dozen. They reckon it was someone they fired. A Dale Grant."

"Why'd they fire him?"

"Smoker and lazy. Apparently, lied about smoking at the interview but was caught one too many times and given the boot."

"What do we know about Mr Grant?" Dropping into his chair, Ben woke his computer.

"Not much. The address he gave them is fake. Have a description." Andy sat at his desk and opened his notebook. "Wiry build, blonde hair, blue eyes, about one-eighty centimetres."

"Best lead so far. Anything else?"

"Was always smiling but didn't socialise. Even when working kept his gym bag close by and never let anyone touch it."

"Still nothing back on the fingerprint we found at the apartment?"

Andy shook his head. "One more thing, guy had a personal hygiene issue. Always stunk of sweat."

Ben stared at his computer screen. Gym bag. Blonde hair. Wiry. Tall. But it was the stench of dried perspiration which took him back to the elevator in Ellie's apartment building. The first time he'd barely glanced at the man as they passed through lift doors. The second time Ellie was avoiding the man in the foyer.

"He runs around with a gym bag but doesn't use the one here. I thought he was chatting me up one time then he told me he isn't into older women." That was what she'd said the other day.

"Shit."

"Boss? Did you just use a bad word?"

Ben phoned Ellie, hand over the receiver. "We're going."

"I just got back."

The call went to message. "Ellie, this is urgent. If you are home, lock the door and stay inside. If you are out, get around people and tell me where you are. Phone me."

On his feet, Ben grabbed his jacket and keys.

"Ben? Got a name for you on the camera from the guest house." Meg hurried out. "Dale Grant. And he lives near Ellie. Like, really close."

FIFTY
CAUGHT

Ellie had no intention of being out late. Not tonight. She'd do and say what was necessary to get more information from Paul, but then she was taking time for herself. Too much happened today for her mind to process and she needed to put it into some semblance of order.

Back at her apartment she'd revisited Paul's purchase order. She phoned two other security firms for quotes, arranging times to meet with both tomorrow at Bannerman House. If they had to spend so much, she owed it to the board and the staff to do due diligence. Paul would be put out, so she had no intention of telling him until then.

She put some wine into the fridge to chill for later. The sliding door was open, and she wandered outside. Below, the traffic wasn't easing. Pedestrians filled the pavement on both sides, a mix of workers going home and early diners coming out. The wine bar already had a line up.

Sliding door locked, Ellie collected her handbag and let herself out. As she stepped into the lift, her phone rang. It was Ben. She tapped the 'close door' button.

An arm stopped them and gym man forced his way in.

Ellie instinctively stepped back.

"Don't answer."

"I beg your pardon?"

"You heard me, Mrs Connor." He hit the carpark button. "We're gonna have a nice chat downstairs."

Was he high? Going to mug her? Except you don't mug someone you know.

His body odour was repulsive.

"Where's your gym bag?"

"What?"

"You normally clutch it against you as though there's gold inside." She lifted her chin, looking directly into his eyes. "It must be important."

"Shut up." Sweat beaded his forehead.

The floor buttons lit as they descended.

"You're gonna help me get a whole lot more cash than I'm already owed." He spat the words.

"Who owes you money?"

Five more floors to ground.

"Little Miss Ellie. Because of you, I've had to put my life on hold. Done things I didn't want to."

"Do you know where my father is?"

"No clue." He crossed the lift to tower over her and she flattened against the back wall. "You stay quiet and come with me. Or I'll kill you, and anyone else we come across."

The elevator stopped and as the doors parted, Ellie saw Ben's face. She dropped to the floor.

"Dale Grant, turn around slowly and put your hands in the air. I will taser you."

Between gym man's legs Ellie saw the taser in Ben's hands. He pointed it at the man's body, but his eyes flashed to Ellie.

"Go ahead. Idiot." Dale grabbed a handful of Ellie's hair and smirked over his shoulder. "Taser me and see how much it hurts her too."

Ellie's fist flew upward, connecting with soft flesh between his legs. Dale screamed and buckled.

She scrambled her way from the elevator onto the concrete of the carpark level, sliding across the floor until Andy steadied her. A second later, Ben dragged Dale out.

Andy released her and Ben was there, enfolding her in his arms until the stench of gym man was gone, replaced by the familiar, safe smell she knew so well.

Paul checked his watch for the third time. The table was at the back of the wine bar, away from the baby grand piano and the noise around the bar. But Ellie was late. He'd ordered a bottle of red, ready for a glass after the day he'd had. A couple of sips and some of the anxiety about where she was lessened.

In the centre of the table, he'd placed a printed copy of the purchase order, his rationale statement, and a list of recent failures of equipment. It gutted him to think how much footage was lost thanks to poor connections or flawed cameras. He'd run through it once Ellie arrived. As soon as she signed the document, he'd place the order. Make sure nobody ever got away with crime again on his watch.

He sent her a text. *In the back corner. Nice glass of red awaits.*

She was probably making herself look nice, not that it could possibly be difficult. Ellie was one of those people who looked great in anything and he'd seen her in everything from jeans to a ball gown. Perks of working closely with Jack was keeping an eye on his gorgeous daughter.

"Pour me one." Ellie emerged through the crowd and slid into her seat before Paul could stand. "I am so sorry to be late."

"Not that late." He filled her glass almost to the top. "Everything alright?"

She was texting. "Sorry, remembered something I need Joni to do." Ellie finished, put her phone away, and gave Paul a quick smile.

He tapped his glass against hers. "To the future."

Ellie barely tasted the wine before putting down the glass. "Have you been here for long?"

"Nope. Just arrived a couple of minutes ago. Sent you a message as soon as I found the table. Are you sure you're okay? You look a bit...dunno."

"Tired? Sad?" Now, Ellie took a long sip of wine. "Both of those apply. I barely sleep worrying about Dad, and now Campbell's in hospital, a bit of me is broken inside."

"And we're no further along finding out who is behind this." Paul picked up the purchase order. "Let me read you something. This is a list I made of all the footage missing thanks to equipment failure. Jack's full movements the day he disappeared. And Dennis'. Campbell's office being unlocked in the dead of night. And yours. Campbell's fall." He raised his eyes. "Shall I go on?"

"I kind of feel it is closing the gate after the horse bolts."

"But what if anything else happens? If you say no..."

"I haven't said anything, but there are competing priorities, Paul. I've been dropped into a mess made by Dad and aided by two men who are unavailable to do so much as advise me. Even the Foundation has to be put on hold while I give my attention to my father's business."

"Shall we have dinner?"

"I can't."

Paul pushed down a rush of annoyance. "You need to eat. Might as well be with a friend."

"I appreciate the offer, really I do. In half an hour I'm having a call with Michael's case manager, so must be back in my apartment."

"What if I bring something up, afterwards?"

Ellie sipped more wine, her eyes on the glass.

Why won't you look at me?

"Or I can cook for you." Surely she'd accept one of his suggestions.

With something like a sigh, Ellie put down her glass, and

looked at him. Her face was serious. "I know you are looking out for me, but I have too much to do. And now I have to take time to find out where Mark is."

"Mark? What do you mean?"

"Nobody has seen him since a few minutes after the police arrived on the executive floor. Joni has no idea where he went, even though she'd asked him to help out one of Campbell's staff."

"You did say people could go home if they were upset."

"Not without telling someone! What if he's missing now?"

"And I could tell you exactly when he left if I had better surveillance. How about signing this now and I can complete the order tonight?" He pushed the papers toward her and felt for a pen in a pocket.

She pushed them back. "Not tonight. Are you sure you didn't see him leave?"

"Why would I? We barely cross paths."

"Funny how we work with people and don't always know much about them." Ellie got to her feet and slung her handbag over her shoulder. "Short of looking up personnel records, I don't even know Mark's surname or where he lives."

Paul jumped up and came around the table. "Why not stay for a few more moments? Another glass of wine?"

"Thanks, but I can't miss this phone call. We'll talk about the purchase order tomorrow." With that, she merged with the crowd and was out of sight in seconds.

He noticed he'd clenched his hands and forced them open. With a grunt, he returned to his seat and refilled his wine glass. Why wouldn't she just sign the damned purchase order? Paul raised his glass to her empty chair. "Mark's surname is Grant. Mark Grant."

FIFTY-ONE
CHANGES COMING

"I'm finished with Paul and going home now. I promise I'm fine, so goodnight. And thanks." Ellie hung up after leaving a message on Ben's phone. It was him she'd texted when arriving at the wine bar. It was the only way he said he'd let her out of his sight tonight.

As soon as Ben was convinced Ellie was unhurt—apart from a slightly sore hand—he'd helped Andy finish the arrest. Dale Grant was doubled over, still moaning and wanting an ambulance. In the end, they'd called one, and Andy left with him.

"Am I in trouble...for hitting him?" Ellie's legs had finally stopped shaking but exhaustion settled on her shoulders. She knew the feeling was an aftermath of adrenaline and would push through it.

"I'll need a statement, but not necessarily about that. Do you want to come in now? Or we can talk here." Ben was back to business, but she'd caught him glancing at her often enough in the last ten minutes to know he was struggling with what happened in the lift.

Ellie had watched the ambulance leave. Uniformed officers followed and only Ben remained in the carpark with her. Other residents had been alarmed, some distraught, at the police activity, but they were dispersing. "Here's the thing. I'm late for an appointment, so can I do the statement thing later?"

"What appointment?"

She'd chewed her lip as he stared at her.

"Ellie, what are you up to?"

"I'm meeting Paul at the wine bar over the road. He wants to discuss the purchase order and I'd already agreed earlier."

"Why?"

"The truth?"

"That would be nice."

"I want to see if he lies anymore. He doesn't know it, but I have a couple of security firms coming to Bannerman House tomorrow to provide quotes. This isn't my money, Ben. If Dad denied his last order—and I don't know this yet—then I need to consider alternatives. Outsourcing if it gets the result we need as a company."

He'd half smiled. "Such a businesswoman."

She'd screwed her face up. "Nope. Doing what I'm trained to."

"Well, you're good at it." He'd walked with her to the doors. "Two things. Text me once you are sitting at the table. Phone me when you are back. If there is more than an hour between those events, I'll come find you."

I don't need a keeper!

But the memory of Dale Grant, sneering at her in the lift, raised the hairs on her arms. She'd agreed to Ben's request.

Now, as she entered the apartment building, she couldn't help looking over her shoulder. The concierge hurried over.

"Mrs Connor? I'll escort you to your apartment."

"Oh, you don't need to...actually, thank you."

In moments she was in the apartment, door locked. She turned on every light, including the lamp over her bed and the bathroom lights. Then checked the sliding door was locked. It was.

Phone on the kitchen counter with the volume up, Ellie opened the wine from the fridge and poured a glass. She needed to eat. The earlier events had played havoc with her stomach. Fridge door wide open, she scanned the contents. Hard cheese. Olives. Feta. Tomatoes. Garlic. Basil.

It took five minutes to make the pastry for a pizza base and then she set it aside with a smile. Hands in flour made her oddly content. As she washed her hands, she zoomed in on the feeling. Images of a casual, yet quality pizza and pasta eatery danced around in her mind. Perhaps near the sea somewhere. And she'd buy a house big enough for Michael to live there. He'd need a full-time carer, but surely this was doable.

She took her wine glass, opened the sliding door, and stepped onto the balcony. The evening was beautiful, warm and it was beginning to quieten on the streets. How she still loved living here. But other dreams were emerging, or more accurately, forcing their way back to her. Long buried beneath her guilt about Michael, and Dad's relentless demands.

You gave my job away.

Ellie understood he'd needed to have Dennis there to take over when she left with only a note to say she'd be back in a few months. He'd had no time to prepare for her going and for that, she'd paid dearly. He almost refused to have her back at Bannerman.

A breeze from the sea found its way to the balcony and she breathed deeply. Gabi never got over Dad buying the house in Canterbury and selling the waterfront home they'd moved into as newlyweds. A home she adored. He wanted something grander and simply sold up without a word. Gabi tried to forgive him and move on in their new and lovely upmarket home, but the lifestyle took a toll on her and then she was gone.

"Why does everyone leave?" Ellie glanced at her watch. Kerry would be calling any minute and she needed to sort her head out first. No more sad ponderings about what might have been.

Back inside, she prodded the ball of dough and moved it to a warmer spot.

The phone rang and she started, then shook her head.

"Ellie Connor speaking."

"Mrs Connor, this is Kerry. Are you free to speak?"

"I am. Thank you for calling me. How is Michael?" Ellie settled onto the arm of a sofa.

"He's well. Lots of swimming over the last day or two which he enjoys immensely."

"Oh, that's good. He was an amazing surfer."

"I'm sure."

There was a silence and Ellie gathered her thoughts. "I'd love to take Michael out for a day or two sometime. Once all this mess with Dad is sorted of course. What would it take to make this happen?"

"Do you think that's wise?"

"I would pay for his carer to come with us. Surely, he can stay a night at my home, and go to the sea for a short time?"

Kerry's voice hardened. "Of course, he can. It might be much harder than you think though. He still is prone to unpredictable behaviour, as you've seen firsthand. He really is best left here, with us, where we understand him."

Ellie pushed away the hurt from those last few words. "I'd like to talk to his specialist at some point. Would you arrange this?"

"Which one in particular?" Kerry's tone held contempt.

"Kerry, what you and your wonderful facility do for Michael is amazing and deeply appreciated. He is comfortable and safe and you all work so hard for the best outcomes. All I want is to expand his horizons a little bit."

"Fine. I'll email you the details of those who make the decisions about his care. If they are happy to let him come with you for a short break, then I'll make one of his carer's available."

"Thank you. You've been most accommodating."

"If there's nothing else?"

Nothing except a personality makeover.

The call ended and Ellie sighed. Was nothing easy anymore? The phone rang again. Ben.

"I'm home. Locked in."

"Good to hear."

"What's happening with gym man?"

"Admitted to hospital."

"Did I do that much damage?" Ellie grinned, but it was borne from a strange sense of unreality. Three minutes in a lift with a maniac.

"Doubt it, but we want to do things in a way he can't wriggle out of. Better to let him have his night of observation and then tomorrow he gets to spend some quality time with me."

"Sounds fun."

Ellie stood and stretched. She glanced at the dining table, covered in paperwork.

"I know you've probably had enough of people for one day, but may I come and see you? I'll only stay for a few moments...I want to be sure..."

So much emotion behind the words. It clutched at Ellie's heart. "Still like pizza?"

"Are you making it?"

"Uh huh. One condition. Bring some sourdough bread and a salad. Any salad. Not much in the fridge again."

"Half an hour?"

"Perfect."

She hung up, smiling. It was perfect.

FIFTY-TWO
USE BY DATE

Sea Angel was the only yacht tied up tonight. Perhaps the other owners thought they might be the next victim if there was a serial killer about. He almost smiled at the image of them all racing to leave the pier.

This was a peaceful spot to contemplate the future. The sun had dipped below the horizon and all that was left were fading tendrils of pink and gold across the sky. He'd miss Melbourne. Best coffee and food. Nightlife wasn't bad either.

His phone rang. "Why are you calling?"

"It's about Dale."

"What has he done now?"

Panic filled the other voice. "Arrested."

"What the hell!"

"Don't have all the details but what I do know is he tried to grab Ellie."

He dropped the phone away from his ear. Under what circumstances would even that idiot do something so dangerous?

"Are you still there?"

He put the phone back to his ear. "Did he hurt her? And, where is he?"

"Hurt her? The little bitch punched him in the balls. Sent him to hospital."

This was too good. His burst of laughter cut into the air.

"Yeah, you laugh. But now he's arrested and will fall apart when he's questioned."

He stopped laughing. "Dale needs to keep his mouth shut. They've got nothing on him, except whatever he's done to Ellie. Have you cleared out of your place?"

The other man grunted. "Dale was the only one who dragged his heels. You and I just need to keep our heads down."

"It'll be worth it. No more calls." He hung up.

Another blip in the plan. He was sick of the problems. Dale's arrest now stamped a use-by date on everything.

FIFTY-THREE
SOURDOUGH AND SALAD

Ellie buzzed Ben up, but left the door locked until he knocked.

"What's the password?" she asked.

"Sourdough and salad."

"And what am I making for dinner?"

"I could just eat these out here."

She flung the door open. "Wrong answer. But come in anyway."

He sniffed the air and moaned. "Oh...how do you do that?"

"Ellie's Pizza and Pasta Bar open for business. Let me throw some butter and garlic on this and it can join the pizza for a few minutes." Ellie took the bread from Ben.

"Your supermarket downstairs has all sorts of nice things. I got what appears to be fresh Greek salad."

"Yum. There's a salad bowl on the table if you'd like to decanter into it?"

Ellie glanced at Ben as he tipped the salad into the bowl. He'd changed from his normal suit and tie into jeans and T-shirt. With his too-long hair, perpetual two-day growth, and the hard condition he maintained, he was more surfer than detective. But that's why people trusted him so readily. People like Michael.

"Shall I pour you another glass?" He was on the other side of the counter, fingers curled around the bottle she'd left there.

"As long as you join me. There's another glass on the table."

Ellie removed the pizza from the oven, pushing the bread in a bit further. "Not bad for a handful of ingredients!" Hunger gnawed at her stomach. Much better than panic, or tension, or shock. "You might need to fight me for it."

He poured two glasses of wine. "I've seen how you fight and much as I want pizza, I'd like to avoid any injuries to my...er..."

"Oh, that wasn't fighting. I was helping you do your job."

How she kept her face straight was a miracle. Something like happiness bubbled up inside and for the first time in forever, Ellie's heart didn't ache. Her stomach was only hungry, and the tension she'd carried for so long lifted.

"Are you laughing?" Ben was suddenly in the kitchen beside her, his eyes dark pools, but ones with mirth lurking in their depths.

Ellie picked up the pizza cutter and waggled it at him. "Out of my kitchen, Detective. You've seen me in action without a weapon so imagine what I could do with—"

Ben captured her hand and gently removed the cutter. "I'd rather not consider it. Why don't we eat on the balcony? I can cut the pizza if you like."

The warmth of his hand crept along her arm, then swept through her body until the heat rose to her neck, then face. She looked away. He mustn't know what he still did to her after all this time.

He released her hand. "Shall I slice the bread as well?"

She nodded. "Um, sure. I'll move everything outside."

Ellie slipped out of the kitchen. She was sure Ben watched her, probably wondering why she'd suddenly stopped the banter. In a few minutes she'd relocated the contents of the dining table to the one on the balcony and turned on an overhead light.

"Ready! Don't you have one of those bells?"

Back inside, Ellie shook her head at him. "Just yell 'service'."

Ben topped up their glasses. Nothing remained of the pizza, and only a few slices of the bread was left. Whatever Ellie touched turned to gold, at least around food. Her earlier happy mood disappeared the minute he'd touched her and try as he might over dinner, the light in her eyes was down a notch.

"Twice in a week."

Ellie tilted her head to one side.

"Home cooked meals from Chef Ellie."

She gave him a small smile and picked up her wine glass. "I admit to enjoying cooking. I'd forgotten how much."

"Then, don't stop."

"I want more, I think." She sipped, then gazed out across the city. "Once Dad comes back, or...well, you know, then I have some ideas I might explore."

"Such as?"

"Not really formed yet, but something around food."

"About time."

She finally looked at him. "I'm single again. Dennis will be out of my life one way or another, so as long as Dad can find a way to keep the business and find someone else...to take my role..."

"Even if he doesn't."

Doubt crossed her face.

"Jack will always want you at Bannerman Wealth Group. He can't help himself."

"You don't know what drives him."

"Oh, Ellie. I do." Ben chose his words with care. "Jack had the childhood from hell. He looked out for his mother and siblings when nobody would only to lose them in a car accident just as things were getting better. One way or another, he dragged himself out of a life of misery. I have more respect for your father than you think. And I don't dislike him, never have."

"Why am I hearing this now? Not then?" Her face was so troubled he wanted to reach across and touch it. But he didn't.

"Would you have listened?"

"Yes."

Ben leaned back in his chair. "Will you listen now?"

"I'm not certain revisiting the past is a good idea. So much happened, Ben. To me. To Michael." Her voice was a whisper. "I've lost my brother because you arrested him."

"*That's* what you believe?"

Sorrow welled inside him. Michael was his friend before he met Ellie and fell so far in love with her there was no coming back. All this time she'd thought he was the reason Michael overdosed. He took another mouthful of wine, using the moment to think. "If Michael could coherently speak, he'd say otherwise."

"Coherently speak? He can't really talk at all."

"Sure, he can if you listen hard enough." Ben said.

"How on earth do you know what he can and can't do?"

"The point is, after prison and once he got clean, he thanked me for saving him. You might not like this, but he knew he was out of control and the arrest and prison time changed his life."

Ellie was on her feet, fury pouring out of her. "He thanked you? For taking him from the career he loved and throwing him behind bars? My God, Ben, will you say anything to make yourself look good?"

"You have no idea, Ellie. No idea! He was a drug addict on

the verge of ruining the lives of other people. If you think for one minute I wanted to arrest my friend—my best friend— then you don't know me."

"Then I don't know you." Her shoulder slumped and she went to the railing, leaning against it with her arms crossed. "Did I ever?"

"Yeah." The anger drained away and he joined her. "You do. You have fine instincts and a beautiful heart. That same heart sees the good in Jack and never the control he has to have."

For a while they both stared down at the street. For the first time in his life, Ben wanted to swap the city for something else. Anything. Mountains or ocean, but not here. Take Ellie and run away, run so fast the sadness and tragedy of their past would be lost forever. His fingers clenched around the railing and his head dropped at the futility of his thoughts.

"I wish we could sail away."

She spoke so softy he thought he'd misheard her. Perhaps he'd wished the words into existence. He shifted his stance to watch her. Her eyes were toward the distant sea framed between buildings.

"Every time I'm on *Sea Angel*, she yearns to be free. I feel her tug at her ropes, teasing me with the promise of a full spinnaker on the open sea."

"She's yours to take."

Ellie turned to face him. Tears sparkled in her eyes. "Remember when I told you there were conditions around her? When Dad gave me *Sea Angel*, I had to work seven full years for him and then she was mine."

"You've done more than that."

"Apparently my taking a year off started the clock again. He said I'd broken our agreement and I was lucky he was prepared to start over." Her eyes never left his. "Exactly like my job. Gone and given away when I only needed the first break from work or study of my life. How long did you and I ever had spent together?"

"Never more than a long weekend."

"We didn't stand a chance."

"Ellie—"

"Is there any wine left?"

Ellie collected the wine glasses and went inside. He grabbed the plates and followed her. She was opening another bottle. "I hope you didn't leave your car downstairs again. Tyres are expensive."

"Andy dropped me off. I'll be discussing the damage done to the last lot with Dale Grant tomorrow."

"How did you know about him?" Ellie sploshed wine into both glasses, her hands visibly shaking. "I know you rang, and I'd missed your calls. But what made you find him and how did you know he'd go to the carpark?"

Ben took both glasses and led the way to the sofa. Ellie sat and curled her legs under her and accepted the glass he offered.

"Meg traced the signal from the camera in the guest house to him. His previous employer identified him as the possible thief of something we found in the empty apartment overlooking the pier. His description rang a bell with me."

"Oh. Do you mean his smell?"

"I do. And there's a camera in the elevator. Your concierge knew exactly where you were and was in something of a panic."

Nothing like the panic I was in.

He'd burst through the fire door and taken the stairs in leaps, only just making it to the elevator as the doors opened. Ellie's face behind her captor almost tore his heart out.

"Did he kill Frank Barlow?"

"No idea." Ben sighed. "Hopefully, he'll be talkative in the morning. His apartment had only a handful of clothes and a bed. Nothing else. And that gym bag he carried? Found it in his car with a balaclava, black pants and top, and bags of pills."

"He was dealing?"

"Dunno. But he will be off the streets for some time. I need to use your bathroom."

"Feel free."

A few minutes later, Ben wandered back, stopping again at the photos on the wall. There was a new addition. Ellie, her eyes alight with happiness, stood on a beach with an arm around Michael and the other around Ben. They'd been dating for a few weeks and he had no idea then about the drugs, or Jack's controlling ways.

"We were happy." Ellie was at his side, her finger tracing Michael's smile. "I found it the other day at the back of a drawer."

"When did you see him last?"

Ellie walked away to the kitchen. "Michael? A couple of days ago."

"I can wash up." Ben leaned on the counter.

"Maybe you should go." She ran water into the sink.

"Okay. You're mad at me."

"All I know is Michael will never be the same. Maybe he forgave you."

"How often does Jack visit him?"

"Dad pays for everything for him."

"I didn't ask that. He won't visit him because—"

"Because what?" Ellie turned the tap off and spun around. "Go on, tell me what your theory is."

"For god sake, Ellie, it isn't a theory. I was there when Jack told Michael to his face what a disappointment he was. His exact words haunt me."

"He would just have been upset."

"Stop defending your father! What he did was indefensible."

Ellie pushed past him, to the front door. "I don't want to hear anymore."

Ben got the message and met her at the door, but he wasn't ready to go. "Jack disowned Michael. He told him to never be in his sight again and never contact you or your mother."

"No." Ellie's voice wavered. "He...wouldn't."

"I was there. Jack said he was arranging an order to ensure he stayed away and would prosecute him for trespassing if he stepped foot back on Bannerman property. A few hours later, Michael overdosed. You want someone to blame? You're looking at the wrong man."

The colour left Ellie's face and her eyes pleaded for this not to be true. Her lips parted as if to speak, then she shook her head and opened the door.

"I'll go. And I'm sorry but you needed the truth."

"Ben?"

They were so close the heat from her body touched his.

He needed to wrap her up in his arms and erase the harsh words between them.

The fire in her eyes flickered out. "I wish we'd never met."

As the door closed behind him, pain cut through Ben's gut. No sailing off into the night.

FIFTY-FOUR
SECURITY ALERT

12 December

Ellie was in her office long before dawn. Whatever sleep she'd managed brought distressing dreams and she'd ended up calling the concierge to escort her to her car. Getting in the elevator was harder than she'd expected, and her heart was thumping by the time the doors opened in the carpark. On her way to Bannerman House, she phoned the control room and asked for someone to meet her downstairs.

She felt weak and useless asking for escorts everywhere, but the alternative was to freeze up or jump at every shadow. It would pass. Glen checked the executive floor and turned on every light, then he left after she refused his offer to stay in the reception area. Ellie helped herself to coffee from the kitchen and locked herself in her office.

The whiteboard mocked her. Dennis was set up but why by Dale Grant? Who was he and what was his motive for his actions? She turned it around, not wanting to think about it anymore.

Coffee helped fire her brain up and she powered through

the paperwork she'd taken home last night. After getting another cup, and locking herself in again, she glanced outside. Daylight was close. Today was about making decisions. Even about Dad.

"He told him never to set foot in his sight again." Ben had said.

No. He wouldn't say that.

"To never contact you, or your mother."

Ellie dropped her head into her arms. Michael's love of family matched his love of life. Of all of them, he was the one who'd regularly track down their mother on some island, flying in to spend a few days fishing with her in pristine waters. It annoyed Dad when he'd return with his broad grin and gifts from his trips, but Michael eventually would make him smile with stories of Gabi's beautiful illustrations and strange food combinations.

She pushed her seat back and went to the whiteboard. With a black marker, she wrote on the exposed side.

Dad

Left suicide note

Phoned later to tell me where to look for note—probably a second note (so he's not dead)

Lied about meeting Dennis to sail

Selling the business and Foundation

Took Michael's special gift of gin—last bottle

Refused to approve Paul's last upgrade (did he want cameras to fail?)

Left his obligations without notice

The words got messier as she scribbled faster, her hand putting in writing what she refused to acknowledge aloud.

Forced me to change careers to help him when Michael became an actor

Gave me Sea Angel and changed the terms of agreement

Told Michael he was disowned

Told Michael never to contact me or Gabi

Gave my job to Dennis
Encouraged my relationship with Dennis
Controls me.
CONTROLS ME!

She stormed away from the whiteboard. At her desk, she turned and with all her strength, threw the marker at it. It hit the board with a satisfying crack and fell to the floor in pieces.

"No more, Dad. I'll make sure you're okay, but no more of this shit." She squatted, arms around her body. "No more."

Always the good girl, the one who stayed, the reliable one. Enough. Jack Bannerman was an adult who did not need his daughter to fill some void in his own being. Whatever game he was playing with his disappearing act, he'd put her at risk.

She dragged herself to her feet. Staff would arrive soon and there were meetings to attend. The police might be finished on this floor, but there was a lot of cleaning to do and putting the offices back together. All the PAs would be busy, and she'd get Joni and Mark to call on assistance from the teams as needed.

Would Mark be here though? Joni had messaged her last night to say she'd not been able to raise him at home. No more missing people. Please.

Ellie took a photo of the whiteboard, then cleaned it. The building was stirring, and she had to fix her makeup.

Mascara removed and reapplied, extra powder added to reduce the redness, Ellie pulled her hair back into a tight pony-tail. If she looked serious and in charge, hopefully nobody would ask her personal questions.

Her heart was empty whenever her mind wandered to last night. Ben needed to keep his distance, for both their sakes, and now, perhaps, he would.

Joni was on the phone behind reception when Ellie returned from her second meeting of the morning. No sign of Mark. Joni waved at Ellie to come to her.

"Thank you again, I will pass the news on." She hung up as Ellie reached the desk. "Oh, this is good news for once! That was Mrs Campbell. Mr Campbell is awake, well asleep again, but he is expected to fully recover!"

"Joni, that is wonderful!" Ellie reached over the desk to hug her. At last something positive in all this gloom. "How is Mrs Campbell holding up?"

"Tired. But she said she'd been a bit upset with you and asked me to tell you personally you are welcome to visit as soon as the doctors allow it."

"Let's hope everything is going in the right direction now." Ellie stepped back. "Have you heard from Mark?"

"Yes, where is he?" Dennis walked in.

"Why are you here?" This was a complication Ellie hadn't expected.

"I work here. So, where is my PA?"

"Let's talk in my office." Ellie said.

Dennis brushed past Ellie. "No. In my office."

She rolled her eyes at Joni, who covered her mouth as if to control either a giggle or gasp. "Let me know when my next appointment arrives."

Ellie sat opposite Dennis, who was shrugging off his suit jacket. "How are you?" His face was drawn.

"How do you think? Thrown in jail for nothing, interrogated for hours, then bang, lost my car to the bloody cops. Lawyer will fight that, of course."

"Good luck. Isn't it mandatory loss for a month if you're over the limit?"

"Where is Mark?"

"We don't know. He left yesterday afternoon and hasn't returned any calls."

Dennis dropped into his seat. "Another missing person?

Joni can fill in for him."

"Joni has plenty to do. If you insist on working, then you'll do it without an assistant."

"Insist on working? What else does a CEO do?"

"Oh. You haven't heard." Ellie crossed her legs. "With you under arrest, Campbell in hospital, and Dad still God-knows-where, the board asked me to take over for now."

"Finally got what you wanted. Not only your old job back, but mine as well."

"Get real. I don't want either but nor do you—or why would you put yourself and other people at risk by driving drunk? Why not go home to Meredith?"

Dennis opened his mouth, then leaned back, arms folded, his expression changing from anger to something…something like regret.

This should be good.

After a moment, he sighed. "I stuffed up, Ellie. When you went to London, after our argument, I thought for sure you'd come back and tell me to leave. So, I left first."

"I had no intention of doing that, Dennis."

"But then, Jack vanished, and Meredith freaked out and refused to stay alone at the house—"

"Cut the bull. There are live-in staff. She could have called her sister, or a friend. This was the perfect excuse for you to be where you wanted." How she kept her voice calm, she had no idea. "You've always wanted Dad's job and you got it, just for a moment. And his wife. Because you thought I was going to leave you." She leaned forward and lowered her tone. "And you wonder why I asked you to see a marriage counsellor with me to talk about communication."

"I'm not with Meredith!"

Ellie smiled. "You're with whoever gives you the best shot at controlling this company. She told you about the pre-nuptial agreement, didn't she?"

"We're still married, El. I'll go see a counsellor. Let's give it another shot."

"Sorry." Getting to her feet, Ellie smoothed her skirt. "That boat sailed."

"I'll sink your damned boat, baby."

"Now you sound like the deranged ex in a book I once read. Didn't work then either." She didn't look back as she left. Dennis spluttering behind her was the best thing she'd heard in days.

FIFTY-FIVE
NEED FOR FREEDOM

An hour later, Ellie left the second of the two security company reps for the day in the foyer, more puzzled than ever. Neither were prepared to quote on the spot, but both were shocked at the low-quality cameras.

Paul wasn't in the control room when she'd taken them there, which was just as well as he'd have taken offence at some of the descriptive language used by the second rep.

"Worse than rubbish."

Will had nodded.

She tapped on Dennis' door and almost changed her mind at his expression. "This is purely about the business."

"What?"

"Why is our security system antiquated if Paul upgrades it every couple of years?"

"Ask Dekeles."

"I'm asking you. What do you know about past upgrades?"

"Why the hell does this matter right now?"

"Because Paul is pushing for me to sign a purchase order."

"Push back."

"I have. But two independent security experts just told me our system is crap. Paul says Dad refused the last upgrade."

"Rubbish. It was done when you were in Sydney for the charity ball. I remember because Campbell and I spent the day working downstairs while it was done. Jack's office and yours were free because of the event you were at for the Foundation."

"Then why aren't they working properly?"

"Probably bought them on the cheap and pocketed the rest. I'm busy." Dennis went back to his laptop.

Joni came back from the kitchen with a coffee as Ellie headed for her office. "Would you like me to bring you one?"

"Thanks, but I over-caffeinated myself this morning. Nothing about Mark?"

"Afraid not."

"Would you ask human resources to send his personnel file to me?"

"Of course." Joni lowered her voice, eyes flashing toward Dennis' office. "You are still acting CEO? Not…him?"

"I am. And I've told him you are too busy to take on Mark's role, so if he gives you grief, let me know."

"I handled Mr Bannerman's moods for all these years. I'll be fine. But you look exhausted."

"I want to find Dad."

"If you don't mind me saying, he wouldn't want you running yourself into the ground."

He should have considered that before doing a vanishing act.

"Thanks for caring about me."

Back in her office, Ellie stood at the window. Always four walls around her, or at least, it felt that way. Was this why Gabi left? No view or sound or smell of the sea from the Canterbury house, and as pretty as the gardens were, and as soothing as the waterfall in the pool, for a person with the heart of a nomad, the restrictions must have stifled her. Dad's house was only a few minutes' drive from the bay, but it wasn't anything like the wild beach front house on stilts they've lived in for the first few years of marriage.

Gabi once told Ellie how Dad bought two yachts. *Wind Drifter* and *Sea Angel*. As Ellie sat on her lap, Gabi's face lit up as she whispered the names and promised they'd sail every summer and even during winter. "No day is a bad day to be on the water."

One winter's day, Gabi proved it by taking *Wind Drifter* and leaving them behind.

"Where are you, Mum?"

When she turned to her desk, she noticed the whiteboard was moved. After cleaning off the one side, she'd pushed it back against the wall to hide her theories on the other. But one end was a good few inches from the wall. A marker lay on the floor. Not the one she'd earlier thrown at the whiteboard.

Her phoned beeped a message alert. Ben. Her heart jumped seeing his name.

Need to ask a few questions about Dale Grant. Can you drop into the station around three?

At least he was talking to her. Kind of.

I'll be there.

First, she needed answers from Paul, and then a trip to the hospital. She collected her briefcase and handbag.

See you then.

She set her phone to remind herself. As she left, she didn't bother locking her door. What was the point?

FIFTY-SIX
FALLING DOWN

Paul wasn't in his office. Nor the control room, but Will knew. "Said he needed to pull the camera apart."

Great. Another one down.

Ellie was proud of herself getting into the elevator and down to the carpark. The doors opened to Paul on a ladder, barking into his phone. He glanced at her and lowered his voice.

Rather than waiting, Ellie put her briefcase and bag in her car, sliding her phone and car keys into a pocket. By the time she walked back, he was off the phone.

"Damned thing keeps going on and off."

"Do you happen to know who went into my office this morning?" Might as well lead with the latest problem.

He stopped to glance down at her. "No. Wouldn't Joni have seen?"

"It was before eight. Nobody else was on the floor and I left to attend to other business. Only now I find something's been moved in there."

"What has?"

"The whiteboard."

He returned to fiddling with the camera. "Sure, you didn't

leave the wheels unlocked on it? Those things have a mind of their own sometimes."

"You're suggesting a huge, heavy whiteboard decided to pull one end of itself away from the wall? How much movement is there in the building?"

"I'll give Will a call and see if he can look. The cleaners were up there today."

"Not at that time and they've been told not to touch anything on that floor."

Paul called the camera a bad name and climbed down the ladder. "See. Everything is falling apart. Any chance you can sign the purchase order?"

"Not until I get some assurances about the company you're dealing with. Your supplier."

At the bottom of the ladder, Paul turned to Ellie, one hand on a rung above him. His body was rigid and she had to control the instinct to step back.

"Same supplier we've always used. Jack approved them years ago and they are quick, efficient—"

"And poor quality. Cheap, Paul."

"Not poor quality."

"I've had two firms in today. Both told me the cameras, monitors, everything, is cheap and nasty. These are security experts who will give us new quotes."

"You've done what?" Paul almost shouted and now, Ellie did step back. "Sorry. Sorry, I didn't mean to raise my voice at you." He ran a hand through his hair. "I'm that stressed about Jack and completely blame myself for not being there when he needed me. I didn't see the signs, El."

"What signs."

He shook his head and began packing up the ladder.

"Paul, do you know something about Dad?"

"Not my place to talk."

Ellie grabbed his arm. "Yes, it is. I'm going crazy not knowing, or half knowing. We found a note he'd written. Like a suicide note. But then he left a message telling me where to find it and that I'd understand. All I can think is that he was going to… hurt himself, and changed his mind. So, there must have been a second letter."

Paul leaned the ladder against the wall. "Let me get this straight. Jack left a note which you just found. But there's no evidence that he's off'd himself. And then a full day or so later, he phones you to say what? To look for the note?"

"It doesn't add up."

"Oh my god. I'm an idiot." Paul put his head in his hands.

"What? What's wrong?"

"You have to find your mother. You have to speak to Gabi."

"What?"

He dropped his hands. "I just remembered a conversation with Jack. It was a few days before he disappeared, and I don't know why I forgot about it. God, I'm sorry, Ellie."

"Forgot what?"

"He was talking about her. Gabi. Wishing he'd never let her go but had kept the old beach house. He said he'd never even been to visit her cabin and how it must be a peaceful place. Somewhere to refill the battery. A place of happiness."

The bottle of gin. It was a gift from Michael, and he'd had the labels made up with the image of a yacht. A particular yacht. *Wind Drifter*.

"I wonder if he's gone to see her. Probably not. I mean, he'd have let you know. Let someone know. Wouldn't he?" Paul stared at Ellie until she nodded.

"I wish it were that. But Gabi isn't even in Australian waters. Hasn't been in weeks."

Her heart pounded as excitement rose in her chest but she controlled her tone. "I have an appointment."

"I'll walk you to the car. Damned upset I wasn't there to help you last night." He fell into step.

Something didn't ring true but Ellie's thoughts were elsewhere. They passed the spot where Dennis usually parked.

"Guess you'll be looking for a new right hand soon." Paul nodded at the empty space.

"Oh, Dennis is here. But no licence or car."

Paul was quiet as they reached her car. "Thanks, Paul. I'll be back...in a bit."

"Sure. Ellie, just so you know, I always respected you. Always." He disappeared back through the carpark, leaving Ellie with the oddest sense of unrest.

Any plans to visit Campbell were replaced by a new mission. Ellie drove to her apartment and parked out the front. All the way there, her heart refused to stop racing as thoughts hammered her. What if Gabi was back? There were any number of reasons why the satellite phone wasn't working, and perhaps the neighbour hadn't seen her come home thanks to the distance between moorings. Or she might be out on the water, sailing along the coast.

To think Dad might be with her, out of communication range but fit and well...Ellie could barely work through the ramifications.

After changing into shorts, T-shirt, and runners, she grabbed a small backpack from her cupboard and tossed in a change of clothes, extra socks, and anything else she could think of. If she was going so far, she'd be there overnight. And if Dad was there, she'd need the whole night to make sense of it.

On her way out, she let the concierge know she'd be back tomorrow. No point having him send out a search party.

In her car, she sat for a moment to think it through. This was probably another wild goose chase. At the best, she'd find Dad with Gabi. And the worst? *Wind Drifter* not moored and Gabi not home. In which case she'd let herself into the cabin and have a night away from all of this. Either way she had to go. She pulled out onto the road.

A dark sedan followed Ellie's car. She went through the tunnel then settled into the left lane on the freeway.

The driver dialled his phone from a few cars back.

The phone rang once before answering. "Where is she?"

"Heading to dear Mumma's place by the look of it."

"Send me your location. I'll be half an hour or more behind so you find some way of slowing her down."

"And then we're done?" There was a long pause. "Dale and I need that payment."

"Sure, Mark. Then we're done."

Mark hung up. The minute that money was in his account, he was out of here. Dale or no Dale.

FIFTY-SEVEN

KALEIDOSCOPE

"Mrs Connor wants this processed as a priority. So, I'll wait for the transaction number, thanks."

Paul glanced at his watch as one of Campbell's team looked over the signed purchase order.

"I'll just need to confirm this with her—" The woman reached for a phone.

"She signed it five minutes before leaving for the hospital to see your boss. If the cameras upstairs had been working properly, we'd have known Mr Boyd had fallen much earlier and got help faster. That's why she's instructed me to begin work immediately on the upgrade. Until the funds are in their account, the supplier won't order what we need."

"Oh. I should really follow protocol for such a large amount."

"Sure. Go ahead. I'm sure she won't mind being interrupted at the hospital." Paul crossed his arms.

The woman checked the signature and nodded. "It won't take a moment."

He watched every keystroke as the details of the account were tapped in, then the amount.

Come on.

"Sorry. It can take a while sometimes. Ah, there we go." She wrote the transaction number on the purchase order and stood. "I'll photocopy this."

"I'll do it. I have to give Mr Connor a copy so I'll bring one back for you."

He almost snatched the paper from her fingers and strode back to his own office. His palms were so sweaty his hand slipped off his door handle.

Get a grip and focus.

One more thing to do. He locked his door and pulled the box from his bottom drawer. Setting it beside his briefcase, he transferred two passports and multiple wads of hundred-dollar notes. From the wall behind he took the photograph of himself with Ellie and Jack. He grinned at Jack's face.

"Thanks, mate. Been a pleasure."

He dropped it into the bin under his desk.

For once, Ben appreciated Andy's good cop, bad cop routine. Because if Andy wasn't being the aggressor, he'd have pinned Dale Grant to the wall by now. Just the sight of the man raised his blood pressure.

Still acting as though he was mortally injured, Dale had tried to avoid being released from hospital earlier, but there was no lasting damage except to his pride.

An hour into the interview and almost nothing had come out of his mouth. Not even a request for legal representation. Arrogant if he thought he didn't need it. Or stupid.

"Let's go over this again. You moved into an apartment on the same floor as Ellie Connor around three months ago." Ben read off his notes but only to avoid looking at the man. "You broke into an empty apartment overlooking the pier where her yacht is tied, even storing stolen bottled water there. And your phone was the recipient of footage from an illegal camera looking over a safe in her father's house."

"Guest house."

"He speaks." Andy pulled up a seat. "When did you install the camera?"

"I didn't."

"So, you have a partner?"

Dale laughed shortly. "Partner implies someone you work with."

"You worked for someone? Were paid to watch Ellie and Dennis? Or Jack."

Hands clenched beneath the table, Ben watched Dale's face and body language. He wanted to talk. They needed the right questions. The right incentive.

"If you help us with this investigation, we'll try to help you out."

"I don't want your help." Dale scowled.

"Bad choice." Andy said. "Won't be hard to make a case against you for the murder of Frank Barlow, the disappearance of Jack Bannerman, and the attack on Ellie Connor. All adds up to one long jail term."

"Yeah, but I didn't touch Frank or Jack. And she attacked me if you remember. We just happened to be in the same elevator, and she went all psycho-bitch."

Ben's hands snaked out before he could stop them, grabbing Dale's forearms. "There was a camera in the lift, idiot."

"What Detective Rossi means, Mr Grant," Andy kicked Ben under the table. "is we have plenty of evidence before we even get to the stash of illegal substances in your gym bag."

Hands back under the table, Ben turned to Andy. "He's not going to talk. I think we need to pass him over to Homicide."

"Sure. I'll ring McNamara and get them here."

"I didn't kill Frank. I wasn't even in the area. Ask Mark about the date because we were at his place all night with some ladies."

"Who is Mark?"

Dale shook his head and looked down. "No more questions. I want a lawyer."

Dennis stormed from his office to reception, banging the flat of his hand on the top of the counter. Joni jumped, and excused herself from the phone call she was on.

"Where the hell is Ellie?"

"She went down to speak with Paul some time ago."

"How long?"

"More than an hour. She was going to see Mr Boyd at the hospital afterwards, and then going to the police station."

"Damn. Do you know anything about this purchase order he wanted signed?"

"Only that Mrs Connor told him she was getting outside quotes first. They haven't come in yet, so I imagine nothing has changed."

"It's changed alright. Finance put through the transaction to the supplier. Can nobody run this place except me?" Not waiting for a response, Dennis stomped to the elevators.

Whatever Dekeles was playing at, he was about to stop it. After Ellie's earlier interruption, he'd double checked his memory about the last upgrade. "Told you." She never appreciated how right he always was. Not content, he'd dug around the records for the past decade of security expenses and almost fell out of his chair at the overspend.

Paul's office was locked. Dennis phoned Will who arrived puffing a few minutes later with a spare key card.

"Stay at the door. Don't want Dekeles accusing me of stealing anything."

Dennis frowned at the flickering monitors. The desk was tidy. Too tidy. Had the moron simply swept the usual pile of papers into his bin? He went to see.

"What the hell?"

"Sir?" Will peered over the desk as Dennis pulled the photo frame from the bin.

They both looked at the wall where it belonged.

"Do you know where he is?"

"Last I know, Mrs Connor was heading down to the carpark to talk with him. He was fixing the camera over the lift."

"And?"

"Couldn't fix it."

"Tell me his car is still there. And by that, I mean go and look!"

Will ran.

Jack. Frank Barlow. Mark. Ellie?

FIFTY-EIGHT

HEADING TO THE CABIN

The road had long since narrowed to single lanes and Ellie needed a break. At the first petrol station, she pulled in.

She filled the car and locked it even out here, in the countryside where cows lowed in a paddock nearby and the traffic was a trickle. After a comfort stop, Ellie stocked up on bottled water and chocolate. She waited as the attendant heated a pie, her growling stomach a reminder she'd not eaten since last night.

Back in the car, she sat for a moment, getting the air con up as she fiddled with the radio. The afternoon was humid, and she hoped any storms would hold off until she was in the cabin. A hand appeared from nowhere to tap on her window and she jumped.

A woman called out. "Your tyre is a bit low, love."

Once she began to breathe again, she checked. If the lady hadn't noticed, Ellie might have ended up miles away with a flat on a country road. In minutes, she'd refilled it and checked the rest of the tyres, just in case.

The road was quiet and would only get quieter. Gabi's cabin was tucked along an estuary near a national park. Access was limited and she'd need to leave her car in a designated area and hike down. It was the perfect deterrent for unwelcome visitors. Possibly even welcome ones. If she'd had more time and the threat of storms was over she'd have sailed *Sea Angel* here instead.

Ellie turned onto the long road heading toward the sea. Her spirits lifted a little. She needed her mother like never before.

"So much to tell you."

Even the bad stuff. Like gym man in the elevator.

Tension gripped Ellie's stomach and she opened a bottle of water. Shouldn't think about him. Ben was there in time and she wouldn't have gone with him anyway. All she'd have needed was a second to reach into her handbag and he'd have been screaming louder than when she hit him.

Ellie's phone beeped an alarm. She pulled over, puzzled.

3pm. Police Station.

Whoops.

She messaged Ben. *Sorry, forgot about coming in. On way to see Gabi. Back tomorrow.*

As she eased back onto the road another car was behind in the far distance.

A message came through, but she'd had enough stops and ignored it. If Ben was put out by her forgetfulness, she would apologise later. She had so much to apologise for. Add it to the list.

Ben tapped a message on his phone, barely paying attention to Andy as he put a coffee in front of him. Back at their desks since abandoning the interrogation, he'd checked twice with the front desk in case Ellie was waiting out there.

"You find her?" Andy moved a pile of files for a spot for his own coffee and sat. "She okay?"

"Ellie is apparently on her way to see Gabi Bannerman."

"Isn't she along the coast somewhere?"

"Trying to find out exactly where as we speak. Ellie forgot about our interview."

"Does she sound alright though? Not still upset about last night?"

Ben shot a look at Andy. "What about last night?"

"Maybe we're thinking of different things. Dale Grant and the elevator?"

"Right. I don't know because all she did was message me. And she's not replying now."

He stared at the screen of the phone as if that would make a message appear.

The landline rang and Andy answered. Then, offered the phone to Ben.

"You might want to take this. Dennis Connor."

Ben mouthed "What now?" and took the receiver. "Yes, Dennis."

"Don't worry, I don't want to talk to you, either."

"So...?"

"So, Paul Dekeles has disappeared. My wife has disappeared. My PA, Mark, has disappeared."

"Mark? What's his last name?"

"That's what you worry about? Mark Grant."

"Damn. Hold on." Ben covered the mouthpiece and leaned toward Andy. "Mark Grant is Dennis' PA. Find out where he is."

"Are you there?"

"Yes, Dennis. You said Paul is gone."

"Aren't you concerned about Ellie?"

"I know roughly where she is. Tell me about Paul."

"The little shit forged Ellie's signature and got money transferred to a wholesaler, but I think it is a front for something else. I reckon he's been stealing from Jack for years."

"Okay. We're on our way. Don't touch anything in his office for now."

"Hang on, I—"

Ben hung up. "Oh, do you think he had more to say?"

Andy chuckled and grabbed his coffee.

FIFTY-NINE
CLOSER

"Are we there yet?" Ellie asked the car, bored from too long behind the wheel. The landscape was dry after a summer with little rain and endless brown paddocks were dotted with giant round hay bales. Across to the west, storm clouds brewed, but so often they fizzled out as soon as making landfall.

She'd tried Gabi's satellite phone again with no response. It wasn't even ringing, so who knows where Gabi was. This might well be one long and tiring drive for nothing. But the further she got from the city, the more her heart lightened. To escape the worry and pressure of the past few days was a gift and reinforced her musing last night about her future life.

The car she'd noticed early was closer and was the same make and colour as Paul's, but then again, the city was full of them. He was probably arguing with Dennis in his office. Maybe he'd even try to get him to sign the purchase order.

Not your problem today, Ellie!

She accelerated

———

Before leaving the station, Ben detoured to the holding cell.

Dale glared at him from behind the bars. "Still saying nothing."

"Your brother doesn't mind talking."

"Shut up."

"Yup. Mark happily told us you are behind all of this. Blames you for everything from Jack's disappearance to Fred Barlow's death. We know he was just an insider."

"Bullshit." Dale stumbled to his feet and grabbed the bars. "All we did was agree to help a friend out. Keep an eye on a couple of people."

"Which friend?"

"Want a lawyer."

"On their way. Who's behind it, mate? If you and Mark are just helping, who is the puppet master?"

Back on his bed, Dale turned away. "Lawyer."

Ben relayed this all to Andy on their way to Bannerman House. "Who, Andy?"

"If Dennis is right, then Paul Dekeles. Syphoning funds through a shell company. Didn't Meg say something about that website you showed her? But what does it have to do with Jack?"

They were met in the foyer by Will. In the lift, he barely waited for the doors to close. "Listen, please. I've seen stuff and I want to know if I can get some protection. Immunity."

Andy straightened. "Protection from?"

"No. Tell me if it is possible first."

"Anything is. And we'd appreciate your help."

Will nodded. "Whole lot of strange stuff been going on here. Doors unlocked when I'd checked them as locked. The night Mr Boyd fell? I was supposed to be checking the floor every half hour but Mr Dekeles sent me on a wild goose chase. He's made me keep quiet about things the bosses should know. But I got kids."

"He threatened you?"

"Kinda. Anyway, I kept this. As protection." He shoved a USB stick into Ben's hand as the door opened.

"What's on it?"

"Mr Bannerman."

Ben and Andy exchanged a look.

"Where is Mr Connor?" Ben set off toward Paul's office.

Will hurried to catch up. "Waiting."

Dennis sat behind Paul's desk, face blank. "About time."

"What have you touched?"

"Nothing. Except this." He pointed at the framed photo. "It was in the bin."

Ben slipped on gloves and picked it up. "Wasn't this on the wall?"

"Give the man a medal."

"Where was the photo taken?"

"Fundraiser last year for the Foundation. In Sydney."

"Is there some significance?" Ben turned it over. The clips at the back were bent out of shape, so he forced them aside.

"Funny story. Ellie asked me when the last security upgrade happened. It was then, while she and Jack were away. She knew nothing about it. Which is why she's unsuitable for the job." Dennis said.

Ben removed the back. "Andy, look."

There was an envelope between the photo and the back.

"Jack's writing. One of his personal envelopes." Dennis stood to see better. "Is it addressed to Ellie?"

"Yes." Ben opened the envelope and slid out one page—almost the same as the one found in the rum bottle. He let Andy read over his shoulder as he silently scanned the words.

Darling Ellie,

Sorry for the cloak and dagger routine, but once you get to the cabin I'll fully explain. Had a health scare and almost did something stupid, until I thought about spending some time with your mother. Get her take on things. See, I've messed up some decisions about the business, and with Michael, and now I want to make amends. Just hope it isn't too late. Paul knows where I am, so he'll fill you in and arrange transport here. I've not told anyone else yet. We'll talk soon.

Love,

Dad

"Holy…" Andy breathed out.

"What? Let me see!" Dennis reached for the page and Ben stepped away with it.

"Police evidence. But I have a question and need a straight answer, Dennis." Ben passed the note to Andy, who refolded it and placed it in an evidence bag. "Whose idea was selling the business?"

"Huh? How is that even important. But it was Jack's. He reckoned his doctor told him it was time to slow down."

"And who knew about it?"

"Campbell. Me. And Mark. He worked with Jack on it rather than Joni. Jack didn't want her upset."

"Not Dekeles?"

"Why would that idiot know?"

Will spoke from the door. "Sir, he did know. He told Mark it would be the end of everything. I thought he meant our jobs."

Ben patted him on the shoulder. "Thank you for speaking up. We'll talk another time but appreciate this."

"What about me? I found this, so do I get some special treatment?" Dennis said.

"Yeah. We won't charge you with interfering with an investigation. Yet." Andy said.

Ben didn't bother answering as he strode out, dialling his phone.

A tractor drove down the middle of the road, fast for its bulk but still slow enough to make Ellie brake and peer around in the hope of overtaking. This stretch offered no option but to sit behind the machine and glance at the increasingly stormy sky.

She backed off a bit when the phone rang, flicking accept on the steering wheel, surprised her phone had signal out here.

"Ellie, tell me precisely where you are."

"I sent you a message. On my way to see Gabi. I think Dad might be there."

"He is."

Ellie gasped.

"Do you know where you are? How far away from the cabin?"

"Are you sure he's there?"

"I need you to listen. Paul Dekeles has been embezzling from the company for years. This whole time he's known Jack was with your mother. He is dangerous."

The car behind closed in. Ellie glanced in the rear vision mirror and almost swerved off the road when she saw who the driver was.

"Ben. He's behind me! Oh, God, what do I do?"

"Are you near a town?"

"No! I'm almost at the parking zone which is in the middle of nowhere."

"Get to the cabin and lock all of you in. Help is coming."

Help had no chance of getting there in time. Ellie veered into the middle of the road and accelerated, squeezing past the tractor just as it reached a bend. She floored it, seeing the tractor disappear in her rear vision mirror.

"Ellie?"

"I can't let him get to Gabi and Dad."

The phone dropped out. Ellie told the car to reconnect, but the signal was gone. She gripped the steering wheel until her knuckles were white. Still no sign of Paul. Her speed was too high to be safe and she prayed nothing would get in the way. She needed a head start.

SIXTY
ABOUT JACK

"Local police are an hour away but heading to the point of last contact now." Andy updated Ben as they took stairs two at a time. "Weather conditions are deteriorating with the risk of a storm."

They burst through a fire door onto the roof of the police station. A helicopter approached to land.

Both men carried rifles and wore protective gear. The noise from the helicopter stopped them talking.

A few minutes later, they were above the city skyline. The Yarra River snaked below, with Port Phillip Bay to their right.

"How long?" Ben addressed the pilot through headphones.

"Depends on the weather ahead. I'll let you know."

"We'll get to her, Ben." Andy checked his rifle.

Ben had to believe him. Treat this like a job, track down the bad guy and keep a family safe.

He pulled a tablet from a bag and plugged in the USB Will gave him. He nudged Andy to watch as the image of Jack's office appeared.

It was night. With only the lamp on over his desk, Jack handwrote a note. He reread it, then folded and placed it inside an enve-

lope which he placed on the desk. There was a handgun beside the photo of Gabi and Ellie. He picked up the gun and loaded it.

For a moment, he stared at the photo, before laying it face down.

He pointed the nozzle of the gun to his head and sat for long seconds gazing out of the window.

With a sudden movement, Jack put the gun down. He screwed the note into a tight ball and tossed it into a bin beside the desk.

"Something changed his mind." Andy said.

The screen went black, then another image of the office from the same camera.

There were no lights on. Paul straightened from behind Jack's desk, the balled envelope in his hand.

"He knew all the time." There was nothing else and Ben ripped the USB out and tossed it in the bag. The helicopter rose and fear stabbed at Ben. Not fear of flying. Fear of not getting there in time.

SIXTY-ONE

DANGER IN THE TREES

The parking zone was nothing more than a dirt carpark surrounded by bush with room for maybe thirty vehicles. Ellie slammed her brakes on in the farthest corner and jumped out. She tossed her handbag into the backpack and sprinted into the undergrowth.

As far from the car as she dared go while being able to see it, Ellie planted herself behind a thick bush, peering through prickly branches. Paul's car went past the entrance and she held her breath.

Keep going.

But it backed up and turned in. It circled the carpark and stopped near her car. When the engine was cut, the silence was disturbed by a long roll of thunder.

Paul climbed out, gazing around before checking her car. He pulled something from a pocket.

"Ellie! Ellie, I'm here and have news about Jack!"

Every muscle tensed until her legs ached to run.

"Why are you hiding from me, out of everyone? I'm your friend. The only one you can trust." Paul walked around her car. It was a knife in his hand, glinting from sun through the trees. "We can go away together, El. Find somewhere private and start over."

He leaned down and slashed at her tyres. One, then the others.

It was you who destroyed Ben's tyres!

Her heart sank. She'd expected him to look for her, giving her the chance to get back to her car and drive the way they'd come.

He opened the boot of his car.

She sent her location to Ben's phone, doubting it would reach him but desperate for help. One careful step at a time, she worked her way through the undergrowth to a narrow path. Ellie had no idea where this would lead and she hesitated, looking left and right. Which way?

The boot slammed.

Ellie ran.

SIXTY-TWO

THE HUNTER, 1

He didn't have time for this. Hours on the road and now a trek through the bush.

A million-dollar detour.

The bag was locked in the boot. One handgun was in a pocket and he carried the other. His rifle was slung over a shoulder and would stay there unless he needed to take a long shot.

Finding Ellie shouldn't take long and with her out of the way, he'd hike down to the cabin and take care of the other two. Pity about Gabi, she'd always been nice. There really was no malice behind what needed doing. After all, Jack was responsible for every cent in Paul's bank account—his very secret bank account—so deserved a thanks. Before he died.

More thunder. He glanced up through a break in the trees. The sky was almost dark with the approach of the storm. Now, which way did Ellie go?

SIXTY-THREE
THE HUNTED, 1

Heavy drops of rain hit Ellie's head and arms as she stumbled over rough terrain. There was a creek and she followed it, remembering it would lead her almost to the clifftop before continuing underground to emerge again as a waterfall partway down.

It was years since she'd walked along it with Gabi, but the memory was clear.

Every sound made her glance back, but nothing was there. Glimpses of open ground broke through the trees. She licked rain from her lips rather than stop to get water.

The humidity dropped as the clouds emptied and rain hammered down, plastering her hair to her scalp. Slow thunder growled in the sky. The bush came alive with heightened smells of eucalypt and wattle.

The storm wouldn't last. Even now, the rain eased. Ellie needed to rest. Her legs screamed with fatigue, her back ached from the weight of the backpack. Should she leave it here?

She began to shrug it off.

"El-lie. I'm here to find you."

Both hands over her mouth to suppress a scream, Ellie took

off and splashed through the creek. Overhead, the heavy whir of helicopter blades forced air into the trees.

Ellie sucked in oxygen as she followed the sound of the helicopter. It appeared for a second above her and she threw her arms up.

Wait. See me!

But it moved away. No rescue. No last minute reprieve. No help.

SIXTY-FOUR
THE HUNTER, 2

Paul crouched in undergrowth until the helicopter was gone. The wind had picked up and no pilot in their right mind would risk flying for long in this weather. He had that on his side.

But Ellie was a problem.

Whatever happened to the sweet, naïve girl he'd adored from afar for more than a decade? He'd watched her make terrible choices in men and almost lose everything by defying her father. All he'd ever wanted was for Ellie to see him. Really see him. Not the man looking after security, even when at her side or behind Jack. But as the man he was.

The helicopter left and Paul continued along the creek.

The night he took Ellie out for dinner, they'd been so close. Over an expensive dinner and candlelight, they'd talked. That one time, he'd almost lost sight of what he'd worked so hard to achieve. Almost.

Ellie chose to treat him the way everyone else did. No respect.

And it didn't matter.

There was a million dollars in his bank, plus all the cash Jack carelessly left in no less than four safes. More fool him.

SIXTY-FIVE
THE HUNTED, 2

For as long as she could, Ellie stayed under cover but close to the edge of the bushland. At some point she'd need to cross the open ground between here and the edge of the cliff and then—if she could find the track—descend to the cabin without Paul finding her.

No longer was she worried about why he was doing this. Every move was about survival. Ben's plea for her to find safety, that Paul was dangerous, was etched in her thoughts. Her body responded out of sheer instinct. One foot at a time and careful of where it landed. Keep quiet. Above all, stay invisible.

Why had the helicopter gone? She strained to hear for its rotors but now, the wind was gusting through the trees, branches creaking and groaning. Was it the police or simply a sightseeing chopper too far off course? How long had she been out here? The layer of dark from the storm confused her.

Ellie stopped close to a large tree and took out her phone. There was one bar of signal on it. She began dialling Ben. Behind her, a crack, something breaking. Her head spun to look, to peer through the undergrowth. The wind was playing tricks, surely. Nobody was there.

"Ellie! Time to give up."

She almost shrieked at Paul's voice so close, and the phone flew from her fingers. It hit a rock and bounced away. With every bit of control she had, Ellie forced her body to stay still, flattened against the trunk of the old gum. The crunch of footsteps through the mass of fallen leaves and sticks approached. Terror rose until she was certain she would die in this lonely place.

The wind dropped. Her heart pounded in her ears.

Get to Gabi. Ben will find us.

Last night she'd lied. She didn't wish they'd hadn't met. Only that her wayward heart wouldn't long for him. Bit by bit, Ellie reined in her rapid breath until she could listen to her surroundings again. And she could no longer hear Paul.

SIXTY-SIX
THE HUNTER, 3

She really must believe she was safe, blended in against the trees. But Paul knew where she was. He unslung the rifle from his shoulder. If he used a handgun, he might miss. Just a bit too far for the accuracy required.

He glanced at the safety and flicked it off, then raised the nozzle. She was gone.

Paul swore aloud as he stowed the rifle. In a few seconds he was where she'd been.

Concentrate.

Was she so brave as to run across open ground? Or rather, was she so foolhardy.

Oh, yes. She was. There was a couple of hundred metres of terrain between here and the cliff edge and Ellie was running as if her life depended on it. Which it did.

He liked that. It showed courage.

Paul strode out of the forest.

Ahead, Ellie was close to the edge of the cliff, doubled over. Out of breath, or terrified, didn't matter.

It's over.

"Oh, El-lie."

Her head shot up.

"I'm here to help you."

His loved how his voice carried out in the open.

She was running again, this time along the edge of the cliff. He followed at a walk, hugging the tree line.

He picked up his pace as she disappeared into the gloom. Somewhere he had a flashlight. His hand dug around in a pocket and found it.

Where was she? He crossed the open ground.

A sudden cry and he knew. In a moment he found a narrow path weaving down the cliff.

The helicopter was back, over the sea and parallel to the coastline. Was it close enough to shoot down? He didn't need to. Whoever was inside wasn't the problem unless it was Ben Rossi. Its flashing lights disappeared down the coast.

"Are you down there, Ellie? You don't need to run anymore. I've come to help. I can get you to Gabi. You came to see her, didn't you?"

Paul unlocked the safety on a handgun.

"Getting a bit over the games, you know. All I ever wanted was to make you happy."

Anger boiled in his stomach. Ungrateful little bitch. Handed everything on a platter and still never happy.

She never loved you.

On the very edge of the cliff, Paul trained the flashlight on the path below. Blood streaked the ground in one spot. She must have fallen but was nowhere in sight.

"Oh, there's a blood trail. I'll bring you a bandage, Ellie."

The path was deceptively steep and slippery from the rain. He took care with his footing, the flashlight weaving from side to side as he checked every crevice and bush. Ahead was a sharp turn and what looked like a cave entrance.

Tiny stones descended from above Paul and he flattened against the rock, hiding the flashlight. Someone was up there.

"Ellie!" Ben called.

Oh, you don't wanna be interfering, Rossi.

"I'm here. But he's close by!" Ellie emerged from the cave entrance, blood and mud splattered over her arms and legs.

Paul turned the flashlight on her. "Gotcha, baby."

"Run! Ellie, run for your life!" Ben bellowed.

"I wouldn't do that, not if you ever want to see him alive again. Make a choice, Ellie." Paul sneered at the confusion in her face.

Then she turned to run.

A shot rang out.

SIXTY-SEVEN
TO TRUST

Partway around the sharp curve the gunshot rang out.

A guttural cry of pain cut through the air.

Ben. No, no, no.

The ground disappeared beneath one foot and she grabbed the branch of a bush, breaking her fall and landing on her side, her knees dangling over an edge. She dragged herself up, scrambling onto the path to lean on the rock face as she caught her breath.

Another shot. Further away.

The heavy clouds parted, leaving an almost full moon rising, reflected in the sea. Gabi used to tell Ellie to see the simple beauty around her. *Nature is bigger than we are. We don't control it, only ourselves.* And Ellie needed to control her panic, or she'd never see Gabi again.

She dug deep. Past the terror. Beyond the fear Ben might be dead. At this moment, there was only one person Ellie could trust.

I trust myself.

Ellie dragged muddy hair from her eyes and continued down the path.

At the base of the cliff Ellie hit the sand running. She dodged the waves battering the narrow stretch until she reached the mouth of the river. She stumbled along its side, scratching her legs on low lying branches in the dark. Back under the canopy of trees, the moonlight was all but gone.

Exhaustion racked her body and her breaths were gasps. But behind her was a killer. For surely, Paul had killed poor Frank Barlow. She'd trusted him. So had Dad.

There was a post and rail fence. Ellie climbed through. *Wind Drifter* loomed through the fog on the river, tied at the end of a rickety jetty. The ground rose. When the bushes gave way to open grass, she paused, scanning the area between here and the cabin. All was still.

Ellie sprinted over the grass to the front door. There was no response to her soft tap, so she peered through the window into the living room. No light or sign of movement. Somewhere in her bag, she had a key to the back door.

Halfway around, a crunch of dead leaves broke the silence. The hairs rose on the back of her neck. She'd just passed a shed and froze, her back exposed to it.

This was it. Paul had caught her and there was nobody here to help her. She slid her fingers into a pocket of the backpack.

Another crunch. Her hand slowly withdrew, fingers encircling a canister.

Why hadn't Paul spoken? Mocked her some more.

He was behind her.

Right behind her.

A hand clamped on her shoulder.

"Ellie? My God, what happened to you?"

"Daddy!"

She spun around and there he was. Jack. Alive and right

here where Ben said he'd be. He opened his arms and she threw herself into them.

"Gab, its Ellie! It's just Ellie." He called over Ellie's shoulder.

"Darling?" Gabi emerged from the dark near the shed and flung her arms around them both.

I found you. I knew I could.

"We heard gunshots! We've been trying to get a phone signal higher up the hill." Gabi released them both. "Are you alright?"

"We need to get inside and lock ourselves in." Ellie stepped back. "You have no idea how happy I am to see you. Dad, I thought you were dead. Everyone thinks you are."

"What? But, honey, Paul knows exactly where I am, and I left you a voicemail telling you where to find my note."

"Paul is on his way to kills us. We have to go inside."

Jack laughed.

He actually laughed.

Ellie's arms and legs were bleeding, she was covered in mud and drenched from the rain. Did he think she was making it up?

"Jack! Take a look at our daughter!" Gabi put a hand on his arm. "Something's terribly wrong."

"I can see that. But kill us? Paul's been at my side for years."

"He let everyone believe you'd disappeared without a trace, even tried to frame Dennis."

"Nonsense. Paul picked me up from the house after the board meeting and drove me down to a quiet spot on the Mornington Peninsula where your mother collected me with *Wind Drifter*. Realised my pen was missing after he left. Did anyone find it?"

"I found it. Dad, I found it under a seat on *Sea Angel* and we all thought you'd drowned. Paul's been stealing from you."

The strangest look passed between Dad and Gabi. Then, Dad sobered. "I know about the money."

Ellie took a step back as her stomach clenched.

"He helped me out once. Can't tell you about it." Dad shook his head. "So, a few thousand dollars here and there meant nothing to me in return."

"I can't believe what I'm hearing. Dad, he probably killed a man. Frank Barlow."

Dad's jaw dropped. "Frank? But why? Paul paid him to keep half an eye on the pier."

"Trouble is, he kept too good an eye on it." Paul limped around the corner of the cabin, waving his handgun. A blood-soaked strip of material was knotted around his leg. He stopped, panting heavily. "And it is more like a million dollars you've turned a blind eye to, and I thank you for every cent."

"Is that a gun wound?"

"No, Jack. I always have a hole in my leg."

"What the hell is going on?" Confusion filled Jack's face and tone of voice.

"Payback, Jack." Paul swayed a bit. "Should have given me an office on the executive floor and a salary to match. And her." He leered at Ellie. "You made her marry a fool when she'd have been happy with me."

"I would never have married you!"

Paul shrugged "And there I was feeling bad for threatening you and your brother. And getting Dale to stalk you in the alley. Did you ever feel like you were being watched, baby?"

"Did you hurt Campbell?" Ellie forced the words out.

"He was becoming a liability, Ellie. Digging around in the past. But your beloved detective is an idiot because I left clues. Did the stapler make you think Mark did it? Or Joni?" He laughed.

Jack lurched forward and Ellie grabbed his arm. "No, Dad."

She pushed herself between her parents and Paul, one hand behind her back.

"You're bleeding. Let me help you."

"You care? Only nicked me, not about to bleed out." His face was pale, and his gun hand dropped to his side. "Why couldn't you have loved me back? We're going to go inside. Home invasion sounds plausible."

"Did you send Dale to attack me?"

"Nope. He did that all on his own, bloody idiot. I simply paid him and his brother to help out a bit. Well, I promised I'd pay them, but that ain't gonna happen. Now, into the cabin."

"We're not going anywhere." Ellie tightened her grip on the cylinder behind her back. "Dad, Gabi, please try to phone for help."

"Get in the cabin!" Paul's hand began to rise.

Ellie rushed at him, her arm outstretched as she forced down the mechanism on the cylinder. A stream of spray burst into his face and he screamed. The gun came up and from nowhere, a shot echoed through the air.

Paul hit the ground. Ellie's fingers gripped the cylinder as a primal cry escaped her lips.

In her peripheral vision, figures appeared through the darkness.

"Ellie!"

Her legs were locked in place, every muscle taut as she released the mechanism. If he moved, she would blast him again.

"Ellie, sweetheart. Drop the canister."

She opened her fingers and it fell. The figures closed in. One was Andy, who trained a rifle on Paul, standing back from the still-visible cloud of spray.

Ben was in front of her. His face was so worried. Why was he so worried?

"You're alive." It sounded silly as soon as she spoke.

He half-smiled. "More importantly, so are you. Where did you get pepper spray?"

"Oh. I guess he forgot, but Paul gave it to me ages ago."

"Good for him. You know it is illegal to carry."

"Whoops."

"Hello Jack." He looked past Ellie. "You've put your daughter through hell. I'm going to have quite an interesting discussion with you soon."

Ellie opened her mouth to stand up for her father. Then, she closed it again. Ben grinned. Did he know what she was thinking?

"I think we should get Ellie cleaned up. And some water, darling?" Gabi took Ellie's arm. She smiled at Ben. "Thank you. I think."

Ellie glanced at Paul. He moaned and rubbed his eyes. Andy was talking on a radio, rifle loosely pointed at Paul. Ben followed her gaze. "Wish Andy hadn't shot him in the other leg. Now, we'll have to carry him."

He reached out a hand and Ellie grabbed it like a lifeline.

SIXTY-EIGHT
A WAY BACK

A bus pulled away from the kerb on a quiet street in west Melbourne. Only one person had alighted, a young man wearing a jacket and jeans, hood pulled up to protect him from the last of the rain from an earlier thunderstorm. He carried a huge bunch of cheap, but pretty flowers, and wore a backpack.

He looked around, unsure of himself. Checked the time and turned back to wait for another bus. His eyes kept flicking to a house up the road. Small, humble, and with its porch light on. The rain stopped and he pushed the hoodie off, running a hand through a mop of brown hair. Someone appeared at the front window of the house, checking through the curtain before disappearing. As though unable to stop, he walked quickly to the front gate.

The letterbox had a name on it. *Blackwell*. He pushed the gate open.

At the door he stood for a moment, then raised his hand to knock. And lowered it with a sigh. He smelled the flowers, then laid them on the doorstep. His shoulders slumped as he traipsed to the gate.

The front door opened. "Hello? Who is it?" An elderly man peered down the path.

The young man froze.

"Who are these flowers for, young man?"

Adam Blackwell turned around, uncertainty in his eyes. "They're for Grandma."

Door now wide open, the older man picked up the flowers and came down the steps to Adam. He stood in front of him, his expression unreadable. They gazed at each other as the rain began again.

"Better come in and give them to her, son."

Adam's mouth opened and his eyes glistened. "I...I'm so sorry about how I left, Grandad."

His grandfather's eyes glistened back. "Me too, son. Me too."

"What are you doing outside, old man?" Mrs Blackwell appeared on the porch. Her eyes widened and a hand flew to her mouth.

"Better take these to her. Go on." Mr Blackwell handed Adam the flowers and patted his shoulders. "Time to go in."

With a wide grin, Adam took the flowers and sprinted to his grandmother.

SIXTY-NINE
RESOLUTIONS

19 December

It was late afternoon when Ellie locked her car and went to find Michael. She carried his early Christmas present, but intended to buy lots more to bring him on Christmas Day. There would be plenty of shopping time since she'd taken the rest of the year off.

Dad was back at the helm of Bannerman Wealth Group after a considerable amount of explaining to the board and police. He wasn't going to be there for long, not with the untreatable tumour which would shorten his life. All he wanted, so he told Ellie, was to sell and make sure his staff and family were properly taken care of. After that, he intended to live out whatever time he had with Gabi. They had plans to sail away. Meredith agreed to a divorce once Dad gave her the house and enough money to live well for a few years.

Michael wasn't in the pool or buildings, so Ellie wandered down to the lake, a quiet spot he loved. She'd spoken to one of his specialists and a new series of tests would commence early next year to evaluate his ability to leave for extended stays with Ellie, once she was in a better position to host him. Her apartment was already on the market and she'd warned Dad that in the new year she'd stay long enough to hand over the Foundation to new owners, and not a day longer.

The lake sparkled and Ellie spied Michael on a bench, his wheelchair to one side. He listened to something his carer said, then threw his head back and laughed. Ellie laughed in response, and Michael's head awkwardly turned. So did his carer's.

Ellie stopped dead and almost dropped the parcel. It was Ben with Michael, a broad grin on his face.

She lifted her chin and got moving, kissing Michael's cheek before settling next to Ben without looking at him.

"So, Michael, does Ben visit often?"

Michael's eyes moved to Ben and a lop-sided smile formed.

"I see. But does he bring you presents?" Ellie tapped the top of the parcel. "Nearly Christmas time, so you'll be getting a lot of these."

"Pe...pee...za."

Ellie's jaw dropped. Michael almost never said anything other than yes and no. "Did you say, pizza?"

He nodded.

"Michael, that is great talking, dude!"

"Be...er."

"Mikey, no, let's keep some things between us, okay?" Ben chuckled.

"Ben Rossi, are you bringing alcohol here?"

"No." Michael's eyes were filled with mischief.

Ellie giggled. She couldn't help herself, and it turned into a heartfelt laugh with Ben and Michael joining in.

For an hour, they sat, and talked, laughed some more, and watched the lake as the evening approached. Ellie helped Michael open his gift. It was a lava lamp and made Michael laugh again. As kids, they'd both had them and each preferred the other, so they'd swapped. Every day, Gabi would put them back in their respective rooms, and every night, Michael and Ellie would do a secret exchange.

The carer came to find Michael, Ellie and Ben accompanied him as far as the building. He grabbed her hand when she kissed him goodbye. "B...en. El...ly. Yes."

She didn't know how to answer, so kissed him again and watched until he was out of sight.

"Walk you to your car." Ben offered her his arm and she took it.

"How long have you been visiting?"

"Since the first day I was allowed in. And I visit when I can. It makes him happy."

It did. Seeing Michael interact with Ben shook all her beliefs and perceptions about what happened before Michael's overdose.

"Sometimes I hate Dad." The words were out before she filtered them. "Michael adored him and it shouldn't matter that he stuffed up, Dad should never have cut him out of his life. Our lives."

"Don't. You'll eat yourself up if you do and then how will you go forward? Your father was raised on hate and abuse and he made his own mistakes, but you see them now."

"Is he going to be charged with anything?"

"He did nothing illegal by going to visit his ex-wife. And they seem happy again."

"They are. But they've gone about it the wrong way. People need to treat relationships with respect. Even the end of them."

She couldn't read Ben's expression. Approval? Or disappointment in her?

"What about Mark and Dale?" Ellie changed the subject.

"Mark is still at large but Dale was kind enough to provide some possible places to search for him. Sounds like both were hired guns, as a manner of speaking. Eyes and ears where Dekeles needed. Hence the unlocked office doors."

They reached her car.

"New tyres? Seems we both annoyed Paul Dekeles." Ben changed the subject. "Andy and I are making sure he is in prison for a long time. Forever if I have my way."

"Yeah." Ellie unlocked her car. "Tyre slashers should be put away forever. Dennis told me he will fight the drink driving charges."

"Bring it on."

"I told him it is yet another reason to divorce. I prefer to stay on the side of the law, not against it. And I know I have to answer for carrying pepper spray." She opened the door and tossed her bag inside. "Are you okay? You could have died."

Ben tucked a tendril of hair behind Ellie's ear. His touch sent a shiver down her spine. "I am. Couldn't believe my eyes when you ran at Paul. Andy had his rifle on him, so Dekeles wasn't going to get a shot off, but then you showed such courage. Even if you almost gave me heart failure. Ellie, I am proud of you."

A glimmer of happiness touched her heart. One day everything would change. She'd follow her dream by the sea and hopefully have Michael with her. There were other ways to do good in the world, even though she'd miss the Foundation. And she'd be free for the first time. Free to live life on her terms. And free to love again.

SEVENTY
ONE YEAR ON

"Service bells! Service bells. Service all the way!" Ellie sang the words in time to a Christmas song playing in the background as she put two bowls of pasta on the pass. They were her last meals of the evening as she was taking an early mark to have a picnic on the beach before the sun was gone. Her small crew were more than capable of running the little eatery.

Half an hour later and she'd boxed up some pizzas, garlic bread and grabbed some beers and was crossing the road to meet Michael. He'd arrived yesterday to stay over for Christmas.

This was his fourth visit and longest one. Each time he stayed, things were a little easier and Ellie longed for the day he would move here full time. She'd bought a sprawling old house near the sea and had it renovated to cater for his visits. There was even a room set up for his ongoing physical therapy. Ambling Fields let one of his carers be with him each visit, Kerry finally softening after seeing how committed Ellie was to making this work.

"El...ly." Michael's smile was worth every cent and every moment of work to make it happen. His carer was Stanley, an older man with a soft voice and kind hands whenever he assisted Michael. Ellie hoped she might steal Stanley away should Michael come here permanently. Stanley stood beside the wheelchair.

"Evening!" Ellie kissed Michael's cheek and grinned at Stanley. "Shall we find a spot?"

As they ate, Michael's eyes strayed to the sea. Ellie knew he was happy here, his whole body relaxed and his speech improved with every visit. Nature at work. If only he could be out there again, on a surfboard.

Be happy with what we've got.

Ellie squeezed Michael's hand.

———

Sunday was the only day the restaurant was closed. Ellie went down there early to collect eggs for breakfast. A leisurely start to the day with Michael sounded perfect.

She came home to an empty house. There was no note, but everything was locked up the way she insisted on. Stanley must have taken Michael out. His van was there, so logic told her it wasn't far, but unease settled in her stomach. She still couldn't help looking over her shoulder sometimes.

She phoned Stanley. "Are you out for a walk? I'm about to cook breakfast."

"We're at the beach. I was about to call because something wonderful is happening."

"I don't understand?" Ellie peered through her front windows. Up where the surfers went in high tide, she could make out Stanley with Michael in his wheelchair. Except…

"Where is my brother?"

"Mr Rossi is with him—"

Ellie hung up and slammed the door as she ran out. Why was he here? She hadn't seen him since Dad's funeral a few months ago. They'd not talked at all about anything other than events of last year, so why now? She'd accepted that their relationship was over for good. More or less.

Feet on the sand, she threw off her sandals and sprinted to join Stanley. Her eyes darted up and down the beach but she couldn't see Michael or Ben. Yet Stanley simply smiled as she reached him, panting. He pointed to the sea.

The tide was low and there were only a couple of kids playing on boogie boards and two men in shallow water, one sitting on a surfboard.

All the hairs on Ellie's arms stood up and tears prickled at the back of her eyes.

"Michael?" she whispered.

A long, slow wave rolled in and Ben, one hand on the back of the surfboard and the other on Michael's shoulder, guided them over it. Michael's laugh carried over the sand and Ellie was suddenly running to him.

Her feet carried her into the warm sea, water splashing around her until she got to the surfboard. The joy on Michael's face was the most beautiful thing Ellie had ever seen. She burst into tears.

"El...ly. Sad?"

She shook her head.

"She's happy, dude. Happy to see me, do you think?" Ben grinned at Ellie. "I'd offer you my hand but need both to keep this precious cargo upright."

Water lapping around her waist, Ellie brushed the tears away, eyes back on Michael. "Looking good, Michael. And those were happy tears."

"Ben. El...ly. Yes?"

Another wave interrupted and Michael laughed in delight again.

"What are you doing here?" Ellie asked Ben once the wave passed.

"Turns out there's a job going locally. Thought I'd check out the surf before I make a decision." All of a sudden, the usual confidence disappeared from Ben's face. "That's if you don't mind me living closer."

The sand moved a bit beneath Ellie's feet, or maybe the tide tugged at her. It couldn't be anything else.

"Your divorce is final?"

She nodded.

Ben may not have had a spare hand, but she had two. One squeezed Michael's arm so he looked up, and the other touched Ben's face as she smiled. "Ben. Ellie. Yes."

Detective Liz Moorland now has her own series which includes characters Pete McNamara, Andy Montebello, Ben Rossi, and others. Begin with Lest We Forgive.

ABOUT THE AUTHOR

Phillipa lives just outside a beautiful town in country Victoria, Australia. She also lives in the many worlds of her imagination and stockpiles stories beside her laptop.

She writes from the heart about love, dreams, secrets, discovery, the sea, the world as she knows it… or wishes it could be. She loves happy endings, heart-pounding suspense, and characters who stay with you long after the final page.

With a passion for music, the ocean, animals, nature, reading, and writing, she is often found in the vegetable garden pondering a new story.

Phillipa's website is www.phillipaclark.com

ALSO BY PHILLIPA NEFRI CLARK

Detective Liz Moorland

Lest We Forgive

Lest Bridges Burn

Lest Tides Turn

Connected to this series through several characters is

Last Known Contact

Rivers End Romantic Women's Fiction

The Stationmaster's Cottage

Jasmine Sea

The Secrets of Palmerston House

The Christmas Key

Taming the Wind

Temple River Romantic Women's Fiction

The Cottage at Whisper Lake

The Bookstore at Rivers End

The House at Angel's Beach

Charlotte Dean Mysteries

Christmas Crime in Kingfisher Falls

Book Club Murder in Kingfisher Falls

Cold Case Murder in Kingfisher Falls

Plan to Murder in Kingfisher Falls

Festive Felony in Kingfisher Falls

Daphne Jones Mysteries

Daph on the Beach

Time of Daph

Till Daph Do Us Part

The Shadow of Daph

Tales of Life and Daph

Bindarra Creek Rural Fiction

A Perfect Danger

Tangled by Tinsel

Maple Gardens Matchmakers

The Heart Match

The Christmas Match

The Menu Match

The Cookie Match

Doctor Grok's Peculiar Shop Short Story Collection

Simple Words for Troubled Times

(Short non-fiction happiness and comfort book)

———

Prefer Audiobooks?

The Stationmaster's Cottage

Jasmine Sea

The Secrets of Palmerston House

Simple Words for Troubled Times

Till Daph Do Us Part

Lest We Forgive

The Cottage at Whisper Lake

Made in the USA
Coppell, TX
30 May 2025

50084366R00229